C000147654

Puma

MANCHESTER
1824

Manchester University Press

The Irwell Edition of the Works of Anthony Burgess

Series editors: Andrew Biswell and Paul Wake

Anthony Burgess (1917–93) was one of the most prominent novelists and critics of the twentieth century. He wrote thirty-three novels, twenty-five works of non-fiction and two volumes of autobiography. Pursuing a parallel career as a classical composer, he wrote a symphony, a piano concerto, a violin concerto for Yehudi Menuhin, and more than 250 other musical works.

The Irwell Edition takes its title from a collected edition outlined by Anthony Burgess himself in the 1980s but never achieved in his lifetime. Each volume in the series presents an authoritative annotated text alongside an introduction detailing the genesis and composition of the work and the history of its reception.

Titles previously published in this series:

The Pianoplayers   Will Carr (ed.)
A Vision of Battlements   Andrew Biswell (ed.)

The Irwell Edition of the Works of Anthony Burgess

Puma

Edited with an introduction and notes by Paul Wake

Manchester University Press

Copyright © International Anthony Burgess Foundation 2018

The right of Anthony Burgess to be identified as the author of this work
has been asserted by him in accordance with the Copyright, Designs and
Patents Act 1988.

Published by Manchester University Press
Altrincham Street, Manchester M1 7JA

www.manchesteruniversitypress.co.uk

British Library Cataloguing-in-Publication Data
A catalogue record for this book is available from the British Library

ISBN 978 1 5261 3273 4 hardback

First published 2018

The publisher has no responsibility for the persistence or accuracy of
URLs for any external or third-party internet websites referred to in this
book, and does not guarantee that any content on such websites is, or will
remain, accurate or appropriate.

Typeset in 10/13.5 Stempel Garamond by
Servis Filmsetting Ltd, Stockport, Cheshire
Printed in Great Britain by
CPI Group (UK) Ltd, Croydon CR0 4YY

Contents

General Editors' foreword

John Anthony Burgess Wilson (1917–1993) was one of the most prominent novelists and critics of the twentieth century, but for many years much of his work has been unavailable. A graduate of Manchester University, he wrote thirty-three novels, twenty-five works of non-fiction and two volumes of autobiography. Pursuing a parallel career as a classical composer, he wrote a symphony, a piano concerto, a violin concerto for Yehudi Menuhin and more than 250 other musical works.

The Irwell Edition of the Works of Anthony Burgess is the first scholarly edition of Burgess's novels and non-fiction works. One of its purposes is to restore 'lost' novels to the canon of available work. The edition will include stage plays, musical libretti, letters and essays.

The Irwell Edition takes its title from a collected edition outlined by Anthony Burgess himself in the 1980s but never achieved during his lifetime. Each volume is edited by an expert scholar, presenting an authoritative annotated text alongside an introduction detailing the genesis and composition of the work, and the history of its reception. The appendices will make available previously unpublished documents from the Anthony Burgess archives held at institutional libraries in Europe and North America, in addition to rare and out-of-print materials relating to Burgess's writing.

The Irwell Edition is designed for students, teachers, scholars and general readers who are seeking accessible but rigorous critical editions of each book. The series as a whole will contribute to the ongoing task of encouraging renewed interest in all aspects of Anthony Burgess's creative work.

Andrew Biswell
Paul Wake
Manchester Metropolitan University

Acknowledgements

My work on this edition has been supported by many individuals and organisations. I would like to thank the Humanities Research Centre at Manchester Metropolitan University for providing the period of research leave that made work on this volume possible; the Harry Ransom Center at the University of Texas at Austin and the Trustees of the International Anthony Burgess Foundation, Manchester, for allowing me access to their collections; Matthew Frost and Paul Clarke at Manchester University Press (and their anonymous readers) for their assistance and enthusiasm; my colleagues Khawla Badwan, Catherine Danks and Isabelle Vanderschelden for assisting me with Burgess's foreign languages; Ellen Datlow and Andy Sawyer for answering my questions about Burgess and science fiction; and Paul Boytinck, whose bibliography to Burgess's work has been a constant companion. Finally, it is my pleasure to thank my friends and colleagues at the International Anthony Burgess Foundation in Manchester. Andrew Biswell, Will Carr, Anna Edwards and Graham Foster have all been unfailingly generous in sharing their knowledge and expertise throughout the preparation of this volume.

Paul Wake
Manchester Metropolitan University

Introduction

Genesis and composition

Discussions of the project that would result in *Puma* began in 1975, in the offices of the independent film production company Zanuck/ Brown, at Universal Pictures in California. Richard D. Zanuck and David Brown, whose *Jaws* was released in June 1975, were evidently on the lookout for the next blockbusting disaster movie. Their discussions began with an interoffice memorandum from Joan Southerden Orihuela, working in the Universal City Studios' Story Department, to David Brown on 8 April 1975. The subject of the memo, and the basis for the abortive film project that would produce *Puma*, was 'When Worlds Collide and After Worlds Collide by Edwin Balmer and Philip Wylie'. The memo offers a brief assessment of Balmer and Wylie's co-written novels *When Worlds Collide* (1933) and *After Worlds Collide* (1934) as possible future film projects, along with a fifty-one-page summary of the plots of the two books. Taken together, the books offer, Southerden Orihuela suggests, 'a good possibility for the ultimate in disaster pictures, in spite of a style that seems old-fashioned now and so repetitious that it fairly screams for an editing job'.[1] Brown evidently agreed that the project was worth

---

1 Joan Southerden Orihuela, 'Copy memorandum to David Brown from Joan Southerden Orihuela regarding a proposed remake of *When Worlds Collide* and *After Worlds Collide*, with attached story synopsis', unpublished type-script, 8 April 1975, International Anthony Burgess Foundation (hereafter IABF), Manchester, GB 3104 AB/ARCH/A/PUM/4.

exploring further and a second (author-facing) proposal was written, setting out the premise for the *'ultimate'* science fiction film 'to be presented to a writer of superb imagination, scientific knowledge and human insight'.[2]

News of the potential project reached the Burgess household, if not Burgess himself, on 21 July 1975 in a telegram from Brenda Leys, who handled dramatic rights for the Deborah Rogers Agency in London: 'Zanuck Brown Universal want you for major science fiction screen play sending novel and back up material Siena please reply re interest.'[3] Deborah Rogers, Burgess's London agent, would write, just four days later: 'Universal anxious for acknowledgement receipt of material and your reaction please contact me soonest.'[4] When Burgess expressed his preliminary interest in the project, prior, it seems, to his having seen the detailed information, Zanuck and Brown responded with delight, describing him as their first choice of author and promising to send him a second set of the materials relating to the project.[5]

Zanuck and Brown met with Burgess in Rome to discuss the project in September 1975, and a contract for a screenplay based on *When Worlds Collide* was drawn up in early October. Burgess's motivations for accepting the project appear to have been largely financial. The reward for the work was generous, with the original contract for a screenplay of 'not less than 40,000' words promising Burgess a payment of $65,000, and when asked by William M. Murray in an interview about the project, 'Why do you want to write a disaster film?', Burgess replied: 'For the money, for the money ...'[6]

---

2 Richard D. Zanuck and David Brown, 'Outline for a proposed major science fiction film by Richard D. Zanuck and David Brown (Universal Pictures)', unpublished typescript, 1975, IABF, GB 3104 AB/ARCH/A/PUM/3.

3 Brenda Leys, telegram to Anthony Burgess, 21 July 1975, IABF.

4 Deborah Rogers, letter to Anthony Burgess, 25 July 1975, IABF.

5 Richard Zanuck and David Brown, telegram to Anthony Burgess, 9 August 1975, IABF.

6 William M. Murray, 'Anthony Burgess on Apocalypse', *Iowa Review*, vol. 8, no. 3 (1977), 37–45 (p. 44). For details of the contract, see Zanuck/Brown Productions, letter to Burgess, 5 October 1976; and Liana Burgess, letter to Robert Lantz, 14 January 1976, both IABF.

Burgess met with Zanuck and Brown again in New York in late 1975 and was evidently working on the project in October of that year while he was a visiting professor at the University of Iowa. There he met Professor James Van Allen, the magnetospheric and space physicist after whom the Van Allen radiation belts are named.[7] Burgess told Murray:

> It was useful for me to come to Iowa because I'd already met Brown and Zanuck in New York and I could see a very great man, Van Allen, who is here in Iowa, and he would be able to tell me actually what will happen if an asteroid or some other heavenly body comes into our orbit – what would happen in terms of the physical apocalypse. He was able to tell me what it would be like if the moon was smashed up and so forth. But this is mere window dressing; this is mere background material. The interesting thing is how would people behave in these circumstances and how can we present little creatures behaving in a particular way. So I suppose my interest is not primarily in apocalypse at all in that sense, but rather in people facing any great disaster.[8]

Despite the implicit suggestion in the Murray interview that Burgess was working on the script for a disaster film, his initial response to the Zanuck/Brown commission was to write 'not a film treatment but a brief novel'.[9] While the two extant drafts of the screenplay are undated, internal evidence confirms that the novel preceded the screenplay. It is possible, to give but one example, to track the spelling of 'ouranological' across the three extant manuscripts. The spelling of the word, a term of Burgess's coinage that is glossed as 'the discipline that binds together the various specialisations necessary to the

---

7 Burgess, who taught a course on the modern novel ('Problems of the Novel') in the English Department of the University of Iowa, talks about his time in Iowa City, and of his meeting with Van Allen, in *You've Had Your Time* (London: Heinemann, 1990), pp. 324–6.

8 Murray, 'Anthony Burgess on Apocalypse', (p. 38).

9 Burgess, *You've Had Your Time*, p. 326.

building of a space microcosm' (p. 99), is unstable in the *Puma* manuscript, initially appearing as 'houranological'. A handwritten annotation to page 53 of the typescript establishes 'ourano-' as Burgess's preferred spelling, and all 'h' versions of the word are corrected by hand until its final appearance on page 82, by which point it appears in its final form. By contrast, neither draft of the screenplay includes the 'h' version of the word, suggesting that by the time of their writing its spelling had been established. The novel, it seems safe to say, came first. Evidently, writing prose fiction was a necessary first step for Burgess when tackling work for the screen – he would do the same a year later when working on Franco Zeffirelli's *Jesus of Nazareth* (1977), writing that he had to compose a 'preliminary novel [...] before I could deal in stark dialogue and camera directions'.[10] It would seem that script-writing, 'a relief from the plod of fiction [...] nearly all dialogue, with the récit left to the camera', began for Burgess with a good deal of descriptive 'plodding'.[11]

While a full draft of *Puma* would be finished by 31 January 1976, a letter from Burgess's wife, Liana, to his New York agent, Robert Lantz, confirms that he was some way off completing the screenplay in mid-January:

> Anthony finds that the project requires a little more research and a little more time, and I am afraid it's going to be much longer than originally planned. He is half-way through and is already approaching 40,000 words. From the contract, which I am enclosing, this does not seem to appear a problem ('not less than 40,000'), although I wonder how serious is the deadline of February 1st. It may seem strange but Anthony finds it an extremely taxing work, very demanding upon the imagination and also such that cannot be speeded up.[12]

In the same letter Liana goes on to note that, 'This second leg of the apocalyptic journey is being covered by Anthony entirely outside of

10 Burgess, *You've Had Your Time*, p. 303.
11 Burgess, *You've Had Your Time*, p. 142.
12 Liana Burgess, letter to Robert Lantz, 14 January 1976, IABF.

the U.S.' The significance of this lies in the fact that while the novel was completed in Bracciano, it had its genesis in the United States, primarily in Iowa City and New York, where Burgess and Liana were living for a time in 1975.

Publication history

The publication history of *Puma*, until its appearance here in this Irwell Edition, is the history of its non-publication in the 1970s, and later of its reworking as part of *The End of the World News: An Entertainment* in 1982.

Conceived as both a film and a novel, the non-publication of *Puma* was a double disappointment for Burgess, who recounts the waning of the film project in *You've Had Your Time* (1990). *Puma* was, he writes, one of the 'scripts for films and television series that were, as I knew while writing them, destined not to be made':

> I was summoned by Zanuck and Brown to Culver City to meet their elected director, John Frankenheimer, but he was busy at Paramount editing a film about Palestine Liberationists dropping bombs from the Goodyear blimp on to the spectators of the Golden Bowl game in Florida. A gesture in the direction of making *Puma* was a storyboard created by Universal artists – four walls covered with a strip cartoon of the narrative. But I could hear the heart going out of the project – something to do with the shaking of the heads of the banks.[13]

This reference to Frankenheimer's *Black Sunday*, released by Paramount Pictures in March 1977, indicates that discussions regarding the film project were approaching their end by early that year, and it seems reasonable to conclude that it had been abandoned by 8 June 1977 when Burgess wrote to Lantz:

---

13 Burgess, *You've Had Your Time*, p. 337. John Frankenheimer (1930–2002) was an American film and television director whose films include *Birdman of Alcatraz* (1962) and *The Manchurian Candidate* (1962).

I have a copy of *Puma* suitable for publication, but I feel inclined to rewrite the whole thing – not just yet though – with a view to expanding it and getting rid of all the inherited elements in it.[14]

By September 1978 the American rights to *Puma* had been offered to McGraw-Hill alongside 'Jesus' in a two-book deal.[15] McGraw-Hill would publish the 'Jesus' book as *Man of Nazareth* in 1979, but at this stage the *Puma* project appears to have been abandoned. *Puma* makes a final appearance in Burgess's correspondence in discussions of a paperback edition of his collected works, to be published by Hutchinson and provisionally titled 'The Irwell Edition'. An undated list in Burgess's hand proposes *Puma* as volume 15 of the series (along with stage adaptations of *Cyrano* and *Oedipus*), while a typed version, dated 23 March 1980, places *Puma* as volume 14 of the series (alongside *MF*).[16] *Puma* is struck from the proposal in a version of the list annotated by hand in November 1982, shortly before the British publication date of *The End of the World News*.

In May 1981 Burgess wrote to his son, telling him: 'I've done 180 pages of my new novel, which I call *The End of the World News*.'[17] That novel, published in London by Hutchinson in October 1982 and in New York by McGraw-Hill in March 1983, weaves together three writing projects undertaken in late 1970s: the 'Puma' narrative (with the rogue planet renamed 'Lynx'); a Broadway musical about Leon Trotsky's visit to New York in 1917; and a series on the life of Sigmund Freud, written for Canadian television. Presented without chapters, the three texts are, as Burgess has John B. Wilson, the fictitious editor of the volume put it, 'shuffled casually together' with the Puma/Lynx material, retaining its original order of presentation.[18]

14 Anthony Burgess, letter to Robert Lantz, 8 June 1977, IABF.
15 McGraw-Hill, 'Publishing Agreement: *Jesus* (Book #1) and *Puma* (Book #2)', 29 September 1978, IABF.
16 Burgess, 'The Works of Anthony Burgess', unpublished letter, 23 March 1980, IABF, GP 1982/83.
17 Anthony Burgess, letter to Andrew Burgess Wilson, 5 May 1981, IABF.
18 Burgess, *The End of the World News: An Entertainment* (London: Hutchinson, 1982), p. viii.

Writing of the projects that make up *The End of the World News*, Burgess claims, perhaps rather disingenuously:

> All three sat in the same folder in instalments of varying length, and when all three were finished I saw that they were aspects of the same story. They were the story of the twentieth century [...] Writing respectively a television series, the libretto of a musical, and a science fiction novella, I had really written a tripartite novel in a form appropriate to the television age.[19]

This claim reiterates the one made in the book's preface, a fiction that presents it as a posthumous publication:

> Perusal of this typescript by myself, and by others on whom I called in the hope of enlightenment, my own powers of literary or sub-literary judgment being only moderately developed, was a process fraught with dubiety and puzzlement. There seemed, despite a double unity – that of the typeface (Olivetti STUDIO 45) and that of the typing paper (Gevafax 701) – and the fact of willed collocation, to be not one work here but three.[20]

That John B. Wilson is cautious in regarding the book as a single volume should come as little surprise. His creator, a certain John Burgess Wilson, concludes a near-identical discussion of the volume with the rather more honest admission: 'I hate waste.'[21]

In 1983, coinciding with the publication of *The End of the World News* in America, the Puma/Lynx narrative appeared as a self-contained narrative in the March and April issues of the American science fiction magazine *Omni* where it was presented as 'an excerpt from his latest novel *The End of the World News* (McGraw-Hill), in which Burgess focuses on the classic science-fiction theme of impending disaster and how normal human beings cope with the coming end of the world'.[22] The *Omni* text, selected from *The End*

19 Burgess, *You've Had Your Time*, pp. 326–7.
20 Burgess, *The End of the World News*, p. viii.
21 Burgess, *You've Had Your Time*, p. 327.
22 Anon, 'Contributors: Omnibus', *Omni*, March 1983, p. 10.

of the World News by the magazine's fiction editor Ellen Datlow, which presents key passages from the Lynx narrative and which makes no reference to Freud and Trotsky, equates to what are chapters 11, 14, 15, 16, 17, 20, 21, 22 and 25 of the *Puma* text. The significance of this extract is twofold: first, its publication in what was arguably the foremost science fiction magazine of the time, alongside work by Jack Dann and Thomas M. Disch, confirms its status within the genre; and second, the extraction of an entirely coherent Puma/ Lynx narrative from *The End of the World News* indicates just how loose the stitches holding the three strands of that book together are.

The version of *Puma* presented in this edition therefore represents the first print appearance of the novel as it was originally conceived. The text has been prepared from the earliest known typescript, completed in Bracciano, dated 31 January 1976 and now held in the Harry Ransom Center in Texas. Burgess's lament that '[m]y typescripts too were fair and therefore, in that market where authors' holographs have a cash value, not easily saleable', is a fair description of the *Puma* typescript, which contains few typographical errors and only a small number of hand-written corrections.[23] In preparing this edition, Burgess's annotations have been followed and his spelling, punctuation and presentation have been retained as originally given. In a very few cases, spelling and capitalization have been altered to remove errors but only where these errors can be confirmed by cross-referencing the manuscript with the two versions of the *Puma* screenplay (both of which are in the collection of the Anthony Burgess Foundation in Manchester) and the first British edition of *The End of the World News*. In all cases these amendments are logged in the endnotes.

Background and contexts

While Wylie and Balmer's *When Worlds Collide* provided the initial inspiration for the *Puma* project, Burgess's novel is by no means a faithful adaptation. When Rudolph Maté's 1951 film of the same name makes an appearance in *Puma*, an old movie watched by the

23 Burgess, *You've Had Your Time*, p. 37.

crew of *America I*, it is dismissed as 'mildly entertaining, but remote and incredible' (p. 218). Burgess echoed this sentiment in his conversation with Murray:

> Now, in the 1930s, I think about 1932, Philip Wylie, American novelist and, I think, a scientist in a way, wrote a book called *When Worlds Collide*, which Paramount has already turned into a film in the 1950s, a very bad film, about a couple of planets coming toward the earth, one planet remaining within orbit somewhere outside the earth and the other actually hitting the earth, and people were able to get off this planet of ours [onto] this untouched planet before the other planet collided. This is a very improbable notion.[24]

Despite this dismissal of the film, Burgess's novel shares a number of similarities with *When Worlds Collide*. Some of these, such as the references to Noah's Ark, stirring speeches by the American president, and scenes of drunken debauchery are unremarkable in novels concerned with the extinction of humankind. Others, such as the Manhattan setting, the moratorium on marriage, the rogue planets passing the earth twice, the destruction of the moon, the brilliant father and daughter team, the writer character (the aptly named Eliot James in *When Worlds Collide*), the attack on the spaceship, and the children as last-minute additions to the crew, do much more to confirm the connection of *Puma* to the work that inspired the project and it is probably this material to which Burgess referred when he wrote to Lantz of the novel's 'inherited elements'. These inherited elements notwithstanding, the novel remains very much Burgess's own and *Puma* is perhaps best understood in the context of his life and work. Three particular contexts might be said to be key to *Puma*'s composition: Burgess's life in New York in the 1970s; his sense of his identity as an author, in particular to his sense of himself as an author of science fiction; and his 'vestigial Catholicism'.[25]

While work on *Puma* was completed in Italy, at the Burgess

---

24 Murray, 'Anthony Burgess on Apocalypse', (p. 38).
25 Burgess, *You've Had Your Time*, p. 64.

home in Bracciano in 1976, its genesis clearly dates back to 1972 when Burgess took up the role of Visiting Professor of English Literature and Creative Writing at City College, New York. This was a period of Burgess's life that introduced a long-term relationship with America, and with New York City in particular. As Burgess told Murray, 'a city is a kind of spiritual entity [...] New York has this soul but has not had a chance to demonstrate it and show it exists; no disaster has been big enough yet to explore its soul.'[26] *Puma*, as a New York book, is best understood in relation to Burgess's *The Clockwork Testament* (1974), a novel written in a few weeks in 1972, and his illustrated non-fiction book *New York* (1976), written for Time-Life's Great Cities series. Further contextual information is to be found in Burgess's journalistic commentaries on the city, notably his *New York Times Magazine* article 'Anthony Burgess Meets New York', and his script for the unreleased film *Gli Occhi di New York* [The Eyes of New York], written in late 1976, and reproduced here as Appendix 3.[27]

Burgess's time at City College and his life in Manhattan, where he lived with his wife, Liana, and his son, Paolo Andrea (later known as Andrew), provided much of the material for *The Clockwork Testament* and it is evident that Burgess returned to this experience, and to *The Clockwork Testament*, in writing *Puma*.[28] Both novels, for example, feature university professors as their main protagonists (Enderby is a minor literary figure teaching creative writing at a New York university) and young female students offering sex in return for 'A' grades. Moreover, the two volumes are connected at a thematic level by a shared concern with death – *The Clockwork Testament*, subtitled *Enderby's End*, recounts the final days of Enderby and it is notable that Enderby's death and the end of the world in *Puma* are connected by an allusion to T.S. Eliot's *The Hollow Men*: 'Not with a whimper'.[29]

26 Murray, 'Anthony Burgess on Apocalypse', (p. 39).
27 Burgess, 'Anthony Burgess Meets New York', *New York Times Magazine*, 29 October 1972, pp. 28, 32, 37–9.
28 See Burgess, *You've Had Your Time*, p. 285.
29 Burgess, *The Clockwork Testament* (London: Hart-Davis, MacGibbon, 1974), p. 110.

If Burgess's life as a lecturer in New York in 1972 provided inspiration for some of the early adventures of *Puma*'s protagonists, then his research for *New York*, Time-Life's glossy picture book, plays a more direct role in the detail of the city that dominates the story. That *New York* and *Puma* were written in the same period becomes evident in the novel's frequent references to the history of the city. Tamsen Disney's essay on 'Otis L. Grosso And Parachronic Fantasy' (p. 38), for example, refers not to an obscure science fiction author but to Elisha Graves Otis, the master mechanic of the elevator business for whom Burgess has much praise in *New York*: 'Otis may be said to have launched today.'[30] Similarly, the names of Brodie's students include the murderer Henry Judd Gray (1892–1928), the librettist Oscar Hammerstein II (1895–1960), and the architect Max Abramovitz (1908–2004), all of whom feature among the many figures whose stories make up the narrative of the Time-Life book. Alongside these gestures towards the city's past, Burgess draws on his life in Manhattan in the construction of his future cityscape. In this he recognises himself as following in the footsteps of the German filmmaker Fritz Lang, whose *Metropolis* (1927) he greatly admired. In *New York*, this connection is made explicit:

> The German film director Fritz Lang, seeing the Manhattan skyline from a ship, was impelled to start thinking of a film project about the city of the future. His film, *Metropolis*, appeared in 1927 and its cut-out, studio-made skyscrapers mingled, in the dreams of this Manchester schoolboy, with the true enfilmed and photographed Manhattan. It helped to make New York seem sinister as well as magical.[31]

Manhattan, as Burgess puts it in an early draft of his *New York* book, 'leads us to a new science-fiction view'.[32]

30 Burgess, *New York* (Amsterdam: Time-Life, 1976), p. 18.
31 Burgess, *New York*, p. 19.
32 Burgess, 'Incomplete draft of *New York City* (*NYC*). Pages 7–35 only', c.1976, IABF, AAT/9, p. 8.

Asked 'Do *you* want science fiction?' in an interview on the publication of *The End of the World News*, Burgess answered 'No, not
really'.[33] This ambivalence towards the genre is played out in the
novel in self-deprecating figure of Valentine Brodie, an 'instructor in
Science Fiction' and the author of 'well-made but trivial fantasies' (p.
34). Early in the novel, Brodie dismisses the genre in an end-of-term
address to his class:

It's brain-tickling, no more. The American cult of mediocrity,
which rejects Shakespeare, Milton, Harrison and Abramowitz,
has led us to the nonsense of running university courses in science fiction. Christ, we should be studying Blake and Gerard
Manley Hopkins. (p. 36)

The class, predictably, are unimpressed. Brodie, as a university professor and practitioner of a form he purports to reject, is perhaps
modelled on Burgess himself, who had taught creative writing at
City College, New York, and was, despite himself, making a name
for himself as a writer of science fiction.[34] Another likely model for
Brodie is Kingsley Amis, whose critical book *New Maps of Hell: A
Survey of Science Fiction* (1960) was based on his lectures on science
fiction at Princeton University in 1959. These two potential models
for Brodie are rather at odds with one another. Where Amis was
cautiously optimistic about science fiction's literary merits – 'This is
not the stage at which one names names, but at least a dozen current
practitioners seem to me to have attained the status of the sound
minor writer' – Burgess's assessment was less positive: 'Why', he
asks in an *Observer* piece on the genre, 'is most science fiction so
damned dull?'[35]

Despite the disparaging remarks about science fiction made in

33 Alastair Morgan, 'Interview', *Literary Review*, February 1983, pp. 21–5, (p.
23).
34 For Burgess on his reputation as a writer of science fiction, see Morgan,
'Interview'.
35 Kingsley Amis, *New Maps of Hell: A Survey of Science Fiction* (London:
The Science Fiction Book Club, [1960] 1962), p. 156; Burgess, 'Galactic
Cuckooland', *Observer*, 2 July 1978, p. 26.

his journalism, Burgess clearly found aspects of the genre appealing. Many of the authors included in *Ninety-Nine Novels* (1984), his choice of 'the best in English since 1939', are associated with the genre, including Brian Aldiss, J.G. Ballard, Aldous Huxley, Keith Roberts and Nevil Shute.[36] Similarly, his personal library, which contains many works of science fiction and is now held at the International Anthony Burgess Foundation and the Bibliothèque Universitaire d'Angers, suggests a sustained, if not overwhelming interest in the genre. Burgess also wrote in support of science fiction writers whose work he admired. In 1972 he was asked to write a brief introduction to an anthology, seemingly unpublished, of stories by Aldiss, Michael Moorcock and J.G. Ballard, and, in 1978, the introduction to the *Best Short Stories of J.G. Ballard*, an essay that Ballard would describe as 'a brilliant and powerfully written statement of the whole case for imaginative fiction'.[37]

Alongside Burgess's commentary on science fiction, much of his own work is readily associated with the genre. *The Wanting Seed* (1962) and *A Clockwork Orange* (1962), both set in dystopian near futures, are regularly cited as examples of science fiction. To these well-known examples might be added his time-travel story 'The Muse' (1968) and his later novels *1985* (1978), a fantasy of a future Britain written in response to George Orwell's *Nineteen Eighty-Four*, and, of course, *The End of the World News* in which a version of *Puma* provides the central strand. There is, then, something rather perplexing about Burgess's understanding of science fiction, and in the final analysis it is hard not to view his attitude towards the genre as the kind of literary snobbery attacked by Amis when he notes the curious double-bind of the science fiction writer who, at best, can hope to 'conciliate the non-science fiction reader into believing that what he is reading is not science fiction and is therefore worthy of serious attention'.[38]

A desire to stand apart from the other 'SF-men' (p. 227) perhaps

36 Burgess, *Ninety-Nine Novels: The Best in English Since 1939* (London: Allison & Busby, 1984).
37 J.G. Ballard, letter to Anthony Burgess, 14 May 1978, IABF.
38 Amis, *New Maps*, p. 152.

explains Burgess's attempt to situate his work within an alternative history of the genre. Eschewing the pulp fiction of the 1950s, or the work of the authors of the 1960s New Wave about which he often wrote as a critic, Burgess identifies with a literary tradition dating back to Daniel Defoe's *Journal of the Plague Year* (1722). Burgess has Brodie make this argument, much to the consternation of his students:

> 'One book I have not mentioned,' he said, 'since it doesn't seem to come into the Scifi or Futfic category, nevertheless seems to me to be the true progenitor of the genre. I mean Daniel Defoe's *Journal of the Plague Year*. This is an imaginative reconstruction of London, England, in 1665, at the time when the bubonic plague was brought into the port by rats from ships plying the Eastern trade. The plague spread rapidly and disposed painfully and horribly of a large proportion of the population, but the city survived and gained a new moral strength from its ordeal. This, I think, is what our genre is about – the ways in which ordinary human beings respond to exceptional circumstances imposed unexpectedly upon them. The bubonic plague, a Martian invasion, global dehydration, the end of the world –' (p. 35)

Here Brodie is at his closest to being the author's mouthpiece, repeating a claim Burgess makes in his introduction to the 1966 Penguin edition of *Journal of the Plague Year*: 'When post-Wellsian science fiction presents its collective horrors – either in word or on film – Defoe is somewhere in the background.'[39]

Burgess's rather idiosyncratic history of the science fiction genre, coupled with a concern for his own literary reputation and a distinctly modernist sensibility relating to literary tradition, offers one possible explanation for the frequency with which *Puma* alludes to earlier literary works. The range of reference will be unsurprising to readers familiar with Burgess's work, including as it does references

---

39 Anthony Burgess, 'Introduction', in Daniel Defoe, *A Journal of the Plague Year* (Harmondsworth: Penguin, 1966), pp. 6–19, 19.

to authors such as T.S. Eliot, Gerard Manley Hopkins, James Joyce, François Rabelais and William Shakespeare. Eliot's work provides not only an authorisation of the novel's highly referential form – Burgess turned to Eliot in response to Brigid Brophy's accusations of similar literary 'stealing' in *The Wanting Seed* – but also its epigraph, which combines lines from 'The Hollow Men' with lines from Seneca's play *Medea*.[40] Hopkins's poem 'Moonrise, June 19 1876', to give another example, provides the titles of Brodie's novels: '*Eyelid of Slumber, Maenefa the Mountain, Cuspclasp and Flukefang, Desirable Sight, The Moon Dwindled* and *The White and the Walk of the Morning*' (p. 34), while Willett's 'Sycophant-varlets, drawlatch hoydens, brattling gabblers, ninniehammer fly-catchers, woodcock slangams, ninny lobcocks' (p. 49) is not, as might be expected from the creator of Nadsat, an invented language but rather is a borrowing from Thomas Urquhart and Peter Anthony Motteux's translation of François Rabelais's *The Heroic Deeds of Gargantua and of Pantagruel*.[41] This stitching together of literary fragments in the novel, recalling as it does Eliot's *The Waste Land*, is unmistakably Burgessian. In *Puma*, Eliot's 'heap of broken images' is reduced (or enlarged) to accommodate a story told to a class of space-faring children by their teacher Valentine O'Grady, 'drawing on his fancy, his background reading, his knowledge of ancient films, the long unfinished chronicle that rested in the Brodie Library' (p. 223).

A third and final context that helps situate *Puma* in relation to Burgess's life and writings is that of his Catholic upbringing. 'Defiantly Catholic in his fictional world-view, though agnostic in everyday life', Burgess was, as his biographer Andrew Biswell puts it, 'a writer who finds it impossible to avoid interpreting the world in broadly Catholic terms'.[42] As Burgess writes in 'The Apocalypse and After' (1983), 'When I was a small Catholic boy living in the

40 For Burgess on Brophy's review, see *You've Had Your Time*, pp. 63–4.

41 François Rabelais, *The Heroic Deeds of Gargantua and of Pantagruel*, translated by Thomas Urquhart and Peter Anthony Motteux (London: Dent, 1929).

42 Andrew Biswell, *The Real Life of Anthony Burgess* (London: Picador, 2005), pp. 318, 229.

middle ages, the end of the world was likely to come at any time.'[43] In *Puma*, the child's sense of apocalypse is realised when, in the novel's opening scene, the rogue planet Puma is sighted during a school nativity play, acted outside during an Australian summer. Interrupted by the appearance of a new star in the east, this comic scene, replete with fidgeting shepherds, poddy-dodgers and pommy bastards, simultaneously recalls the second coming of Christ and, through its antipodean setting, the self-inflicted apocalypse of Nevil Shute's *On the Beach* (1957).

The development of this religious strand in *Puma* is one of Burgess's main innovations. While the end of the world is couched in biblical terms in *When Worlds Collide* – which *Puma* follows in connecting the spaceships that will save the elect from destruction and Noah's Ark – only in Burgess's novel is the parallel between Noah and the Flood given any sustained consideration. This comes in the addition of the televangelist Calvin Gropius, a figure described by Burgess as 'some great Billy Graham kind of character'.[44] Gropius, working from the Book of Revelation, regards the end of the world as the Last Judgement of Christ: 'Take warning, then – drunkards, fornicators, scoffers, blasphemers, adulterers, liars. Hell exists, hell waits' (p. 52). As Burgess tells Murray:

That's the real apocalypse, that's the one thing we daren't believe, we feel it's incredible, impossible to believe. Supposing it were true? Supposing there were a Last Judgment, and there was Christ ... there's no reason it shouldn't. Without heaven, hell is as Joyce described it. Catholics have this; Catholics have this all the time.[45]

43 Burgess, 'The Apocalypse and After', *Times Literary Supplement*, 18 March 1983, p. 256.
44 Murray, 'Anthony Burgess on Apocalypse', (p. 38). 'To say that the evangelist Billy Graham is highly dispensable must, I know, seem blasphemous to many', Burgess wrote in 1973 in an unpublished essay about Billy Graham, titled 'People We Could Do Without', IABF, Journalism Box J, p. 1.
45 Murray, 'Anthony Burgess on Apocalypse', (p. 45).

Here Burgess is referring to hell as it is described in the third chapter
of Joyce's *A Portrait of the Artist as A Young Man* (1916), a novel
which the young Burgess read during his own crisis of faith on
the recommendation of L.W. Dever, his history teacher at Xaverian
College: 'when I came to the school retreat and the two sermons
on hell I found myself outside literature. I was terrified.'[46] It is
against this backdrop that the novel's conclusion – the story told
by Valentine O'Grady to the space-faring descendants of Brodie,
Gropius and Goya – should be read. That story, which closes the
frame opened by the nativity play in Chapter 1, revisits the Puma
narrative as an origin myth: '"Who built the ship?" asked Val desperately. "God or somebody," said Fred Greeley. "It doesn't matter.
It's here, that's what matters [...] There's nothing but this," he concluded. "All the rest is science fiction"' (p. 224).

Critical reception

To talk of the critical reception of *Puma*, unpublished in Burgess's
lifetime, would of course be premature. It is, however, possible to
extract some comments from reviews of *The End of the World News*,
the book in which a version of *Puma*, close to the original but by no
means identical, appears.

The End of the World News was met with mixed reviews both
in Britain and the United States. The most positive came from J.G.
Ballard who, writing in the *Guardian* (28 October 1982), described
the book as 'a brilliant extravaganza'.[47] Michael Wood, writing in the
New York Times appears to have quite liked the novel but remained
noncommittal: 'Some future critic will have to sift all this [Burgess's
prolific output], sorting wheat from chaff, but at the moment even
what may be chaff looks pretty good. *The End of the World News*

46 Burgess, *Little Wilson and Big God* (London: Heinemann, 1987), p. 140.
   Burgess includes two parodic Joycean hellfire sermons in *A Clockwork
   Orange* (London: Heinemann, 1962) and *Tremor of Intent* (London:
   Heinemann, 1966).
47 J.G. Ballard, 'Senses of an Ending', *Guardian*, 28 October 1982, p. 16.

appears to be chaff.'[48] Anatole Broyard, in a *New York Times* review, was less positive in his assessment. Noting the book's subtitle, 'An Entertainment', Broyard remarks, 'In Mr. Burgess's case, the term suggests that he entertained the idea of writing a novel, but he either could not or would not rise to it.'[49] Most damning of all was the *Christian Science Monitor* review in which Roderick Nordell asked 'what *would* be worth saving at the end of the world?', only to conclude that *The End of the World News* 'retains Burgess's franchise on technical ingenuity but perhaps not a place for itself on that spaceship'.[50]

The book's tripartite structure was to become a common feature in reviews; of the three sections, the Lynx narrative, described by J.D. Reed as the book's 'most complete tale', attracted the majority of critical attention. It is these comments that come closest to offering a critical response to *Puma*.[51] For Broyard, Burgess's science-fiction apocalypse is the 'most effective' part of the novel, though ultimately one that disappoints. His review deserves to be quoted at length:

I think that a man of Mr. Burgess's accomplishments should be able to come up with a few fresh ironies about the end of the world, instead of the same old saws about science versus art. In the spaceship that leaves the earth with a handful of survivors, there are, with one exception, only scientists, and the ship's library is dedicated exclusively to technological subjects.

The only exception is Val, a science-fiction writer and the husband of one of the women scientists on the spaceship. It is his job to write the story of this expedition in space, and I think that Mr. Burgess's identification with him is deep enough to give Val some appeal. In fact, his treatment of Val suggests

48 Michael Wood, 'A Love Song to What Would Be Lost', *New York Times*, 6 March 1983, p. 3.
49 Anatole Broyard, 'Triple End of Innocence', *New York Times*, 12 March 1983.
50 Roderick Nordell, 'Burgess Novel: Ultimate Questions, No Answers', *Christian Science Monitor*, 11 May 1983, p. 9.
51 Roderick Nordell, 'Burgess Novel: Ultimate Questions, No Answers', *Christian Science Monitor*, 11 May 1983, p. 9.

that Mr. Burgess might have written a very good science-fiction novel if he had been more interested in entertaining the reader rather than himself.[52]

Reid Buckley, writing in the *American Spectator*, was of a similar opinion, noting the 'apocalyptic third storyline is fun' but regretting the fact that the characters were little more than stereotypes:

> Willett is the Bohemian who Breaks Molds, Brodie is the Nice Guy, the Liberal Humanist, the Error-Prone, Sinning, Everyman (but *lovable*). Brodie's wife is the Blonde Intellectual Iceberg (that is, she freezes Brodie's libido). Hubert Frame, her Man of Science father, is wooden, predictable, and entirely dialectical. Others in the cast are mini-series television [...] This is *bad* stuff, and *bad* writing, and it is the more inexcusable because it is served up by a pro whose craft never entirely deserts him.[53]

Wood was more positive, reading the Puma/Lynx narrative as:

> a love song to what would be lost if the world went away: all its colors and tastes and smells and finally forgivable mistakes. It is an old song but a good one, made attractive not by its newness but by its steady virtue and the liveliness of Mr. Burgess's arrangement of it.[54]

This assessment must have satisfied Burgess, who claimed: 'The man in *The War of the Worlds* who, facing the probable endtime, mourns the loss of tinned salmon with vinegar remains more memorable than the Martian death rays.'[55]

What today's readers will think of *Puma*, here disentangled from

52 Broyard, 'Triple End'.
53 Reid Buckley, 'The End of the World News', *American Spectator*, August 1983, IABF.
54 Wood, 'Love Song', p. 3.
55 Burgess, 'Endtime', in *Homage to Qwert Yuiop: Selected Journalism 1978–1985* (London: Century Hutchinson Ltd, 1986), pp. 12–16, (p. 16).

the Trotsky and Freud narratives, remains to be seen. While the novel might invite reflection on Burgess's better-known writings about the future – *A Clockwork Orange*, *The Wanting Seed* and *1985* – it is also deserving of consideration in its own right. Perhaps, on the evidence of *Puma*, Burgess might be regarded as a writer of 'pure' science fiction, an 'SF-man' to use his own phrase. Or, perhaps more likely, he will be recognised as an apocalyptic writer who is more interested in humankind's response to the destruction of the world than he is in the scientific subject of his futuristic fictions.

Puma

To Liana
– till Catday

Here on the final pyre
See that page with its curled ends
Rolling into the fire.
Here's what the poet sang:
'This is the way the world ends:
Not with a whimper. BANG.'

One

All this happened a long time ago, children, so forgive me if I am vague on detail. But the date and place are sure. The date was December 18 and the last day, evening rather, of the Christmas term. The heat was seasonably intense, and the school nativity play was being held in the open air. Three hundred-odd parents and children sat on plastic chairs in the playground of St Bede's Primary, Nowra, New South Wales, and watched Jack Tamworth, Joey Warwick and Bertie Domville as shepherds watching their flocks by night. Their stage was a set of planks on trestles, the sky they sat under a real one. The Southern Cross spoiled things rather: you were not supposed to be able to see the Southern Cross in Palestine. But the three boys sounded like real shepherds. Mr Lithgow, the English master who had written the script, had given them real sheepmen's language.

'Who's that joker there then?' asked Joey Warwick.

'A bloody poddy-dodger,' Bertie Domville said.

Ronald Birchip, one of the older boys, winged and nightshirted as the Archangel Gabriel, was coming towards them, bare feet making the boards creak. 'Hail, O ye fortunate shepherds,' he said, giving the Australian Labour Party salute.

'Sounds like a pommy bastard,' Jack Tamworth said.

'Have ye not seen that star rising in the east?' said Ronald Birchip, pointing firmly at the horizon. 'It is as a sign. A great travail in the heavens has brought to birth a fiery wonder, and this night it shines over a lowly stable, where the Prince of Peace, himself a fiery wonder, shall be brought to birth by a virgin.'

'What's a virgin?' asked Joey Warwick.

The headmaster, Mr Maitland, frowned round at Mr Lithgow. Mr Lithgow had, in the interests of realism, gone too far. This was supposed to be a reverent occasion. But Gerald Bathurst, a reporter on the *Wagga Wagga Sentinel*, a small yachtsman and former air navigator, winner of an astronomical quiz on Channel 37, was saying to Lithgow: 'Christ, there's a bloody coincidence.'

'What is?'

'There *is* a new star in the east. Look.'

'I can't see anything.'

'God has a great sense of showbiz, I'll say that for the bugger. Look, man. A bloody star in the bloody east. Can't you see it?' Some of the audience was going shhhhh.

'No. Are you sure *you* can?'

'Me tight? On three schooners and a rusty nail? I know the sky. I look at it, remember? I'd be doing an onomy column not an ology one for the rag if anyone was bloody interested.'

Shhhhh. Shhhhhhhh.

'Look,' said Mr Maitland, 'this is supposed to be a holy occasion.'

'A scoop,' said Bathurst. 'A sky scoop. I'd better go and get some background dope from Canberra.' He started to get out and trod on the little toe of the right foot of the stout lady next to him. Ow. Shhhhh.

'I can't see anything,' said Lithgow.

Whether he could or not, boys and girls, it was at last available to his naked eye and to all naked eyes in the southern hemisphere. Puma. Puma. It had once been thought to be an asteroid, or minor planet. The gap between Mars and Jupiter had long been known to be full of minor planets, scraps of celestial nonsense spinning round the sun. Round, many of them, many of them small. But some not all that small and some not round at all. There was one in the shape of a canister of toilet cleanser, more than a hundred kilometers long. Hector. A lot of them had good old classical names, just like toilet cleansers – Ajax, Hercules, Vesta, Juno. But there were also names of unclassical origin – Victoria, named after an ancient empress; Brucia, because the man who discovered it did so with a telescope donated by a lady called Miss Bruce; Marilyn, named after some-body's daughter. After the first Great War of the twentieth century, the American Relief Administration had helped Soviet Russia get over a devastating famine, and Soviet astronomers had responded by discovering a new minor planet and calling it ARA. It was because certain astronomers had their instruments trained on that gap in the sky between Mars and Jupiter that Puma was at last (I intend no pun) spotted. Asteroids were despised by some starmen: the vermin of the sky they called them. But others dedicated their lives to those spinning bits of rubbish.

There were two men, one in Florida, USAMC, the other in Lilienthal, Europe (Teutphone Province), who laid equal claim to the first sighting of Puma. The American, whose name was Pulham, wanted the asteroid to be called Pulhamia. After all, there was a Pickeringia, a Blenkinsopia, a Piazzia, a Gaussia. The Teutphone invoked the same precedent when he demanded it should be called Mannheimia. The Global Astronomic Sodality, GAS, bade them compromise and call it PUMA. Why not MAUP, the unimagina-tive Teutphone wanted to know. Puma seemed, soon, to be rather a fitting name. The radio signals that the heavenly body pulsed out had a curious snuffling intonation, like some great cat on the scent of fodder. Puma was not, as we know, an asteroid. (A megasteroid? cried Pulham. Pulham's Unattached Mega Asteroid?) It was a major planet, though not of our solar system. It seemed to have been the satellite of a star unnamed and unlocalised. By some gravitational vagary or other it had become a maverick, a heavenly rogue. That night in Southern Australia brought its first whisper of tidings of great horror. It was of earth's size but its density was at least ten times greater. It had wandered into the stream of earth's history and, at leisure, proposed bringing that history to a close. Astronomers knew about Puma. They knew the worst, though not all were pre-pared to admit it, even to themselves.

There had been a number of blepophone calls to Professor Bateman of the Canberra Observatory. Eyes other than those of Gerald Bathurst had been sharp. Bateman's secretary gave unsensa-tional information. A name and a vague destiny. Puma, a heavenly body in Sector G476, now at the beginning of a period of clear visibility in the southern heavens. In a few months the northern hemisphere would see it too. It would get into the gravitational pull of the sun, then go haring off again into the unknown. A flash in the heavenly pan, so to speak. Bateman and his guest, Professor Hubert Frame of the University of Westchester, USAMC, knew more and better, or worse.

They had finished dinner, which for Frame had been mostly Australian burgundy and cigarettes. Frame was sixty, of a dangerous thinness, a man worn down to intellectual brilliance and a pathological appetite for tobacco. He was an ouranologist, and his official title at the University was Coordinator of Space Travel Studies. He had come to Canberra to give the Israel Goodman Memorial Lecture on Early Ideas Concerning Magnetospheric Storms and Electron Activity Relations. During the talk he had not coughed at all, an act of will supposed Bateman, but he was coughing enough now. The talk, which had seemed to some to be delivered in cartoon balloons of cigarette smoke, had been well received. He was free now to relax, cough, and talk with his old friend Joe Bateman. Bateman said, as so often before:

'You ought really to give them up, you know. How many a day is it now?'

'Eighty. Ninety. A bit late to talk about giving up, wouldn't you say?'

They were in Bateman's study, a pleasant room full of russet leather, mediaeval astrolabes, small highly coloured fish of the South Pacific in dim-lighted square glass tanks, group photographs, swimming trophies. 'That cough must be a nuisance.'

'I take these,' Frame said, showing Bateman a packet of Rasps Extra Strong. It bore a picture of an old man coughing his heart up. Frame fed himself a pastille and lighted a fresh Cataract from the stub of the old. 'The two go well together,' he suck-puffed, breathing out eucalyptus like a koala-bear. And then: 'The Responsibility of the Scientist. We've all been asked to give talks with some such title at one time or another. I've always refused. The question is: what do we tell them?'

'We tell them, if by *them* you mean the so-called Fourth Estate, that Puma, when it gets close enough, will exert a palpable gravitational pull on the earth. They'll want to know what that means, so we tell them. Tidal waves, earthquakes, seaquakes. Then Puma snuffles off.'

'But,' said Frame, after coughing, 'comes roaring back.'

'I like to believe that none of us is really sure about that, Hubie.'

'We're sure. We're damned sure. We're sure all right.'

'One thing at a time,' Bateman said. 'Sufficient unto the day, and so forth. The first job is to convince the heads of our respective executives that they'll have to declare a state of emergency.' He looked out at the heavens beyond the open french windows as he went over to the little bar to get cognac. The term *emergency* had led him to cognac.

'A national matter, then.' Frame coughed it out. 'In the long run it will have to be a national matter. What they nowadays call a provincial matter.' Bateman nodded as he poured cognac for them both. It was Australian cognac. *Beware of French imitations*, the commercials said. They both knew in what way it was a national, or provincial, matter. Bateman said, handing a brandy balloon over:

'Politicians are a nuisance. They won't be able to blame this on anybody. They can't make party issues out of it. Coalition governments. They don't like those.'

'You'll speak to your P.M. tomorrow?'

'Who am I to speak to the P.M.? That thing up there will get bigger, then somebody will want to know what it is, and then a question will be asked in the House, then they'll get on to the Minister of Science and finally they'll get on to me. That question, of course, may never be asked. No time for frivolities with so much important party legislation to go through. Politicians make me sick. *Bloody sick.*'

'My poor dead wife's first cousin,' Frame coughed, 'married our President's sister. It's an involuted mode of getting to the White House. God works in a mysterious way. It so happens that our President's son Jimmy is to marry shortly – the assistant woman counsellor at West Point. There will be junketings in the nation's capital. I shall be there, as a marginal relative. Jack Skilling will hear all about Puma amid flowers and California champagne. Ten days' time.'

'Of course,' Bateman said, 'we reckon without Legrand. For all we know Legrand may be telling them about the End of the World already. Headlines in *L'Univers* and *Figaro* and so on.'

'The French are an excitable lot,' Frame said in a new gust of smoke and eucalyptus. 'Nobody will believe him. But I shouldn't be surprised if Burgos is preaching doom in Valparaiso. After all, they'll have seen Puma there by now. Look, like a damned idiot I find myself out of cigarettes. I could have sworn I had another pack. You don't by any chance –'

Bateman smiled. It was a good smile on a sixty-five-year-old retired army kind of face, seawindsuntanned. A fit man, strong and paunchless, a non-smoker all his life, he took from his jacket pocket a twenty-pack of tipped Robotti and handed it to his friend. His friend, in manic eagerness to tear the pack open with his nails, nearly shredded the contents. 'Bless you, Joe,' he said, a Robotti wagging from his lips.

'How will you get on?' Bateman smiled. 'There'll be no tobacco up there.'

Frame frowned a second, as though he thought Bateman meant heaven. Then he smiled and said, coughing: 'I shan't be going. I'll be lucky if I see the thing completed. If it ever is completed. If it's ever even damned started. Politics again,' he smoke-sighed. 'Big words. The survival of the race through its most useful representatives. The trouble is we've inflated language to the limit. We need to get an epic poem written just to show the bastards the awesomeness of what they're up against, the responsibility of those who rule our race in the face of it. Milton, thou shouldst be living at this hour.'

'Has your doctor been saying something?' Bateman frowned.

'I don't need a doctor to tell me. I *know*. I'm thin, I'm tired, I coughed something up the other day. Tired, yes. Very tired. Ready for sleep.'

'You can sleep on the plane.'

'I meant in a bigger sense.'

'I know damn well what you meant. Is your bag packed?'

'Yes, except for those films. The evidence, the ineluctable, the incontrovertible.' Bateman handed over the envelope that had been lying on a small fretwork Indian table. Frame weighed it in his hand. 'We were always talking about working for the future. And this is what the future is.'

'Man will survive.'

'Why the hell *should* he survive? For the sake of who or what?'

'For the sake of the future.'

'The future.' Frame gave out the word in two brief bitter coughs. Then he drank off his cognac and went to the bedroom with the envelope. He packed it between his shirts and his other suit. The ineluctable, incontrovertible. He was glad he had smoked himself to death. When he came out coughing to the central living-space into which all the rooms of the bungalow disembogued, he found Bateman waiting to take him to the airport. He was looking glumly at the huge wall telescreen, on which a giant newsreader rainbowed out the end of the news. The new star in the east was a godsend bit of froth to end on, after all the weighty items about terrorists and politicians. Nativity play at a school in Nowra, Christmas star, the real thing, no tinselled stage prop. Then a crack about no virgin births having been reported in New South Wales and the unlikelihood of three wise men coming from the east, namely New Zealand, the New Zealanders being traditionally known as poms without brains, or brynes. The newsreader smirked himself out, shuffling his papers together, and Bateman switched off a commercial for Manegloss. He led his coughing friend to the car. It was a gorgeous antipodeal night. Their trained eyes saw Puma well above the horizon.

They travelled silently for a time towards the southern tip of the metropolitan Commonwealth Territory. 'A future,' Bateman then said, 'for Vanessa. You want that, surely?'

'Vanessa wandering through space, generating generators and genetrices of generations. It sounds pretty dull, doesn't it?'

'There'll be generations who've never known anything else. Born in a spaceship of someone born in a spaceship of someone born in a. Give Vanessa my fondest regards. God, what a pity, what a bloody damnable –'

'Yes yes yes.' Brian, Bateman's police technical supervisor son, was to have married Vanessa Frame, but Brian had been killed by rioters in Ballarat, Victoria. Vanessa had been doing research at the Ouranological Institute in Melbourne at the time. All of five years ago. 'And when I consider the son-in-law who's been wished on me instead – Half-assed dilettante, not even good in bed so far as I can put two and two together. There'll have to be an end to that marriage. Candidates chosen singly, not in tandem. He may, of course, die in a bar brawl. He may have a sudden accession of self-denying nobility. Val as Sidney Carton. Most damned unlikely.' He went into a fit of coughing. They saw the lights of the airport. They slid into Traflane F. 'Whatever she says, I stand on that single nomination – her. Not because she's my daughter but because she is what she is. She doesn't have to be fed into VOZ or PIT or UNY or whatever damned computer it's going to be. She's the only one who can take over from me. And if she starts insisting on damned Val going with her –'

'Women are strange.'

'Strange? Daisy and I were married for thirty-five years and I never knew the first thing about her. And here's Vanessa saying she loves that half-assed no-good. Strange is not the –' He broke into coughing.

'When you say *take over*,' Bateman said, now steering towards the ANSWER terminal (Air New South Wales East Runs), 'you don't mean totally in charge?'

'No. Just my aspect of the venture. As for overman or overwoman, that'll be up to VOZ or PIT or UNY.' He got out of the car. 'No need to see me off. Parking's too much of a problem. Will you be at GAS in February?'

'Yes. Bring Vanessa if you can. Thanks for coming. You gave them all something to think about. Watch that cough.'

Frame dozed in his first-class couchette speeding east towards the United States of America, Mexico and Canada. His cough shook him into waking, so he injected a miniampoule of S9 into his wrist. That would quieten the cough for an hour or so, but he didn't like the after-effects – nausea, shivering, constipation. He fell into a dream. Someone was calling him from downstairs. 'Get up, you lazy little runt. Out of that bed, boy.' It was his father, back home in Lafayette, Indiana. Hubie Frame, a child again, called down: 'But I *am* up, *am* up, *am* up.' Even in the dream he wondered why he was calling that, never having been much of a liar even as a boy, patently still in bed. He awoke, and his brain was ready to remind him that a lot of his dreams were verbal, and that here was a palinlogue. Amup was Puma. Now why was his father, who, if anyone was, was with God, or in the dream perhaps *was* God, calling him down? But, of course, *get up* meant *come down*. And vice versa. The time was coming when notions of upness and downness, backness and frontness would cease to have meaning. Earth Puma thrae amup thraaemup rhumptaea.

A whirring noise below told him that the capsule containing passengers for San Francisco was being released. He drew back the curtain that had hidden his gaze from the stars to find daylight outside, and below the city. Then down hurtled the capsule. He rang for the stewardess to bring him orange juice, coffee, and a packet of Lombard cigarettes. While waiting to be served, he began to cough and felt something slimy and sickening come up into his mouth. He spat it into his handkerchief and then ceased to cough. Dissolution. Pmrhuaaet.

Soon Manhattan lay below and, children, Professor Frame had a terrible vision. The city was washed in huge swirling seas of ochre and greenish egg-yolk, mounting in regular rhythms ever higher and higher, till they broke in spray from the pinnacles of the Newman Tower, the Patmore Center, the Scotus Complex, the Outride Building, the Paternoster Convention City, the two hundred storey Tractarian Folly. And then the island split down the middle and from the wound thus made fire leapt and smoke billowed. The fire was lashed out by the waves but came back again, snarling. The towers crumbled and went down into momentarily gaping holes in the ocean, and then all was covered in dun hell smoke, puffing and bellying. Then, boys and girls, ladies and gentlemen, the city was as it was, proud, the skyscrapers thrusting like swords sprung from dragons' teeth, lovely in sunlight, and Frame and his fellow-passengers were told to prepare for landing.

Two

Valentine Brodie, husband of Vanessa, was delivering his last lecture before the Christmas break. He was a handsome man of thirty-eight, with a well-trimmed black beard and rather unhappy hazel eyes, a strong nose at variance with the weakish chin hidden by the beard, a fine forehead and a slight beer-drinker's paunch. Val and Van, he and his wife were known as, or Lentine and Nessa. The VA their names held in common was a motif woven into the curtains, cushions and bedspreads of their apartment, and all the books on their shelves belonged, so the book plate proclaimed, to VA. BRODIE. This assertion of a common initial and post-initial was somehow pathetic, since their marriage was evidently failing and could not be saved by a coincidence of letters. They had in fact first met at a party where pairing was effected through identical first-name initials, had gone about together thereafter, considered that they had fallen in love, married.

Val was an instructor in Science Fiction, and he was himself quite well known as a practitioner of the form. Paperbacks of his well-made but trivial fantasies were to be found in college bookstores, but also in airports, tobacconists, and pornoshops, and they existed also in cassette adaptations and microfiches. The best-known were *Eyelid of Slumber, Maenefa the Mountain, Cuspclasp and Flukefang, Desirable Sight, The Moon Dwindled* and *The White and the Walk of the Morning.* But he was too modest to deal with his own work in the two courses he ran; he began with Cyrano de Bergerac and ended with Bissell, Hale and Galindez. He was now addressing a group of graduate students in the Englit Complex of Westchester University and was recapitulating the point on which he had begun three months before.

'One book I have not mentioned,' he said, 'since it doesn't seem to come into the Scifi or Futfic category, nevertheless seems to me to be the true progenitor of the genre. I mean Daniel Defoe's *Journal of the Plague Year*. This is an imaginative reconstruction of London, England, in 1665, at the time when the bubonic plague was brought into the port by rats from ships plying the Eastern trade. The plague spread rapidly and disposed painfully and horribly of a large proportion of the population, but the city survived and gained a new moral strength from its ordeal. This, I think, is what our genre is about – the ways in which ordinary human beings respond to exceptional circumstances imposed unexpectedly upon them. The bubonic plague, a Martian invasion, global dehydration, the end of the world –'

'That's what you said when we started,' said Dan French, a lanky student with a slow bray. 'And what some of us said was that that killed the whole idea of the genre. And there you are, you see – this plague book you talk about gets right away from it. You might as well say that old Anglo-American guy, Harry no Henry James, was an SF writer because he wrote about how people responded to things. I mean that's what the novel qua novel is about. Right? People responding to things. Right?'

'Exceptional things is what I said. And on a large scale. Would you accept that a book about the end of the world and how it affected people in, say, Cincinnati or Columbus would be scifi?'

The class began to wrangle unprofitably, as it usually did. A bright boy named Juke Harris put everybody right. 'Science fiction,' he said, 'has to have scientists in it. I mean, even this plague book thing of Doc Brodie's has a thing in it which can only be dealt with by scientists, doctors of medicine being kind of scientists. If the book is based on some big unexpected thing that scientists are concerned with, then it's science fiction.'

Judd Gray said that the job of scifi, futfic really, was to prophesy. To get us ready for things going to happen in the future, right?

No, said Penny Dreiser, it was to give us the future in the present, because none of us would get the future in the future. Then, to Val's slight embarrassment, they started asking about one of his own books – *Cuspclasp and Flukefang* – which was about people in a state of neurosis induced by a headache pill which had unforeseen side-effects, and this neurosis made them believe the end of the world was coming any minute, and they were all most ingenious in their suppositions as to how it was going to come – a great explosion at the centre of the earth, a world epidemic that wiped out whole populations in seconds, a war with nerve gases and poisoned water, air pollution, invasion by fierce warriors from outer space. Then a cure was found for the neurosis, people began to live again, and the end of the world came in a form that nobody had expected. What they wanted to know was why Val had just ended his book like that, with those words 'in a form that nobody had expected', without saying what the form was.

Val said: 'You're always saying that scifi should open up the imagination. Well, the book ended with everybody's imagination wide open. They'd had all the kinds of end of the world that anybody could think of, so what was left? That's the job of the reader's imagination to find out.' Cheating, said some of his class. The writer had certain obligations to his readers. Life asked the riddles, the writer's job was to try and answer them, and so on. 'Science fiction is, let's be honest, ultimately a triviality,' said Val. 'It's brain-tickling, no more. The American cult of mediocrity, which rejects Shakespeare, Milton, Harrison and Abramovitz, has led us to the nonsense of running university courses in science fiction. Christ, we should be studying Blake and Gerard Manley Hopkins.' This was indiscreet, he was also surprised at the vehemence with which he condemned the very thing he was being paid to promote. Cunningly, a dark musky girl with the top buttons of her shirt undone, Tamsen Disney, cut into the shouts with:

'How does Dr *Vanessa* Brodie think the world is going to end?'

There was an interested silence then. Everybody knew Vanessa Brodie, if not with more than a superficial acquaintance with her professional brilliance, certainly with a total awe at her beauty. Some

of the men students thought more highly of Valentine Brodie for
his being the consort of a goddess than they did of him as a writer
and teacher. He slept with her, handled her divinity in the flesh, and
then came down to earth to teach Science Fiction. Everybody now
listened closely to Val's words: it was almost, but not quite, like
creeping into their bedroom and watching invisibly, by courtesy of
an old SF writer called H.G. Wells.

'My wife,' he said – a mild thrill of concupiscence went through
some of them – 'well, she has little time for that kind of speculation. She leaves that to us humbler children of mere fancy. Anyway,
her eyes are on outer space –' (ice-blue eyes, some of the students
knew, saw them now, on outer space) '– and the only danger from
there, apparently, is so ineffably remote that it's not worth considering. Some asteroid, for instance, hurtling in and perhaps smashing
Greater New York. Or Moscow. The Martians are *not* coming. Nor
the Venereans, nor the Uranians. The earth will die when the sun
dies. Man may starve himself to death by his stupidity, or cease to
breed. Nothing apocalyptic, anyway. Leave all that nonsense to the
SF men.'

'How about Puma?' asked Margaret Hammerstein.

'What about Puma?' asked Val.

'Well, there was this news item on TV. They showed this thing in
Australia, a film that is, and said that it was an intruder from outer
space, Puma, that is. What does Dr Vanessa say about that?'

Was there a touch of insolence in it – *Dr Vanessa*? No, just verbal
economy. 'You're not to worry about Puma,' Val said soothingly.
'It's going to spin round the sun and then spin away again into space.
Plenty for the scientists to be interested in, very little for the science
fiction writer.'

'But,' said Margaret Hammerstein, 'there's this scientist in South
America – Caracas or Rio or somewhere – who says it's going to spin
towards the earth and cause trouble.'

'My concern,' smiled Val, 'is science fiction, a very minor com-
partment of literature. And now – a happy Christmas and do some
serious reading during the brief break. Try *Paradise Lost*. In the sense
that the material of the poem is theological, it can be called a kind of

science fiction.' As the class shambled out, he called Tamsen Disney. 'Your essay,' he said. 'The one on Otis L. Grosso And Parachronic Fantasy.' He spoke the title with mock-pomposity, smiling. 'It's in my office.'

Her lips smiled back, but her eyes were hot. 'I want an A.'

'It's not worth more than a C.'

'I want an A. I've got to have an A.'

'We'll see about that.'

They took the elevator together to the top floor. Though they were not the only ones in the cabin, she boldly put her warm hand in his cold hand. When they had entered his office and locked the door, her mouth was at once on his. He trembled as he undid the buttons of her shirt that were still buttoned and fondled her pert firm breasts. Paradisaical fruit, lovely in waning but lustreless. Her flesh was brown with a fine black flue. 'Wait,' she said, and peeled off her tight trousers. This was the prized, the desirable sight, unsought, presented so easily, parted me leaf and leaf. He kissed the fire at the coynte. He took her on the broadloom carpet, groaning. Afterwards she said:

'An A. I want an A.'

'You've got an A.'

'Now.' Naked, he crawled to the desk and her essay and a red pencil and gave her a great big undoubted A. 'There.'

She looked at him and said: 'Why are you so *hungry*?'

'Hungry?' he said. He took a bottle of vodka and two plastic cups from his filing cabinet. He poured. 'There, take this in your right hand and say after me.' Then, not jocular but sad: 'All right, hungry is right.'

'She doesn't want you, won't let you?'

'Rather the opposite. I don't want her. I want to want her. It would make things so much easier all round. But I can't want her.'

'She's one of the ten most beautiful women in the world.' Tamsen was referring to the results of a poll in *Wesches*, one of the student magazines. Gracie Flagg, singer; Doris Cosby, actress; Vanessa Brodie, scientist. Third, not bad.

'Perfection,' Val said, as though he were giving a lecture, 'is lovable by definition.' Sitting gloomily, tousled, in shirt and underpants and bare feet, he gave himself more vodka. 'To perfection,' he gloomily toasted.

'You mean,' she said, thrusting her own cup forward, 'she puts you down all the time.'

'She doesn't mean to do anything except be loving and a good wife. She cooks superbly. She has the most brilliant scientific brain in the world, after her poor coughing father. Her body is a wonder. She loves sex. She knows all about it too. She's read all the books. *Let's try Hamsun Three*, she says, and then she shows me. Then I lose whatever erection I have. I shouldn't be telling you all this. You're a student.'

'A good student. I just got an A.'

'You see what she's done to me,' he groaned. 'She's made me corrupt.'

'She looks to me like an iceberg,' Tamsen said. 'If I were a man I'd prefer something a bit warmer. Someone like me.' She smiled. 'I don't suppose you're in a hurry to get home. I'm going to the Gropius rally tonight. We still have two hours if you want them. Why don't you get a mattress in here? Or cushions or something soft anyway.'

'I don't intend to make a habit of this,' he said primly.

'That sounds like the voice of post-satisfaction. I could soon get you into a pre-satisfaction state again.'

'I have to get home. People for dinner. She'll cook a superb dinner. White wines chilled to perfection. Red wines *chambré*. Her father's just back from Australia.' He kissed her breasts.

'Something to do with that Puma thing?'

'Oh, to hell with that Puma thing.' The prized, the desirable. When they had finished, and then finished the raw vodka, she said:

'There ought to be an A plus.'

'That would be going too far. That would be perfection.'

'Still, I'll be writing other essays.'

'Over which I shall be quite dispassionate.'

'Post-satisfaction. We'll see, we'll see.' And then: 'I'm going to the Gropius rally.'

'You said that. I suppose you want me to ask why. Why?'

'It's the best entertainment in the world. Beats all your science fiction. He scares me so that I wet my pants.'

'Ah.'

'All that thunder about hell and damnation. Miserable sinners writhing in the unquenchable fire. I get excited.'

'And what do you do afterwards?'

'Writhe. With Maureen and Edwin and Archie and Minnie and Benny Goodhue.'

'Women are insatiable.'

'I'll be thinking about you. Or perhaps not. That paunch of yours turns me off.'

'It's a gesture in the direction of human imperfection.'

'Quite a nice little poem. I must remember that.'

Three

'More chocolate mousse?' said Vanessa Brodie, all in gold with a scooped décolletage. Her father shook his head smiling and lighted a tipped Frick Giant. 'Australia's done your cough,' said his daughter, 'a lot of good. Unpolluted air.' It was a kindly game she played; she knew the worst but saw no reason for facing it, not yet. 'You Muriel?' she said to Professor Pollock. Muriel Pollock nodded greedily and scooped to her mouth the bit that was left on her plate. She said, tactlessly:

'I ought to start smoking, I suppose. It kills the appetite.'

'More than the appetite,' said Frame brutally. Vanessa looked at him reproachfully and said:

'Val?' Val shook his head unsmiling.

Nobody could deny the charm of this living-room with its dining-alcove set in a wall-and-ceiling silver scallop shell. VA monograms on russet curtains, chunky coarse-looking grey armchairs from Bonicelli, Milan, that were masterpieces of comfort. On the lime-green walls paintings by Paxton, Loewy, Treboux and Voorhees. A bronze bust of Vanessa by Hebald, queenly neck exaggerated as to length, breasts brazenly or bronzely offered. Stereotelescreen discreetly covered by a different kind of screen – tapestried nymphs and centaurs by Piers Widener. Cassette-disc-tape-machine in a Whitney-Stanford cabinet. Drinks bar by Franchot Tilyou. Perfection. Val took out a five-pack of cheap cigars, lighted up and saw Vanessa's nose wrinkle. Vanessa pressed a gold lozenge and almost at once a tasteful steel coffee-cart came purring aromatically out of the kitchen. Val went over to the bar and brought back Untermeyer New York cognac (*beware of French imitations*).

'I suppose,' said Muriel Pollock, tactlessly again, 'I might as well start eating myself to death.' She was very fat, though not primarily through gluttony. Being fat, she had decided to use her condition to justify gluttony.

Frame looked coldly at his son-in-law, not attempting to conceal his dislike, even for his daughter's sake. 'I take it,' he said, 'you will understand what er Dr Pollock refers to?'

'Muriel,' Val said, looking coldly back through his rank smoke, 'is responding jocularly to a certain foreknowledge possessed by the Science Department. Something to do with a certain heavenly body.'

Frame grunted. 'You write fantastic little books,' he said. 'I've read none of them, but I should imagine the situation she and I and my daughter have to think about might well come into your er fantastic province.'

'You mean,' Val said, resentful of the term *my daughter*, 'I am unfortunately in the family and have to be informed, since I am bound to find out sooner or later in some other way, probably from *your daughter*, about something I am professionally unworthy to be informed about.'

'*Please*, Val,' said his wife.

'Sorry, Van. Sorry, sir. The rumour's right then, is it – the one from South America? About Puma.'

'Puma,' said Vanessa, in the somewhat pedantic tone she sometimes used, especially when most femininely dressed, 'is, according to all the calculations, preparing to approach the earth and exert a gravitational pull which will have a devastating effect on its structure –'

'And also its inhabitants,' Val finished for her. 'And then?'

'Then it will go away,' Muriel said in a childish little voice, as though referring to rain.

'Supposing,' said Frame, 'the world should come to an end –'

'Ah,' said Val. 'When is it going to happen?' He drank off his coffee with relish and pushed his cup to the machine for more.

'Nobody,' snapped his father-in-law, 'said anything about it going to happen. The sort of thing that Puma will do to the earth will not necessarily mean an end to it.'

'It will go away, will it?' Val said to Muriel. 'For ever and ever? Or will it come back again and be even more devastating the second time?' The scientists looked at each other as to say: never underestimate the intelligence of a lay brain. Frame said:

'We put it to you as a hypothesis. In a science fiction situation – ridiculous idea, science fiction, ridiculous phrase – what would you do about the end of the world?'

Val relighted his rank cigar. He said: 'The situation's not uncommon in science fiction. Indeed, it's rather a cliché situation. If the work of fiction isn't to end with everybody dead, then somebody builds a sort of Noah's Ark and a selected few, the cream of mankind, gets into it and, by the grace of God or somebody, finds a new and highly habitable planet after a short cruise in space.'

'The cream of mankind,' repeated Frame, then drank a mixture of coffee and cigarette smoke. 'And who's to decide who the cream of mankind is?'

'It's easy,' Val said. 'A combination of high intelligence and high physical fitness, beauty too I suppose, with probably a longish family record of these qualities well attested.' He saw Muriel nodding dumbly. What he was saying was, of course, very cruel. 'One might,' he said, in palliation, 'regard high intelligence and special scientific attainments as outweighing the physical qualification. But if you wanted to breed, as presumably you would, you couldn't afford to perpetuate too much unfitness.' He grinned. 'As I see it, looking round this table, only one of our present company qualifies. She, of course, qualifies shiningly.'

'You admit,' said Frame, 'that *you* don't qualify? Hypothesis, remember, no more. We're talking about a book. A character made in your image wouldn't qualify, you admit that?'

'I'm moderately fit,' Val said, 'though there's a history of cardiac weakness in the family. Also a tendency to bronchitis. As far as intelligence goes, who am I to judge? If specialist scientific knowledge is a prime desideratum, then I'm out. I'm a dabbler, a literary man, a sort of poet even. My book would probably end with a poet-hero, made in my image more or less, composing an ode as the world ends. A useless thing to do, but my breed is probably useless.'

'This man,' Frame said, 'would be married. Married to –'

Val again showed his quickness. 'To someone like Vanessa. He would see the spaceship smalling in the heavens, with this Vanessa character tearfully but bravely and dutifully and invisibly waving goodbye. Is,' he said, 'that what is going to happen?'

'No!' This was Vanessa, her face and neck flushed.

'Not science fiction then,' Val said. 'I knew it wasn't. Funny, I've written fictional accounts of people responding with shock and horror and disbelief and so on to these words of ultimate terror, and here I am – here you are too – well, wanting more coffee.' The coffee-machine was chuckling quietly away, ready to give them more.

'A hypothesis,' Frame said. 'That's all.' He was showing flight fatigue. He began to cough. 'As they say, we'll cross our bridges when we –' He coughed.

'I know what you think of me,' Val said hotly. 'I'm a bit of shit compared with that policeman son of your Australian buddy –'

'Not before Dr Pollock,' said Frame. 'Will you give me a lift home, Muriel? A delightful dinner, Vanessa. May we have many more.'

'Next Wednesday,' Vanessa said. 'Christmas dinner.'

'Will there be Christmas in outer space?' Val asked. 'Or is Christ too unscientific a figure?'

'*Please*, Val,' said Vanessa. Muriel Pollock got her bag and coat in a swift waddle to the master bedroom and back. Frame coughed good night. Vanessa kissed his cheek, also Muriel's. They left. The host and hostess heard a cough receding down the corridor outside the apartment. Val gave himself brandy. He flopped down with it on the Bonicelli settee.

'I never loved him,' Vanessa said, standing, superb in her gold, before him as he frowned up hopelessly. 'You've always known that. It was just father's idea. It's you I love, now and always.'

'Why, Van, why why why?' The frown had changed to a look of sheer weariness.

'That's not a question anyone asks. You know I love you. Why can't you love me a little?'

'Take it,' said Val, 'that I'm not worthy of you. I mean it. My not being worthy of you gets into bed between us.'

'There was a time when you didn't talk of worthiness. Love doesn't say that sort of thing. What made you change?'

'Knowing you better. Knowing that you contain me as you contain Frobisher's Hypothesis and the Deuteroastral Doctrine and – oh, all the rest of it.' She was down on her knees before him. He could see the twin swell of her breasts, naked, hugged by gold, and should have felt desire but didn't. He knew it would be easier if he could feel desire. Many a marriage sustained itself on desire and nothing else, and there were simple secret devices for promoting desire.

'Put that glass down,' she said, and was on the settee beside him, warm and gold. He closed his eyes, trying to evoke an image of the body of Tamsen, or one of the others, all the same one really – dark, musky, hot, ignorant. He dealt cruelty coldly, hating himself, saying:

'This afternoon, after my class, I had a girl in my office. A student. A little slut of a girl. Not worthy to dust your desk computer. She remarked on what she called my hunger. Hunger. I was hungry.' She drew away from him, as he'd expected. He looked at her eyes, ice-blue, not quite knowing what he wanted them to register – disgust, hurt, puzzlement. It looked, he thought, like puzzlement. Or was it pity? He had not put down his cognac glass. He drank, looking at her over the rim.

'Quite a number of men are like that,' she said calmly. 'There's a book by Montrachet, *Nostalgie de la Boue*. They can't take sex as a communion between equals. They want sex as dirt, as possession. I don't blame them, you. But I'm a little disappointed, I thought you were learning. I'm not as good a teacher as I thought. Perhaps you ought to read Montrachet. There's that thing also by Peter Nichols –'

'If,' he said, 'or when – Tomorrow morning I shall wonder if I dreamt it, this Puma thing. Then I shall ask, and it will have been no dream. But if this happens, happened, and you had this science fiction thing, the cream of which you are the cream, and –'

'I'd never go without you,' she said firmly.

'After what I've told you, and the other things I could tell but haven't?'

'I refuse to have it, the failure of love, of a marriage. We'd go together, we'd learn somewhere, *you'd* learn.'

'And if I refused to go? Granted, of course, that they let me go?'

'That would have to be one of the conditions,' she said. 'I know I won't admit it to myself, not yet, but I'll have to soon. Father's going to die. What I know he taught me. I've a duty to science, which means to the race. But I'm not having this cold impersonal choosing by computer. If father claims the right to a nomination, without the intermediacy of computerised *fairness*, I claim the right too.'

'What good am I to the race? I've a brain like a jumble stall. I'm a moral rubbish dump. My sex life, as you so kindly tell me, is just snuffling in the dirt.'

'Don't think about the race. Think about *me*.'

'You fall short of perfection, then. There's human virtue in you, meaning corruption.' She said nothing, she looked at her golden nails.

'Your father's in charge, is he, or will be?'

'I told you about last month's meeting of Natsci. He was re-elected president.'

'I didn't take it in, not in this new context. You've all known about this for some time, have you?' She nodded, eyes on him. She said:

'You'll know all about it soon enough. There's time to take it in, time to get ready. Time to get all we can out of –' She made a limp but graceful gesture which seemed to signify the room they sat in, meaning culture, marriage, perhaps sex, and also nature outside, candyfloss, beer in low bars – no, probably not those. 'We'd better go to bed.'

'No.' He did a vigorous headshake. 'Christmas is coming. When, by the way, is the other thing coming? The final thing?'

'About this time next year.'

'So this is our last Christmas.' He stood up. 'I'm going downtown. I must drink in as much of imperfect humanity as I can while I can.'

'I'll come with you.'

'No, Van. You don't like that sort of thing. Besides, the simple pleasures of the poor and lowly would collapse in face of your frightful perfection. I shan't be all that long. Moreover, I have some thinking to do, don't I? I find low bars conducive to thought.'

The nuclear-powered hangline from Roelantsen Station got Val to 57th Street and Third Avenue, Manhattan in a little over twenty minutes. The streets and bars were lively. Snow and Christmas were in the air. There were drunks, there was violence. Underprivileged Teutprot youth picked quarrels with privileged blacks and browns and blackbrowns, jeering and provoking in their underprivileged argot: 'A sniff in the krotevar, that what you want, yeled? A prert on the dumpendebat?' Val drank his way from bar to bar – GNYs straight up with four olives, plain Manhattans – and found the stores on Fifth Avenue doing a great trade. Outside Yamasaki's, all lights and evergreens, a Santa Claus twice as fat as Muriel Pollock, and God knew she was fat, was having trouble with a gang of rowdy Teutprots. They were telling him to jall his little bell up his yahma and flute his beard up his rucksuck. This Santa Claus was having no nonsense. 'Scum,' he cried. 'Droppings.' He was hitting out with a great glove that was probably loaded with shot, for it caught one boy on the ear and sent him scudding to the gutter. 'Witless turds,' he told them. An under-manager looked on uneasily from the nearest entrance to the store. Five boys set snarling on Santa Claus and ripped at his red robe. Underneath he was wearing old grey patched slacks. They ripped at those too. Santa Claus cried unsaintly language and hit out viciously. To the under-manager he called: 'Why don't you help, you snot-nosed bastard?' The under-manager responded to this with a frown that boded no good to the name-caller but with nothing more helpful. Val himself now stepped in. He was quick on his feet, despite his little paunch, and he had tricks with his fingers that he had learnt when, many years before, he had been a schoolteacher in the Astoria district of Queens. He and Santa Claus quickly sent the young louts flying. Then two policemen came from round the corner, and the thugs did not feel like renewing their assault. The under-manager said:

'What was it you called me then, Willett?'

'A snot-nosed bastard, I think. Also, now I have leisure and breath, I might add that you are a slabberdegullion druggel, a doddi-pol jolthead, a blockish grutnol and a turdgut. Also a coward.'

'You're fired, Willett. Give me that outfit.'

Willett tore what was still untorn, so that he now stood in ordinary sinner's clothes, with a red fur-trimmed Santa cap on. This latter he thrust into the under-manager's face and draped him with the ripped mass of red cloak, enough for a yacht's sail. 'In the classic phrase,' he said, 'I quit. You shitabed and lousy rascal.' To Val he said, 'Thank you, my galliard friend, let's go and drink.'

They entered a bar, full of red lights and tinsel for Yule, on 53rd Street, full of cheerful drunks who seemed to know Willett well, for they hailed him with 'Hi, fat Jack' and 'Well, if it ain't old Hohoho himself' and, more soberly, 'Behold the great Courtland Willett in poison.' Val learnt from this that Willett was probably an out-of-work actor who had, inevitably, made his name once as Shakespeare's Falstaff. Courtland Willett: the sort of phony name an actor might take on. Willett, having ordered beer in litre-tankards and quadruple Scotches to go with them, must have seen this onomastic scepticism in Val's eye, for he said:

'To give you the full version – Robert Courtland van Caulaert Willett, Dutch and English ancestry freely mingled.' He took from an inner pocket a cigar in an aluminum sheath, the longest Val had ever seen, withdrew the brown fumable tenderly, struck a match on his trouser-seat, and lighted up with relish. 'A gift,' he said through smoke, 'from a passer-by who had seen me on the boards in better days and well-remembered. I played Gargantua once in a stage-version of Rabelais's bawdy masterpiece. That he had seen, also my Falstaff. My Hamlet, alas, was not a success. Too fat, they said, too scant of breath – precisely, I pointed out, the words that the Queen uses of the prince in the fencing scene. Who, by the way, is to pay for these potations? I suffer from a disease which used to be called shortage of money.'

'I have money,' Val said. 'I received my professorial salary this afternoon.'

'Then we have no worries,' Willett said contentedly. There was a talk programme on the stereotel conducted by a thin sly man and his fat jackal. An actress with bosom well on show was saying: 'Yah, I guess so, yah, that's about it, I guess.' Willett at once inveighed against the silly stereoscopic faces:

'Sycophant-varlets, drawlatch hoydens, brattling gabblers, ninniehammer fly-catchers, woodcock slangams, ninny lobcocks.'

As if aware of this invective, the talk-show master said that that would be all for tonight, tune in tomorrow night, and commercials for Roundy Cupcakes, Kingfisher Kingfish in Eggbatter, Beadbonny Mock Caviar came on, all of which Willett denounced as filth and poison. Val felt a great sadness. He saw clearly, as in a film-version of one of his own novels, a great spaceship looking for a thousand years for landfall, full of men and women with thin exact minds who would not know who Sir John Falstaff was or ever dream of using a term like 'woodcock slangam'. The dirty delightful world, full of whores and rogues and bad language, was going to come to an end. He ordered more drink and found that Willett was now thundering against the Calvin Gropius rally that was being broadcast from Westchester's own stadium. Gropius's exhortations to repent were thoroughly drowned by Willett's 'Codshead loobies, flutch calf-lollies, idle lusks' and so on, but one of the cameras picked up members of the congregation, and among these was Tamsen Disney, her lubberly student companion with a hand on her left breast. Well, let them all get on with it – dirt, life, juice and panting.

Gropius's exhortatory organ was a gnat-squeak compared with Willett's poetic thunder. He was giving the bar Shakespeare, Milton, Dylan Thomas and Gerard Manley Hopkins:

'Heart, you round me right
With: our evening is over us; our night whelms, whelms and
will end us...'

The poets had always had words ready for the end of the world. It had been expected from the very beginning: the generation of Noah was not far ahead from Adam. The man sitting nearest the television screen made a change to another channel, and even Willett was quiet as they looked at a blown-up image of Puma, all the way from Australia. It was a mere blob of light, no more. A parsonical voice-over was saying with unction: 'Puma in the heavens greets Christ the tiger.' And then the choir of the Mormon Tabernacle of Salt Lake City was singing an old American carol:

'Star of wonder, star of light,
Star with royal beauty bright,
Westward leading, still proceeding,
Guide us with thy perfect light.'

Willett, a man as ready for big globular tears as for drink, poetry and invective, started to cry, saying: 'My childhood. Turkeys as big as sheep and Christmas puddings like cannon-balls, and the flaming sauce reeking like a blaze in a brandy-cellar. Gone, gone, for ever-more gone.'

'Gone for everybody,' Val said. 'No more Christmases. Let's make the best of this.' And he ordered another round. Those who heard him took his words to mean that the great past was dead and the endless future would be thin and mean and unloving. A young whore was also, encouraged by Willett's huge tears, weeping for her lost innocent childhood. Willett had his arm round her and was soon kissing and fumbling her heartily. An old man took his false teeth out and did a comic caper about the bar-room to the accompaniment of somebody's harmonica. The bar-tender sang about working on the railroad. A girl called Elsie did a drunken tap-dance on the counter. A man came in with snow on his shoulders. Christmas was coming. At the end of the night Val could not make it to Westchester. He was taken home by Willett – a wretched single room which fitted its lessee like a pair of roomy trousers – and the two snored amicably till morning.

Four

What Val Brodie and Courtland Willett saw on the telescreen in that lively Christmassy bar was, between the talk-show and the star of wonder, the final phase of Calvin Gropius's Christmas rally in the Westchester University Stadium. His live congregation alone was about fifteen thousand and his teleauditors must have amounted to some fifty-odd million. It was chilly on the Stadium benches, but the chill was mitigated by the opportunity to sing stirring march-type hymns and stamp and gesture to them, under the direction of a white-sweatered athlete, Zwingli Gilroy, D.D. Some of the less devout members of the congregation fought the cold with hip-flasks. But the subject-matter of Calvin Gropius's address was considerably chosen. In earlier days he would have been called a hot gospeller.

'Fireballs blazing in the intestines,' he told the microphones. 'The body a furnace compounded of many furnaces, and all stoked to white heat by the diabolic agents of divine punishment. Ah yes, you students, you professors, you men and women of intellectual learning, you rationalists disposed to scoff at the plain words of the Lord, consider this – that because you have cast off the troublesome burden of inconvenient belief in eternal and condign punishment you have not thereby changed the divinely ordained reality. Why should your visions necessarily be the counterparts of God's truth? God is made not in your image but in his own. Sin, you say, is a mere clouding of reason. But sin, as the word of the Lord howls into ears that will hear not, is a stinking reality, an eternal and terrible viola-tion of celestial purity. I too have had my visions, and they have been visions God-given not products of erring reason. I have seen, have smelt, tasted, heard, touched the endless endless endless terror of the fiery pit. Yes, the Lord has been good to me in order that, so I am bold to believe, I may transmit his goodness to you. Take warning, then – drunkards, fornicators, scoffers, blasphemers, adulterers, liars. Hell exists, hell waits.'

After the thunder of his catalogue and chilling or warming affirmation, Calvin Gropius spoke more softly. 'A star in the east,' he said. 'We have been told of a new star in the east. The folks down under,' he said folkily, 'have been vouchsafed a look at its pinpoint of fire. It has come at Christmas, as a star came for the first Christmas two thousand years ago. A prodigy in the heavens signalling a prodigy on earth – so it was then. And may it not be so a second time? Our Lord Jesus Christ promised the faithful, warned the sinful, of his second coming. And his second coming would serve not the sowing of the divine word but the reaping of the harvest. Yes, the harvest – which means not only the gathering in of the wheat but the burning of the chaff. The burning, the burning, the consigning to the furious flames of the pit of doom. May not the time be coming? May not the star be a herald of his coming? The star whose image we see on our television screens will rise for eyes unaided by science in our own hemisphere – in God's good time. Nature's good time, one may say – the time of the burgeoning of life after the long winter. In the spring we shall see it. May our hearts be pure and ready for it. For if it is the harbinger of Christ's second coming, as I believe it to be, let us be purged and clean and have no fear of the judgment.'

The augmented notes of an organ swelled, rose into the crystalline air, and the congregation too rose rustling like the rising of a wind. They sang a hymn composed by one of Calvin Gropius's henchmen, the poet and musician Wyclif Wilcock; D.D., Mus. Doc.

'We fear thy anger, Lord,
Less than we love our sin.
O may we soon begin
To cut the devil's cord
And let thy goodness in.'

Among the members of the congregation who were not singing was Edwina Duffy, a young colleague of Val's. She ran a course in Devotional Poetry, more popular with the devotional than the poetical. She was interested in the nexus between religion and sex, adept at picking sexual imagery out of holy poets like Watts and Wesley. She had even written a well-regarded article for the *Sewanee Review* on the true meaning of the sticking of the lance into Christ's side when he was dying on the cross. Out of his side came blood and water, said the Bible. Really, she alleged, his final emission was of semen, and the blood-water-lance collocation was obliquely expressive of this. She was not singing because she was too moved to sing. Gropius had an effect on her nerves that was wholly sexual. The voice itself, despite or because of the grotesque magnification by microphones, was like a shot of some powerful aphrodisiac, and the broad handsomeness of the evangelist, undiminished by distance since he was projected stereoscopically on to a great silver screen, set up shivers in her that could not be confused with the effects of winter night cold. Her boyfriend, Nat Goya, had refused to come with her to the rally. 'Orgyporgy,' he had said. 'Superstition. Nonsense.' She had accused him of ingratitude. He did not understand the accusation. He soon would, she told herself, as she made her way out through Mouth D, a mousy girl disregarded by most, a thin creature demure and nun-like. Her ardour was hidden; not for her, or for men who glanced incuriously at her, the flaunting of breasts in a sweater or wagging crupper in tight pants.

It was but a brief walk to the brilliantly lighted staff carpark, where her yellow Goodhue Seven awaited her animating key. There was much activity there tonight, the moving out of many cars. The atmosphere was devotional, meaning sexual. Hell, she was thinking, hell. Hot dark hell, raging. A nether cavern. The sexual significance must always have been evident.

She drove down Gottlieb Way, turned right on to Hammerstein Avenue, left on to Greeley Street, stopped outside Pell House, an apartment block where many of the young single professors lived. The doorman who let her in nodded knowingly. She rose in the elevator to the nineteenth floor. 'In,' cried Nat Goya. She went in. He was a

thin hard young man with very little hair. He sat at his desk in underpants only for the heat, marking papers. He was in the Department
of Microagronomy and was reputed to be potentially brilliant. He
looked at her, unsmiling, as if she were another paper to mark. She
smiled, and her face was transformed to that of a courtesan. She put
off her demureness with her clothes. So far the one word spoken had
been 'In'. Soon it became the second word, this time spoken by her.
Microagronomy was far. To delay his ejaculation he repeated over
and over to himself the chemical symbol for monosodium glutamate:
$HOOC (CH_2)_2 CH (NH_2) COONa$. But this was soon transformed
into meaningless vocables – *hook chacha coona hook chacha coona* –
which matched the rhythm of his thrust. She, at the moment of their
joint climax, felt herself being impregnated by Calvin Gropius who,
for a reason she could not at first comprehend, wore a bright star on
his brow. 'The second coming,' she said.

'What?'

'A poem by Yeats.'

'What's a poem by Yeats got to do with it?'

'And what rough beast, its hour come round at last, slouches
towards Bethlehem to be born?'

'I don't see what the hell that has to do with –'

'Never mind,' she said. 'Rhythms get into your head when you
– The mystical state,' she added. He frowned. But soon enough he
could see a point in that business about the second coming. Later,
while they drank instant coffee from mugs, she said: 'Gropius is
remarkable.'

'In what way remarkable?' he growled.

'The energy. He goes on about God and Christ but it could just as
well be about Belial and Beelzebub. Great big blind crashing sexual
energy. Bethlehem and the rough beast. There were three beasts in
that manger and two of them were gentle.' She put down her cup of
coffee, which she had hardly touched. 'Come on,' she said. 'Time is
so short.'

'What do you mean – time is so short?'

'Oh, come on.'

'Let me finish my –'

'*Come on.*'

Calvin Gropius was not aware, in a particular sense, of the effect his rally, personality, words were having on Edwina Duffy. In a general sense, of course, he was well aware of the sexual impact that was in a manner a secondary articulation of the evangelical impulse. It was all in the Bible, like everything else. Salome and John the Baptist, for instance. That pouting little sexpot, surrounded by the drooling lechers of the Galilean court, fell not for one of them but for an emaciated burning-eyed incarnation of the primal force of the universe. God, devil, demiurge – words, words, words. Gropius, taking fruit punch with the committee of the Student Christian Body of Westchester, could see how the wide eyes of the girl members were devouring him. He was neither gratified nor repelled. Religion and sex equally spoke of life; they met in the agricultural myths out of which the most sophisticated faiths were generated. But he never, on these social occasions, tried to take advantage of his charisma. He was a family man of fifty-five, with three grown-up sons. He was four times a grandfather. He kept himself physically fit, chemically subdued the timely greyness of his hair, visited his dentist every three months, not that he should be attractive to women but that the Lord's truth should be attractive to them. And to men, of course, as well.

Despite his worldly appearance, children, he was not what you would call a worldly man. He had a small ranch in Arizona and a penthouse apartment in DeWitt Towers, East 35th Street, Manhattan. He had a million dollars in the bank, no colossal sum at that time, and few worries about the material future. But about the future of his soul, and the souls of his fellow-men, he was sincerely concerned. He believed in holiness, a loving but just God, the redemptive powers of Christ's blood. He believed that man had done all that he was predestined to do through sheer skill and intelligence, and that now man must look, more than ever before, to the needs of the spirit. He saw self-indulgence all about him, too much wallowing in the pleasures of the flesh, too much cruelty and unkindness and selfishness, and he desperately wished to play some part in the spreading of the regenerative word. He was always delighted to be able to talk and pray with the young, and the ingenuous and ingenious spiritual enquiries of the young he took most seriously and endeavoured to answer with earnest and candid appeals to divine reason as presented in the Holy Bible. The future, he considered not unreasonably, lay with the young.

'The Second Coming,' one lank-haired girl of Korean extraction was saying. 'Does that mean Christ has to be born again, like that first time, or will he just step out of heaven at the age he was when he died, all ready for the Last Judgment?'

'The Bible says nothing of a second birth,' Calvin Gropius told her. 'One birth was enough, as reason must tell you. Christ exists, as man and God, waiting in heaven for the day. The day may be soon.'

'You say that,' said a young man who was going through a phase of devout scepticism, 'because we've come to the end of the second millennium. They were saying the same sort of thing in the year 1000, but the world didn't come to an end. Why should there be a sort of magic in the number 2000? And why, for that matter, should you have to bring a star into it? It all sounds like a lot of superstition to me.'

'Right,' said his girl friend. 'You really believe the end of the world's coming? How?'

'We have to be careful,' Gropius said, 'in interpreting Holy Scripture. There's a rhetorical level of meaning and a literal one. I don't seriously believe that this whole structure of the earth is going to collapse in smoke and flame and the sky is going to be filled with the sort of scene Michelangelo painted on the wall of the Sistine Chapel. I believe rather that men and women will become more aware than ever before in history of the nature of good and evil and that they'll finally take sides. Some men will be on the side of Christ and some on the side of the devil. Then there'll come the final conflict and the end of man as history has known him. Man will have to start again, as after the Flood.'

'The fire next time,' said a black youth, called Stanley Baldwin.

'Yes, the fire of human conflict. That fire will be the judgment. The righteous will survive it, but the righteous will be few. I speak

Christ's word to millions, but do not in my heart believe that more than a wretched little percentage will be among the saved.'

'So it's not going to happen *now*?' said the Korean girl. 'We're just going to start getting ready for it now? You mean there's plenty of time really?'

'Never plenty of time,' Gropius said sternly. 'To make our souls ready requires all the time that life can give. But do not think that you can stop the conflict happening that is predestined to happen. The forces of Communist darkness have rejected Christ, they have defined their good, but it is not Christ's good. An underfed and overpopulated world, led by Antichrist, will beat at our doors before this coming year is out –'

'That you prophesy?' said the sceptical youth, who was deep down the profoundest believer of all. 'That you know?'

'Armageddon,' said Gropius. 'The last great war, fought by Christ's powers against the forces of Antichrist. The judgment is contained in the very notion of Armageddon. The righteous who die will sit at God's right hand. The righteous who survive will build the kingdom of righteousness on earth. It's all in the Bible.'

'Another glass of fruit punch, Dr Gropius?' asked the wide-eyed girl secretary of the SCB, who had, Gropius noted dispassionately, as nice a little Christian body as he had ever seen.

$HOOC(CH_2)_2\, CH\, (NH_2)\, COONa.$

Hook chacha coona hook chacha coona.

Five

Jimmy Skilling, younger son of the President of the United States of America, Mexico and Canada, by the President's second, dead, wife, was duly married to Flavia Rowley, a social counsellor of the West Point Military Academy, at the White House in Washington on the Feast of Childermass or Holy Innocents. Professor Hubert Frame, by virtue of his dead wife's marital kinship with the First Family, was, as he had foretold, among the guests. Having, on the Feast of St Stephen, coughed up another grey gobbet of lung, he was not disposed to cough now. Still, in view of the gravity of the discussion he proposed with the President and the need to hold it without hacking interruptions, he had had two special injections – one to inhibit the cough reflex, the other of a nicotine surrogate, so that his starved body would not fidget. It was thus as a cigaretteless man that he faced Jack Skilling in the holy of holies of the home of the head of the executive. The President, hands folded, inclined his head in a listening pose, the furled flag of the Union behind him.

Jack Skilling was the first Canadian to assume the highest honour that America could accord a citizen of the Union. The addition of the Canadian provinces, along with the single province of Mexico, to the existing fifty-three states, had been seen as inevitable as early as 1980, beginning as an act of defensive unification against the increasing threat of Russchin and its Latin American satellites, a single military command begetting a centralised executive control in Washington. The British Commonwealth had gone into liquidation in 1979, save for sundry pockets faithful to the old sentimental ideal – chiefly Gibraltar,

New Zealand's southern island and Newfoundland. Jack Skilling had been born a member of that Commonwealth in Toronto, but had come early to New York City, there to be made mayor three terms running on an independent ticket. His candidacy for the Presidency was inevitably supported by the majority of English-speaking Canadians, and many citizens of the old Union had hopes that the Canadian tradition of comparative incorruptibility in politics might regenerate the White House. This was in spite of Skilling's far from immaculate record in City Hall, but it was recognised that New York could corrupt even the incorruptible. The general faith in Skilling as President had not, in the last four years, in fact been misplaced. The first New York mayor and the first Canadian to achieve the supreme office, he was also destined to be the last. But there was probably no better man around to preside over his country's final dissolution.

'Puma,' said Frame. At once Skilling took from a side table a copy of that morning's *Pravda*. He showed the headline without saying a word:

ПУМА – АМЕРИКАНСКИЙ ЗВЕРЬ!

'So,' said Frame. 'We might have expected that. The American beast in the sky. Single-minded, the Russians, I'll say that for them. How about the Chinese?'

'It ties up,' said Skilling, 'with the Year of the Cat. They follow the Russkie line, of course. The claws are paper, though – that's their foreseeable variation. As for the Presidium, it's already acting on the er astronomical data and making its salvatory preparations.'

'What kind of preparations? What kind of salvation?'

'A spaceship.'

'Ah.' Frame nodded. 'So you already know what I want to talk about.'

'Two things, isn't it? The need to plan a national evacuation to the centre of the American land-mass. The need to prepare our own spatial salvation. Or is that second project too previous?'

'The position is,' said Frame, 'that Puma will, after its devastating perigee –'

'How devastating?'

Frame, somewhat surprised at himself but realising the inadequacy of words to the situation, impulsively picked up the presidential paper-knife and walked a yard to the large terrestrial globe which, with its inset lights that marked capitals and strategic areas, shone like a Christmas tree in the afternoon gloom. Frame, gritting his teeth, sliced all the way down Africa, the plastic yielding easily. He jabbed and ripped at all the coastlines of the world, then stopped, breathless. 'Earthquakes,' he said, 'seaquakes, reawakened volcanoes. That's the gravitational pull. Sorry about that, by the way. I'll have another globe sent to you tomorrow.'

'No,' said the President, 'it's as well to have a true picture. I see you've put some of the lights out – London, Paris. There goes New York. There goes Washington.'

'Puma,' said Frame, 'will, after this devastating prologue, go away. It will circle the sun, joining our planetary system. But in the opposite direction to us and our sister planets. Then it will return, having, on the other side of the sun, come to some complicated conclusion as regards the solar pull and its own rotation. All our calculations point to its colliding with the earth – a glancing blow, a head-on crash, an irresistible tug. Its mass, as you know, is considerable.'

'Thank you,' Skilling said. 'I've already heard all this, of course. I won't look elsewhere for denial or confirmation. Your word will do for me. So,' he said, 'doomsday. Catday. Day of the Big Cat, the Final Catastrophe or Cataclysm. Politics,' he said, 'being the art of the possible, all the possibilities I can see relate to – putting off the end. Mass-evacuation from the coasts. The possible. How much of the final truth is it possible to tell the people?'

'It's easier for the big communist collectives,' Frame said gloomily. 'It's taken for granted there that nobody must know the truth. I'm no politician, but I can see no way out of the telling of the half-truth.'

Skilling smiled. 'Humankind,' he said, 'cannot bear very much reality. A poet said that. A ruler's job is to promote the bearability of life. This is the half-truth the people will be told – that a *temporary* quitting of the coastline will be necessary. And after that –'

'Temporary? There'll be no coast to go back to. As for the little island-nations – no hope, no waiting for the Day of the Cat. My people,' Frame said, 'came from England. No more England.'

'After that,' said Skilling, 'we get beyond the art of the possible. The presidential voice speaks soothing words over what's left of the communication media. And the Presidium will wave at us from space.'

'The request I make,' said Frame briskly, 'is that America be permitted to save something better than its mere rulers.'

The President grinned sourly. 'You mean its mere scientists?'

'No, no, no.' Frame was impatient. He longed for a cigarette, that injection having begun to wear off, and had no cigarettes. The President was a non-smoker. 'There are people, politicians among them, who would face with some equanimity the idea of floating for ever in space, round the sun, a new planet, or one of the moons of Jupiter. Life going on on a kind of endless cruise, complete with fornication and old movies on TV. An ark with no Ararat at the end of the voyage. My proposal is not one to appeal to politicians, nor to the man in the street. I want to see our civilisation preserved. I envisage a spaceship voyaging for centuries, millennia if need be, fraught with our achievements – books on microfilm, stereoscopic records of our architecture, music, thought, philosophy. I envisage it manned by fine bodies housing great brains, breeding a new generation, teaching it – the process going on for thousands of years if need be. And then, some day, landfall. A remote galaxy, a habitable planet. A fresh start for humanity, but not from scratch. This, I may say, is no mere dream. My daughter and I have long worked on the theoretical logistics of such a project –'

'Ever since you knew about Puma?'

'Long before, long long before. You understand the intricacies, the problems of coordination of the various specialisations involved. A ship to be totally self-sufficient, indefinitely, eternally – producing its own food, manufacturing its own tools – a city, a country in miniature, a civilisation in microcosm –' He coughed with embarrassment at the incipient swell of rhetoric. The politician brought him down to earth. He said:

'What do you want from me?'

'I want,' said Frame, 'a government grant without limit. Money will soon cease to mean very much. I suppose really what I'm asking is the resources you'd grant an army. I want a square mile in central Kansas, fenced round – it could be called, perhaps, a Center of Advanced Technology. CAT.' He grinned without mirth and waited for the inevitable question.

'Why Kansas?'

'An area which is, according to the seismologists, less likely to be disturbed by earth tremors than any other in the Union.'

'The obvious choice, then, for a centre, of government.'

'Keep government away,' warned Frame. 'We need isolation. Our project will be unpopular, will be totally misunderstood. It will be regarded as privileged self-salvation, not what it is really is –'

'And yet,' said Skilling, 'it is precisely that. A lucky few who are going to live, who are not going to face disaster. You, your daughter, your scientific friends –'

'My daughter, yes. Me, no. I'll not last out the year. As for the others – a matter of cybernetic choice. Leave it to the computers. We know the specialisations needed. We look for the best – physically, genetically. Men and women in equal numbers, for evident reasons. But no married couples. Perfection doesn't go in pairs, not in a world given over to imperfection. Mating in space, the creation of a new race that's never known earth –'

'The Space Race,' said the President. 'Your daughter's married, isn't she? To this science fiction man – my poor wife was very fond of him, incidentally –'

Frame cut in growling. 'There has to be a divorce. Or something. There's a problem there, but it can be solved. We can't afford the dead wood of paunchy fantasists. Fifty. I had in mind fifty. And room for the doubling of that population.'

'And what do they populate?'

'Tallis,' said Frame promptly. 'Tallis. The bare hull of Tallis. The CAT team, if I may call them that, will fit out Tallis to what I may term the Frame specifications.'

'Fill the frame with Frame,' said the President, a quick man with slogans. 'Who, by the way, told you you won't last out the year?'

'Never mind,' said Frame. 'It's true. Can we have Tallis?'

'Tallis,' frowned the President. Tallis was the latest of the space laboratories, very large, its propulsion mechanism already installed, due for launching six months hence. 'You talk,' he said slowly, 'in terms of a single venture. May there not be others?'

'Of course there may be others. There will be. And, if you'll permit a prophecy, there'll be a great deal of quiet talk soon, or perhaps not so quiet, about the saving of national cultures. China and Russia have been regarding themselves as mere provincial aspects of a single ideological entity, but you say that the Russian Presidium is thinking of its own skin – not the yellow ones of its Oriental comrades. I can't somehow see Europe wanting to save European culture. The Teutphones and Francophones – why the hell can't they be called what they used to be called, by the way? – the Germans will want a German space colony and the French –' He grinned. 'How is Canada going to feel about it all?'

'Nobody's going to feel anything about anything,' said this Canadian. 'There are going to be no plebiscites, no newspaper campaigns, no flags waving. There are going to be a host of Mayflowers and Speedwells and Santa Marias set up not by states but by free associations of experts. Is that what you and your colleagues – and I don't mean just American colleagues – have in mind?'

Frame nodded. 'It's the state's task to provide what only the state can provide – the resources of an army. Now how about Tallis?'

'It's fortunate in a way,' said Skilling, 'that the Communists are compelling us to set up a state of emergency. I can see no problem with a *carte blanche* emergency budget. Yes, you shall have Tallis. What, by the way, is going to happen to Lunamerica?'

'Thank you for Tallis,' Frame said. 'As for our Moon State – you realise that Puma may gain a satellite at our expense? That the moon may follow big heavy Puma and desert frail little Terra? I refer, of course, to mass, not to size. The moon is a woman.'

'What do we do about our Lunamericans?'

'Leave them there. They'll have their troubles, but they'll be smaller than ours.'

'State of emergency,' brooded the President. 'Congress will

respond more readily to talk of Commie threats than to something much more – palpable. I can hardly believe it. End of our historic cities. Of the America of our founding fathers. And yet I feel no particular depression. A lot of problems are going to be solved.'

'Such as?'

'A world overpopulated and underfed. Puma at least saves the world from Armageddon. And at the end of it all there's no justice. The overfed save civilisation.'

'Try to save it. Try to.'

'Where will Tallis make for?'

'Jupiter,' said Frame promptly. 'And, just beyond Jupiter, turn left for outer space. I think, by the way, Tallis must be renamed. Poor dead Tom Tallis won't mind. America, say. The spaceship America. America I. No reason why there shouldn't be other salvatory programmes – America II, III, IV. The more the better. As for Europe, I fear the sole hope lies in spaceship Europa, but there'll be failed attempts at a France, a Germany, an Italy instead. Best not think of the rest of the world.'

'You've enough on your plate with America I. Another question. How much do you know about the er composition of Puma?'

'I know what's in your mind,' said Frame. 'Is God destroying the earth in order to supplant it with a nice new fresh clean one? Will Puma be the new earth? No. Puma has no atmosphere. Frozen hydrogen ready to melt and vapourise when it gets close enough to solar heat. No, kill that hope in yourself, Mr President, kill it in others. We're facing the end of the world.'

Six

VOZ, the cybernetic monster which was the pride of Westchester University, was fed with the necessary data and disgorged fifty choice names. If the presence of the name Vanessa Brodie – demaritalised to Vanessa Mary Frame – was foreknown, this could not be attributed to nepotic cheating. A female specialist in ouranology, specifically trained by Professor Hubert Frame, healthy and of impeccable genetic antecedents, was required, and there was only one candidate, poor Muriel Pollock being too old and morbidly obese to qualify. But surely, boys and girls, ladies and gentlemen, if single status was a condition for membership of the ultimate élite, there was sharp practice proceeding? Was not Vanessa, despite the anagraphic fiction just alluded to, still married to Valentine Brodie, formerly lecturer in Science Fiction but now, at his urgent request, transferred to the Department of Drama? The answer must be yes and no.

During dinner one evening in early March, while they were engaged on the main course, Val choked on a mouthful of chicken Marengo when his wife, without preamble, said:

'Tomorrow morning I cease to be Mrs Brodie and revert to my *nom de jeune femme*, as the Francophones so delicately put it.'

Val spent fifteen seconds of concentration on the dislodgement of a small bone from his throat. He eventually, gasping, said: 'This is very sudden.'

'Oh come, you know it's only a formality. No marrieds on the CAT team. So now we're both perfectly qualified.'

Val stared wide-eyed. She had fed him two incredible hunks of information at the same time, as well as this chicken Marengo. He did not know what to say first. He said: 'But – is this – I mean – is it *legally* possible?'

'The filing of a divorce petition is being taken as the equivalent of a resumption of unmarried status. The divorce petition will be filed tomorrow morning. I take it that you're not going to oppose it.'

'What,' he gasped, 'are the grounds?'

She smiled sweetly, carving delicately at the fried egg that rested on a golden crouton. 'The Muslims have a useful short word – *nusus*. It means the unwillingness of one of the marital partners to cohabit with the other.'

Val had nothing to say to that, but he was surprised to find his penis twitching. Perverse, how perverse the human instincts. He said: 'You said *we're* qualified, *we*. You mean I was fed into that computer? On what possible basis could I possibly be considered to be –'

'You're number fifty-one. A supernumerary. Archivist, historian, diarist, documentarian. Do you consider yourself unqualified?'

'But this sounds like cheating. There must be hundreds, thousands – I mean, how did you work it?'

'Totally against father's wishes, I may say. And it wasn't *worked*, as you term it. Consider the qualifications required. Writer – not enough. Writer with style well-regarded by the critics – great narrowing of the field. Writer with smattering of science. Writer under forty. Writer healthy and –'

'I'm not all that healthy.'

'– Writer with Celtic blood. We have to watch the racial balance. Your family comes from Dundee, Scotland.'

'It sounds like cheating to me.' He brooded, brooding Brodie.

'Writer acquainted with Framean ouranologistics.'

'Cheating, cheating.' He pushed his plate away, frowning like Napoleon. 'I'm not going, you know. It's not fair.'

'Finally, writer opposed to élitism of any kind. You're going, my boy. It's not going to be a matter of choice. You'll be under quasi-military orders.'

'And if I disobey?' He grinned. 'Am I sentenced to death in a year's time?'

'I don't think the thought of anybody's actually disobeying has as yet been entertained,' she said in her prim way. 'I should imagine you would be put into the work-force.'

'What work-force?'

'The CAT work-force. The hewers and hammerers. The camp-builders.'

'Will they know what they're building?' He took a sauced cooling fowl-bone between thumb and index and nibbled.

'No,' she said, pushing away her plate. 'They won't exactly. The story is that Tallis will be the last word in spacelabs. That is, shall we say, retrospectively true.'

'Tallis?'

'Tallis. Taken over by CAT and renamed America. Tallis the selenologist is being accorded the ultimate honour.'

'An ignorant mob,' said Val, 'that doesn't know it's working its guts out to save a select fifty. I wouldn't mind working as one of the mob. I'd preach revolt.'

She looked steadily at him, elbows on table, hands delicately enlaced. 'Yes, you would, wouldn't you? This – democratic spirit of yours was something required by the programme. Anti-élitist. The common touch. But you mustn't let it go too far. You'd probably be shot. And don't start saying that everybody's going to die anyway – nearly everybody. There's still precious time ahead, more precious than time has ever been. Life can be good, you know, and life certainly isn't going to be dull. You won't want to be shot, believe me.'

Her cold blood chilled him. When the coffee-machine came in, it dispensed a beverage that seemed hotter than usual. He warmed his hands on his cup.

'Think,' she said, 'what the project means. It's nothing to do with the saving of a few select lives. It's concerned with the salvage of a civilisation.'

He tasted the words. 'Where did the idea come from? What committee worked it out? It doesn't sound like your father, God proleptically rest him and his finished lungs. He's always been a great growler against what man's made of the world. Is it you? What the hell do you know of civilisation?'

'If,' she said, 'by civilisation you mean the flea-bitten French and Florentines and British who produced rags of poetry and cynical amorous caterwaulings and big stone wedding-cakes to the glory of what they called God – well, yes, it doesn't interest me much. But I believe in knowledge and the transmission of knowledge and the dream of setting that knowledge to work again – some day, somewhere.'

'Is there a somewhere?'

She looked down at her hands and then up, fiercely, at Val. 'Yes,' she said. 'Yes. Yes.'

That identical vocable was being breathed by Edwina Duffy at that very moment, naked in the naked arms of young Professor Nat Goya in the tumbled bed of his apartment. It was an injunction to him to thrust home seed which, she prayed, would make her pregnant. This evening's love-making was not, to either of them, a mere casual satisfying of appetite breaking into the labour of paper-marking. It was an anticipation of the consummatory act. It was sac-ramental. They now knew they loved each other, and tomorrow they proposed being married before a magistrate in Trenton, New Jersey. Secretly. A secret. Their secret. For the moment, anyway. Edwina's parents in Hawaii did not approve of Nat Goya. Nat Goya was still supposed to be affianced to a girl in Charlottesville, Virginia. Unpleasantnesses were always best put off. They would get down, they had decided, to announcing their happy state during the Easter vacation. All the time in the world. Nat now smiled, kissed Edwina, and went to the little kitchen to make instant coffee.

'No. No. No.'

That vocable was now being uttered very sharply by Vanessa Brodie, Frame as she would be again tomorrow. The coffee, not instant, that had been served by her handsome modern machine, was serving as a prelude, not postlude, to an amorous impulse. Not the fulfilment, the attempt. Val was surprised at himself. The cognac he had taken with his second and third cups of coffee might have had something to do with it. But his impending liberation from matrimony's bonds, the restoration of what had once been called, children, existential freedom might have fired his glands more effectually than alcohol. He was, yes, surprised at himself, but also, in a manner, to some extent, not surprised. He was a sort of novelist, he was empirically interested in human nature, he was given to observation and introspection. Still, he gaped at himself as he tried to take his still lawful wife in his arms, lewdly, as it appeared to himself (lewdly? Because love, or at least decent ordinary affection, wasn't coming into it?), and was not really surprised when his wife fended him off with her triple no.

Hands limp by his sides, Val said: 'Our last night together as a married couple. It seemed to call for, you know –'

'You're beastly. But you'll learn. There'll be all the time in the world to learn.'

'Yes,' said Val. 'No.' And he went out to get the hangtrain and find his fat friend in Manhattan.

'Yes. Yes. Yes.'

The words were being spoken in colourless clinical confirmation by Dr Emile Fouilhoux, carcinomologist and personal friend of Professor Hubert Frame. He gave a yes to each röntgen image of Frame's pulmonary economy, as the two sat together – long after office hours – in Fouilhoux's surgery. 'So,' said Frame, 'how long do I have?'

'Strictly speaking,' said Fouilhoux, 'you shouldn't be with us at all. Why did you do this to yourself?'

'I've always liked cigarette smoking,' said Frame. 'Probably because both my parents were violent anti-smokers. They both died, incidentally, of lung cancer.'

'Six months ago,' said Fouilhoux, 'pneumometaphyteusis might have been possible – you know, lung transplant. All I can suggest now is that you enter the Bodenheim. You'll need looking after.'

'I've work to do,' Frame said.

'You'll do no more work.'

'I must. Important things are happening.'

'You're functioning on a minute area of lung. I can give you a supply of DCT3. It won't help all that much, I'm afraid. You ought to be connected to a pneumosurrog. That means the Bodenheim.'

'I need six months. No more than six months.'

'You'll be lucky to get that,' said Fouilhoux gravely. 'Very lucky.'

Meanwhile Val and his huge friend Courtland Willett were coming out of one bar off Broadway and making their way to another. There was a bright light in the sky, not the moon. The moon had still to rise. The air this night was remarkably clear. 'Look,' said Willett, 'Venus.'

'No,' said Val sadly. 'Puma.'

'Venus,' affirmed Willett, 'the planet of love. My God, you can feel it snuffling around you tonight – love, the burgeoning of green things, spring.' He began to recite loudly, with round gestures:

'Tomorrow will be love for the loveless, and for the lover love.
The day of the primal marriage, the copulation
Of the irreducible particles; the day when Venus
Sprang fully-armed from the wedding blossoms of spray
And the green dance of the surge, while the flying horses
Neighed and whinnied about her, the monstrous conchs
Blasted their intolerable joy!'

People in the street paused, open-mouthed or derisive, listening and looking. A policeman said: 'Okay, okay, break it up.'

'Love,' said Willett, ignoring the cop. 'The next transit of Venus was due in 2004, so I read or thought I read, but things must have gotten speeded up. How much money have you?'

'About thirty-five dollars. And my credit cards.'

'Good. We'll go to Madame Aphrodite's. Appropriate, highly. That's Venus up there,' he said to a young flashy black.

Madame Aphrodite's was a house of pleasure on East 44th Street. The titular owner was as much a myth as her divine namesake, and the place was run by a certain Mrs Simona de Lancey, a black woman of fifty-odd and startling handsomeness. 'No trouble,' she said to Willett. 'I want no trouble tonight, nor no poetry neither.'

'Love,' said Willett, gesturing so widely that he hit from a flower-table in the vestibule a plaster statuette of love's goddess (Botticelli version). 'We come for love.'

'You can have that, baby.'

Val was both surprised and not surprised when he chose, from the bevy presented in the sitting-and-drinking-room, a girl of lissom and chill blue-eyed beauty with whom, in her patchouli-scented cubicle, he made love sobbingly. No dark musky creatures of swamp and jungle tonight. 'It seemed you needed that, honey,' said the girl afterwards. They both lay, smoking, sipping whisky, listening to Willett proclaiming from another room of love:

'People in the streets are dancing, kissing each other.
Cats are wailing in most melodious counterpoint,
Bitches have had a miraculous accession of heat.
In the Bronx Zoo there must be amorous pandemonium,
Probosces wantonly wreathing, capillary erections
Of leopards and panthers. Probably even the tortoise
Moves with a sort of leisurely impetuosity.
And the air is full of the headiest distillation,
Chiming madly like bells. It's like a
Gratuitous Christmas, an antipodeal Christmas...'

'Nuts,' said Val's companion, whose name was Stella. 'He's nuts.'

'An antipodeal Christmas,' muttered Val. 'That's when the world began to change.'

'What's that you're saying, honey?'

'Never mind,' Val said. 'My friend Courtland Willett isn't nuts. Far from it.'

Nor was he. Although he mistook the identity of that bright planet, he was not wrong in supposing that its gravitational pull would produce certain glandular and psychic changes. Another three weeks and people would be driven to impulses they would, at first, be aware of as quite uncharacteristic. Love, yes, but also jealousy, rage bred of no clear motive, religious mania, dementias of various kinds. A radio was now turned up in another cubicle, in order that Willett's rhapsody be drowned. But he had already finished and

was audibly at work on some act ecstatic but sub-poetic. The radio
sang:

'Pounce on me, Puma,
Puma, Puma.
For I'm in the humour
(It's no idle rumour)
Tonight.'

Seven

These, for the record, boys and girls, were the names and specialisations disgorged by VOZ. They are names you will know, names still living among you. Some of them.

Abramovitz, David T., bibliothecologist
Adams, Maude Quincy, ouranoclinician
Audelan, Vincent, hydroponist
Belluschi, Robert F., microbiologist
Bogardus, Sarah, engineer
Boudinot, Louise, engineer
Cézanne, Miguel S., electronologist
Christian, Katharine, heliergonomist
Cornwallis, Douglas C., physicist
Da Verrazano, Gianna, microbibliothecologist
DeWitt, Felicia, biochemist
Durante, John R., engineer
Eastman, K.O., diastemoploionologist
Eidlitz, Mackenzie, energiologist
Ewing, Georges Auguste, diastemiconographer
Farragut, Minnie, physicist
Forster, Sylvia, hupologistics engineer
Frame, Vanessa Mary, coordinating ouranologist
Fried, Sophie Haas, ouranoclinician
Goya, Nathaniel, microagronomist
Greeley, William, diastemopsychologist

Harrison, Belle, cybernetologist
Hazard, Ebenezer, supplies coordinator
Herodotus, Alger, physicist
Irving, Guinevere, atmospherologist
Jumel, Lilian, engineer
Kopple, Grayson, mellonologist
La Farge, Gertrude, maieutist/general secretary
Lopez, Fred K., engineer
Markelius, Sven Maximilian Josiah, oicodomicologist
Moshowitz, Israel, morphoticist
McGregor, Herman A., ploiarch 1.
McEntegart, Angus, ploiarch 2.
Nesbit, Florence, mageirist
O'Farrell, Terence, rapticologist
O'Grady, Lee Harvey, astunomicologist
Opisso, Rosalba, diaitologist
Parkhurst, Ethel Armand, engineer
Piccirilli, Attilia, electronologist
Prometeo, Susanna, anacoinotic engineer
Reiser, Deborah, physicist
Roelantsen, Julius C.C., electrical engineer
Sennacherib, Betsy, morphoticist
Skidmore, Owings Merrill, expert in domestic scediastics
Thackeray, Jessica Laura, biochemist
Untermeyer, Fernando S., ouranoclinician
Velasquez, Wouter van Twiller, diastemographer
Wolheim, Fernando Alexander, petrologist
Yamasaki, Minoru, botanical engineer.

Note the pitiful lack of Mexican names, the very slight preponderance of males, the absence of the name Valentine Brodie, which came after the above list had been completed, and the fact that here, to my computation, you will find forty-nine instead of the fifty scheduled. The fiftieth name, or fourth taking it alphabetically, was Paul Maxwell Bartlett, whose official title eschewed Greekish pretension and was simply Head of Enterprise or HE, or, in the eventual colloquial of the team, Boss Cat. His importance requires that we take a closer look at him than can be accorded to any of the others, except, of course, those in the human foreground of our narrative. *Who's Who*, 1999, gives the following curriculum vitae:

BARTLETT, Paul Maxwell; Coordinating Principal, Combined Space Research Projects of Columbia, Princeton, M.I.T. and Univ. of Pennsylvania; Bronze Star 1989; Legion of Merit 1990; Presidential Unit Citation 1991; DSM 1992 (U.S. Navy Special Attachment with temp. rank of Rear-Admiral); Ph.D. (Harvard), D.Sc. (Cantab.), hon. Ph.D. Univs. of Toronto, Pasadena, California, Washington State, etc.; *b.* 17 Dec, 1958; *s.* of Maxwell Everard Bartlett, D.D. and Dorothy Aline Goodhew; unmarried. *Educ.:* Choate School; Harvard; Trinity Coll., Cambridge; Sorbonne. Professor of Astrophysics, Univ. of Delaware, 1985–86; Member, U.S. Federal Satellite Commission, 1986–87; Adviser, U.S. Defense Project Achilles, 1987; Commander, Mission Philoctetes, 1988–1992; Professor of Ouranology, M.I.T., 1992–95; Delegate, Global Diastemic Organisation, 1995–6; Visiting Distinguished Professor, Univ. of Tokyo, 1996–98. *Publications:* Into Space, 1988; An Enquiry into Anti-Matter (with L.B. Moran), 1990; The Future of Man, 1992; Critique of the Hopkinsian Radiation Belt Doctrine, 1993; What I Have Learned, 1995; Scenarios Relating to Project Discipline, 1998. *Recreations:* Athletics, biography, political philosophy. *Address:* 10A, 366 West End Avenue, New York City. Tel: (212) 6894–4400.

A skeletal summary, no more, mere logarithms of ability. No one, meeting the man even casually, could be unaware of the intelligence, the scientific hunger, the dynamic of intuition, the great gift of leadership. Further enquiries into his life and personality would disclose a total lack of vice – he ate sparingly, drank only on social occasions, had no notable sexual life – and a balanced sanity of mind and body very rare outside epic fiction. Large, handsome, strong, vital, he was a flame on the tennis court, a fish in the swimming pool, a thudding menace in the boxing ring. But he was urbane, eloquent and lucid in conference, and he even wrote well. Those books of his which had a 'popular' pseudo-philosophical theme – as opposed to the uncompromisingly technical works which had made his name in the inner circles of science and scientific strategy – showed that he thought deeply about man's place in the universe. He had read widely outside his own fields, and his *The Future of Man*, for example, was heavily footnoted with citations from Heidegger, Reich, Jung, and Teilhard de Chardin.

Most of his non-scientific reading, however, was, as his *Who's Who* entry indicated, in the area of a concept which may be vaguely termed, ladies and gentlemen, as the 'man of destiny'. He believed that some human beings were better, or certainly cleverer, than others, and that these were destined to lead. His favourite biographical subjects were Metternich, Napoleon Buonaparte, Cromwell, Winston Churchill, and, alas, Adolf Hitler. All these men had risen to power and fallen from it. He was concerned with tracing the course of the human parabola in each story, probing for the weaknesses but at the same time trying to analyse the strengths. His interest in political philosophy was narrower than was appropriate to an American democrat. He read and reread *The Republic* of Plato, Hobbes's *Leviathan*, and Prauschnitz's *Doctrine of the Elite*. From his study of Aristotle he remembered that the term democracy denoted a perversion of government, not a wholesome ideal to be propagated among nations unlucky or stupid enough not to have discovered its beauties for themselves. *Demos*, after all, meant 'the mob'.

One recreation he must have regarded as too trivial to be recorded. As a temporary high-ranking officer of the U.S. Navy, he had disclosed not merely a powerful physical bravery but also a martinettish temper that served marvellously when quick decisions had to be enforced. He was, it was quietly recognised, a natural leader. His professional colleagues were glad to see him return to civilian life. He himself was eager to get on with research unhampered by considerations of national defence, but he did not forget the simple joys of command. Often in his apartment, behind locked doors, he would put on his naval uniform, which he kept clean and pressed, and enact, all alone, a tense moment on the quarterdeck, using a vocabulary derived from old films like *Mutiny on the Bounty*. He never troubled about anachronism and would order keelhauling, would himself even lash out occasionally at the furniture with a cat-o'-nine-tails normally kept locked in the documents safe. All this represented a harmless diversion which, to one in his high-strung position, was sweetly cathartic.

When the letter conferring the highest power of his career arrived, Paul Bartlett was dressed as a civilian, ready to set off for the weekly inter-university conference in Dalrymple Hall on the Columbia campus – within walking distance of his apartment. The letter was headed with the presidential seal, a note stated that the paper would self-destroy an hour after the opening of the envelope, the letter itself informed him that he was appointed head of a most secret enterprise and that he was to report at Lindsay Airport, Concourse D, Green Lounge, at 0400 hours on April 2nd. There was another letter, inviting him to dinner at the home of Professor Vanessa Frame the following evening and would he please blepophone if he was unable to come. Bartlett smiled to himself; he thought he knew what all this was about.

Next evening, as he got into his car for the drive to Westchester, he noticed that Puma was well above the horizon and now about half the size of the moon (both were just starting their first quarter). The citizens of Manhattan, not easily moved by anything, were nevertheless fascinated by Puma. Some stood in the streets gawping up at it, some – complementing the Russian allegation – swore it was a Communist device for observing American ballistic installations, others had become religious and spoke of the Day of Judgment, yet others – chiefly the idle young – were making a cult of it and banging drums and shrilling pipes and swinging asses and hips nightly at it. On some, highly impressionable, psyches it was producing an instability manifested in various bizarre forms – sudden bad temper, often of a murderous kind, in normally placid temperaments; placidity in the normally violent; incursions of poetic inspiration among stolid bank managers and insurance brokers; satyriasis; sadism; a longing, as in pregnancy, for strange foods. Bartlett knew from one of his medical colleagues that the menstrual cycle, especially in girls under twenty, was being disrupted. He himself had been aware of incipient bouts of light-headedness. Coming, a couple of days before, out of his office in Dalrymple Hall, he had felt impelled to embrace a not very personable secretary of the department. Shocked at himself, he had laughed off the aberration. 'A touch of the Pumas, Sybil, sorry.' Librium seemed to help some. Tablets called Pumoids were on sale at Mens, Sana, Corpore and other fine pharmacies.

At the house of Professor Vanessa Frame, he found his hostess lovely in black silk, a science-fiction writer called Brodie slightly drunk, and Professor Hubert Frame in shocking condition. He was encased from waist to shoulders in a noisy respirator plugged into a power-point on the wall, equipped also with batteries for travelling between point and point. He had not seen Frame since the last Natsci conference, when he had been smoking and coughing much but seemed vigorous enough. Now he was clearly a dying man. Vanessa he had met at some great science convocation or other; the SF man he did not know at all. The genre he practised Bartlett certainly despised as having little to do with science; he wondered what the man was doing here.

The dinner was one of Vanessa's finest – watercress soup with croutons; roast duck with orange, braised celery; English sherry trifle. But Bartlett was not given to the refinements of the senses, Frame was too ill and Brodie too bleary with drink to eat much. Vanessa said, as if to excuse a meal she had foreknown nobody would eat, something about the days of the *haute cuisine* being numbered. 'We're joining the army,' she said.

'*Your* army,' Frame said to Bartlett. Bartlett frowned slightly. It was as if he were an appointee of the Frames, a puppet general. The Frames talked too freely of the project in the presence of this SF soak. Bartlett put it to the soak bluntly:

'Where do you come into all this?'

'Some day,' Brodie said, 'on a distant planet in an unfathomably far galaxy, schoolchildren will read a book with some such title as *Annals of the Star Trek* or *How Civilisation Was Saved*. I shall have written that book.' Bartlett grunted. Bartlett said to Frame:

'Where is the place?'

'Classified information,' Frame gasped. 'We'll all know when we get there.'

'But somebody knows.'

'The President knows. I know.'

'But I'm not permitted to know,' said Bartlett. 'Interesting.'

'We have to watch security,' Frame wheezed, his respirator wheezing with him.

'We? Who's we?'

'The project,' said Vanessa, 'had to start somewhere. It started with my father.'

'And presumably with you?'

'Well, yes. My father trained me.'

'Back to this *we*,' Bartlett said to Frame. 'You yourself are going to Station X or Y or whatever it's called?' Frame seemed to wheeze yes. 'In what capacity?'

'Adviser,' Frame said. 'Adviser as to what? As to the implementation of the project.'

'Look,' said Bartlett, 'how far am I really in charge?'

'Oh, all the way,' Vanessa said. 'As soon as you know what you're in charge of. Have you a Z class decodifier? At home?'

'Of course.'

'Well, then –'And as if she were fetching a cold dessert from the sideboard she went to the sideboard and fetched a bulky bound typescript with RPT(3a) printed on the blancmange-coloured cover. She gave it to Bartlett. Brodie grinned faintly and Bartlett saw the grin. He looked the grinner in the eye while he addressed the other two. He said:

'I'm not particularly sure that I shall require advice.'

'You'll get it just the same,' Frame said.

'You don't look particularly healthy to me.'

'That's my concern.'

'It's the concern of the project. Do we travel together on April 2nd? I take it for granted you know everything.'

'You have a camp to set up,' Frame said. 'A work-force will have been dispatched to erect the basic living-units. Army, of course. You're an ex-serviceman, you'll know the kind of discipline needed.'

'I'm navy.'

'I know. The army knows more about setting up things on dry land than the navy. That's just the way things are. The personnel of the project will be travelling in separate small groups. Staggered. Security again. My daughter and I will arrive at CAT on April 12th.'

'And er this gentleman?'

'Dr Brodie,' Vanessa said, 'must be in on things from the beginning.'

'That's right,' said Val Brodie. 'In on things from the beginning.' The coffee had arrived. Val brought cognac from the bar, zigzagging slightly. 'You haven't touched your claret, I notice,' he said. 'Perhaps you're a hard-stuff man, like me. Let's drink to the salvaging of civilisation.'

'I don't drink,' said Bartlett.

'None of us will drink,' said Val with sudden gloom. 'An end to drinking. But what sort of civilisation will it be without drink? Or,' he grinned at Frame, 'without tobacco?' Frame grunted.

Bartlett waved the typescript grimly. 'I'd better start reading this now. So, if you'll excuse me –'

'That's right,' Val said. 'You start reading it now.'

'Were you ever in the service?' Bartlett asked him, getting up.

'Alas, no. Always a free civilian.' Bartlett nodded, as to indicate that all that was going to change. Then he left, without thanking his hostess for the dinner. 'Friendly sort of bastard,' Val said.

'He's what's needed,' said Frame.

'By me, no,' Val shuddered.

'*You* are not needed.'

'Let us not start that again,' cried Vanessa. 'Shall I put you to bed, father?' For now there were three bedrooms in use in the Brodie-Frame apartment.

'Let's hear the President first. Ten o'clock.'

They caught the end of the nine-thirty telenewsummary. Disaster in Portugal, they caught: devastating tides overbearing Aveiro, Odemiro and Comporta. It was a long way away. The culprit filled the screen: Puma, in high colour, very flushed. The President of the United States came on, easy, smiling, unpanicky. His words, he said, were addressed to the entire Union. He would use English first, Spanish after. What he had to tell them about was a very simple matter of elementary science, a question of gravity – that strange thing they would all have learned about at school: Newton and the apple and so on. Everybody knew how the moon pulled tides just as the earth pulled apples. Well, the moon, old friend, was being temporarily joined by the planet Puma, a new friend, in exerting a gravitational pull on the tides of a force not known before in history. Coastal dwellers would be in some danger. Accordingly, the Federal government was joining state and city governments in establishing certain emergency facilities to be employed during the period of greatest hazard. All coastal dwellers who had (a) their own transport and (b) friends and relatives in Nebraska, Colorado, the Dakotas, Oklahoma and other central states were advised to make their own arrangements to effect temporary – temporary only – evacuation within the next three weeks. Coastal dwellers without one or the other or both of these advantages would be transported free, where necessary, to special emergency camps or hostels, where necessary, in the scheduled safety zones. There is nothing, said the President, to worry about. The Communists are not coming with bombs and gases. Nature, neutral nature, nobody's enemy, is making things a little difficult for us, no more. In a month or so, when Puma's transit takes him away from the earth, things will be as they were before. He smiled, wished everybody good luck, and then began again in Toronto Spanish. A typical politician's performance. When he had done, the local station gave another such show, this time with the Mayor of New York, who spoke about reporting times, places, the need to keep cool. Business would go back to normal after a brief exciting interim, in which the Federal government was making itself responsible for the basic amenities of evacuated life. He repeated this in Spanish and Kuo-Yü.

When Hubert Frame had been put to bed, Val disclosed himself as sober enough. The irresponsible artist act had been chiefly for the benefit of their cold masterful guest. He put his arms gently about

Vanessa's cool body and kissed her gently on her cool lips. 'Shall we,' he asked gently, 'commit an act that is technically fornication? An act which, I fear, will not be officially approved of when the great work begins?'

She smiled and, there on the living-room floor, she collaborated in the exordia of the act – the baring of her shoulders and arms and breasts and back, a delicacy of caressing which grew ever more ardent, and soon the two of them lying naked together, and his tenderness modulating to a fire, and then:

'Not like that,' she said. 'Not that way at all. Let me show you.'

'Oh, my God,' he groaned.

'You know it. It was Plate 4 in *Hamsun*. I showed it you, you know it.'

'Oh, Jesus Christ.' He was up, dancing into his pants, flaccid.

'You don't love me,' she cried from the floor. 'That's the trouble, you just don't –'

'Has everything to be science? Every fucking thing? I know now that I don't want your kind of civilisation to be saved. Is there no room for for for clumsiness and humanity and imperfection and drunkenness and and –'

'And whores,' she sobbed. 'Filthy whores. Goats and monkeys.'

He grinned sourly. 'That's from *Othello*,' he said. 'I didn't know you'd read any Shakespeare.' And then he slammed out to get drunk in Puma-crazed Manhattan.

Eight

The first floods did not seem so very terrible. On April 3rd, the day after Paul Bartlett's departure for a place unnamed, water came swirling in over the Battery, the Hudson roared and hit at the quays, the East River sloggered at the United Free Nations Building and dislodged its bas-relief emblem on the riverward wall (a bronze pregnant female figure with arms raised towards a solar cornucopia). The waters were quick to recede in the normal tidal rhythm, leaving streets no dirtier than usual, but the timider citizens began their exodus. On April 11th there were earth-tremors in the Bedford-Stuyvesant district of Brooklyn, an area of the borough habituated to calamity. There was also water at waist-height on Fifth Avenue, swift however to go gurgling down the gutters. Bad things were happening abroad but, in the interests of maintaining American tranquillity, few of these were being divulged through the regular channels of communication. Still, stories of the entire destruction of Auckland, New Zealand, were leaking in, as well as of the deaths of innumerable coastal towns on the Malay archipelago. As for San Francisco, already totally evacuated, there was as yet no report of unusual seismic activity. This, to many, seemed more ominous than tranquillising. Nature was dabbling, yawning, taking her time.

At eleven o'clock on the evening of April 12th, Vanessa and Val and Professor Frame were packed and ready. Their plane did not leave till four in the morning, but Vanessa, the cool, the careful, never liked leaving things till the last moment. Besides, there was the task of recharging Frame's batteries for the car journey to Lindsay

Airport. On the aircraft he would be able to plug into one of the galley points; at CAT he would be permanently set up in his own bedroom-office. Permanently? He gave himself four months. The machine strapped to his body was an ingenious device that, with the aid of a catalyst known as DCT3, converted oxides to oxygen which rhythmically flooded his bloodstream but enabled him to expire the wastes orally, so that he had a normal supply of breathed-out gases for the speech process. But his heart, he knew, was not going to last much longer. He was on the blepophone now, saying goodbye to Muriel Pollock, whose fat face was clearly tear-streaked on the bleposcreen. Meanwhile Val bit his nails.

'What time do we leave here?' he asked.

'About two-thirty,' Vanessa answered. 'Why?'

'I think I'll go into town. A last look. A last drink with, you know, friends.'

'You'll do nothing of the kind.'

'Let him,' glared Frame, putting down the handset and automatically switching off poor Muriel's image. 'Let him. Let him be late if he wishes. We shan't wait. We have our orders.'

'I shan't be late,' Val glared back. 'You old bastard.'

'Father,' Vanessa cried in distress. 'Val. Oh, why can't you both –'

Val stamped out. Frame said: 'As the word *bastard* has been used, let it be used again. Why do you say you love that *bastard*?'

'I don't know. Love isn't a thing you analyse.'

'I'll tell you why. You love him as a chunk of raw material you think you can mould. Pygmalion and Galatea in reverse.'

'Who? Never heard of them. Oh, I don't know. I think it's because – he's so chaotic.'

'Exactly. You want to do something with that chaos.'

'No, no, not that. There's something in me that – responds to chaos. To imagination, indiscipline, call it what you like. Or perhaps to a different kind of organisation than science can provide. You know what I mean.'

'Poetry. Verbal narcotics.'

'It's not altogether sincere of you,' she said primly, 'to sneer at narcotics.'

'I hope he gets drowned.'

'The tides are quiet tonight. Because of the winds or something.'

'Beaten up, then. Killed.'

'You *are* an old bastard,' Vanessa said. The word sounded terrible on her cool tongue. 'You like him really. You're more alike than you'll admit.'

'There was only one man for you.'

'I never liked him.'

'Never mind, never mind.' Frame closed his eyes, weary. 'I'll sleep a little.'

So Vanessa, troubled greatly in one part of her mind but coldly organised in another, completed the packing of her hand-luggage. Some book to read on the journey, a book totally unconnected with the project, a book chaotic or submissive to a different kind of organisation than science could provide? She looked at the hundreds of books they were leaving behind. She picked out one – a volume of poems by Val, his first publication, a private printing done in Iowa City at the state university's Windhover Press. The little collection was called *Searfskin*. 'Not my flesh,' he had told her, 'not even my skin. The parings of my skin. I was getting small things out of the way in preparation for the big things.' But the big things had never been written – only pitiable romances based on hypotheses scientifically untenable. She read a poem at random:

Why would you not yield
As the field to the plough
As the cow to the milking
As the silk to the weaving
As the leaves to the wind
As the skin to the peeling
The bell to the pealing
Pealing pealing pealing
Our lives away?

She wept a little. She had no great capacity for tears, but she wept a little. And she packed the little book in her little bag.

Puma was bright and bloody tonight, seeming to stand like an ornamental artefact, as Val stood and looked up an instant on Fifth Avenue, on the pinnacle of the Partington Building, balanced, if you looked from one particular angle, like a blood orange on the tip of a finger. On Fifth Avenue a group of yellow-robed monks, hair shaven, gave exotic song to the heavenly body, banging little drums, tinkling little cymbals. In St Patrick's Cathedral, interdenominational or panchristian since the Fourth Vatican Council had dissolved Roman Catholicism in favour of a kind of Hookerian faith that, in the face of the menace of oil-rich Islam, might reconcile all Christian sects, a night service was in progress which was crammed to the doors. Val, unseduced by religion, went to Jack's Tavern on West 46th Street, there to find his friend Willett in full flood. Willett, who had recently completed a small acting stint for television (he had played Orson Welles in a dramatisation – somewhat indiscreet, seeing the need to keep public panic down – of the creation of that ancient radio adaptation of the other Wells's *War of the Worlds*, and its devastating effect on a public whose naïvité the present American public had long outgrown) and was in funds, was drinking away and inveighing against a Calvin Gropius rally that was being televised:

'Shitabed scoundrel, slapsauce druggel, jobbernol gnatsnapper, codshead looby, turdgut.' But many of the customers told him to hold it, shut it, pipe down, quiet friend, they were interested. The point was that Gropius's audience was restive, shouting back, not willing to accept his slavery to the Bible and his attempts to impose that slavery on his congregation. To Val, what words of Gropius got through seemed not unreasonable, granted his theological premise:

'There are times when God warns – and if you will not have it that it is God directly sending us these prodigies in the sky and on the earth, at least take it that times of fear have come upon us – warns, I say, each and every one of us to take stock of our lives, examine our faults, consider that mankind approaches a judgment –' He tapped his bible vigorously and tried to recite from the Book of Revelations, but his voice was overcome by the collective voice of a huge block of opponents that, well drilled, was on its feet, shouting slogans, waving banners. LIVEDOG, said the banners, LIVEDOG LIVEDOG, and the slogans took up the name – 'Live for Livedog, Kill for Livedog'. Val saw that the name was compounded of God and Devil spelt backwards. He nodded to himself – a science fiction situation. Evil? That didn't perhaps come into it. The new god was beyond morality, the ultimate supernatural to be appeased. Puma was his body.

'Where's this?' he asked the bartender.

'Sacramento, California.'

California, seedbed of crank faiths. He watched the screen intently, and even Willett, despite odd grumbles about codshead jobbernols, had eyes of interest on it. The meeting was being disrupted by the Livedog body but a purely secular element had crept into the proceedings – young men and women stripping off their clothes and engaging in the movements of bacchanalia – frotting, mock or real buggery, fellation – to the tune of 'Pounce on me, Puma'. The scene was cut off rapidly and commercials supervened, the sanity of salesmanship – cars, carboats, boatcars, traveboxes, realtors seeking to buy not sell. 'Out of here,' said Willett.

'You know I'm off tonight?' Val said.

'Off? Where?' Val saw two Pumas in Willett's great bloodshot eyes.

'CAT. Center of Advanced Technology. Where I don't know. Highly secret.'

'Off, then.' Willett nodded. They were walking towards Sixth Avenue (which had once been called the Avenue of the Americas). 'The wind,' he said. 'It's changing. There'll be trouble before the night's out. Man is born to trouble, yes yes. In my fifty-five years I've seen as much as any man. I can smell something on that wind. Puma, cat, catastrophe. I'm a wordman, I can read things too. Is there going to be an end of trouble?'

'I don't know,' lied Val, loyal to something – her? 'I'm wanted as a kind of literary recorder of this moon project.'

'What's this? People escaping to the moon?'

'Not escaping exactly. The moon, I understand, may leave earth's orbit and become a satellite of Puma. Think of what that means to scientists. Science fictionists, too. Puma snuffles off, its moon with it, scientists observing, busy as hell. Me with them.'

'You should sound excited.'

'Oh hell, I don't want to go. I'm an earthman, like you.'

Willett grunted. 'Let's go and eat. Something gross and sustaining. Beef pudding and sausages and stewed tripe and jam pudding. Great grumbling spuds roast in their overcoats. Beer by the quart.'

'Quart?'

'You won't have heard of quarts. Too young.' He quoted loudly to the crowded street:

'Oh I have been to Ludlow Fair
And left my necktie God knows where
And carried halfway home or near
Pints and quarts of Ludlow beer.'

A young Teutprot did a lip-fart at him. 'Lob-dotterel,' remarked Willett evenly. 'Noddie-peak simpleton. Idle lusk. Saucy coxcomb. Look,' he said to Val, 'I don't like the look of that.'

'Christ,' Val said, 'I know her.' An alley off West 46th Street, full of upturned garbage-cans, torn garbage-bags, refuse blowing on the growing wind, was also full of fighting youth, girls as well as boys. One of the girls was Tamsen Disney, scanty clothes near torn off her, not alone in that. 'I won't,' she was screeching, 'I won't.' One of the boys, a leering Teutprot, was dressed in a jersey that said LIVEDOG. Who the hell made those, wondered Val in a segment of his mind. Christ, was commerce behind everything, even the end of the world? There were one or two opposing sweatshirts marked PUMA, worn mainly by blacks. 'Sacrifice, baby,' panted and grinned a Livedogger. 'The loving Lord demands a human sacrifice, baby.' Willett picked up a rolling empty whisky flagon by its single finger-ear. 'We can't do a damned thing,' said Val, fearful. Willett said nothing; he waded in; he hit. 'Wrong side,' panted Val, as Willett hit out at a black. Tamsen seemed to be on the black side. 'Any side will do,' roared Willett. A point in the struggle, in which language had been reduced to pinpoint monosyllables of outrage and pain, came in which Tamsen was clutched quite naked in Val's arms and clutched back at by dithering fingers. Tamsen did not seem to

recognise her temporary saviour, for she hit out at him with teeny
fists. 'It's me, idiot,' expired Val. 'Val. Val Brodie.' She screamed,
for some reason, all the more for that. Willett was doing well, roaring Shakespeare or somebody. Then whistles pierced like toothache.
'Jesus Puma,' somebody tried to yell. 'The fucking millicents.'
There were grey uniforms as well as blue. The militia, the minutemen, the emergies, the specials, some fucking thing. Val and Willett
were quick to be grabbed, Willett, whisky-flagon brandished in air,
bashed ouch ouch on the shin with a nightstick. It's trunch trunch
truncheon does the trick, wrote somebody, Kipling, Beerbohm,
somebody. The sticktrick ready for Val Val opposed with desperate
arms, crying: 'We tried to stop it. Look at us. Christ. We're not.
Kids.' Kids streaking off, torn and limping, were frankly shot at, gun
raised, eye closed. 'Oh Jesus, let 'em live,' moaned Val. A black van
had drawn up. Tamsen, naked, well-mauled by cops' hands, was one
of the first in. 'In, in, gog damn it, in, bastards.' Val followed Willett,
hopping, crying, feebly now, about fucking blasted shitabed scrotflogs or something.

It was black as hell inside the van, full of noises, including the odd
cry from, presumably, Tamsen: 'Hands off, fucking pig' and so on.
Then she, or some other girl, seemed to throw a fit, all threshing legs
and dangerous fingernails. Some boy or other howled high-pitched
like a woman. 'Dark dark dark,' quoted Willett, 'we all go into the
dark.' Somebody opposite responded urbanely: 'The vacant inter-
stellar spaces, the vacant into the vacant.' Others, angered, shouted
to the quoters to shut their asses. 'Thou toilest not, neither dost thou
spin,' said Willett for some reason. And then: 'Nips.' And then: 'Try
some of the other words backwards. Intellectual sustenance for our
long ride, ladies and gentlemen,' he announced. He seemed crazed,
delirious, but calmly so. They couldn't tell whether they were going
down or uptown.

Downtown, well downtown, they knew when the van stopped
and the door was pulled open. City Hall area, place of nicks and
lockups. 'Out out, you little beauties,' sneered a one-eyed red-haired
sergeant, cap back to look like a black halo. Val felt sudden panic. He
shouldn't be here, he had a plane to catch, it was all a mistake. 'Look,

sergeant,' he said desperately. 'I'm looking, me boyo,' the sergeant replied, and stamped a heavy black boot on Val's aesthete's sandal. Val limped in, howling. In, he found, a great hydraulic hoist without door which rose creaking.

'Tide-time,' said Willett with nodding satisfaction, sort of, looking out at the East River. The water was rising, wind-lashed. 'Wait for no man.' Tamsen was shivering. Val gave her his jacket. 'Why,' she said, 'it's Professor Brodie. He gave me an A plus,' she told the others. Nobody was interested. The hoist stopped at the third floor, brightly lighted. 'Out,' said the accompanying sergeant. 'Look,' said Val, 'I demand to see the captain, the lieutenant. I've urgent business, I've a plane to catch. A letter with the presidential seal. Here, somewhere.' He reached towards his inside jacket packet, meaning Tamsen's right breast. 'Okay, feller,' said the sergeant, 'we'll bleep the President right away.' Then Val remembered that Vanessa, the faultlessly efficient, had both their letters of authorisation in her leather carrying-file. 'Let me at least –' And then he let it go, arms dropping, body drooping. Bleep my wife. My wife? The clever woman, Dr Frame.

They were not formally charged. That, they were told, would come in the morning. They were shoved ten in a cell, white walls, open clogged toilet, ineradicable zoo-smell, men together, Tamsen off somewhere with his jacket and his pack of five cheap cigars. Willett took out a footlong (whatever a foot was) silver torpedo and released a cigar, not at all cheap, of aromatic gooseturd colour. He also produced a nailfile and sawed the monster in half. He gave Val the half with the round end. He struck a match on his behind. They smoked. Their eight fellows snarled or moaned, black and Teutprot together, LIVEDOG confronting PUMA. 'Am up,' said Willett. 'Go, devil.' And then, laughing, 'Toilest.'

'What am I to do?' said Val. 'What the hell am I to do? They'll go without me.'

'And without me, for that matter,' said Willett. 'Don't worry. There's much of interest still in the world. *I* won't go without you.'

Nine

Up in the air Vanessa was going through the sounds and motions of sobbing but gave out few tears. Dry ducts, deficient ducts, no room for tears in her trade, but her distress was genuine. Her father, seat turned into a bed, respirator wheezing away, put a dry mottled hand on her lily one and said softly:

'Nothing could be done. He was terribly knocked about. Unconscious. They gave him an hour to live.' He looked at the clock above the cabin-curtains. 'He's dead now. Rest his soul, such as it was.'

'You're. So. Heartless.'

'You were always telling him not to go out and get drunk the way he did.' There was a little too much satisfaction in his voice. She looked at him, dry-eyed but all grief, and said:

'How do I know you're telling the truth?'

A good question, he thought. 'I'm your father. You heard me speak to the Commissioner.'

'You didn't have the bleposcreen on. How do I know who you were. Speaking. To?'

'He was carrying his ID card. No doubt about who it was. A tavern in the Village. The Minetta or some such name.' Not too bad at the fictional craft or art of lying, Frame told himself. Not too bad at all. 'Believe me, dear, it's for the best. In these times. These aren't normal times.'

'I. Loved him.'

'There was only one man for you.'

'How can you be. So. Heartless?'

A glockenspiel-surrogate high A came from a megalal, and then a synthetic voice gave news. 'Strong tail-winds may reduce our flying time and our ETA may be brought considerably forward. The highest tides yet recorded during the present tidal phase are presently ravaging the eastern seaboard. Land evacuation schemes are being implemented.' The artificial Standard Yankee twanged off.

'He's better off,' said Frame, 'as he is. Dead, I mean. A badly wounded man trying to cope with all that panic. New York City. A very undisciplined place.'

'You're so.'

'Sure sure sure sure. You'll get over it, honey, think of the future, your work.'

'I don't want to. Live without him.'

'Duty. Think of your duty.'

Few in the cabin seemed to be thinking of their duty. The windows being blacked out, none knew precisely whither the totally automatically piloted plane was bound, though they had fair ideas about general direction. Still, of course, there was only one general direction from New York – westward, but not too much so. There was a subdued atmosphere of hilarity, as on a holiday magical mystery tour, abetted by bottles passed around by hearty men like Skidmore the scediastist and O'Grady the astunomicologist. Deborah Reiser the physicist was agiggle, as were also Florence Nesbit the mageirist and Gertie La Farge the secretary-maieutist. Young Nat Goya brooded. He was in love, married, and his wife was pregnant. He thanked God that she had already left Westchester – four days ago, in fact, not too much time really – and, that very evening, while he was completing his packing, he had received her call from her aunt's house in Fort Worth, Texas, where she was already installed and safe. She had by telephone told her parents of their marriage, prematurely true, but the times asked for prematurity. They were not, apparently, unhappy about it. He had longed to match her sweet voice with her sweet face, but her aunt was old-fashioned and did not believe in blepophones, new-fangled nonsense which made people brazen-faced and give too much away with their expressions. As soon as he got to this place where they were going he would call Edwina. He would call her every hour of the day until married quarters were arranged or, perhaps before that, furlough. It was, after all, only like the army all over again, and this time he seemed to be, though still a civilian, a kind of high-ranking officer. Married quarters with a servant. Besides, the project would not last long. The money would be good apparently. They needed money to put a home together. Real estate prices had, inevitably, gone dramatically down in Westchester County but, with the passing of the bad weather, they would rise again. If only he'd been able to put down a deposit now. He heard old Frame say to his daughter: 'Duty. Think of your duty.' He had only one duty, and that was to the best girl in the world. Dearest, sweetest, sexiest Edwina.

Duty. Back in jail in downtown Manhattan, Val awoke from an uneasy sleep to hear Willett's voice singing something about duty. 'All intrepid captains and mates,' he trolled, 'and those who went down, doing their duty.' He la-la-lahed a few measures of presumable orchestral fill-in, bowing strongly a fiddle of air, and said: 'Walt Whitman's words. Vaughan Williams's music. That sounds like a regular sea symphony outside. Jesus. Cacophony rather.' Val came fully awake to hear swishing and roaring, the tumble of what sounded like a ton of bricks not far off, their own cell shaking like a brig on the high seas. Their cellmates were coming awake like a slowish scale, *molto accel.* at the end, do re mi fa... 'Jesus, Jesus,' a black prayed, 'ah meant no harm, main, there's only you.' Somebody started as though struck by taut leather – a knout of water, indeed, had hit him. Christ, this was the third floor. Willett, on tiptoe, was looking through the bars. 'We're at sea,' he said. Val, looking too, saw marine night sky, most bitter waters, a sickly yellow high wall going down from a wave-strike, flickering floodlights on it, moon and Puma peekabooing through thick clotted cloud.

'An eighteenth-century sailor's life,' said Willett. 'A jail sentence with the risk of drowning added. We'd better get out of here.' This seemed to be the view of many, not only in this cell but in the neighbouring ones. Willett strode to the corridor-bars and yelled louder than most. The religious black with PUMA on his vest called on

Jesus. A flurried officer appeared in waterproofs and shining wellington boots. He had keys. 'You birds had better swim for it,' he confided. 'No room on our choppers.' He ground metal and conferred freedom. His fellows had done likewise with the other cellbirds. The corridor was full of panicky freed. The liberators, dressed ready for water but destined for the air, were getting into the hoist. Some of the liberated tried to join them, but guns pointed. The red-haired sergeant of their welcoming committee of a few hours back said, pointing a heavy black Politian: 'Heavy waters, heavy, heavy. Swim strong, swim strong and good.' The hoist rose.

'That,' said Willett, 'will not come back again.' Some of their fellows, following a long reflex, were ready to take the stair down, but a thin Slav cried: 'Water. The fucking sea's gotten in. There.' He pointed. A tentatively lapping tongue of wet green, dirty-flowery with foam, carrying like a silly gift an empty Gelasem pack, protruded from the stairwell. Then came vivid lightning, blueing everything an instant, and, a second or so after, clumsy blunderbussing thunder. 'Don't like this, man,' said the black for Jesus, ostensibly Puma. 'Don't like this one little bit.' A white sneered: 'This is what your fucking Puma has done to us.' Willett said: 'It has to be up, gentlemen. And risk the bullets.' They waded and splashed to the stairs.

It was a long climb – seven more storeys. Willett cursed out of Rabelais with what breath he had left. Val's head was first to peer out of the roof-door, obligingly open. He saw helicopters taking off into murderous squalls. One roared inaudibly with frightened policemen fearful of being pitched out by the craft's yawing. The waves were good creamed mid-Atlantic, the rain hissed down diarrheally, moon and Puma peered coyly, arcs flickered and flickered and then went out. Manhattan's street-lighting all went out. There was an infernal red glow from somewhere in New Jersey. Val came in again and, with the aid of three heavy-shouldered louts, shut the door against the chaos. Lightning blued out a brief message; thunder, at greater length, confirmed it. 'No good,' cried Val. 'We'll have to wait till the tide goes down.'

'It's coming up, fuck it,' dithered a weedy Teutprot, one of Livedog's boys, pointing. Water, not much slower than they had been, was dancing up step by step, that empty Gelasem pack still being pathetically proffered, a full Götterdämmerung six-pack making heavier weather of the ascent. A cool black slopped down, grabbed a can from the sodden cardboard harness, popped it open and drank. 'Thirsty,' he then gasped. 'You could have waited,' said the thin Slav. 'They're being delivered to the fucking door.' There was a shove past Val and Willett by some dozen cursing, better be drowned in the open fucking air, and Willett gravely nodded assent to their act, seeing the swift rise, tread by tread, of the flood. The roof had amenities not previously noticed – a kind of tough metal bus-stop shelter, probably for the use of roof-guards, if there had been such things, people, too late to bother about that now, in wet weather; a twenty-foot radio tower. Some men were in one; others considering, if the water should further rise, the salvatory value of the other, which swayed terribly in the wind but was toughly haw-sered. Moon and Puma obligingly, with the sporadic aid of lightning, fitfully illumined these. They also showed Willett, who was peering out from the parapet, something he was gravely interested to see – a vast torn wood and metal advertising hoarding raft-like nudging the parapet-corner as if impatient for someone's embarking. The sky-lights showed, foreshortened, a vast flat naked girl enthusing over Pippet, whatever that was, something comforting and desirable, stimulating, something. 'Aboard,' yelled Willett to Val. 'Impossible,' shook Val. 'Aboard,' buffeted Willett, buffeting him aboard.

The raft bore them some little way uptown, soaked, shivering, lurid in lightning. It made manically, already dissolving to plank and lath, for a building high enough to have still twenty or so storeys showing above the flood-level. The name of the building flashed an instant in Egyptian italic – THOTHMES. Hotel? Damned silly name for a. The raft hit the façade clumsily but kindly just beneath a window-sill and then disintegrated further. Willett grabbed a metal support before it leapt into the tiger-jawed waters and hit with it at the window. He was pulled away and then shoved back. He hit and hit inaudibly, but the window was responding. Willett stepped on to the sill with remarkable grace for one of his hugeness, then fell in, glass yielding. Val was borne away and screamed. He was borne back and grabbed, grabbed and was grabbed. Willett pulled him in there, to lovely dryness. It was a hotel, a bedroom, abandoned, lightning showing brutally a bed unmade. Val wanted to lie on it, made or not. 'Up,' insisted Willett, over the thunder.

To their surprise there was dim light on the corridor, evidently a domestic generator snug above the waterline. But the elevator bank seemed to have fed on some deeper power, for it would not work. The two walked to the emergency stairs and clattered up, taking their time this time. Val, ridiculously, looked at his watch, ticking healthily away, time and the hour running through the roughest night. Three-thirty-five of a wet morning. He'd never get that plane now. To be on the safe side they climbed five storeys. Safe side? The building was shaking; probably it would hold, though, till the tide went out, if it went out. Little explosions popped from all over the city. Through a landing window they saw the greater towers of Manhattan lightning-drenched but still standing. 'This,' panted Willett, 'will. Do.'

They came out on to dim-lighted deep purplish corridor-carpet. Many doors were locked, but one, *Rameses Suite* in cursive metal on the wall by it, was open and welcoming. Hasty evacuation here – bed a Laocoön of sheets, an open wardrobe even displaying neat suits. In the bathroom fine towels unused; toilet articles, male, on the marble wash-deck. A sitting-room with bar. Another bedroom, bed made or perhaps never used. The lights were dim, emergency obviously, but to their joy there was hot water in the taps. Val, drinking raw gin naked at the bar, let Willett soak his mountainous body first. In heavy jocularity he dialled 4 for room service. A mechanical voice said that room service was temporarily suspended. The telescreen gave out nothing. The radio quacked urgent official words, unintelligible under static. There was nothing in the refrigerator except soft drinks and fruit-flavoured yoghurt – papaya, bosenberry, butterscotch and bitter orange. Healthy fare, but it would not do for Willett.

Ten

The advance party had done good swift work on CAT. An electrified wire perimeter enclosed a square mile of flat earth on which little grew. In the middle, flown in by the end of March, lay the great hulk of the moonliner Tallis, its name already deleted but its new name America not even yet stencilled in. Surrounding it, but at a respectful distance, were prefabricated huts of great solidity, for work, for sleeping, for minimal recreation. The huts on the periphery housed army troops. The fifty élite were lodged, in greater comfort and privacy, nearer the squat ship, each hut divided into four large apartments, each apartment accommodating two men or two women, but never a woman and a man. There was a small assembly hall, or lecture-theatre, equipped with cinematic apparatus. It was here, the morning of their arrival, that Professor Frame had proposed, in a near-final moment of glory, to outline the project to the CAT team. Paul Maxwell Bartlett, brutally but reasonably, had pointed out that for a dying man to speak, in the inspiratory way that was needed (he stressed the *inspiratory* cruelly), about a project concerned with salvation, with, yes, life, was out of order. Head of Project, he had insisted that he himself give the inaugural address. There was a brief argument, in which Vanessa joined, but there was no question as to who must win.

Bartlett wore black leather and very well cut black boots. He stood on the little dais and surveyed his buzzing audience without fear, with a measure of histrionic contempt rather. Vanessa's heart was heavy, heavier still when Bartlett began with: 'There should be fifty-one of us here, but there are only fifty. Dr Valentine Brodie, cybernetically appointed our official chronicler or archivist, met an unfortunate, indeed fatal accident last night in New York City. We shall, I think, contrive to find without difficulty a substitute for him among ourselves. The recording of events is a task hardly to be termed scientific. It calls for no specialist skill.' Vanessa sobbed drily and those near – Felicia DeWitt and Mackenzie Eidlitz – looked at her with brief curiosity. Then they gave all their attention to Bartlett. He had more cruelty to deal out before he got down to business. He said: 'The founder of the project we call CAT, Professor Hubert Frame, is, as you will know, with us here, though in a very marginal capacity. He is a sick man and is confined to his quarters. He is not a member of our team, though without his brilliant work, and that of his daughter, who is fortunately very much with us, this team could hardly have been brought into existence.'

He paused, did an upstage turn, then swivelled abruptly to frown at them all. 'Professor Frame,' he said, 'is going to die, but we are going to live. The whole of the population of these United States is going to die, but we are going to live. Civilisation as the world has known it is going to die, but it is also, with us, going to live. It is our duty to salvage human knowledge in the face of human cataclysm. The day of the cataclysm is coming, Cat Day as we may call it, and the identity of the world-destroyer is known to you all. Puma, most vicious of cats, is already showing his claws in earthquake, seaquake, moonquake, flood. Soon he will leave, but only to circle the sun for a year briefer than ours. Then he will return and make straight for our hapless planet. Before that day, Cat Day, our preparatory work will have been done, and our ship, laden with the fruits of men's enquiries, a self-sufficient microcosm of our creation, will be making for Jupiter, our first posting-inn on the long journey to another world. That world may never be reached, but our search will never give up. We shall breed new generations of spacemen and spacewomen, and they in turn will breed. We are not ourselves, we are man. Man must survive, and we humble insufficient creatures are the chosen instruments of his survival.'

He relaxed as far as his temperament allowed, smiling grimly as if to deprecate the rhetorical tone he had, in justice to the poetic implications of the project, been compelled to employ. He said: 'You are all specialists in various fields relevant to the scope of the project. As philosophy was once regarded as the clearing-house, or interpretative unifier, of the various sciences, so we may regard ouranology as the discipline that binds together the various specialisations necessary to the building of a space microcosm. Dr Vanessa Frame, our coordinating ouranologist, is, as it were, the possessor of the blueprint of the ultimate body –' There were smiles and sly glances at Vanessa, sex rearing its blessed head even now, but Bartlett seemed unaware of the double entendre. 'You, the engineers, clinicians, physicists, even librarians, are, as it were, the several organs of the body. My function? It is quite simply to control, maintain project discipline, be ultimately responsible – to whom, you may ask? I say to the spirit of future man – for the success, if one may use so utilitarian a word, of the whole glorious and terrifying venture.'

Professor K.O. Eastman, a bronzed lean diastemoploionologist, was tentatively raising a finger to raise a point. Bartlett made a dismissive gesture, like a karate chop. 'Wait, please. Questions later. Or rather, I hope to anticipate all possible questions before I have done. You all know where you are – in the state of Kansas, between Hays and Hill City, an area chosen for its centrality and hence immunity from tidal damage, also its negative seismic record, also its comparative isolation. You know where we are, but, I must say it now, you will never be in a position to divulge our whereabouts to the outside world. Security must be absolute. Doomed mankind, if they knew of us, would be envious and, in the final phases of apocalyptic panic, be very willing to destroy us and the hope of the race. You, and I with you, are prisoners of the project. You were chosen not solely for your supreme skills, not even solely for the combination of those with superlative records of personal and ancestral health. You were chosen also because you have no family commitments. You leave friends behind, true, even perhaps mothers and fathers, but you are unburdened by responsibility for wife, husband, child. The time will come for mating and the duty of breeding the first space generation, but that must wait. Our primary dedication is to work.'

Nat Goya was raising his hand in a dithering manner and stuttering a vocable that sounded like *but*, but Bartlett waved his proposed interruption away sternly. 'To help us in our work, we have a military body of engineers, technicians, pioneers, both male and female. The restriction that applies to ourselves applies also to them. They too have no family commitments, are granted no furlough, but they have a sufficiency of amenities and have been instructed in the great advantages of belonging to the project. The true nature of the project, of course, they do not precisely know, nor must they. But, even if they knew, they would be content to remain here till the end, having been made to realise – through televisual and other forms of indoctrination – the horrors proceeding, or due to proceed, in the world outside. They are well-disciplined and are under superb officers. They are unarmed.' A chill went through his listeners as he said: 'Arms there are in this camp, but under my personal control, securely locked away in a hidden armoury. They will never be for the use of the military.'

'But,' dithered Nat Goya, 'there must have been a –'

'Silence,' cried Bartlett. 'Wait. You will wish to know about supplies. In terms of commissariat we are already remarkably equipped. In terms of the materials necessary for your work, the basic requirements stipulated in the Frame prospectus are already in process of fulfilment. You will indent for further supplies, from hydraulic cranes to microfilms, through Dr Hazard.' He nodded towards a squat black man of superb musculature, who rose slightly, bowed slightly, frowned much. 'I can assure you that security will not be jeopardised even minimally in such necessary contacts with the outside world as are involved in the securing of your supplies.' He glowered at his audience an instant as if he knew how much they wished to jeopardise security and supplies were mere self-indulgence. 'Three centres – Kazan, Barnum and Wollcott – are at the disposal of the project. Loading will proceed by automation after telecomputerising of needs. Pilotless vehicles will pick up supplies. One final, perhaps minor, point. To emphasise the essential unity of your various tasks, to promote a sense of quasimilitary discipline, you will wear uniform. It will be the uniform that I am already wearing. It is smart

and serviceable. The Quartermaster, Lieutenant Wetmore, will be at
your disposal all day in his store. If there are questions you wish to
raise, perhaps you would be good enough to arrange an appointment
with me through my secretary Miss La Farge. And now Dr Frame
will discuss matters of allocation with you.'

He strode out, and Vanessa came forward, organised the lowering
of a cinescreen and the projection of images of the interior of the
spacecraft, and prepared to talk about the allocation of specialist
zones of activity. But young Nat Goya dashed after Bartlett and
caught him as he left the building, prepared to march purposefully
to Project HQ and his office. 'Dr Bartlett,' he said, 'there must be
some mistake.'

'Mistake?' Bartlett frowned as the Kansas sky frowned.

'I'm a married man.'

'You're a –'

'Married man. With a child expected.'

Bartlett said: 'Impossible.'

'But it's true. I can show you the –'

'Nonsense. Computers don't lie.'

'They do if they're wrongly programmed. The information on me
couldn't have been up to date.'

Bartlett drilled him doubly with fierce Napoleonic eyes. 'You can
take it that your marriage is dissolved. I see no alternative to that.
Like all of us, you're married to this project.'

'That's absurd. I'm married to a girl I love. I want her here.'

'*That's* absurd.'

'Or I want to opt out of this. If it means having to die, I'd rather
have it that way. With her. With our child.'

'No.' Bartlett shook his head very sternly. 'Oh, no. There's no fat
on this project – except for that Brodie man who isn't here anyway.
You're the only microagronomist we have.'

'There's Belluschi. There's Audelan.'

'No,' Bartlett said. 'You need to have your priorities regularised.
Report to Dr Adams after Dr Frame's briefing session. A session,
incidentally, which you should be at.'

'Dr Adams? Dr Maude Adams?'

'I'm ordering you to go to that session, Dr Goya.'

'You mean I'm to be brainwashed? Into forgetting my wife and loving the fucking project? No, Bartlett, I'm not having it.'

'I should hate to have to use disciplinary measures so early in the in the –' Bartlett twitched minimally. 'Go on, go. And report to Dr Adams afterwards.' He took a stick microphone from his breast pocket and intoned a frequency. 'Provost captain? Be good enough to send a sergeant and two men to AHE. At once. Thank you.'

'Christ,' said Nat Goya. 'Police state tactics. All right, I'll go.'

'You're going to have an escort,' Bartlett said. 'Until you're made to see sense and behave in a civilised manner.'

'Civilised manner. Oh Jesus.'

That expletive, children, was being used partly as a vocal gesture of shock, partly as a genuinely pious ejaculation, by another man at that moment. Dr Calvin Gropius, with his wife Maria and his eldest son James, were proceeding by car towards Dallas, Texas. They had flown to Oklahoma City from Sacramento, California, after the disastrous rally which had been cut off from the eyes of Val Brodie and Willett and the other televiewing drinkers of that New York bar now drowned in dirty flood water. In Oklahoma City James Gropius had resided until the earthquake destroyed his home but not, he, they, thanked God sincerely, his wife Jennifer and their daughter Jessica. These two, having been forewarned in a dream, the mother's, had gone to the home of John Gropius in Dallas, where they still, as a blepophone call had confirmed, rested in safety. Calvin Gropius, learning of terrible events on the Californian coast while still in Sacramento, had also learned of seismic disturbances inland. He had blepophoned James's number in Oklahoma City, but a recorded message at the central exchange had said that all private lines were temporarily out of order and that the caller should contact 405 5534–2349. This turned out to be a highly operative number, that of a temporary rescue centre on the outskirts of the city, and Calvin Gropius had made eventual contact with his son. The times seemed to call for a family reunion. The Will Rogers airport was still functioning, though the Thaw, Whitehead and Toscanini car-hire services were all equally disorganised. It had eventually been a matter of stealing a Durango 99, idling outside the terminal building while the driver went in to get news of flights, so James presumed. James stole the car, but he told his father that he had been merely lucky enough to hire it. He now drove it towards Dallas, just having crossed, by a very solid and imperturbable bridge, the raging Red River.

'Jesus, Jesus, help us all, forgive us all.'

The news trickled in faintly over the car radio. The citizens of New York caught unprepared, the disastrous flooding of the Potomac and the evacuation, to a location not yet announced, of the Federal Government, the end of London and the whole northern French coast, a fissure all the way down the great continent of Africa, Russia's blaming of the destruction of Leningrad on the filthy capitalists of America. How much was true, how much mere improvisatory rhapsodising it was hard to tell: the announcer stuttered and kept breaking into his endless bulletin (as if to find time to invent new enormities) with a record of a Utah choir singing Sullivan's 'Lost Chord'.

'What's going to happen, Calvin? What's going to happen?' Maria Gropius kept up the hopeless litany. She was a mature beauty of fifty, smart, well-read in the Bible, not over-intelligent.

'I don't know, I just don't know.'

'You should know, you ought to know.'

'Quiet, dear, quiet. Or else pray, yes, pray.'

'What's going to happen, mom,' said James, 'is that we're all going to be together. Dallas is a safe place, nothing much happens there. John will be there, and Rufa and the kids, and Dashiel's coming over from Fort Worth. And Jay and Jay will be waiting for us, safe and sound and lovely.' He meant Jennifer and Jessica, his wife and daughter.

'But what's going to happen to all of us?'

'A guy told me,' said James, driving into a filling station, 'that this will last only a couple of weeks. Puma will come closer and then go. Then there'll be a great calm, a lovely great peace, and we'll all get to thinking it never really happened.'

'But there's our apartment and Rachel and Judith.' Rachel was the cat, Judith the Teutprot servant.

'It's high, mom, real high. Safe as houses.' He pondered the simile and its ineptitude and growled: 'My stamp collection, all my fucking – Sorry, dad, mom.'

'All right, son, you're overwrought, God will forgive you.'

'I guess I just forgot myself. Sorry again.'

The filling station was attended by a tough thin old man who knew his Bible better than either Dr or Mrs Gropius. At least, he knew it better in its Italian version. '*E vidi*,' he recited, filling them with Sharpas Super. '*Ed ecco una nube bianca, e sopra la nube uno seduto simile a un figlio d'uomo, avente sopra la sua testa una corona d'oro. All a dere*,' he said. 'In a da Bibbia. Enda world coming.' He was an Italian Protestant, one of the Mid-West Florio congregation. He gave them accurate change and wiped their windows, exhorting them to repent in Italian. They nodded tiredly. He went to his seat, picking up a pornograph in bright colours and reading it with relish. The Gropius family went on to Dallas.

'Jesus help us, Jesus forgive them.'

It was beginning to grow dark, and Puma was rising, red and big and veined like a bloodshot eye. The moon seemed smaller. Mrs Gropius shivered and resumed her litany:

'What's going to happen, what's going to become of us, Calvin?'

Calvin Gropius, very weary, said:

'Oh, for Christ's sake, shut up, dear. Put your trust in the Lord.'

'Yeah, I guess we ought to do that,' said James cheerfully. 'Put our trust in the Lord, like you said.' He had earned his living as a salesman of sanitary installations in presbyteries, manses, and other sacred residences. As for a less peripheral concern with religion, well, he left that to his father. One holy guy in the family enough.

'Family enough,' said Dr Adams, a very lissom dark-haired woman of thirty-two, to Nat Goya. 'That's what he said? The project is family enough?' She leaned against the surgery wall, legs crossed, arms folded, looking at Nat Goya, who sat in a kind of dentist's chair. 'All right,' she said to Sergeant Tiziano and his two men. 'You can go.'

'We got orders, lady.'

'The term,' she said coolly, 'is *doctor*. I have a right to see my patient alone. *Sergeant*.'

'He told us to stay, lady doctor.'

'Who?'

'Boss Cat we call him.'

'Boss Cat,' she grinned. 'Very good. I myself will see *Boss Cat*, sergeant, and explain about responsibility and that sort of thing. All right, go.'

'If you say so, doctor lady.'

'I do.' And they left. Then she searched the beautifully appointed surgery for microphones, even telecams. She found a minute microphone, no bigger than a coin you will have seen called a *dime*, in the wall-plug of the examination light, and she pulled it out. 'There,' she said. Then she wrote rapidly on a prescription block: 'Not happy at all about these dict. methods. Youre a free man. Im going to give you a water injection. Maybe other mikes.' She showed this to Nat, then stuffed it in her white jacket pocket. Then she filled a syringe with water and watered Nat under his epidermis. 'Come back at the same time tomorrow,' she said, 'and I'll see how you're getting along.'

'Thanks, Doc Adams.'

'Not at all, *Doc* er Goya.'

'I see now that he's right. The project is family enough.'

'You'll see it even better when you wake up tomorrow morning.'

He grinned and left. Having left, he did not grin. Sergeant Tiziano and his two dogfaces were in the corridor. 'Has our orders,' the sergeant said. 'Did it, did she?' They looked. 'This arm,' Nat said, showing. 'Yeah, she did it all right.' Nat Goya went away. The escort did not follow. Medical science had its own built-in escorts.

Nat got his briefing indirectly from Drs Belluschi and Audelan. 'Tomorrow at 0800,' Dr Audelan said. 'The foodfields are here, you see, in Bays 3, A, B, and C.' He had a plan of the spaceship. Nat Goya hardly listened. His idea was not to be here at 0800 tomorrow, but on his way to Fort Worth.

Two men, children, had actually settled into Fort Worth, having come all the way from New York straight, not via that place in the state of Kansas. There were wicked men in those days, and these were two of them. It was not their primary aim to be wicked but to make money fast and easy, and wickedness was unfortunately involved in the process. They had a fine old Sicilian name, Tagliaferro, and they were the children of the famous Don Tagliaferro, who had christened them Salvatore and Gianni. Gianni, naturally enough, called himself Johnny, but Salvatore kept his name as it was. It was kinda a holy name, meaning saviour or some such *sacra merda*. Their father, and the rest of the great family of Tagliaferro, had regarded the coming of Puma as an impertinence hardly to be fought but best ignored. They were in Princeton, New Jersey, a fine old university town full of fine old Sicilian names. Salvatore and Johnny had argued loud and long with their father, a thing never known before, and had said that this heavenly visitant was going to be the death of New York and possibly of New Jersey too. Salvatore had read a book, a pamphlet really, full of the prophecies of an ancient guy called Jack the Seer, and this book gave a nasty prospective account of life in the year beginning on Lady Day, 2000. Floods and earthquakes and other disasters. Bad for business. They had talked with a guy in a bar who had told them to go west, young men. So they had come west to look after aspects of the family business in Fort Worth, Texas.

The Florentine Hotel had long been fronted by a third cousin called Paolo, or Paulie, Praz, a suspiciously northern-sounding surname. But Paulie was responsible for certain irregularities, involving heavy nest-feathering, and had been taken, on instructions from Princeton, New Jersey, for a little trip to Lake Arlington, where leaden boots had helped to effect a rapid quietus. The boys who did the job were trusted death-mechanics of the Tagliaferro family and they had been given a fine long holiday, as a reward, at the Fontainebleau Hotel in Miami, Florida.

The installation of a non-Sicilian, even a non-Italian, as manager was not, in those days, irregular. Protestants, it was known, could be trusted more than Catholics. Customers liked to see a fine upstanding American college-boy type in charge of a gambling palace. It made them feel easier. Sicilians, for some reason, had rather a bad name. This guy Dashiel Gropius was okay; he was the son of a big

Protestant sky-pilot, hence a walking guarantee of cleanliness and fair dealing. He had done well, the brothers discovered on examining the accounts. He was no womaniser, no drinker. He read books in his spare time. He liked running things. The hotel cuisine was good, though a bit Frenchified. The brothers were happy to set up in a couple of nice suites in their family hotel and consider the extension of their business in the Fort Worth area. Their families they had sent to live in another family hotel in Peoria, Illinois. They did not want them here for the moment. They wanted to sample local talent. Besides, the inevitable trouble involved in extending their business (with the Maranzana family, for instance) might be dangerous for their wives and children. They would send for them later.

Salvatore, however, was troubled. He spoke, troubled, in the Trapani dialect of West Sicily, to his untroubled brother. He said: 'Suppose it happens. We were told at school by the nuns. The end of the world. What do we do?'

'Nothing we can do. A short life and a happy one.'

'You think it can happen?'

'Anything can happen.'

Salvatore was silent for a space, still troubled. Then he said: 'Hell. You think hell exists?'

'We were taught it exists. The Church says it exists.'

'If the end of the world came, that's where we'd go? We've done bad things. We'd go to hell for them?'

'*Babbo* has done worse, worse than killing.' He was referring to their father, Don Tagliaferro, who had once cut off a man's penis and made him eat it, or as much of it as he could. 'Hell, we were taught it's there. The big thing is to put off dying. Of course, *babbo* won't go, not with all the masses. Better get those *puttane* in Illinois buying a few masses. They've nothing else to do.'

'But we may not be able to put off dying. It's coming, Gianni, I can feel it in my balls. What do we do?'

'Now? Have a drink. Always best to have a drink when the cold hand hits you on the back of the neck. *Un whisky liscio?*'

Eleven

Val Brodie, in silk shirt, Taxis woollen suit, both baby blue, and soft Gucci shoes, sat at a dawn meal with Willett, whose bulk had made it difficult to find anything fresh to wear. He had, however, unexpectedly, bizarrely, come across male Scottish evening dress in the *Ptolemy* suite, as open and rapidly evacuated as their own, and he now wore kilt, sporran, even stocking dirk below and, above, an oversize pyjama jacket and a bulky hunting coat of leather with pockets for hares and rabbits, possibly even stoats. The tartan, Val knew, was that of the Mackenzie clan.

They ate alone in the top-floor restaurant, though they were not sure whether they were alone in the entire hotel. They heard odd movements, as of a great upset stomach, doors banging, feet hurrying, but these might have been engineerings of the tidal gale which, though, was now dying down. The restaurant had its own emergency power supply, like many in those days of overloaded, strike-bound public supplies and comparatively cheap nuclear installations. They had litres of fruit juice from the refrigerator, steaks, cold game pie, ice cream with strawberry preserve, champagne (Ballarat, 1994), brandy (Zacatecas, b.o.f.i.), much coffee. 'The skywalk,' Val suggested.

'Hole up here for a bit,' said Willett. 'Nothing wrong with here.'

'My view is,' Val said, 'that the tide will rise even higher tonight. Higher still tomorrow night. We want the highest hotel in Manhattan.'

'The Neogothic?'

'The New Gotham, yes. There ought to be a skywalk from the roof here. We'll see after breakfast. No hurry. More brandy?'

Skywalks, ladies and gentlemen, were a feature of the Manhattan skyline in those days. There was much helicopter traffic, many heliport roofs, some of them in the service of hotels. You could disembark from the chopper, walk by skywalk to the reception area on one of the upper floors of your chosen midtown hotel, then, more often than not, be taken *down* to your room. Having finished their bottle of Zacatecas, washed it down with more champagne and coffee, and lighted up long Tchaikovsky panatelas taken from the restaurant's smoke-case, Val and Willett went up, following a notice that said THE GARDENS OF ALLAH MOST HIGH, to a ruined mass of greenery on the roof. They saw that there was indeed a covered skywalk, battered somewhat by the gales but still intact. The skyscrapers, they were glad to notice, still stood in proud defiance and had also sheltered the skywalks from the fury of the sea and the sky. They looked down to see the water-level falling as the sun rose. When it fell totally, they knew, they would see a street littered with thousands drowned.

'New Yorkers,' Willett puffed sadly. 'They will not be told. Everything left to the last minute. Public orders ignored. Public orders badly given and hardly at all enforced. Too much individuality. Too much incredulity. New Yorkers have seen everything and live in a perpetual state of fear. There is nothing new to make them feel new fear. Millions dead, I have no doubt. The subways choked with dead. How many, I wonder, will have got through the tunnels to New Jersey?' He shook his head puffing. 'This highway or skywalk or whatever it is leads to the roof, by a series of gentle stairs and corridors, of the Witherspoon Hotel. Then we mount, gently again, to the Valentino. Then the Neogothic.'

'New Gotham.'

They walked, peering through the tough durovit at the skyline. The Brooklyn Bridge was shaking in the wind. They thought they could see the plinth where the Statue of Liberty had once been. Soon, on its heliroof, they stood beneath the gigantic sign of the New Gotham. But the A and M had gone, dislodged by fierce winds or struck by lightning, and the hotel spoke of what would now never happen, though it had often been prophesied – the coming of a new

savage disruptor of western civilisation from the fierce lands of barbaric warriors. A morning wind suddenly blew fiercely, straight out
of the dawn. 'For God's sake –' Willett cried tardily. The huge false-
gold G, evidently only hanging on by a single nail, flew down at Val
and clonked him on the temple. Then it clattered and clattered on the
roof and lay still. Val too, down, lay still. He had fallen heavily. 'G,'
said Willett to himself, 'coming from the wrong direction. Val, Val.'
Val was out and bleeding badly. His teeth madly clutched a panatela
still smoking. 'Val.' Then: 'Jesus Christ all damnable mighty.' Willett
threw both panatelas away and dragged Val by his armpits. It was
difficult. 'G,' said Willett bitterly. Panting, nearly expiring, he got
Val wound round him like a sousaphone in a fireman's lift.

Val came to in twilight, wondering where the hell he was. 'Thank
Christ,' Willett said. Quick, drink this, these I would say.' He gave
him a powerful analgesic ready watered, then hot strong tea, heavily
sweetened and rum-laced, from a thermos. 'A foul headache, I should
think,' said Willett, 'but the cut isn't deep. I checked. I medicated and
bound. But I was getting worried. You've been out too long.'

'How long?' Val felt the bandage round his forehead, felt pain
rattle in his skull like a stone in a gourd.

'G hit you yesterday morning.'

'Yesterday mor –?'

'You were right about the tide getting higher. It seems to have
engulfed that Egyptian place we stayed in. Here seems safe enough.
This is the penthouse suite, called for some reason the *Ezra Winter*.'
Val took in blurred and agonising luxury – apple-green walls, olive
curtains, chunky fawn furniture, a cocktail bar. He was lying not on
a bed but on a great couch as big as a bed. 'We are not alone,' Willett
continued. 'There are others here with the same notion as ourselves –
to ride out the storm, wait for a total tidal recession, and then – Then
what?' he asked. 'Or will talking exacerbate the pain?'

'I think I'd better sleep,' Val said.

'But you've done nothing but sleep. No, unfair. It wasn't sleep.
Will you eat something? No. Look, I'll leave you in peace for an
hour or so. I have dancing lessons to give.'

'*Dancing lessons?*' But Willett had gone. Val, shaken fully awake by this revelation of the frippery of dancing going on (seriously, too: *lessons*, for God's sake) while New York drowned, meantime being shaken like a rat by a terrier, suddenly felt a deeper and more awed affection for Willett than he had previously known. Willett had, then, dragged him here painfully, knocked out by G, whatever that meant, and tended him. If he had been alone last night's sea-sky bacchanal would have done for him. (Out as long as that, for God's sake.) He slept, hearing the wind rise, feeling protected. He woke to dark with a monstrous light on him and screamed like a child. Then he knew: Puma. Puma, yes. The destructive planet intruder. But surely Puma had been different – a red sore eye, all veined? Now Puma had a silver disc attached, its circumference edged in red, glued to the planet below its centre. The moon and Puma, lord and vassal, were joined tonight in a one-way tug. Then his senses, shocked to deadness by the vision, came alive to fear of the consummation of all things coming. His room rocked like a ship's crow's nest, the whole slender strong hotel beneath him creaked and groaned like the same ship's main mast, hail and rain whipped the window, fire tore at the sky and thunder rumbled open-mouthed punctually a second after. The pain in his head temporarily knocked away, he went tottering to the window to look down and was shocked by what he saw: cream-topped waves dragoning and burling three storeys down. This must surely be the tide's limit. In panic he went to what he took to be a bedroom but saw only glacial bathroom white coloured silver and blood by the fireballs in the heavens. 'Willett,' he called, back in the living-room, going to first one door and then the other. There was no sleeping Willett, only two neatly made beds. He shook his way to the corridor and found dim blue light, as in that other hotel so long ago, an emergency supply holding up. He heard faint music. He followed it and came to a well-carpeted broad stairway leading up to what was called THE JACOB RIIS BALLROOM. He climbed the stairway and swung open a massy door, blued gilt in the dim light. What he saw astonished him more than the tidal madness without, the silver and red fireballs.

Candles, candles, candles. A stereogram thundered out civilised defiance at the elemental rage clawing and bouncing the building:

the *Blue Danube* waltz belting from wall and wall and wall, men and women, youths and girls swirling, with Willett a loud master of ceremonies, beating out the time on the floor with a bandmaster's mace, crying: 'Dignity, grace, rhythm, for God's sake.' Faces sweated in candlelight, bodies swung, turned, swayed. This, thought Val sadly, this: you'd never get this in a spaceship. He sat down on a chair by the door, comforted by light, people, harmony, civilisation. Never get this in a fucking spaceship. He decided to go down with *this* ship, so long as Willett was captain. Earthship, that had weathered so much, that held the dust of great men in its bowels. To hell with that cold contrived future in the heavens, the spaceship horror. To his sudden shock he thought he saw Vanessa among the dancers. But no. And then he saw Vanessa, cool, unperturbed, watching meters, taking readings. A woman he knew, a woman who had been his wife. The heavens were hers; he would crumble to nothing with the dirty earth. His body relaxed in heroic resignation. Only the dead were great. He left the dancers, went back to the *Ezra Winter* suite, fell into one of the beds, raised his fist feebly like a wool-stuffed Beethoven at the tempest in the heavens, then passed out like a child.

He awoke to daylight and near-tranquillity, to find Willett, half Scot, half American hunter, looking down on him.

'How do you feel?'

'Better. That was a hell of a night.'

Yes, I'm aching all over. So are the others, I should imagine. Oh, you mean the tide. I think we've had the worst of it now. Time and the hour run through the roughest – Perhaps I've said that before. Shakespeare. I played Macbeth in Minneapolis, at the old Guthrie. Shall I bring you breakfast, or do you think you could manage to walk to the Pickwick Coffee Shop? A Mrs Williams and her daughter are running it, enjoying it too. There's nothing like occupation. It's on the floor below this.'

'If you could bring me some orange juice and coffee –'

'But you must be *starved*.'

'Yes, I think I must be.'

'Ham and eggs. Steaks. Corned beef hash with poached eggs.'

'I'd better wash.'

And so they ate breakfast, in cheerful enough company. There seemed to be a general feeling that New York, the world for that matter, had seen the worst. A man called Mr Weill was bitter about lost trade, the ruination of stock, the difficulty of restarting a men's garment store. A Mrs Wolheim tried to cheer him up by recounting something she said she had heard, thinly, distantly, on a radio broadcast from what was now called Federal HQ, meaning presumably the new Washington: no shortage of government money to tide (ha) over, a mere matter of going to specially set up FBF (Federal Bureau of Finance) offices and drawing a hundred dollars a day. In inland towns and cities, of course. New York, no. Mr Terhune said there had to be a boom coming when all this was over, especially in the construction trades. The mortician's trade too, said a Mr Steinway gloomily: all those bodies to be collected, identified, interred. He was revealed later himself to be a mortician: the gloom was a professional mask. Val held his peace. After breakfast he would talk to Willett.

After breakfast he talked to Willett, up in their living-room over a bottle of Presidio cognac (b.o.f.i.). There were certain things that Willett had certainly guessed; now he was to have as near professional confirmation as he could possibly hope to obtain. 'You know,' Val said, 'or I think you know –'

'Yes?'

'That it's all going to be over.'

Willett nodded vigorously with even a sort of satisfaction. The satisfaction of not having to leave the party before it finished? Everybody saying good-night together? 'I couldn't understand,' he said, 'why there was such humming and hahing. Why couldn't the big men be out with it? I always thought scientists believed in the dissemination of truth.'

'The truth is very hard liquor. Panic. Murder. Wait till the people learn the truth. Not from others' lips, from their own agony.'

'What precisely is going to happen?'

'There's going to be a period of calm and tranquillity. Optimistic clearing-up, I suppose, and a lot of free money around, a lot of goods to be used up. The sensible will know the worst from the fact of the general prosperity. No future to save for, no more virtue in thrift. No money spent on war, defence.'

'How about the moon?' asked Willett.

'The moon?' It seemed, on the face of it, a frivolous question. 'The moon,' said Val, 'is, I think, already been drawn into the gravitational field of Puma. Puma's mass is very much greater than earth's. We'll miss the moon during our period of tranquillity. No more destructive tides. No poetry, either. No popular songs. A lot of our literature will become meaningless.'

'Not meaningless,' said Willett. 'Just sad. My son,' he said, 'is on the moon. I used to get letters from him. I don't suppose there'll be any more letters.'

'I didn't know you had any family,' said Val, surprised.

'Oh, yes. My third wife left me six months ago. I have a daughter in Beckley, West Virginia, another in Philadelphia, two sons, twins, inseparable, in Springfield, Illinois. I never hear from any of them, but I used to hear regularly from George. George on the moon. He's been around the moon a bit, has George. Maupertius, Clausius, Cassini, even Hell. Has there been trouble on the moon?'

'Moonquakes? Without doubt. And now the moon is dragged away from us. But it will be back.'

'With Puma.'

'With Puma.' Val traced ellipses and circles on the coffee-table with a brandy-wet finger. 'Puma is entering into its first year as a member of this planetary system. It will be a brief year – about two hundred and forty days. There seems to be some ancient inexplicable law about distances having to be maintained between planets. I've had it explained to me, but I was little the wiser. Remember, I'm only a writer of fantasies, not a scientist at all. *Am*,' he then said bitterly. 'Why do I keep saying *am*?'

'Go on about Puma.'

'Remember that earth itself goes round the sun. At present our position, ironically enough, is favourable to us. We could have been much closer to Puma. But in the fall the two solar orbits will be very close indeed. The gravitational pull of Puma, which we're feeling already, will then be irresistible.'

'So it's earth that will do the colliding?'

'We shan't think of ourselves as the assailants,' said Val. 'Even the specialists are using Ptolemaic terms, not Copernican. We suddenly think geocentrically. We always have, really. We will to the end. Puma will rise, with our moon sidling round it. Puma will approach. Puma will be incredibly large in the sky. Puma will hit. But every bit of our soft and shifting geology will yearn towards the tough male mass of Puma. We offer ourselves, as children of earth, to the jaws of the beast. Sorry,' he grinned. 'That's the writer coming out. The bad writer,' he said with disgust.

'I take it,' said Willett, 'that this place where you were going was not what you said.'

'No. A spaceship, taking civilisation in microcosm into the great darkness, looking for a new light, a fresh habitable planet. Strictly speaking, I should be out there in the middle of the American land-mass looking for it. A soldier who's lost his outfit looking for his outfit. I'm AWOL.'

'But you don't know where it is?'

'No, and I don't care where it is. You and I stay together.'

Willett took in several litres of air and then let them out noisily. 'Your place,' he said, 'is not only with the duty you were chosen to do but also with the wife of your bosom.'

'I'm freed from the duty by not knowing where it is. That frees me also from my wife. I don't love my wife. Perhaps I'm not capable of loving a woman. Going to bed, yes, feeling a transitory tenderness. But engaging the mind, the psyche, of a woman – no. Perhaps that's why I failed as a writer.'

'You didn't fail as a writer,' Willett said. 'I read one of your books – I think it was called *The Desirable Sight*. There was a passage in it I liked. Let me see if I can –' He sat back, shut his eyes tight, then hawked as if to bring up the passage from the back of his throat. 'Somebody says something like this: "The future hasn't come into being yet, and the present is a hairline thinner than the thinnest imaginable hair. There is only the past, and the glory of the past is not order – for order is an abstraction imposed by that non-existent thing called the present. The glory of the past is riot, profusion, a chaos of flowers. But there is another glory too. The past has beaten the forces of destruction: possibility became fact, and fact cannot be willed away ever, not even by God. Let us not dream of the future which does not exist and can only exist by becoming the present. Let us not dream of living in the present, since the present has no existence. Let us glory in having added more and more to the past, increased the chaotic profusion of its flowers."' Willett coughed modestly and took a swig of brandy. 'Something like that.'

'It sounds good the way you say it. You almost make me believe in myself.'

'I was always good at learning off that sort of thing,' said Willett with complacency. 'Fine words, sound. They don't have to mean much, of course. Still, you didn't fail as a writer.' He looked at the wall-clock. 'I have another lesson to give,' he said. 'This time the mazurka.' He left. Val watched his big back on its way to his duty, along with the rest of his huge frame. He smiled with sad affection.

That night was the most terrible of all the terrible tidal phase. Both Val and Willett woke, heavy with brandy, to the smashing of windows, the unwished bounty of red and silver light, lightning like giant probing tendrils, sea and thunder vying for intensity of terror of sheer ragged noise, and the silver-red medallion of the sky-partners in destruction flashing in and out of the torment of clouds. Val felt his hair turning to a nest of upright bristles as he tried to say: 'Christ, look, the water, it's up to, up to –' It was crashing, dirty grey-green-white sloggering knouts, at the window-sill. Willett said nothing; instead he grasped Val's arm in rough fatherliness and dragged him out of the room. The corridor was already filling with pale people dressed as for lifeboat drill, dithering, women ready to scream. Willett cried:

'The whole damned creation is doing a mazurka. We must make for the Partington Building. The highest in Manhattan. If that isn't enough – well, we've had good times together. Come on,' he barked. And he led the way to the sky-reception area, already filling with thirsty water. On the heliroof, fearful of being dragged down by the hurricane to the sea that filled the streets, they made, thirty or so of them, tight embracing groups of eight or ten, turning themselves into a single tottering beast with many legs and arms, wheeling drunkenly to the nearest covered skywalk. It swayed furiously as they went across it in pairs and trios. Somebody, Mrs Stoke or somebody, screamed that it was going to go down, but Willett's voice thundered, 'Damned nonsense.' They came into the terrible open again on the roof of the Newman Tower, whipped and pushed and dragged savagely, drenched breathless, jeered at by the intermittent monstrous light up there. A single beast of sixty legs, they sidled towards the next skywalk. Val, clutching tight a frail girl called May Roth, felt her slipping, was conscious of the vibration, if not the noise, of desperate screaming. She was pulled from the joint grasp of the weakening arms by a violent windstream and was to be seen, sickeningly, backing, backing as in a dance, to the roof-edge. She went over, arms out, as if begging for applause. Thunder gave it. 'On, on,' Willett's great silent mouth must be yelling.

They nearly all made the final pitch to the vast roof of the Partington Building, which spread out on all sides of the strong slender tower, like a playing card poised on the tip of an inkpencil. Willett and Val were among those who had reached that desperate near-haven when the violent voices of air yelled derision at the swaying tunnel poised over an infinity of black Atlantic, and they saw the desperate pleading arms of the others, their useless crying mouths, as the skywalk buckled at an Olympian wind-buffet into an inverted V, sending some sliding straight into the maelstrom, others fighting to hold on to the inverted apex of the deck of the skywalk, bleeding hands slipping, and then, gracefully, taking its time, the skywalk was an arrow pointing to Puma as in protest, then it fired at the ocean below and plunged.

The way into the Partington Building via the roof consisted of an ornate deckhouse, now much punished, with a fancy ironwork gate tormented by the elements to a nest of serpents. That gate, broken free at the catch and soundlessly clashing, offered no opposition to their entrance. They – Val, Willett, fifteen or so others – found themselves broken and without breath in a great empty upper hall, whose tasteful chairs and tables danced drunkenly from one wall to the other with the sway of the entire structure. There were no bedrooms to seek in this tower dedicated to commerce, but there was a restaurant some three floors down. Under the emergency lights of this comfortless carpetless space, it was enough for now to lie desperately filling dry lungs, hoping dawn would come soon, feeling grim satisfaction that, if moon and Puma were to get them now, they had done their utmost, scaled their highest mountain.

Twelve

Men were at work painting AMERICA on the hull, using a uricon-based mix guaranteed to resist indefinitely the encroachings of the abrasive dirt of space. Silver on black – simple, elegant. It had not yet been decided whether to add a I to the name. There were, it was known now, other spaceships in preparation, all to be christened after the land of their creation – II, III, IV: the line would stretch literally till the crack of doom. To call this protoploion anything other than plain America was somehow to diminish the achievement, to make it appear primitive and experimental and, in a sense, already a dead thing.

It was a big ship, with space to spare, endowed with a quality of excess or marginality essential to what was no mere vehicle but a whole self-contained world. The ploiarchal, or navigational, area was small in comparison with the living and working quarters; the nuclear propulsion device was negligible in size, as were the power generators or heliergs. The whole structure was three decks high. One would go upstairs to bed – fifty double cabins, ten bathroom-toilets, a large laundry. The middle deck housed the galley, under the control of Dr Rosalba Opisso, the dining-hall, the recreation area (cinema, games-room, library, microviewing booths). The main or first deck was dedicated to work. It was a university in miniature, with microarchives, lecture-rooms, computer, laboratories. A sterile area of some size, at the stern of the ship, was given over to the essential task of providing food – protein surrogates, vegetable matter, complex vitamin constructs. There was, near it, an engine for converting the waste products of the body into aliments. Below this deck lay the intricate electronic economy of the whole organism, including a gravitational magnetotechnasma of brilliantly original design. Dr Guinevere Irving was in charge of the air, the flow of the carefully controlled mixture that converted the perpetually outbreathed into the perpetually inbreathable. Hospital and clinical surgery were tucked away in a side-pocket that covered the whole height of the ship. There was more, much more. Children would be born, brought up, educated. The eventual dead would be disposed of unwastefully – converted to fuel and alimentary matter.

Running all round the ship at mid-deck level was a walk of a more than a kilometer in perimeter, but there were no windows or lights looking out on to the dispiriting show of space. Instead, there would be, according to Owings Merrill Skidmore, regularly changed exhibitions of art, microfilms blown up in gorgeous original colour. And there would be plants, flowers, even trees – cunning artefacts looking like the real thing, whatever the real thing was, ladies and gentlemen. More than anything, there would be the illusion of vast sky, clouds, birds winging.

Young Nat Goya, microagronomist, had promised himself that he would be out of the concentration camp in whose midst America was set, before any work was begun. He had simulated to Boss Cat Bartlett, whom he cordially detested (nor was he alone in this), the lineaments of a man brought, by cunning medicine, to single-minded devotion to the enterprise. He was no longer, his faint smile said, a devoted husband and potential father. But he plotted a getaway.

He had wandered round the camp, just inside the electrified periphery, looking for an unattended gate, but guards were omnipresent, efficiently changed every six hours on the dot, and, though they were not equipped with firearms, they had nasty-looking coshes and nightsticks. There was no need of perimeter floodlights, since the whole Kansas sky was a nightly day, what with bright red Puma and the silver moon. To burrow under the wire was a dream derived from old scratched movies about prisoner-of-war camps in World War whatever-it-was, I, II, III. To diminish Nat's chances, a disaffected corporal named Stanford Everard Whiteboy had himself attempted escape when on guard duty, making a run for it. Brought back, he had been brutally, physically, punished, publicly too, on the orders of the military commandant, Colonel Fernando Jefferson. His best way out, so it seemed to Nat, was by means of one of the driverless vehicles, remote-controlled by Captain Truslove's transport section. He had wandered round this area, on the pretext of looking for Dr Ebenezer Hazard, supplies coordinator, who was supposed to be there consulting about a particular bulk order on the depot at Kazan University and the number of vehicles required to bring it in. Nat had a brief opportunity to examine the structure of a Speight van. He was even able to look underneath it and observe the simplicity of design – the axles, a kind of hook perhaps intended for traction, and a long laterally placed metal bar probably used for the yanking open of a kind of booby hatch which afforded a view of the engine not provided by the lifting of the hood. Nat, being an adoptive New Yorker, knew little about automobiles, either gasoline-powered or nuclear-driven. About this kind of autoautomobile he knew nothing at all. But it seemed to him that he might conceivably fit himself for a brief space under a vehicle like this, hands gripping that hook, or perhaps a bit of rope affixed to that hook, feet resting painfully on that lateral bar. The vehicle would leave the camp and, at a decent distance down the road, he would let go and drop, relaxed, flat as a corpse, and be free.

As an earnest of his forthcoming desertion of the project, he worked very hard on his side of it, supervising the installation of the auzesis trays and even manhandling some of them himself. He scrupulously requested permission for a further injection of the magical substance from Dr Adams, telling Boss Cat that he had had a disturbing dream of his wife weeping and did not wish any more such incubi. Dr Adams, who was now close to open expression of her dislike of Bartlett, gladly injected him with water.

It was when the moon had become a frank satellite of Puma and Puma already seemed to be retreating that Nat went to Dr Hazard with an urgent indent for heliodiscs and even asked when he could expect them.

'There's this order going out to Kazan tomorrow,' said Dr Hazard, unsuspicious. 'I could telly this addition to it now. There'll be two Speight vans leaving at 0800.'

'I'd be grateful if you would. Twenty, HD/369 gamma size, as I've written down here.'

'No trouble.'

The following morning nobody could but be pleased at the sight of Nat Goya, in tracksuit, jogging around the camp, young, athletic, shaking out harmful juices, sweating away useless impertinencies like sexual desire. At one point, near the transit lines, he got a stitch, also a crick in the calf, and limped panting, looking for a place to rest. He did not think anyone saw him when, lying low, he inched under a Speight van. He took from his tracksuit pocket a little thick hemp, fixed it to the traction hook, and knotted himself a handhold. With difficulty, as in a bed too short, he managed to fit his soft-shoed feet on to the pullbar. His watch had recently given him the time – 0751. He would not have long to wait. The position was agonising, but he did not have to endure it long. Not long to wait at all now.

At 0800 the first of the long day's camp sirens sounded dismally, as though an air raid were expected. Promptly vehicles began to move, one at a time, down a shallow ramp. To his joy, Nat found that his was one of them. There was one behind him, which would present a problem when the time came for his drop: he did not want to be mangled by unstoppable wheels. He was aware of a gate sliding automatically open. He heard the yawn of a guard and another guard say 'Fucking Jesus.' Then he was on the road. The position was desperately painful, and he would have, he thought, to endure it for several kilometers. What electronic eyes were peering beyond the confines of the camp he knew not. He must take no chances.

After, he judged, twenty minutes of agony at high speed, his hands on fire and his feet numb, a thing happened he should have expected but had not. The vehicle came to a sudden halt, as also the vehicle behind. There was a traffic light to be obeyed, and the automatic drivers were automatically obeying it. This meant that he, Dr Nat Goya, was in a town or village or on the outskirts of one. He dropped.

He dropped, boys and girls, ladies and gentlemen, sore, half-dead, but unharmed. He dropped, swiftly crawled out from under, painfully stood, saw a sidewalk and limped to it, then looked about him. The light changed and the cars went on their way. He had arrived in a town of one street only and he had arrived, apparently, unnoticed. There were few people about, and those that were saw with little curiosity a young man in a track suit panting, stiff, having perhaps run too much before breakfast and now probably wanting breakfast. There was, he saw, a place in which to take breakfast – Jack, Joe and Curly – as also an Untermeyer general store, a Stokes dress shop, a grim building called Beulah Chapel. He went to see Jack, Joe and Curly, but not for breakfast. He wanted to use the telephone. He had coins, he had made sure about that. He had the number. He nodded at an old man slurping coffee and at an unshaven young man in dirty white behind the counter, Jack, Joe, not Curly, because he was bald. Or perhaps because he was bald he was called Curly. Facetious nicknames. He went to the telephone, heart desperately thumping. He knew the number by heart. He dialled with a tremulous finger. He nearly fainted when he heard her voice.

'Darling, angel, sweetheart, it's me.'

'Who?'

'Me, Nat, your husband, remember?'

'Oh, thank God, thank Christ, oh Nat, I love you, I love you, I. Where are you, Nat? Here?'

'Not yet, honey, not just yet. I'm –' The name of the little town was up there on a police notice about a certain escaped and danger-ous Geoff Grigson. 'I'm in a place called Sloansville. I escaped.'

'*Escaped*? Oh, darling, darling, come to me.'

'Yes, escaped. It's a camp called a Center of Advanced Technology and it's in Kansas. They're building a spaceship because the earth's going to be smashed by Puma, and I'm on the project, but they won't have married people and they didn't know I was married, and they tried to give me something to make me forget I was married. And I'm on my way to you, angel, sweetheart, dearest one.'

'Oh, my love, oh, my dear love.'

'I love you, I love you, and I'll be with you before nightfall. For now, angel, my love, my love and all my love. Till then. Mmmmmh.' He kissed the dirty mouthpiece.

'My dear dear dear love.'

He had said enough, he thought. Action, out of here. After some orange juice. He was thirsty as hell. Then he saw, and his heart sank. He might have known, he might have. But she must not be touched, not she. Boss Cat, in his regular black uniform, was walking in, smiling. There was a car outside. Nat feigned not to see. He said to Jack or Joe or Curly:

'What's wrong with your phone? Why isn't your phone working?' And he winked furiously and desperately, using the eye to the lee of Boss Cat.

'There's been these earthquakes, feller. Lotta lines down.' The old coffee-slurper said, perhaps using too much embroidery:

'It's a crying shame, I guess, when a young feller away from home can't get through to his folks. And the mails ain't working too good neither.'

'A cup of coffee together, I think,' said Boss Cat. 'And then we'll be on our way. You enjoy your run, Nat?'

Primed by that word, Nat tried to make a run for it. Waiting for him outside was the man called Lee Harvey O'Grady, the astunomicologist, a man with a stormy plump very Irish face, also strong muscles: Nat felt the steel of them as he was grabbed. He had wondered idly what astunomicology was. Now he thought he knew, or would know.

O'Grady and Bartlett sat comfortably on either side of Nat on the way back to CAT in the automatic automobile. Bartlett said: 'It was, of course, very foolish. What worries me is that you didn't realise the foolishness. That argues a lack of intelligence. I wonder sometimes at the viability of cybernetic selection. You see, you were nowhere to be found in the camp. Therefore, you had to be outside the camp. There was only one way for you to leave. It was all very foolish. The question is: what are we going to do with you?'

'Throw me out,' mumbled Nat. 'I'm no good to the enterprise.'

'You're no good to the enterprise,' Bartlett agreed. 'As for throwing out – Throwing, I would say, comes into it, wouldn't you agree, O'Grady?'

'How about security?' asked O'Grady. 'Has he jeopardised security?'

'We got him in time. Throwing, I say again. Throwing *to*, not *out*.' O'Grady grunted and smiled dourly at the same time. Nothing more was said about this throwing. Bartlett confided: 'A certain Dr Damon Scribner is being summoned. You know him, Nat?'

'My field,' Nat said. 'Mid-Western University. Author of *Space Trophimonistics*.'

'Correct, correct. Ah, here we are.' The gate swung open to admit them. The sergeant of the guard saluted Bartlett grudgingly. 'Sergeant Rogers, isn't it?' said Bartlett pleasantly. The sergeant nodded grudgingly. 'Be good enough to conduct this officer to the Provost Captain.' To Nat he said: '*Throwing to*. You know your Bible? Daniel and the lions. But not Daniel this time, Nathaniel.'

'My name isn't Nathaniel,' said Nat. 'It's Nathan.'

'A matter of small importance. A name will hardly be worth attaching to what you're going to become.' And he and O'Grady the astunomicologist marched off, leaving their vehicle to find its own way to the transport park.

The disciplinary action chosen for Dr Adams was less drastic. She was arraigned before a court of which both judge and jury were the same man. The entire CAT team was ordered to attend. The time was 0600, a recessive Puma, along with its moon, lazily setting. The place was the assembly hall. Despite the untimeliness of the hour, there was little yawning. Bartlett sat at the little table on the dais; Dr Adams, dark, lissom, smart in her black uniform, stood before him. Bartlett said:

'This is a court of law. Our laws are emergency laws and our procedure must be emergency procedure. Dr Maude Quincy Adams, you stand accused of violation of an order. You were instructed to administer to Dr Nathan Goya a particular medicinal injection, designed for his own physical and mental good and for the good of the project. You failed to obey the instruction. Do you admit this?'

'Oh, I admit it.'

'Have you anything further to say?'

'Yes. A question first. What has happened to – my patient?'

'You will not ask questions. You may make, if you wish, a statement.'

'Very well, I state this. That the purpose of this mission, as I see it, is to salvage human civilisation –'

'A tautology. Civilisation is necessarily human.'

'No. Your view of civilisation is an *in*human one. If the civilisation we are met here in this camp to salvage is merely a matter of books and theories and gases and test tubes, then it is not worth salvaging. Justice, compassion, fairness, humour – even a modicum of decent human inefficiency: where are these? It is not only my opinion that the dictatorial methods you are using will wreck the project. You were in the United States Navy. You probably know the phrase *a happy ship*. You are at this moment commanding a very unhappy one.'

Bartlett sighed and shook his head. 'The time will come for what you call compassion. Also fairness, humour, though never never never, under my command, inefficiency. But the time is not yet. This project is the most daring the world has ever seen. It must not fail. We must transform ourselves into machines until we are assured of its success. Then the virtues you speak of will have time to flower. Not before.'

'What,' asked Dr Adams again, 'has happened to Dr Goya?'

'Dr Goya,' said Bartlett, 'is unfortunately no longer with us. *Unfortunately* – a conventional term I ought to apologise for using. Dr Goya should never have been chosen in the first place. His substitute will be arriving tomorrow.'

'What,' repeated Dr Adams, 'has happened to Dr Goya?'

'Dr Goya,' said Bartlett patiently, 'has been struck off our strength.'

'He's dead, isn't he?'

'Dr Adams,' said Bartlett sternly, 'we are concerned at the moment with your er – misdemeanour. You say you admit to having er perpetrated it. We must think of an appropriate disciplinary response to that.'

'*We*,' mocked the accused. '*We* are not allowed to think of anything.'

'I, then,' said Bartlett. 'I do not propose to dismiss you from the project –'

'Meaning *liquidate*,' said Dr Adams.

'But I hereby direct that you receive rehabilitatory treatment from Drs Fried and O'Grady. I hereby direct Drs Fried and O'Grady to initiate this treatment as from today. And I shall arrange for a military escort to accompany you, Dr Adams, as you proceed on your regular duties, until such time as I am satisfied that rehabilitation has been effected. This court stands adjourned.'

The incineration of the battered body of Dr Nathan Goya took place in the camp crematorium at 0300 hours. There were no obsequies.

Thirteen

Summer came, and the licking of wounds. There had been too much tide; now there were no tides at all. The moon had left the sky, but it was still, though very dimly, in contact with the selenostations of earth. Thin messages came through from Vitruvius, Zagut and Schneckenberg. A farewell message came from Sheepshanks. The moon had been very badly knocked about, and now it was nearer the sun and very hot, except at night, when it was very cold. It was very near to its new host, whose barren features had been closely annotated. Much hydrogen steaming away, scars of ancient space battles, an interesting axial irregularity.

The United States Government was revealed as having moved, with the disastrous flooding of the Potomac and an earthquake that destroyed the White House, to Dallas in Texas. The Trinity river there had overflowed its banks and made a lake of Rochester Park, but Highland Park had been untouched and the Dallas Country Club, with its imposing gateway on Mockingbird Lane, its fine drive leading to a splendid building overlooking Turtle Creek, was now the presidential residence. There had been no word about the recall of Congress. An emergency situation still obtained; power lay undistributed among the three arms of federal rule; the President was a kind of Boss Cat Bartlett, but a milder and more intelligent one.

In early July, a day after the uncelebrated Day of Independence, he talked with his aides, Bidu Saarinen and Florenz Zenger, both New Yorkers. They walked in the grounds of the New White House, as the Dallas Country Club was now called. The white paint was, on this fine day full of butterflies and birdsong, being renewed. You required two things only for a White House: a president and a can of paint. Jack Skilling, visibly older since his Christmas meeting with Professor Hubert Frame, stooped, his right leg painful and making him limp, his hair greyer and sparser.

'Well, Flo,' he said, 'what are you going to do in outer space?'

'Read Toynbee. Perfect my chess-game.'

'Yes,' said the President. 'I shall read all of Henry James. James and games. Is it worth launching fifty billion dollars' worth of iron-mongery just to keep a handful of the élite in austere leisure? What do you think, Bid?'

Saarinen shrugged, wiping his sweating purple forehead with a snowy handkerchief. 'Life is curiously sweet,' he said. 'If we can't see real butterflies we can read about them and see them flashing on a cinescreen. I'm grateful for the chance to live out my life – even in dead outer space.'

'No guilt?'

'No guilt, sir.'

'No sense of our taking advantage of our position?'

'Why should we be over-modest, sir?' Zenger said. 'We have skills, we have knowledge. If we reach a new earth, or if our children do, we shall know how to set up a community. With the help of the others on America IV. Scientists, I mean.'

'No,' said Skilling. 'That's not it at all. We're just glad at the prospect of saving our skins. But I'll be frank with you, gentlemen. I hope to be cut off before then – in my boat, in a hunting accident. I've no right to outlive one of the best presidents this country ever had, the woman-ising handsome clever bastard.' The others knew whom he meant – a man who had been assassinated in his forties in this very town.

'Do you propose to prepare a statement?' asked Saarinen.

'About the end of things and the salvation of the presidential staff? No, I don't think so. I think we have to pretend that the horror's all over. The return of life to the littoral, the reconstruction of shattered cities – why not? We don't, thank God, have to worry about money. But the time for the welfare handouts is finished. Man justifies his existence by work – backed, of course, by federal grants-in-aid.'

'It all seems a terrible waste,' said Zenger. 'Do you propose the rebuilding of Washington?'

'Why not? The White House, the *real* one, must go up again. Meanwhile the President stays in Dallas.'

'And Congress?' asked Saarinen.

'I don't think we need be in too much of a hurry to recall Congress. God knows how much of Congress is left. God knows how much of America is left. As for the outside world – I refuse to think of it, I want to eat lunch today.'

Already eating lunch in a fine house on Fitzhugh Avenue, southeast, children, of State Fair Park in this same city of Dallas, was pretty nearly the whole of the Gropius family. This was John Gropius's house, John being the second son of Calvin and the vice-president of the Newbold Construction Company. His wife, a pretty woman named Rufa (after her father Rufus – a silly name, it was generally thought, doggish, wuffing, inappropriate to a woman so soft, gentle, undoggish, even unbitchy), was feeding their youngest, Sam, with a spoon and gently chiding their middle child, Joe, who was splashing Jello on to their eldest, Wilhelmina. James, Calvin's eldest, was rejoicing still in his reunion with Jay and Jay, Jennifer and Jessica. There were so many stories coming in still of bereavement, some grotesque, some heart-rending. The dream; Jennifer never tired of recounting her dream. It was a very simple dream, highly biblical with its angel warning of fire coming to the city, its resounding injunction in high Jacobean diction: 'Go ye then to Dallas, safe in the Lord.' And, by Christ, thought James, here they were, safe in the Lord. Though he could have done with less talk of the Lord now that the troubles were over and the government money was coming in and everybody should be having a damned good time. It was the old man who kept grimly going on about the Lord.

There was only one member of the Gropius family absent from the table. This was Dashiel Gropius, the youngest son of Calvin, whose work kept him in Fort Worth. The great hotel he managed, the Florentine, on Arlington Heights, was at the moment booming, what with the influx of coastal refugees into the town, the lavish cash hand-outs from the Government, the leisure which was so easily filled with stage entertainment and gambling. For the Florentine, modelled on many a great hotel in Las Vegas, a noted gambling city, children, offered not solely bed and board but also song and dance and a variety of games of chance – roulette, blackjack, craps, as well as what were called fruit machines and, more popularly, one-armed bandits. Calvin Gropius was not happy that his son should be engaged in such profane work, but he accepted philosophically that at least one of a brood must react against the father of it, and that one great religious prophet was probably enough for any family. Still, he would have been happier if. Never mind. He was addressing his family, less Dashiel, gravely over the dessert and coffee.

'You delude yourselves, as does most of the country, and perhaps most of the world that is left, that we have had our disaster and that we may now resume life as it was before.'

'Don't preach so, Calv,' said his wife Maria. 'Not to us, dear.'

'Life as it was before,' repeated Gropius, 'except that we no longer have a moon.'

'Such a shame,' said Rufa, tears in her eyes. 'Little Sam will never know what it was, the moon, I mean.'

'Oh, it will be back,' said Gropius grimly. 'And nobody will be happy to see it.'

'The moon.' John Gropius waved the moon away, like an appendix or other unnecessary organ. 'We can do without the moon.' There was no money in it, he seemed to say.

'That planet will be back,' said his father, 'lugging our moon along. I have been talking with men at the state university in Arlington. They say that the population at large has been kept in ignorance to avoid panic. They approve of this, as I do myself. The presidential policy, in so far as such a thing may be said to exist, is to allow the people to resume life as it was before, to meet an unavoidable end without special preparation for it.'

'Spiritual, you mean?' asked Jennifer.

'No,' said her father-in-law. 'Spirituality is not the affair of government. Though there was a time when it was, in Geneva, Switzerland, under the man whose name was given to me at the font. And once in New England, many centuries ago. No. I mean, alas, that the final disaster will hit a land disorganised. For to what can organisation lead? To anyone's salvation? Not this time, ah no. Chaos, and government impotent.'

'It's a long time off, dad,' said James, chewing a nut.

'We shall never celebrate Christmas again,' said his father. 'Think of that. We shall never see another spring. Unless unless unless –' He sighed, closed his eyes, opened them. 'Why should the righteous be destroyed with the sinner, O Lord?' He was looking up at a spot of dried damp on the ceiling. He looked now intently at his family, including little dribbling Sam, and said: 'You remember Genesis 6?'

Oh Jesus, thought James, nodding brightly.

'Listen to the word of the Lord,' Calvin Gropius said, giving out the word, which he knew by heart: '"And God saw that the wickedness of man was great in the earth, and that every imagination of the thoughts of his heart was only evil continually. And it repented the Lord that he had made man on the earth, and it grieved him at his heart. And the Lord said, I will destroy man whom I have created from the face of the earth; both man and beast and the creeping thing, and the fowls of the air; for it repenteth me that I have made them."'

'That always seemed kind of unfair to me,' said James. 'I mean the beasts hadn't done any harm.'

Calvin Gropius ignored him and turned his fierce eyes on his daughter-in-law Jennifer. 'What comes next, Jennifer?' he said. Jennifer said:

'"But Noah found grace in the eyes of the Lord. These are the generations of Noah: Noah was a just man and perfect in his generations, and Noah walked with God. And Noah begat three sons –"'

'Yes yes yes,' her father-in-law said impatiently. 'Where is the ark for the family of the righteous?' They looked at him. Then John said:

'You mean it ought to be us?' His father said:

'If only God would speak. An angel spoke to Jennifer here and saved her from the burning city, Oklahoma City. The Lord spoke to Noah.'

'It was a dream,' said Jennifer brightly. 'If you like, I'll dream a dream and he can speak to you through me. I'm good at dreams,' she added simply. Calvin Gropius resumed reading from the holy book printed in his brain:

"'And God said unto Noah, The end of all flesh is come before me; for the earth is filled with violence through them; and, behold, I will destroy them with the earth. Make thee an ark of gopher wood...'"

John, whose trade was ordering the construction of things, like God himself, said: 'It was simpler in those days. Nowadays Noah would have to build a spaceship. If by the destruction of the world you mean, you know, what the professors are talking of. It won't happen, you know, dad. But it shows where the Bible goes wrong. I mean, it's not a good guide for today. If God destroyed the earth, Noah and his sons would have to get off in a spaceship. And they couldn't do it, could they? They'd have to get somebody to build it for them, and have a government grant of fifty billions or so.' John had an instinct for estimates.

'Look,' said Calvin Gropius with such concentrated ferocity that his wife wondered about this Puma disease she'd heard of, men going wrong in the head because of the gravity or something. 'Listen. If anyone is going to be saved, we are. We are the righteous. I've preached the Word to this whole nation, and to other nations too – well, Great Britain, South Africa anyway, that French trip was a flop because of the language problem – and if anybody has the right to call himself the patriarch of this nation, it's myself. And if I'm Noah, you are Noah's family.'

'Would there be animals?' asked twelve-year-old Jessica. 'Clean and unclean beasts, like it says?'

'It's a nice idea, dad,' said John, getting up from the table, his table, this was his house. 'If it was just a matter of an ark of, you know, gopher wood, I could put that in hand tomorrow. Cost you about a million, done properly. Well, perhaps not tomorrow. Next month, say. There's talk about a lot of contract bids coming up. The Coast, naturally. I'm on my way. See you all at dinner.' He kissed his wife and kids and went out humming 'The animals went in two by two, hurrah, hurrah'.

'If anybody's to be saved,' said Calvin Gropius, 'it's us. And now – grace after meals.' He joined his hands and closed his eyes. 'James,' he said, opening them, 'stop chewing. John,' he said, 'should not have gone out like that. Never mind.' He closed his eyes again and started to give thanks for the lamb chops and the Jello.

Fourteen

When life began to return to New York City, Val Brodie and Willett (at last dressed as a non-Scot) were holed up in the penthouse suite of the Peter Minuit Hotel, which overlooked Park Avenue. They had undergone bad times together, but there was now a sense of deflation, of the rebirth of normality and law and order and cops and having to pay bills, which made them almost nostalgic for great waves and winds tugging at them. Periodically, in this fine tideless summer weather, they would go out on to the balcony and look down at the rapid restoration of the old civic pattern. The bone-dry streets had been cleared of dead and other debris by a kind of pressed militia under brutish men with guns and mouths ever ready with insult and obscenity. Val and Willett naturally wished to keep out of the way of any improvised conscription that was going around, but they recognised that forced massive man-power was needed to dry out, clean up, polish what had once, children, been known as the Big Apple. An apple was a kind of fruit: you will have seen a picture of an apple.

They were subsisting, not too tastily, on canned goods they had lugged from various store-rooms of hotels at various skywalk levels, not that many skywalks had survived the ultimate high tide. In the clothes-closets of their two bedrooms they had the entire spectrum of Hiss Soups, Seth Low Tasty Stews, Mensch Spongemeats, Piccirilli Pasta Treats, Moshowitz Kosher Puddings. They had cases, agony to manhandle, of hard liquor and Marquis de Lafayette Good American wines (b.o.f.i.), as well as some genuine vinous relics of dead France, Spain and Italy. They had instant coffee and a water-heater. The water was pretty foul and had to be thoroughly boiled, so they drank mostly from the heady wholesome bottles. The question was: what were they going to do?

Val had been studying the whole business of the impending collision of earth and Puma, mainly with the aid of a couple of paperback books he had picked up from a bookspinstand in the skyreceplevel smokestore of the Rutherford Hotel. The books, like everything else, had been soaked but had dried out in humps and bumps and bleary lines of blurred type. The books were called *Astronomy*, *Folks* and *Ah, The Stars* – silly catchpenny titles. In the early evening, after a meal of Hiss and Seth Low and Moshowitz and good Baton Rouge brandy (b.o.f.i.), Val tried to explain what he saw as the situation to Willett, who was in a kind of white moygashel tent-suit. They both smoked long Joe Papps, of which they had a fine store, as well as of disposable gas lighters.

'Here it is, you see,' he said, showing a bumpy diagram to Willett. 'There's the sun, a hell of a size, and then the planets sort of keep their distances, as in a kind of ritual dance. Mercury's nearest, then Venus comes next, then Earth, then Mars, then you get the mansize stuff – Jupiter, Saturn, the big boys – then Uranus and Neptune, fairly bulky, and last tiny Pluto, right out on the edge, sometimes called the asshole of the solar system. Now what I don't understand is why Puma doesn't smash up Mercury or Venus or, for that matter, following the rule of the dance, just get in, say, between Venus and us and go spinning merrily around, minding its own fucking business. I mean, why *us*?'

'And why, for that matter, does it have to have our moon, with poor young George on it?'

'What I don't want to start thinking about,' said Val, 'is some kind of predestined pattern, with God knowing all about it, creating man, knowing before he created him that he was going to be a wicked bastard, and so setting up this nice little cataclysm to get rid of him.' He looked gloomily at the diagram before him, the page a terrain of little hills, the crude colours run together with the (punitive?) waters.

'It may not happen,' said Willett. 'The general view is that it's not going to happen.'

'Scientists have been wrong before,' said Val. 'I mean, the forecasters let everybody down very badly over the first of the tidal waves. Still, I wish to Christ I'd listened more carefully when Vanessa and her father were talking about it.' He glumly traced on the diagram with a chewed pencil the sun-routes of both earth and Puma and couldn't see for the life of him how a collision was inevitable. 'If,' he said, 'it's *not* going to happen, we ought to start deciding what to do with our lives.'

'There'll be no television for a long time yet. Nothing for me. No theatres. I have money, of, course.' And he patted his right breast where a wad of hundreds lay. They had robbed, both of them. They had found a remarkable phenomenon in the Chemical Bank Skywalk 30 – a safe opened by lightning. They had also found cashboxes and cashdrawers here and there, full of crisp or soggy green. 'But, God, God, life's more than having money. You, I take it, will start teaching again.'

'I had my orders,' said Val. 'I ought to do something about reporting somewhere. But where? And,' he said fiercely, 'we ought to stick together. You and I, we're a sort of gestalt.'

'What's a gheshtalt?'

'One person combining with another one, or more than one, to create a fuller sort of organism.'

Willett grunted, not unkindly, and said: 'I think we might risk a stroll through the city. I wonder if there's anybody running this hotel yet? Anybody interested in the paying of bills and so on?'

'There's no maid service. The elevator doesn't work.' Their room was dry enough now, though tatty, everything lumpy or wrinkled. They had had those sheets and mattresses out on the terrace in the hot sun. The armchairs had steamed out their load of damp in the same blessed fire. Still, a sense of grubbiness pervaded; there was a strong smell of ditches and marshes and rotting apples.

'The worst of being up here,' said Willett, 'is not the going down but the coming back again. I wonder if there's anything *really* happening down there? Bars, Madame Aphrodite, that sort of thing.' He went to the balcony to peer at the street-scene. People, no cars. 'Christ,' he said, 'there are lights coming on.' Val came to see. There were, too. Lights, one or two flickering skysigns – OLMSTEAD, VOORHEES, ISIDOR STRAUS.

'We'll go,' Val said.

'How do we get back?'

'We climb the stairs.'

'Are you mad?'

'It's only fifty floors.'

'You *are* mad.'

When they went out, somewhat furtively, on to the corridor, locking the door with the lockcard that had been kindly waiting for them on the hallway table when they first entered (the door being then flung wide, clothes scattered, the evacuation of the former tenants evidently having been hasty), it was perhaps with no surprise that they found the elevator working. This did not elate Willett at all; he did not relish altogether the end of the days of anarchy. In the reception hall below, however, they found nobody. Some quirk of a time-switch somewhere had brought light and power to the hotel. They cautiously went out on to the sidewalk. They walked south of a very green Central Park and found people, not many, walking dogs. 'Mad, mad,' said Willett uneasily. 'It's almost as though it never happened.' They saw signs of reconstruction work – men working nights, floodlamps already flooding. On 57th Street they entered Jerry Towle's Bar and Grill, a place they could not remember having seen before. It smelt of a very damp grave, but there were drinkers and a cheerful barman.

'Scotch,' said Val. 'Very large.'

'Very expensive,' said the barman. 'There won't be no more Scotch when existing stocks is finished, friend, friends. There ain't no more Scotland.'

'Jesus,' said Willett with awe. 'Television.'

The other drinkers had been watching a blank crackling screen, waiting. In very crude and blotchy colour the stars and stripes fluttered to the blurred noise of 'The Star Spangled Banner'. Then there came the cheerful face of the President.

'Christ, he looks old,' said Val. The President said:

'My friends, I speak to you from the White House, Dallas, Texas, the present centre of government until such time as a certain other White House, in a certain city in the District of Columbia, has been rebuilt and restored to its former glory. We have had, to say the least of it, difficult times. Now we count our dead in resignation to the will of heaven and, in obedience to the law of life, start to reconstruct our shattered country. You will hear rumours, put about by the forces of subversion for its own sake, to the effect that the worst is not yet over, that the destructive planet Puma will plunge back into our, alas, now moonless sky and resume, on a greater scale than before, its wanton work of destruction. This rumour is wicked and false.'

Willett and Val looked at each other over their whisky. One never believed a politician. Or did one? Some of the drinking watchers were believing.

'The world has known many disasters. But man has always come through, by his skin and teeth. I would ask all of you to remember that the disaster that has struck the whole world has been blessedly merciful to these United States. Our littoral has been devastated, and the devastation of the rampant seas has pushed far inland, and where it has not pushed the earth itself has not been slow to erupt in its own mode of devastation. But our basic resources remain intact – skill, materials and equipment, of which, on a nationwide scale, but a fraction has been lost to us. Work, rebuild. Be, during this difficult time, obedient to the civic and federal authorities. Let life go on. God bless you all and good night.'

That was the end of the evening's television, except for five minutes of commercials – CRUNCHTHUMP GRAVELATORS, WARREN AND WETMORE WETMIX, IF IT'S GOODY'S IT'S GOOD, and so on – followed by an ancient movie of a rich girl falling from a horse and developing brain damage. This latter broke down after the doctor had delivered his prognosis, and the service sputtered out. An old man without teeth sat next to Willett and said:

'Sure is good to be back. With my wife's folks in Oshkosh, Wisconsin till the lakes flooded. Then in Indiana. Sure is flat, Indiana. My daughter's there with this guy. I tell 'em why don't they get married like regular folks, but there's no telling the younger generation.'

Warmth, warmth, human warmth flooded in. Scotch at ten dollars the shot warmed, warmed. Soon Willett was going on about flutch calf-lollies, turdy-guts and shitten shepherds, referring chiefly to a group of droop-mouthed youths in, God bless their stupidity, Puma shirts.

'Sure has what they call a vocaburary, your friend here.'

Girls came in, and Willett had his arm round one gat-toothed giggler with surprising speed. 'Honeybunch,' he called her, 'piggesnie, heartsease, bedworthy bundlesnuggle,' and so on. She giggled. Then two men in uniform came in, one with a clipboard, the other with a pistol in a somewhat verdigrised holster. The uniform was a sort of overwashed blue, connoting some store that the floods had got at. In default of collar-dogs or breast-badge, they wore armbands which said NYC CLEARUP. They picked on the droop-mouthed youths first.

'Work-card?'

'What's a work-card?'

'I think,' said Willett, 'it would be wise to get out of here.' He unhanded his heartsease honeybunch. 'Some other time,' he told her. 'A matter of an urgent appointment.'

Outside the bar-room door another NYC clearup man was waiting, armed. 'You wait,' he said, 'till you've been seen about in there, buster.'

'Ah, Jesus,' said Willett.

'Work-card?' said the man with the clipboard, inkpencil at the ready. He was the overbearing sort who never learns humility, not even from world disaster.

'Never heard of work-cards,' Willett said. 'Sounds like an unwholesome innovation. I am an actor, freelance naturally. I work when I'm able to find work. My friend here is a university professor.'

'Work-card?'

'What *is* all this?' asked Val.

'If you've no work-card you get temporary drafted into the city clearup force. Thirty dollars a day and all found.'

'But Christ, I can prove,' said Val, 'that I'm on the staff of –' But, of course, he couldn't prove anything. 'What do we have to do?' he said in resignation.

'You wait outside there with Officer Grogan till we collect ten. Then you march.'

'Where to do we march?' asked a little chewing man they had pressed.

'You'll see, brother.'

Outside Val looked up at the sky and said to Willett: 'Do you see what I see?'

'What do you see? Oh. Oh yes. You'll see, brother, indeed.'

'Not much point in clearing up,' said Val.

Fifteen

You will have been perhaps wondering, children, ladies and gentlemen, how Professor Hubert Frame was getting on during this eventful spring and summer. Lying quiet in a little white room in the CAT hospital, his respirator plugged into the mains (the camp, of course, had its own generator), often under sedation, his heart action kept steady if faint through Dr Sophie Haas Fried's administration of the drug Diegerticon 5, he was informed regularly as to the progress of the great work by his daughter Vanessa, who also told him frankly – not caring much whether there was a hidden microphone about or not – about the unhappiness of the ship, the fervent and growing dislike of Boss Cat Bartlett.

'Dislike or distrust?'

'Oh, he's the soul of efficiency. That's the trouble. Efficiency through tyranny. Just a life of hard work and sterile devotion to the cause. To him, really. More and more he talks of loyalty to him.'

'I heard some story of exemplary harshness. I'd like to know the truth about poor young Goya.'

'Bartlett says it was the military going too far. But now there's O'Grady ready to try the latest astunomological techniques on dissidents. Maude Adams has been turned into a most efficient automaton. I never saw the necessity of an astunomologist on the team.'

'Hm,' said Frame, in the faint voice which was nearly all exhausted breath and very little glottis. 'It comes from the Greek for policeman. The Natsci committee, as you'll remember, was worried about space hysteria, hysterical dissidence, the need for an expert in pacification. One can never be sure. Policeman sounds horrible, of course. O'Grady is highly qualified in techniques of pacification.'

'That sounds horrible too.'

'Yes. You think O'Grady ought to go?'

'I think Bartlett ought to go.'

Frame could see, clearly (sorry) framed in his window, the great bulk of Puma, bloody red, with a tiny moon beside it, newly arisen and ready to terrorise coastal evenings again. 'We're not in charge of the project, Vanessa. We invented it –'

'You did.'

'– But we're not in charge. We don't tell anybody to go. Bartlett could deliver you to the murderous rapists, presumably, and on me he could literally pull the plug. I think, however, I ought to have Bartlett in here.'

'You won't *have him in*, father. He's not a schoolboy, you're not a school principal. He might one of these days deign to come in.'

'I think I have certain rights. Perhaps if you told him I'm going to die. I am, of course.'

'I'll ask. Request. Bow humbly and beseech.'

'I ought to have a talk with him. The Bartlett file – it just didn't give any real idea. Does any file? I've been thinking of someone else – someone with a useless file. Val, I mean. Before I – go –'

'Don't talk about going. Don't talk about poor Val.'

'How do we know it's – *poor* Val?'

'What do you mean?'

'Oh, never mind. He wouldn't have lasted five minutes with Bartlett, from all you tell me of Bartlett. Or – mad, isn't it? – Bartlett might not have lasted five minutes with *him*.'

'What a strange thing to say. You never liked Val. You despised him.'

'I suppose I despised in him what I despise in myself – self-indulgence chiefly. My self-indulgences – tobacco, this project. His? Drink, fornication, science fiction. Perhaps I should have fornicated more and smoked less. Val at least had the grace to keep his science fiction between hard or soft covers.'

'I will not have you saying that – self-indulgence? *This*? What can you mean?'

'Do ask Bartlett to come and see me. I shall have to sleep soon.'

Bartlett was chiding Dr Louise Boudinot and Dr Georges Auguste Ewing in his office, while O'Grady sat silently beside him. Ewing was saying:

'Christ, wouldn't you say you'd reached the limit, Bartlett? If a man and woman can't – Christ, we'd done *nothing*, and even if we had –'

'The time,' said Bartlett patiently, 'will come for fornication, but the time is not now.'

'You call that forn –' gasped Louise. 'A kiss fornication?'

'There's no time for fleshly indulgences,' said Bartlett. 'There was a point 05 error, a significant error, in the calibration that Drs Irving and Herodotus were engaged on. And they were merely pawing each other.'

'Holding hands,' said Ewing.

'What do you suggest, O'Grady?' asked Bartlett.

'Nothing now. Put out a general warning. Next time a dose of eireneutis 6a.'

'Christ,' said Ewing.

'Gamma report in tomorrow,' ordered Bartlett.

'I need at least another two days,' said Ewing. 'I have to stay up all night two nights running. Be sensible.'

'Dr Adams will be glad to be of help,' Bartlett said. 'Overjoyed.'

'Jesus Christ.'

When Vanessa was admitted, Bartlett this time alone, she found him affable. 'A drink?' he said, going to his fruit-juice cabinet. She told him her father's request. 'Yes,' he said thoughtfully. 'He has a certain claim on my time. Though he must have read the progress reports.'

'He finds reading difficult.'

'I'll go now. No need for you to come. Perhaps you'd be good enough to check on whether Dr Ewing's gamma report has actually been *started*. I don't trust Ewing. Ewing needs treatment.' He gave Vanessa no time to reply but marched out. When he got to Frame's room in the hospital, next hut to Project HQ, he entered without knocking.

'Good of you to come, Bartlett. Sit down.' Bartlett remained standing. He said:

'Was there anything particular you wanted of me?'

'When will you be ready?'

'Six weeks to the day. Everything is going as planned, except for some extra work still to be done on the gravity apotha. It seems to be a matter of accepting Puma's pull in the initial stages and then effecting a tangential glance-off, using Jumel's megaproagon.'

'I've no doubt of your having,' sighed Frame, 'every technical aspect of the venture under control. Have you, however, ever considered what the venture is really for?'

Bartlett smiled slightly. 'The salvaging of civilisation in microcosm. Your phrase, I think.'

'Ridiculous, isn't it, Bartlett?' Bartlett smiled still, though more uneasily. 'How much do you believe about that civilisation nonsense? When I spoke to the President, eons ago, months ago, I spoke of man's achievements in science, art, architecture, music, philosophy. False political rhetoric. What do I care about those things? What do you care?' Bartlett held his smile but let the uneasiness out, like a slowly expelled breath. 'This project was designed for the glory of Hubert Frame, scientist and smoker. But who will give him the glory?'

'When America reaches America Nova, the name Frame will be given to the first community established there. That is already laid down in the conspectus.'

'Again I ask: what do you care? What's in it for you, Bartlett?'

'I was chosen. I do my duty.'

'You do your duty,' said Frame with what sarcasm his dyspneal voice could give out. 'But what reality do you serve? Beauty? Love? Truth?'

'Power,' said Bartlett without hesitation. 'Power is the reality. Manifested at so many levels – the power of one heavenly body over another, of one man over many –'

'Fifty men and women,' said Frame, showing no surprise at Bartlett's avowal. 'Not many to have power over.'

'You're wrong. A race of my making will colonise America Nova, wherever it is. I have no doubt that man will survive, the kind of man I shall mould. I shall fix the parameters for ever once the voyage is begun. I have already thought much about the – desirable image. I shall make the new race.'

'So your fellow astronauts are in for an unhappy time. At least you don't give me the hogwash you give to them, or so my daughter informs me – a time of totalitarian discipline to be followed by an endless era of happy freedom. That argument never worked, did it? The end justifies the means, but the means determines the nature of the end.'

'Unhappy,' said Bartlett, having picked out that one word and disregarded the rest of Frame's breathy flow. 'Human emotions are a great nuisance. I have fine brains and fine bodies working for me, for the project, but their emotions are a damned nuisance. Soon there'll be leisure to eliminate emotions – love, hate, that sort of hindrance, that sort of nonsense. What we take with us into space is not the whole of human experience – just a part of it, the useful part. No literature, music, art. Those are disruptive, dissident. Man will have a new chance. A chance to understand the nature of power.'

'God help them, God help me. I wasn't big enough to *frame* such a venture.' He stressed the verb-name bitterly. 'I should have listened to my son-in-law more than I did. I can't give you my blessing, Bartlett. Perhaps in hell or purgatory I shall have a wry laugh at *homo Bartlettius*, learning the reality of power in Bartlettland on Bartlett, habitable planet of the Bartlett galaxy. But there are other ships going into space, Bartlett, other Americas. Remember that.'

'Space is very big,' said Bartlett. 'Big enough for more than *homo Bartlettius*. Well then, I go without your blessing. Have you anything more to say?'

'No more commerce between us, Bartlett.'

'You're probably ready to die, I should think,' Bartlett said coolly. 'Shall I – pull the plug on you? A corporal work of mercy, as the Christians put it. Pull out the plug, wait five minutes, push it back in again. Professor Frame is dead. A grand burial with the buglers blowing taps. If you want a really big funeral you'll have to have it tomorrow. The day after tomorrow the troops are leaving. They've done their work.'

'I should like,' said Frame with equal coolness, 'to see the great ship before I go. See what might better have been left as a dream – a hunk of science fiction. Will you grant me that?'

'Gladly. Some day next month?'

'If I'm still alive.'

'Oh, that can be arranged. No problem there. Keeping people alive is one aspect of power.' And, with no more words, he left.

The day after the next day the troops went off in their blacked-out aircrafts to their bases in Kansas, Indiana, Illinois, as far south as Kentucky and Tennessee, leaving a cadre of a platoon, corporal, sergeant, lieutenant for residual work. Bartlett insisted on a kind of passing-out parade. He wore naval uniform for the occasion. It was noticed by the observant that he had promoted himself to full admiral. He was smart, every inch an officer. When the troops had gone he presided, still in admiral's uniform, over a special dinner in the mess at which, exceptionally, alcoholic beverages were available. He gave a little speech:

'Now, ladies and gentlemen, we enter into the final phase of the operation. The er donkeywork has been completed. Now it is all a matter of fine eye, keen brain, total utter and ultimate dedication to the preparation of Bartlett.'

There were murmurs, even vinous laughs.

'My apologies. America, as we rather too grandiloquently call it. A slip of the tongue.' It was not. Everybody was damned sure it was not a slip of the tongue. And then Bartlett quoted: 'We few, we happy few, we band of brothers.' A chill of a new kind went through the assembly. Nobody had heard Bartlett quote poetry before. Dr Abramovitz and Dr Da Verrazano smiled zombyishly. They did not seem to have heard the line before. After several sessions with Dr O'Grady their professional bibliothecological knowledge had become severely limited. *Tom Sawyer*? *Hamlet*? *A Clockwork Orange*? Never heard of them.

Sixteen

Edwina Goya was still with her aunt Melanie in Fort Worth, Texas. Aunt Melanie was a widow of pre-Puma vintage, not badly off, living for the day, a bridge-player, a great sceptic who called that big light in the sky, *our* moon circling about it, a lot of wicked nonsense. 'Thief,' she said sometimes, '*arrant* thief. Stealing like that and then coming back to mock at everybody. Sneering at us from the sky.' She was not above shaking her fist at it and shouting at it to go away. It did not go away.

Her house was in Haltom City, south-west of Richland Hills, a decent well-built stone house on Conkling Avenue, just by the People's Burial Park. There was enough room in it for two women not to get under each other's feet, but Aunt Melanie saw little of Edwina. Edwina kept to her bed, nursing her belly (everything going just fine, little lady, Dr McBean said) and reading devotional poetry, thinking in a confused way about what had happened to Nat, not doubting that he was alive, doubting totally that she would ever see him again. She repeated to herself the name of the town that poor Nat had muttered, as though his pursuers were near, with great speed: Sloansville, in the state of Kansas. And if she went to this CAT place, they would of course welcome her in, would they not, saying: come and join your beloved, there he is, see, over there. The trouble was that, with the growth of the child in her womb, the memory of Nat became dimmer in inverse proportion. To resume love, Nat and herself, for the brief time left? Less important than to ensure the survival of the child she carried. Otherwise, what waste, what colossal wicked waste. A child crushed in the ultimate ruins. What was God's view of all that? Her volumes of devotional poetry returned no answer.

Sometimes she read the Holy Bible – it made little sense for her, or for the world on which Puma was to pounce – chiefly because its diction and rhythms were inextricably woven into her memory of the patterns of one particular voice. The voice was that of Calvin Gropius, a man who proclaimed for her the vital energy that transcended, or lay immanent in, all the quotidian details of life. In a sense, Gropius was the father of this child kicking in her womb. She had had but to invoke his image, and the image of his voice, when lying with Nat, for her to be flooded with a force of intolerable vital joy. And if she loved Nat it was, she had to be honest with herself, solely as the catalyst of the rending ecstatic process. Her child, Gropius – the two concepts danced in a rhythm which she could now read. It spelt *survival*. Gropius. Where was he now? Perhaps dead, shattered in earthquake or engulfed in tigrine waters. But in a sense he could never die. He transcended the accidents of both disaster and decay. If anyone on the doomed earth should survive – The two; she saw the two together. Her child and the avatar of divine, super-divine energy.

'Edwina,' said Aunt Melanie one morning, bringing her ungrudgingly her breakfast tray – coffee, toast, papaya juice, 'Edwina, Jonathan's coming home.'

'Jonathan?'

'Oh, come, child, *my* Jonathan, your cousin Jonathan. He's coming on leave. Private first class Jonathan Putnam, *my son*. Now you'll have somebody to talk to. Somebody your own age. My Jonathan. Do you mind changing bedrooms, dear? This was always Jonathan's room.'

'Jonathan. I've not seen Jonathan since – He came to see us in Hawaii, didn't he? Hawaii –' Her mouth squared for tears. Her aunt would stand no nonsense, saying:

'Stop that, girl. No news is good news.'

'Dad and mom, oh my God. Hawaii sank like a stone. All of it. Like so many stones.'

'Be cheerful now. Take what comes, girl. Your mother was my sister, remember. But I'd like to kill that great fat thief of a thing up in the sky.'

Jonathan was not of Edwina's age; he was somewhat younger, demonstrating youth in pimples and gawkiness. Edwina came down to the fine homecoming dinner Aunt Melanie had prepared. Jonathan ate heartily of the roast turkey, stuffing, sausages, cranberry sauce, roast and mashed potatoes, braised celery, strawberry shortcake to follow. Edwina picked at a bit of cheese and a breadstick.

'Come, dear, eat,' said Aunt Melanie. 'Remember you've two to feed.'

Jonathan was slow at taking in the meaning of this: he was still only a private first class in the Engineers. But then his face beamed. 'Gee, that's good news,' he said. 'And when do we get a look at your husband, Edwina?'

'Never, as far as I can tell,' Edwina sniffed. 'Never. Excuse me, I think I'll go to bed.' She got up from the table, her half-eaten breadstick clattering down to her plate.

'Oh, come, girl,' said her aunt. But Edwina had gone.

'What happened to him?' said Jonathan, wiping turkey gravy from his uniform shirt with a napkin corner. 'Was he in the coast floods?'

'No, he was in a thing called Cat or something and they wouldn't let him out. She's not heard from him. Of course, as I keep telling her, Jonathan, he may be alive and well and get furlough as you've gotten it.' Jonathan's mouth was wide open. 'Don't show what you're eating, dear. It's not nice.'

'Cat, you said? C.A.T.? The moonship project? Christ, mom, that's where I was.'

'But you said you were working on electrical generators in Kansas, dear.'

'Yeah, I know, mom. I didn't say more 'cause it's still supposed to be, you know, T.S. We were told no talking about it on furlough. But that's what it was, the moon job. Finished our work, so off we march, fly. So, then. So that's where he is, was. Small world, kind of. What's his name?'

'A Jewish kind of name. Goy? No, that's not Jewish. A Spanish

kind of name. There was some big painter with it, Edwina tells me.
Goya. I said before, Jonathan dear, don't open your mouth like that.'
    'But I know about the guy. Doc Goya. He got out.'
    'So Edwina said. He got out and telephoned to this very house.
Then they seem to have taken him back in again.'
    'Yeah, they took him back in again. And then I was on the incin-
erator party. He's dead, mom. Gee, that's terrible. Eddy's husband.
Gee, that's awful. There was a lot of, you know, talk about it. This
guy they had in charge, Boss Cat they call him, was terrible.'
    Jonathan's mother was thoughtful. She brought a bubbling per-
colator of coffee in, set it down, was thoughtful. 'The question is,
Jonathan, whether we let the poor girl live in hopes. Or out with it.
Our family was all brought up on the truth.'
    'It's a terrible thing to have to tell her.'
    'I think she ought to know, Jonathan. You're the one who knows
the truth. You're the one to tell it, dear.'
    'It's the kind of thing,' said Jonathan, a veteran in army *mores*,
'you tell a guy only when he's drunk. I mean, there was this guy in
our outfit, when we were still at Camp Pollock, Dayton. His pal, his
closest friend, you know, got chewed up by one of these excavators
they call crushers. They got him very drunk and then they told him.
It cushioned the shock, the medic officer said. Instinctively correct,
he called it. He was okay when he'd gotten over his hangover.'
    'You're not getting Edwina drunk,' said his mother.
    'But suppose I take her out, mom? You know, on the town. A
couple of drinks only, you know. Tell her quite quietly.'
    'Well,' said his mother, drinking coffee thoughtfully. 'She has to
be told somehow, Jonathan. Poor girl. Poor boy, for that matter.'
    It was not until two nights later that Edwina consented to go out
with Jonathan in his Poe speedbird, Edgar Allan as he called it, and
as other Poe-owners called theirs. Though only a private first class,
he was not unwise in the techniques of holding off bad news. He
took her to the Malinda on Sagamore Hill, to the Comanche off
Lancaster Avenue, Meadowbrook. Puma and his stolen moon were
big in the sky, and there was much drunken excitement about. She
had two martinis and he talked about pals, officers, the time when he

had had two days shore leave in Hawaii when on his way to Fiji and they had, he thought, swum together. Treacly water with Diamond Head looking down. At the mention of Hawaii she wished to cry. He quickly got on to a movie he had recently seen in camp, *Baa Lamb's Ass*, meant to turn you on but it didn't. He had had a girl friend there in the other ranks' dining hall, a waitress, sort of. A sweet potato of a girl, Cindy Woolworth by name. She said:

'Let's go to the Florentine. Arlington Heights.'

'But that's a great big gambling hotel, Eddy. You wouldn't want to go there.'

'Gambling. It's a picture of life. Take me.' He didn't understand, but he paid for their drinks (plain coke for him, driving) and they went off. The Florentine was massive, gaudy, not at all Florentine. Its Italian connections were not, after all, at all northern. It was, after all, owned by the Tagliaferro brothers who were very southern. 'I like it,' said Edwina, brightening as she sat at the huge leather-bound bar in the main gaming-hall. People were gambling away C-notes like quarters. A handsome, broad, sleek man in his thirties, in space-depth blue tuxedo, white-teethed, abundant black hair, armed with a controlling vitality she found disturbingly familiar, came up to the bar and said to the head barman:

'Put the new price plan in operation at nine-thirty, Jack. That's on the Chivas Regal. Let the Claymore run on as it was.'

'Check, Mr Gropius.'

'Everything okay, Jack?'

'Everybody thirsty, Mr Gropius.'

The man laughed and turned away from the bar. Edwina put a hand out and touched. He turned, smiling.

'Your name,' she said, 'is Gropius?'

'That's right, miss or madam. Dashiel Gropius. In charge, as they say. Is everything going all right?'

'Are you,' she could hardly get the words out, 'any relation to.'

'I'm always being asked that,' said Dashiel Gropius. 'The answer is yes. My father is, for his sins or mine or somebody's, the great Calvin Gropius. Does that answer your question and quieten your heart, miss or madam?'

'I need to see him,' blurted Edwina. 'I *must* see him. A very important message. Is he around?'

'Around? Here? That's good,' said Dashiel Gropius. 'No, he never comes to the haunts of sin, not even to preach. He's in Dallas. He wouldn't thank me for divulging his er present hermitage, but that's where he is. At Number 57, Fitzhugh Avenue. South-east of State Fair Park. Go and see him. Go and pray with him.' And, smiling pleasantly, he went into the smoky brilliant electric gambling area.

'Thank God,' said Edwina. To Jonathan's surprise, she kissed him, swiftly, sweetly, on the lips. 'You're a blessing, Jonathan. If it hadn't been for you – Let's have another.'

Jonathan was glad to buy another. He said:

'Eddy, there's something I have to tell you. But not here. Over at that table there. See, that guy's leaving.'

'Very mysterious. Why can't you tell me here?'

'You may want to be somewhere, you know, dark and quiet. It's bad news. Does Cat mean anything to you? You know, C.A.T., Center of Advanced – I mean, I was there. My outfit was there, doing the dirty work. It's about, about, well, I guess you know who it's about, Eddy.'

'Nat's dead, is he?'

'Doc Goya he was known as. A good guy, clever and, you know, young. I'm sorry, Eddy.'

She betrayed no expression, sad or otherwise, but drank off her martini thirstily. 'Another,' she said. And then: 'I thought he might be. God rest his soul, as my devotional poets would say. Thank you, Jonathan.'

'Don't thank me, Eddy. I just thought, well, mom thought –'

'No, thank you for bringing me here. Everything's going to be all right now, I think. Everything.'

Seventeen

Val and Willett were employed on the ghoulish work of unblocking the Ghersom Tunnel which ran under the Hudson and connected, along with other tunnels and very battered bridges now under repair, Manhattan with the New Jersey mainland. Ghoulish because the blocking had been done by cars with corpses in them, as also by corpses without cars. Val and Willett operated a Marquet truck on which cadavers were piled; they drove it to Dump 4; they tipped their freight into a great hole to which, at the end of the day's work, Puma and moon in their crescent phase rising, fire was set. There was an unofficial team that stripped the bodies of whatever was unspoiled and still useful – watches, rings, dental bridges, money, credit cards and the like. This was the ultimately ghoulish. No, not quite the ultimately. There was a dribbling mad necrophile who had to be kept away from fleshly mauling. He was eventually shot by Murphy, the man in charge of Dump 4.

It was this Murphy who, during the lunch break, came up to Val and Willett and their bread and cheese and beer (rations were issued at the Dorothy Draper Museum, at present a work-force hostel, when the parties left in the morning). He had a little book in his hand and said to Val:

'This you?' He thrust the book, a lumpy water-spoiled paperbook, at Val's nose. Val saw his own picture on the back cover. 'Found it on one of the stiffs.'

'Good God,' he said, taking it. 'I'd almost forgotten this existed.'

The title was *Not to Call Night*. The blurb said: 'This brilliant first novel by one who bids fair to become a great name in world SF...'

'I had a look at it,' Murphy said. 'There ain't nuttin doidy in it.' This seemed to be a reproach. A man said, chewing cheese:

'Doidy? A doidy book?'

'*Not* doidy, Milligan,' growled Murphy. 'If you want sumpn doidy I'll take you to see *Baa Lamb's Ass* at the Angus Wilson.' The workers looked at Val, flicking through the book with tenderness, surprise, distaste; looked at him with the mixture of awe and contempt that working men will always accord chance-met writers. Dis guy's a rider. What's he ride? Not rider, stoopid, he writes books. Doidy books?

'Read us some out,' said Milligan. 'A sex bit.'

Willett jocosely grabbed the book from Val, opened it at random and began to improvise: 'Panting with desire she seized him and said "Now, now, I can't wait." He held her off contemptuously, disdaining the proffered opulence of her naked flesh. Then she...' His voice faded out. He looked at Val, frowning. 'When did you write this?'

'The date's opposite the title-page. 1990. 1986. A hell of a time ago.'

'You remember what it's about?'

'The blurb says. About a heavenly body preparing to hit the earth, isn't it? False alarm. A lot of earthquakes, though. Is that right?'

'Listen,' said Willett. 'Listen carefully. There's a character here called Bodley. Dr. Bodley. He says: "If I had to choose a site comparatively immune from seismic shocks, however hard they hit the rest of the American terrain, I'd opt for a little place called Fordtown in the state of Kansas, midway between Hays and Hill City." Where did you get that information? Guesswork? Pure fiction?'

'Ain't nuddin doidy in dat,' said Milligan.

'I used to work pretty hard on background,' said Val, brows knitted; trying to remember. 'The critics were always quick to leap on writers who hadn't done their homework, as they put it. I should think that's a chunk of exact information. Why?'

'Idiot,' bawled Willett. 'Shitabed lobnoddy, foolish loggerhead. Your turdstrewed catcamp is in such a place. Didn't they ever talk about the kind of place they were after? Your wife, your wife's old man?'

'A spot,' Val said, 'comparatively immune from seismic activity.'

'That's where we're going,' Willett said.

'You guys are going,' said Murphy, who had been listening intently but without comprehension, 'back to woik.'

'There are other places,' Val said. 'The United States is full of good quakeless land.'

'We've got to go somewhere,' said Willett, 'and soon.'

'I told you the position,' Val said. 'I'm off the team now, no doubt about it. Discharged dead, probably. And you've never been on it.'

'We'll cross that bridge,' Willett said, 'when we come to it. We'll negotiate that tunnel,' he varied.

'Back to woik,' said Murphy, and he blew a whistle.

'Till when?' asked a polite educated dark man who alleged he had taught Arabology at Columbia. 'When do the floods start again? We have our preparations to make.'

'Don't know nuttin about that, buster,' Murphy said. 'We goes on till the Mayor says to stop.'

'Fuck the Mayor,' said the dark man evenly and without rancour.

'You don't wanna say that, buddy. That's kinda like what they has on the old movies. High treason, it's called. You wanna watch that mouth, little buddiuddy.'

Dump 4 was on the New Jersey side of the tunnel. At three in the afternoon, Val jerked the lever for the last time and sent corpses thudding into the great hole. The scavengers leaped about, frisking like rats, opening dead mouths, tugging at dead fingers. 'Okay,' said Val. Willett let in the clutch. They were off. Voices shouted after them. They fancied they heard gunshots. In three quarters of an hour they were on the outskirts of Newark. Their truck was gasoline-driven. They filled up from a self-serve pump, stuffing dollars into the mouth of the machine. Fat gas glugged in. Opposite Val noticed a shop with a temporary nameboard tacked on: WHITEHEAD GUNS.

'Guns?' said Willett. 'You can actually buy guns?'

'The inalienable right of all Americans. Guaranteed by the

Constitution. The pursuit of happiness, also of enemies and harmless uneatable animals. Come on, we need protection.'

An old man, chewing an afternoon bever, was glad to serve them. 'It's lead,' he said, 'that does the protecting. Had 'em in lead, all of 'em, down there in the cellar. When I came back from my sister Ethel's in Macon, Georgia, I found all gone but the cellar.' He cackled. 'But it's cellars that count. Wine, guns, money. You can't beat cellars.' He sold them a Hamster hipfirer and two .45 Schultz pistols, together with much ammunition. They paid out hundreds of dollars.

Near Reading, Pennsylvania, they ate ham and eggs and cheese-cake in a diner and stocked up at a hypermart on canned goods, at a liquor store on liquor. Puma's crescent was a grotesque lewd mockery of its attendant moon's. Reading had had little trouble last time and expected no more this. But outside Harrisburg they found an end-of-the-world group shouting hysterical slogans about repentance, to the laughter of passing motorists. At a motel outside Pittsburgh they stayed the night. It had been a long drive but the truck was speedy. Tomorrow they would need something speedier, as well as more comfortable. They had their eye on a Tallahassee '00, parked outside Chalet 9A. They lay on the twin double beds in the same room, smoking long Columbus panatelas.

'Hopeless,' repeated Val.

'A matter of degrees,' Willett said. 'One thing's less hopeless than another. To stay in New York would have been ten point hope-lessness. A day added to life – it's something. Even to be in Kansas will be something like three point hopelessness. Besides,' he puffed, 'besides, I have rather a fancy to be saved.'

'Why?'

'A bonus. A gift. I don't insist on it, of course. A man's a fool to insist on anything. I'd rather like,' he said innocently, 'to be in a spaceship. It fulfils a childhood dream.' Rain suddenly burst from a million simultaneously pricked bags in the Pennsylvania sky. When, like a brilliantly organised hissing high-violin effect, it had played a few bars in *moderato* tempo, lightning performed jaggedly on the skyline visible through the wide uncurtained window and hundreds of drummers thumped thunder. Then there were, as from an extra orchestra hidden in the wings, deeper thumps and grumbles afar. The coke-bottles on the middle bedside table rattled together, and their contents danced, even splashed. 'An earthquake,' said Willett. 'North of Pittsburgh. We got out of New York just in time. The tides will be starting again.'

They were determined to get some sleep on this trip. Val had a bottle of five hundred Aupnia tablets. They took two each, washing them down with shaky coke, and settled to sleep. Sleep came tardily, but it came. Their portable alarm-clock, picked up from the travelling-bag of another westward fugitive in the hypermart when he (she with him) was paying his snakelong check, woke them at six. Crescent Puma and moon setting, the rain stopped, the distant seismic rumbles still audible, flashes on the horizon, they got up wearily and stiffly. The sleepers in Chalet 9A slept still. The Tallahassee 'oo would not yield to Willett's omniclef. 'Bugger,' he said, in stage Britishry. 'Let's try that one over there.' He meant an Abaco station-wagon in high-gloss aubergine. It started like a dream. They were on their way, bags and guns rattling at the back.

They breakfasted at a diner just over the Ohio border, five miles or so from Wheeling, and made Columbus easily by midday. Again, as they sped on with full bellies, the sky yawned open and vomited haily rain, lightning did its act with thunder grumbling after. Just beyond Dayton the car broke down. 'Christ pedicate the bastard,' swore Willett. Val got delicate fingers to work on the guts under the hood, but to no avail. 'Christ blast its soul to fucking Tophet.' They couldn't get the thing to work. The tank was half-full of gas. 'Christ deliver it a fiery message of abomination.'

The name of Christ was being used less blasphemously in the headquarters of Calvin Gropius, 57, Fitzhugh Avenue, Dallas. It was also being used less frequently. Gropius found the New Testament hardly relevant to the situation he knew was coming. The Book of Revelations was good for pertinent rhetoric but hardly for a programme of action. The holy name was much more in the mouth of his visitor, Mrs Edwina Goya, widow and prospective mother. Outside the rain whished down, and more damp began to appear on the living-room ceiling. Do you not consider yourself,' asked Edwina, 'the living vicar of Christ?'

'That's what they call the Pope,' said Gropius. 'If there still is a Pope.' He and his family – Maria his wife, his son James, his two daughters-in-law, his grandchildren, the other two sons being at work – looked at the thin strange girl with the swelling belly, not too curiously, certainly not fearfully: they were all used to cranks, it was an occupational hazard.

'Listen,' said Edwina, on the edge of her dining-chair, 'I have the facts, I have the knowledge. I'm not talking now like one of the chiliastic fanatics of California. The world is going to end. Not with the Lord coming in glory, flanked by archangelic brass. Just a very unfortunate cosmic accident, something to be explained solely by physics and not at all by theology. Do you understand me? Going to end, and going to end soon. And there's a spaceship being made ready in the state of Kansas to salvage a load of scientists. Is this right? Is not this flying in the face of the Lord's will? Doesn't the Lord Jesus Christ want the righteous to be saved, not the knowledgeable?'

Gropius looked warily at her. He knew the eyes, wide, capable of adoration. He said:

'I must confess I have waited for a sign – a message – a dream, perhaps.' Jennifer said brightly:

'I'm the one who gets the dreams. There was this one before Oklahoma City got hit by the quake, and this angel –'

'Yes, yes,' said Gropius wearily, 'we've heard all about that. What you say,' he told Edwina, 'makes sense, all too much very sad sense. In the days of Noah, righteousness and the woodworker's skill were enough. Christ's own life shows how these two attributes were, in a sense, cognate. Today, alas, we have an age of specialisation. Righteousness is one full-time job, technology is another.' That last neat phrase had actually been spoken by his son John at dinner the previous evening.

'Well, the ship is in preparation,' said Edwina, 'and I know where. It's your duty in Christ to confront them, confront the head of the team, and make your demand in the Lord's name.'

'Don't you tell my husband what his duty is,' Maria began to say, but her husband cut in with:

'They will laugh. They will tell me to run away. The Lord's word means nothing to the atheist scientists.'

'So,' said Edwina, 'you have so little faith in the power of the word of a messenger of the Lord. You did not show this lack of faith when you were preaching at your great rallies.'

'It was different then,' mumbled Gropius.

'Different, yes,' said Edwina. 'No danger threatened then. Religion is a toy for the good times, is it, not a weapon for the bad?'

'Don't speak to my,' began Maria, but her husband said:

'What am I to do?'

'Demand. And if demanding is not enough, threaten.' James Gropius gave a little laugh, very short. 'The Lord's men were never afraid of fighting giants. David felled Goliath with a boy's catapult. Joshua ordered the moon to stand still. Moses fought. Fight. But threaten first. That's the Lord's way.'

Gropius looked at his loved ones. 'And if it were true,' he said, 'that there were this chance of the salvation of the righteous, a bare chance only, would you come with him who has followed the path of righteousness and preached the word of righteousness to the many?'

James shuffled in his chair. His connections with religion had always been marginal – filial, hygienic. He heard the big words and thought: Jesus Jesus that crap again. Jennifer said:

'I'd rather wait for a dream, I think. I mean it was the Lord's angel in Oklahoma City, and that was only an earthquake. For the end of the world I think I ought to have another angel telling me. Though,' she added, 'this is Dallas. Perhaps the angels don't like coming to Dallas.'

'They came to Sodom,' said Edwina. 'Look, there are other ways than dreams. The way of an unknown woman coming out of the blue in a hire car and a yellow raincoat. A messenger of the Lord, if you like.' Maria Gropius pursed her rouged lips. James said to Edwina:

'What's in it for you?' It was said without insolence. He had said it often before, in his gleaming trade, to men who brought visions of big orders – the toilets of the new Holy Cinema in Ponca City, for example, which was to be devoted to holy movies – *Quo Vadis*, *Ben Hur*, *The Exorcist*, that sort of thing. He waited for Edwina to answer. Edwina said:

'I don't mind whether I live or die. But I have this child within me. And the father of this child, the earthly father, has been done to death by the atheist scientists who run this atheist project which must be redeemed by the touch of the Lord. I want this child to live. Because I believe this child is the Lord's child.' She looked firmly at Gropius, and Gropius separated his neck from his shirt-collar. 'Without my message you would have no hope of salvation. There is hope now, good hope. Not certainty, but hope. That's what's in it for me,' she told James.

James nodded. That seemed fair. 'You want in on Noah's Ark,' he said. Edwina said:

'The certainty can only come about through the strength of the Lord. Through the Lord's threat and, if the threat fails, the Lord's thunderbolt.' Thunder afar heard that and grumbled assent.

'Guns,' said Gropius. 'You mean guns? I never handled a gun in my life, except for duck-shooting.' He turned to his wife and said, 'Maria, sweetheart. Would you come, dressed only in the hope?' James grinned at that, mom naked except for the hope. They might let her in, at that.

'It's not going to happen,' said Maria.

'*It fucking well is*,' hissed Edwina, neck stretched forward, goose-like, lips spread. 'And don't say anything about language, language, because the time is come to stop dithering and act. The time is very short,' she said to Gropius. 'If we leave, we should be leaving tomorrow.'

'But,' Rufa said, breaking her wide-eyed silence, 'it's Sam's birth-day the day after tomorrow. We have this little party.'

'I'll be back this evening. No need to invite me to dinner,' she added, as Maria looked doubtfully at the table, not enough places, not enough roasting beef. 'It's your duty in Christ. God send you the fucking dream, if that's what you want. Good afternoon.'

'A queer girl,' said Jennifer, as they heard her car start. 'Sometimes she sounds religious and sometimes she doesn't.' Calvin Gropius ached nostalgically for *true* religion: a great lighted rally in a vast stadium, bible-thumping, the crowds coming down to the front to pledge themselves to Jesus, a light supper after, eyes of adoration. He then felt sick.

'I don't know,' he said, 'I just don't know.'

Edwina drove grimly to the Florentine Hotel. There was the faint gut-rumble of an earth-tremor, the rain emptied passionately. She parked outside the hotel's main entrance, where there were already many cars. Inside, gambling and drinking proceeded, passionate as the rain. She asked a sort of under-manager for Mr Gropius.

'He's busy right now.'

'This is important,' said fierce Edwina. 'It's about his father.'

'His dad? Well – wait here, lady. See what I can do.'

Edwina waited, the sort of under-manager blepophoned. The image of Dashiel Gropius was disclosed in high colour, shirt-sleeved, working at a desk. 'Send her up,' he said.

She went up in an elevator, accompanied by the sort of under-manager. He knocked at a heavy-looking door of embossed oak. A light flashed. Edwina went in. Dashiel Gropius politely rose. 'Good afternoon, miss, madam. We've met before, I think.'

'Listen,' Edwina said. 'Listen carefully.'

'A drink?'

'Martini. Listen, there isn't much time. Whatever they tell you, we're in for big trouble. The trouble's going to be so big that there's no point in government doing anything about it.'

'Puma?'

'Puma. There's going to be a collision. Now, please don't look at me as if I'm mad. I'm not a scientist, but my husband was. He's dead now, but he told me everything before he died. The government ordered the building of a spaceship – maybe more than one, I don't know. But there's certainly one standing ready in the state of Kansas. I know where, I know precisely where.'

'Where?' He gave her her martini, which she drank thirstily.

'Never mind where for now. I've been trying to persuade your father that his duty is to get his family together and get on that spaceship. With me, too. I have a child to save. To hell with me, but this child has to live. Do I make myself clear?'

'Go on.' But he drew nonchalantly on a long gold-tipped cigarette, faintly smiling.

'Christ,' she said, 'we've all seen too many movies, even read too many trashy books. About the end of the world, I mean. It's just a piece of old-fashioned folklore. But now it's really going to happen. How can I make you believe me?'

'Why did you come to me anyway?'

She smiled a smile faint as his own. 'You're a man of action, I suppose. A man of the world. I don't think it's going to be a matter of the great Calvin Gropius crying "You know who I am, God's voice. Let my family into the ark." I think it's going to be a matter of a fight.'

'Do I look like a fighter?' he smiled, more broadly.

'Ah, shit,' she said. 'I know all about gambling. It's dirty work and dirty people are behind it. People get shot. I should imagine your bosses have names like Leopardi and Tortarella and Bonicelli.'

'A bit like,' he agreed. 'The Tagliaferro brothers, to be exact. Nice people but excitable. If you talked to them about the end of the world they'd probably believe you, making the sign of the cross all the time. Tell them about a spaceship and they'll say, or Salvatore will, "bought one a dem for my eldest kid." As for fighting, they'll fight. They're used to it. Sub-machine guns in guitar-cases, Frobishers, Magnolia sevens with thirty-centimeter silencers. Whether they'll fight for a Protestant Voice of God is another matter. Besides, I don't think father would like to have them on his ark. Not even as animals.'

'You don't believe,' she said sadly. 'I'd go myself, alone, yes, but that's not what the thing's about. Your father's a great force, bigger than he knows, and I don't think it's anything to do with what he believes.'

'I think I agree with you there. I always felt that. That's why I got away from him at the age of fourteen. I wanted to be a force of my own, not just a satellite. I think I see something else you mean. He's anti-science. Instinct, superstition, myth. You think he's a force that ought to be saved.' He grinned. 'In order to save others. Martians or something.'

'Not Martians. Look,' she said, 'you're bright. Why do you do this kind of thing?'

'Because I'm bright.' Silently he went to the bar and brought her another martini. She was parched and took it gratefully. He said: 'I got a message this afternoon. From Ottawa, Illinois. Southern Chicago's in ruins. An earthquake.'

'You're not kidding?'

'I'm not kidding. It happened last time, earthquakes, tidal waves. It's happening again. It can't go on happening, can it? It's got to end somewhere.'

'Call the first time a warning. Get on that spaceship before that too is in ruins. That spaceship's bigger than Chicago. It's the hope of mankind.' Rhetoric, rhetoric – how the hell did one keep rhetoric out? 'I wanted to believe, like everyone else, that the damned intruder was just looking in, then moving off. Or getting into a rhythm of coming and going. I see now how plain the whole thing is, and I wonder why nobody believes. Last time the earth was in one position. Now it's in another. *It's going to happen.* What are you going to do?'

'Are you seeing my father again?'

'Tonight, after dinner.'

He grinned. 'I can see you're not the sort of messenger mom would want to invite *to* dinner. I think I'll be there.'

That night the two crescents were bigger and, it seemed, much closer. There were earth tremors in Fort Worth. There was some panic in the gambling halls of the Florentine, quickly calmed, however, by drinks on the house. Dashiel Gropius, getting in his car, *believed.*

Eighteen

The maimed, indeed dead, Abaco station-wagon provided at least shelter for Val and Willett while hail rattled down from the black sky and the cracking and frank opening of the earth could be heard in desperate rumbles from all over the horizon. They sat glumly in the assailed and rocking Abaco, pushed into a layby, watching healthy vehicles push west. Lightning attempted crude forky images – the number 58729, a caricature of a long-dead maiden aunt of Willett's, a firework setpiece of the battle of Marengo, a collapsing city skyline, a word that looked like BANANAS. The crass thunder imitated nothing but itself, or the drums of a Berlioz orchestra imitating itself. Then: 'Good Christ,' cried Willett. He saw lightning swoop down and knife, with many blades, something on the road far ahead. An explosion, then the great pile-up. Squealing of tardy brakes, torturing of metal, all audible under the hail. Car after car after car after car concertinaed into car after car after car after car to make a long sorry polychrome shattered metal monster python. Thunder roared silly triumph; the Abaco rocked beneath Val and Willett like a boat. They had to sit there open-mouthed, looking at the long metallic chaos sprinkled, dredged, full-floured in hail. Till the hail left off. Then they got out, each with pistol stuck in belt, Willett with the bigger gun slung by its sling over his shoulder, Val wearing a bandolier of bullets, their pockets stuffed with bullets. They squelched down haily grass off the main road, Willett looking back to deplore waste a moment – all those cans, all that liquor – and they proceeded, squelching in their heavy work-boots, by a deserted and long neglected side-road towards the border of Ohio and Indiana.

Eventually they came to a farm. A scrawled poster-sized message in the window of the farmhouse said, supererogatorily, GONE AWAY. A few forlorn chickens clucked, in a field a horse grazed with a companionate donkey beside him. The field was riven by a great smoking ditch. Dirty greasy cloud rolled richly over the sad farmscape. Val and Willett had no difficulty in forcing the warped front door of the homestead. Inside they found the comforting musty cabbagy smell of a house long lived in but never well aired (enough air outside without having to have it in too) and a gross black cat that mewed its neglect. They found unrefrigerated milk not yet sour and gave the cat a basin of it. It ran grrrrring thirstily. They found a flitch of smoked bacon and a basket of brown eggs. There was no electricity working, no gas, so they made a fire in the old-fashioned kitchen fireplace, using chairs for fuel, and fried a fine early supper, washing it down with canned beer and applejack.

The sky had cleared and was brilliant with firepoints, but Puma and moon, steadily continuing lunation and pumation, were vast and approaching the half, moon visibly, if one watched long enough, rounding to hide behind her master. The two watched from the great bed of the master bedroom. 'It's going to be the moon,' Willett said after a time. 'The moon will hit us first.'

'The moon will regret it,' Val said. 'It will shatter to bits and pieces.' And then: 'Us? What do you mean – us?'

'We are earth,' said Willett simply. 'We're not *mind* careering in outer space. We're tree and grass and root and dung and water. Earth, earth is us. What a shame, what a fucking shame. There has to be a God, there has to be an eternal sensorium just to hold the memory of the smell of tobacco and frying bacon and the look of gentians and dawns. Otherwise, what a waste creation was.'

'The universe can afford waste.'

'Well, I say balls to a universe that can afford to waste a Keats or a Shakespeare. Balls, balls, balls.' And then Willett, having taken four knock-out tablets, bawled himself into heavy sleep.

Heavy, but not night-long. Val awoke in the not to call night, the white and the walk of the morning, to hear sobbing. Incredibly, from Willett's bed. He lay rigid, not daring to intrude on a man's sobbing. A woman's sobbing was different, you could always attempt to do something about a woman's sobbing. But a man's. Willett sobbed on, and he seemed to be sobbing in his sleep. Words came from a long way back, or down, and they made little sense. 'Prophet. Zoroaster. Met his own. Image walking. In the garden.' Then a great howl, like the crying of the dying earth itself. 'My dead child. My dead.'

Val whispered to himself: *The earth is dying.* And the dying wasn't noble, tragic, like I am *dying, Egypt, dying.* Cracked, bludgeoned, smashed as Michelangelo's David had been smashed three years before in Florence, Italy, smashed by a madman rejoicing in the act of smashing. The lovely earth smashed, pulverised, spurting out the waters and gases in its belly, cracked and battered by an insensate lump of nothing that did not even have the human grace to be mad. The already dishonoured earth, man's great rubbish-dump, sick with slow poisons. And now, soon, a very undignified death.

As though he had, from deep sleep, conjured Val's awakening to the end that he might be an audience, Willett suddenly said: 'Ah, there you are.' He lay calm, his great eyes open and rested. 'I had the most remarkable dream,' he said. 'There was a great pie, as big as as big as, oh, Kansas City. And it was full of beefsteak, onions, ox kidneys, lamb chops, oh, many other edibles, all smoking away, and also fresh fruit – raspberries, gooseberries, all fresh, mind you, Adamfresh. And it didn't seem a bit absurd that these things – fresh eggs too, brown ones, straight from the hen – should be all together. And another absurd thing. They brought in a great dusty bottle of wine, a Jeroboam or Nebuchadnezzar or something, very big, and the date on the label was 1616. I couldn't see the name of the wine, the letters were all dancing about, but the taste was superb. Impossible, really. It ought to have been vinegar. Perhaps it had long turned to vinegar and then it turned back to wine. That's what I thought in the dream, anyway. Superb.' Willett then smacked his lips, turned massively on his left side, and at once began snoring again. He interrupted the snores to erupt into a big bed-shaking guffaw. Then sleep unbroken till six by Val's watch. Val could not sleep. Curiously, he was no longer depressed. He was excited, eager for the day. Shyly the sun rose.

They left the nameless farm in the old way of picaresque novels – one, Willett the heavy, on horseback, Val, lighter, on the placid donkey. When they came to swifter and less uncomfortable transport, they would kiss and fondle the beasts goodbye and leave them to Indiana grass. Now they took a maze of small bad roads towards Indianapolis, a hell of a long journey. They ate bacon sandwiches in a noon full of cloud swirling in and choking the bloody sun. Behind them the noise of violent earth tremors. Ahead, so far, nothing. They had yet to discover that much of the state of Illinois was jaggedly rent, from Chicago to Decatur, and that the city of wind lay in ruins, the wind singing fiercely over it.

Hooves were still plodding inferior roads when they came, at nightfall, to a scene of riot. It was a town called, so a signpost had signalled, Carson, a one-street nothing. Puma and moon illuminated ghastlily liquor-maddened dancers. A store, indeed stores, had evidently been broken into, and strong waters were glugged down, sicked up, used in jocular baptism. The whole small population was circling in a claw-buttock dance to an old man's drunken accordion – major triad followed by dominant ninth, one, two, one, two – and the banging of a big battered drum by a boy. Val and Willett sought to ride through unnoticed, but Val was pulled from his donkey and, with greater difficulty and much post-Rabelaisian language from him, Willett from his horse. They were offered bottles of Roma Rocket, whatever that was, and a fluid that reeked like coarse calvados. Naked girls, ill-favoured, offered sweat-wet bodies. Some men were piling chairs, tables, anything inflammable, in the middle of the single street. Val and Willett fought off their hosts, who then became truculent, so yielded at least to the offers of drink, though not to the proffered steaming mots. The speech was mostly unintelligible – thick deformation of some local version of English – but it seemed to be about certain fundamentals: drink, fuck, riot, end is upon us.

A man with only a torn shirt on, lustily aswing below, whooshed canned gasoline on to the mess of wood. A naked middle-aged woman, aswing above, threw a flaring butane lighter. The fire broke at once into a scarlet paean to fire, leapt high. Its worshippers leapt about it in a leaping dance. 'Out of here,' said Val, looking for a way out.

'The burro,' someone yelled, 'the fucking donkey.' They were not yet ready for a human burnt offering; a donkey, parody of human servitude and long patience, a long-eared Jesus, would do for the moment. They wanted to seize the living beast and drag it to the flames. Val's heart sank, knowing that now he had, for the first time in his life, to use violence. Man should ennoble himself, awaiting his end in dignity. It could not be avoided, this drawing of the pistol ready loaded, the thumb trembling on the safety-catch. Thank Christ, he did not have to fire. Willett was in there first, cracking a loud shot Pumawards, then another. The gesture was enough. They mounted, kicking bare sweaty bodies, gun-butting hairy arms. They slapped their steeds' necks and got out at a half-gallop, singed.

Ten kilometers on or so they came to a burnt-out farm, with corpses of cows, chickens half-burnt, scorched legs pathetically pointing up at the causative horror in the sky. They took shelter in the barn, their beasts with them comfortably chewing hay. There was plenty of light, God knew. They feared being jumped on by Puma-mad wanderers in the dark. They still had a hell of a long way to go. Hungry, they gnawed at a half-raw rooster. Sweet water dripped from a yard tap. They slept fitfully. They woke to the heaving of the earth, though gently, as of a great body in sleep. Great hail-balls crashed down for nearly an hour. Dawn was sick-coloured, clouds scudding thinly, swiftly. 'This is no life,' said Val. 'This is no fucking life at all.' His head ached, his limbs creaked, his arse was on fire with the jolting ride. Their beasts lay on their sides, their flanks heaving in sleep, unresponsive to the dawn. It seemed a shame to wake them. They set themselves to walk to find an abandoned vehicle.

Having trudged a bumpy road in silence, they came to a main road empty of life, with a grounded signpost pointing to Columbus. Ohio? No, they were out of Ohio. America was full of Columbuses. To their surprise and cautious joy they saw a Howard Johnson motel intact, mock steeple and all on the contingent restaurant. Cars were

parked or abandoned in the carpark, which was bumped up grotesquely by a past mild tremor. They went into the restaurant, empty
but clean, chairs set neatly on a floor that sloped, but not sufficiently
yet to topple the flimsy functional furniture. They found sour milk
and horrible dry buns. They munched, then filled their pockets
with candy-bars. They went, munching, to look at cars and found a
Trussel 95, a veteran Oldsmobile, a shining new Duffy. The Duffy
did not need the attentions of the omniclef: the ignition key was set
firmly waiting to be turned. Thanked be Almighty God.

When they came close to Vincennes, along a highway crammed
with cars and bodies crushed, the highway itself bristling with huge
sharp chunks of broken road, they saw the Wabash in terrible frothing flood. They ran along its flouncy horrible skirt till they saw
a nameless steel and concrete bridge swaying frighteningly. 'We
can do it,' said Willett, who was not driving. They could and did,
but the bridge responded to their speed like a dead tooth in a live
mouth, wagging perilously to the puff of speech. Then they were in
Illinois. Thirty kilometers along a near-ruined highway they saw the
hair-raising deep slash, north-south, that stretched down the state.
To right and left it spread without visible end. They got out of the
car, stood on its muddy edge and surveyed it.

'It's possible,' said Willett. A kilometer-deep slope to a trough
of turbulent water that did not, for all its fury, look deep, a
kilometer-high slope beyond to flat country. Tree-trunks lay everywhere, the disturbed earth gave off a smell of spring, ploughing.
The horizon all around challenged them with interested grumbles.
See what you can do, man. A flock of black-white birds soared
up from nowhere, twittering, were lost in a sudden swoop of
bitumen-coloured cloud. 'All right?' said Willett. Without a word
spoken, they coasted down, zigzag, avoiding stones, tree-trunks,
sculpted boulders. The car sploshed in the fat furious broth of the
trough. The wheels turned impotently, the engine strained. Then, as
if destruction were on their side, a subterranean belch followed by a
head-high spume, grey as bad meat, lifted them. They sailed up the
slope, the car agonised. They stuck in a tangle of oak-roots. A tremor
bore them clear, sailing an instant in air. They were in a flat placid

field. The thunder roared derision, but where was the lightning? It was not thunder, it was the earth straining, boiling, breaking.

'I could lie down,' quoted Willett unconvincingly, 'like a tired child and weep away this life of care.' Then he banged vigorously his companion on the shoulder and said: 'Enjoying it? It's life, God help us. It's something to tell your grandchildren.'

'If,' said Val, 'I have to slaughter the whole fucking crew, you and I are getting on that ship.'

Howls premonitory of slaughter were heavily audible to Dashiel Gropius in Fort Worth. They came from one of the Tagliaferro brothers, probably Salvatore, crying useless revenge. Dashiel's suite faced theirs on the top floor of the Florentine, a floor which was not a corridor but a carpeted area on to which the four suites, one at present unoccupied, opened. Dashiel could guess what the howls were about – failure to get through to the Albergo in Peoria, Illinois; earthquake news from Springfield, Illinois, before radio communication with the outside world ceased. Dashiel was packing a bag and wondering what to pack. Shirts, socks, shoes, a suit. It seemed petty, inadequate. This was not a weekend trip to Florida. This was a trip to the ends of space. They hoped, they hoped. He packed a box of Havana Hermositos and a half-litre flask of white rum. He would travel in leather boots, suede one-piece catskin, heavy hunting jacket. The tremors that had been picking delicately at Fort Worth suddenly bit, hard. He was pitched nearly over. He sat down, sensibly waiting for the spasm to end, smoking a gold-tipped cigarette. Well, whatever lay at the end of the journey, it was all over here. The power had failed at the city plant and here there was no emergency supply – typical Tagliaferro false economy. Last night a minimal tremor and lights out had started screaming, swearing; a man had broken his leg. That was while he had been out, in Dallas, with that girl Edwina and his family. The Florentine was finished. The brothers must know it was finished, but one thing at a time. A passion of grief behind locked doors had first to spend itself.

When the earth quietened, Dashiel took from a drawer the .45 Beaufort he had never had occasion to use, together with the two still sealed yellow boxes of ammunition. He loaded the gun carefully and stuck it in his belt, the soft leather belt that gave a waist to the catskin. The light from the window, though it was full morning, was dim, all boiling ferrous cloud shot with tarnished silver. He packed the rest of the ammunition.

Quite a girl, this pregnant Edwina. John had been the prime scoffer. She had railed against him, but he had prevailed, on behalf of himself, his family, James and Jay and Jay. He had, he said, the finest possible shelter under the house, proof against doomsday the builders had said. It had its own power supply, refrigeration, heating, the lot. It was stocked with enough canned food to last a year, even with ten incumbents. It had an independent water supply and a waste-products converter. Damn it, everybody, was he not in the construction trade? Had they not all lived under long threats of atomic war? Well, the shelter was now to prove itself under the actuality of something less terrible. The horrors would pass, and they, not he, their father, would emerge on to an earth ready once more for reconstruction, while he, their father, went into outer space and to certain death shouting impotent biblical texts.

The girl, Edwina, had told him not to be a fucking idiot. She had drawn on the living-room wall, plain, cream, and apt for drawing, the irrefutable simple diagram that spelt doom. John was not impressed. It was really all to with having known the biblical language of doom from babyhood. It was a dad thing, a bible thing, nothing to do with real-life possibilities. Dad's thunderings had not helped; rather they had made the diagrammatic reality suddenly become remote and mythical. 'All of us, Noah's family, seek the ark of salvation, armed with the Lord's righteousness' and all that jazz. Poor mom had not known which way to turn. She had said:

'John's right, Calv, John's practical. I'll stay here with them till things blow over. I mean, it's only like you going off to preach, dear, isn't it, and it always gave me a bit of a headache, that Sacramento rally last time was terrible, and I said to you never again.'

'But this is different, this is the end, this is the last day, the Day of Judgment.'

'Yes, dear, the Day of Judgment.' Indulging him, 'the Day of

Judgment' being as much the furniture of their family calendar as the Fourth of July, except that it was never today or even tomorrow.

'Your duty as a wife, as the helpmeet of the last living servant of the Lord.' Oh Jesus, all that crap again, James's grin kept saying.

'I'm a mother, too, Calv. Don't forget that.'

And then dad, in his divine foolishness, had said: 'This girl here, this brave Edwina, she knows her duty.' Mom's eyes had gone hard at that. A long agony of contrary gravitational pulls – my boys, my boys, my dear grandchildren; my husband in the potential clutches of a designing female (more, more: whose is that child she's carrying? Is it possible, is it just possible, men are all the same, even the holiest, holy, what in God's name does *holy* mean?). Then many tears and holding on to her strong sons and snatching her grandchildren in desperate arms, but finally the brave tearful decision. Very well, her duty. Dad put strong arms about her. 'Praise be to God, who has shown his servant the light. Praise him, praise him.' He had very nearly called for a fucking hymn, with Jennifer at the piano.

Dashiel did not care greatly whether he was saved or not, in the primary bodily sense. The soul was a doubtful entity, religion was proving itself mere crap in the face of true doomsday. The thing to do was to act, go through the motions of action. The girl Edwina was no fool. She could cite scripture when she needed to, but her arguments were hard and practical. If anyone could lead them on to that salvation-ship it was the charismatic Calvin Gropius. Must the Lord's Word perish with the perishing earth? She had a child to save, and she was right. Why let the miraculous process of gestation end in destruction: a child brought forth only to die directly. But for him, Dashiel, action, just that.

Was that child really his father's? Could it be possible? Was that why she burbled, becoming briefly mystical and foolish, about the divinely appointed mission of the child? An illegitimate Gropius messiah, a divine by-blow? The world was full of surprises. He grinned at the banality of that, hearing a sickening long rumble on the horizon.

Well, now the walking out. Quietly, leaving the brothers to their grief. There was not much point in staying to explain, say goodbye. He took a deep breath, squinted about the dark room as if to remember its comforting details in exile, then prepared to leave. He was not in the least surprised when the door opened and Johnny Tagliaferro came in, leaned on the little bar and looked at Dashiel, white, strained, but ready for more than a wallow in the tub of grief. Johnny had instincts.

'I thought,' he said, 'you might be leaving us, Dash. I thought you might be telling us you'd be leaving us.'

'I didn't,' said Dashiel with care, 'want to intrude on your grief. Everything's over. We all have to go our own way.'

'Grief,' said Johnny. 'That's a short sharp word for what Salvatore's going through. A bad language for grief, the English language. He wants to kill the whole world. Me – I get over it. Nobody lives for ever. Lucrezia and little Gianna – I gave them a good life. But Salvatore wants to kill the whole world.'

'A good reason perhaps,' said Dashiel, 'for my not wanting to say goodbye to him. He might see me as the only killable bit of the world available.'

'Naw,' said Johnny. 'He loves you like a brother, like he loves me. But now he's on to hell and he's going to hell and his wife Susanna and those kids he adored are angels looking down on him burning in the fires of hell. I tell him he'd been a good man and only killed three guys that were bitter enemies anyway, and leave out the violence that didn't kill, and he'll go to purgatory. But then he screams that the pains of purgatory is what he doesn't want either. In a bad way, is Salvatore. Where you going, Dash?'

'I'm going with my father and mother.'

'Lucky you still got them, Dash. Me and Salvatore, we ain't so lucky. And where are you going with your father and mother, Dash?'

'I don't really know, Johnny. Nor do they. We're going with somebody who knows where to go.'

Johnny thought about that. Then he said: 'Your dad's a big name in the Protestant religion, right? He's got connections? He's gonna get you and the rest of his family out of what they call – what is it, Dash? Bloomsday, boomsday, doomsday?'

'Nobody gets out of it, Johnny.'

'So why move? Why not stay till the roof falls and puts you outa your misery?' He grinned affectionately. 'Or makes Salvatore's miseries begin.'

'You've got to do something. You've got to move. You may be moving to something worse than what you get sitting still, but you've got to move.'

A renewal of howls of grief came from Salvatore's room. Johnny shook his head indulgently but also in mild sadness. 'We gotta give him time to make good acts of contrition, pay for a few masses, see a priest maybe. Your dad's a kind of priest?'

'Protestant. Not what Salvatore wants.'

'Still, we're coming with you, Dash boy. Sit down. Have a drink, a good stiff one, *liscio*, wait till we're ready. Where you go we go. Salvatore might even turn Protestant. I've heard a lot about your dad. Always wanted to meet him.'

There was a large explosion in the centre of Fort Worth. Lake Arlington could be heard roaring like an angry sea.

Nineteen

Puma and moon were gibbous and menacing over the state of Missouri. Between St Louis and Jefferson City, Val and Willett became fully aware for the first time of what the term *pumatic* might mean. 'Pumacy,' Val the wordman muttered, 'pumatic asylums.' The whole of the small town of Wilcock was a pumatic asylum. Its buildings were down and its drainage ruined, and it stank of incontinence like any ward given over to cortical decay. The people were bedding down in the ruins, eating raw flesh and poisoning themselves with foul water. As Val and Willett tried to drive down the single street, there were men decorated in rooster feathers, armed with cudgels, brisk to stop them and ask their business. A much befeathered fat young man who stank of raw alcohol asked: 'Are you on the way to the putting out of the big light?'

'If,' said Willett carefully, 'that is what you require?'

The fat young man turned to his henchmen with a gap-toothed sneer. 'To talk of requiring,' he said, and they laughed. To Val and Willett he said with truculence: 'Don't let the big light hear you. You must abide the rising of the bigger light. Come out for the eating.'

'We've already eaten,' said Val. 'Thank you very much.'

'Eaten, yes, as the won'tcocks will. You must eat of Smith to put off the doom.'

'Smith?' asked Willett. The befeathered group pointed. The toothless bald head of an old man leered from a battered and bent lamp-standard. He had been bound to the lamp-standard by the neck, and his belly had been roughly slashed open. Finger-joints and toes had gone, and there was evidence that thin slices of flesh and skin had been shaven off his limbs and torso. Days dead, perhaps weeks; there was a rich scintillacy of maggots in his belly-hole. Val retched. Willett of the strong stomach was unmoved. He said: 'We have eaten of the grandfather of Smith. In a far place of many waters.' And he kicked and punched Val. 'On our way,' he growled. The car growled, pushing forward, and the feathered belaboured it with sticks. Thunder spoke from the western horizon. They turned to it, as though to interpret its loud DAAAAAA. The car got away, Val still retching. There were loud shouts of 'Eh! Eh!' behind them, men waving cudgels feebly running.

'Drawlatch hoydens,' growled anew Willett at the ghastly sky-lights. 'Gaping changelings. Lubbardly louts. Jeering companions. Oh, Jesus. Well, better to go out in madness, perhaps.' The car coughed. The car jittered and jolted.

'A matter of gas,' said Val. The fuel-needle signalled nearly nothing.

'Jesus Jobbernol Goosecap Christ All Grouthead Gnatsnapper Mighty.'

They had to abandon the car and trudge towards Jefferson City. Afar, down a side-road, they saw what looked like the ragged remnant of a battalion marching. The soldiers coughed and coughed, as from Somme mustard. 'Keep in step there,' yelled their sergeant. What was their mission, whither were they marching? Would they march in mindless automatism till the world ended? Willett quoted, growling:

'These, in the day that heaven was falling,
The hour when earth's foundations fled,
Followed their military calling
And took their wages, and are dead.'

There was a great abandoned factory, half in ruins, though with a chimney smoking blackly in the red and silver light, near to a town called Houseman. There was a great carpark, and there was a brace of orange and violet trucks with the name ILLIONS on them. Simple omniclef stuff. This time Willett drove. The next variety of pumacy they saw was at, and Val Brodie shuddered, Brodie. But it was of a kind long known in America – a group of white-robed end-of-the-worlders, crying wolf no longer. An emaciated elder spoke to a congregation bearing torches that stank of animal fat:

'...And I saw a new heaven and a new earth: for the first heaven and the first earth were passed away; and there was no more sea. And I saw the holy city, new Jerusalem, coming down from God out of heaven, prepared as a bride adorned for her husband...'

Since the time when, a bride adorned for her husband, Maria Gropius had vowed obedience, a deep-down potion of truculence must have been preparing itself. Now she was tasting the strong brew and spitting samples of it at Gropius. Gropius was driving silently. To the right the Ozark mountains were leaping, like the mountains in the Song that is Solomon's. The Bible was true after all. Literally true. Behind their car, whose back was loaded with Maria's useless clothes, jewels, frivolous gewgaws, was, he knew, the car of their son, Dashiel, and his companion was Edwina Goya. Behind again, though this he did not know, was the flashy Concordia 'oo of the Tagliaferro brothers, Johnny driving, Salvatore in the back surrounded by a whole arsenal – Kopple sub-machine guns, Lefferts hipfirers, a Munsey Angel, pistols galore. Salvatore knew no Shakespeare, but he was paraphrasing a speech of King Lear's with more punch and economy than the self-indulgent master had ever used: 'Why should a fucking mouse have life and they be fucking dead?' In the leading car, which had just skirted Tishomingo, Maria was showing equal fight:

'You've no right to do it, Calv, you've no right to drag me, and I wouldn't be going with you if it wasn't for the little foul-mouthed bitch back there with Dashiel, it's a wife's duty to save her husband from sin, I'll say that, I've always said it, but you've no right to talk about any other kind of duty, duty to the messenger of Christ's word and all that shit...'

'What did you say then? What was that word you used then?' This was absurd. The sky was red and silver fire, heavy oily cloud-scuds, noise barely excluded from the big saloon by the closed noise-excluding windows, and here was she nagging away as if the world were going to go on for ever, which, of course, was what she believed. A knowledge of the Bible, he admitted to himself sadly, distractedly, was not necessarily cognate with the possession of intelligence. He said:

'You're distraught, dear, and no wonder. But get this now, once for all, into your thick skull, dear, that the girl has one thing in mind and one thing only, and that is to save her child, and she thinks that I'm the only man in the world who can do it. A lot of people, Christ help them, have believed in my supernatural powers, God help me. But she's right about the other thing she says, that the Word of the Lord has to be taken into the high places, and I'm the only man, God help me again, to do it.'

'High places. Word of the Lord. All that shit when the roads are crammed with wrecks of cars and the rivers flooded and those mountains over there shaking with the earth tremors. Why are we going to Kansas? Why couldn't we stay in Dallas till it's all over?'

'It's not going to be all over, dear, for the hundredth time. This is the End of the World. Remember the phrase? *The End of the World*. It's in the Bible – the Last Day, the Day of Judgment – *remember?*'

'Oh yes, the Day of Judgment.' And then, less sarcastically: 'Oh Jesus, oh Jesus lover of my soul.' For the road in front of them was cracking and throwing up slivers of itself. They lurched as on a switchback. 'Stop the car, stop it. Oh Lord Jesus save me.'

'I'm going on. It's our only hope.'

She screamed as an elongated trapezoid of crumbling metalled road flew at the windshield. 'Go back, Calv. Turn round and go back.'

'No, we're going on. Pray, dear, pray hard.'

'I *was* shitting well praying. Oh Lord Jesus forgive my sins.' They sped into sudden calm. 'Tell me,' she said, 'tell me the truth, Calv. We're near to God now, so you have to tell me the truth.'

'What truth, for God's sake? I've always told you the truth, haven't I? I've always told everybody the truth. God's truth.'

'I don't want God's, I want the real truth. I mean that girl. Tell me the truth as you hope to die. Is she carrying your child?'

'Oh God preserve my sanity. No. Or rather yes.'

'Ah, I knew, I knew.'

'Her child and fifty thousand other children are my children. Will that satisfy you? I've spent my life fornicating. I'm a ravening sex monster.'

'There's no need to be sarcastic, Calvin. You're not a sex monster. At least, you've never been a sex monster with me. If we're on to the truth, you've never been all that good in bed. You've got to admit it. Have you?'

'I've always had other things on my mind.'

'I'm going back, Calvin, while there's still time. I'm young still, I have my life to live.'

'Sex, is that it? You're thinking of getting someone who's good in bed? Not like me, your husband, faithful, always faithful, always too damned faithful. Christ, even the patriarchs had handmaidens.'

'Was she your handmaiden, Calv? Tell me the truth. I promise to forgive you.'

Ahead the road was blocked by a fallen sequoia. He had to stop the car. Behind him he was aware of the following cars coming to a halt. Who was in that third car? That car had been with them all the way from Dallas. Well, let who would seek salvation. He said: 'Go back, and let me do my duty. A man's duty comes first.'

'You've always let your duty come first. Never your wife.'

'I've given you children. Your children have given you grandchildren. Go back to them. Let me concentrate on my duty with a clear mind.'

'That's what you've always wanted, isn't it? To be alone. With a *clear mind*. Thank you, Calv. Thank you very much.'

'Let's not part like that. Let's part in love. Confident in the Lord's love and his salvation. We shall meet in heaven, Maria.'

'The sweet by-and-by,' said Maria. 'All right, get out. You can go with that foul-mouthed bitch behind. Dashiel will keep you from any funny business.'

'For the five hundredth time –'

'And when you come back from Kansas with your tail between your legs, don't expect me to be waiting with the pot-roast ready. I may be in Miami. I may be at Palm Springs. I'm entitled to a bit of life without the shitting Word of the Lord in my ear all the time.'

He sighed, getting out, yielding the wheel to her. 'So,' he said, 'it's come to this.'

'Yes, Calv, it's come to this. See you in the sweet by-and-by.'

She turned the car deftly and took the road back. Things were quiet for the moment, as though the very perturbed elements were awed to silence by this demonstration of woman's perfidy. Wearily, Calvin Gropius went over to the car of his son. There was a side-road somewhere back there. That might get them on to Guthrie, where they aimed to spend the night. Maria Gropius had already sped past it, not, unlike Lot's wife Sara, looking back.

And so, by their two diverse routes, ladies and gentlemen, our parties worked jerkily towards their unforeseen conjunction in sal-vatory Kansas.

Twenty

Professor Hubert Frame had his respirator batteries charged and was ready to examine what was the final concrete expression of his long theoretical studies. He could not walk, of course. O'Grady's strong arms lifted him without effort from his bed into the solitary wheelchair that the camp clinic possessed. His daughter stood by, sniffing. 'Stop sniffing, girl,' he said. 'Nothing to cry about.' Bartlett, in smart black with a CAT brassard on his left arm (a stylised puss, back view, sitting up straight), was ready to escort him to Bartlett, America rather. Frame, as he was trundled through the twilight, gibbous Puma and moon newly risen, admired the wide sky, which he had not seen in its fullness for many months. 'The increase in size,' he breathed, almost inaudibly. 'Astonishing. Double acceleration, of course. One is reminded ironically of those old comic films. In which two lovers. Running from opposite directions. To. Embrace each other. Cannot slow down. So go past each other. Miss. Won't happen here. No missing here.' He was taken to America, great, hugely elegant, where the whole team waited. He, Bartlett, Vanessa, O'Grady got into the elevator and were lifted gently to what was known as Level A. When the dying professor appeared on the ring concourse, as it was called, the whole team subduedly clapped. Frame waved feeble acknowledgment.

He was taken round, elevated to Level B and then to Level C. There was no doubt of Bartlett's efficiency, alas alas alas. The concentration on living space, the human need for sheer spatial freedom, had not entailed any skimping on technical essentials. The

ploiarchal area, for instance, where Drs McGregor and McEntegart
flicked their switches in demonstration, made their screens glow, set
talking their radiocommunication devices, was positively palatial.
Frame heard reports come through from Americas II and III, from
the Australasian Southern Cross, from the Franco-German-Italian
Defrit, stupid unrousing name. Moon stations came in faintly. Frame
admired the three-layered hospital, the artificial heavens, the incredible foodfields, the ample bedroom area which, when the population
started to grow, would still be ample. He admired the automated
foremator, which would fabricate you a garment in one second after
the pressing of a size-button. He frowned at the appearance of Dr
Maude Adams, the two bibliothecologists, others. They looked dead,
themselves automated dead matter, going through certain essential
motions. He said sharply to Bartlett: 'Have you been pacifying?'
    'It was necessary.'
    Frame grunted and said: 'I think, ladies and gentlemen, we ought
to toast our enterprise. Is there any champagne aboard?' There
wasn't. Bartlett frowned; O'Grady shook his head, frowning. Frame
grinned bitterly and took from a roomy side-pocket a leather-bound
brass flask. 'Whisky,' he said. 'Irish,' he specified, making a cheeky
mouth at O'Grady. 'A token sip, doctor?' to Dr Adams. O'Grady
tried to intervene. Bartlett put out an arm to hold him back, saying:
    'Alcohol is expressly forbidden to certain of our crew-members.
A matter of –'
    'A matter of depacifying,' said Frame. 'Drink, doctor. Drink, I
insist.' She drank, dead-eyed. Frame had to stop her drinking by
pulling the flask away. An automatic drinker. To Vanessa he said: 'A
word in your ear, my love.' He gave her the word. 'This is it. I might
as well go here.'
    'No!'
    'Yes. One thing still on my conscience. I lied to you. I said that
Val was dead. He may be, of course, now. But I knew nothing of his
er biotic status at the time we took the plane here. I'm sorry. I didn't
want him on the project. I think I was wrong. I'm sorry. He may be
alive, he may even be trying to reach you. I have a dying man's hunch.
Hope. Hope that he'll come to you.' Vanessa put her hands to her

face, white. She couldn't even sob. To the assembly at large Frame now said: 'Ladies and gentlemen. I have lived a full life and now I am going to end it. A full life, but not a successful one. I know nothing, despite the fullness. I know much of science but nothing of life. Now it is too late to learn. But it is, remember, now time for you to begin. If you want a motto to blazon over that great screen there, the one that will show you the pulsing universe you travel through, that is now showing you earth and Puma moving inexorably to collision, the motto might be this: *Scientia non satis est.* Knowledge,' he translated, 'is not enough. Let us now see how well your cadaver-recycler works. Eat me, drink me. Rather sacramental, isn't it? God be with you, which is the meaning of goodbye.' He smiled, switched off his respirator, breathed desperately, wide-eyed, blue-skinned. His eyes looked poisonously on Bartlett an instant, and then they looked on nothing. His head collapsed on to his right shoulder. There was a silence. Dr Adams, of all people, led the few who sobbed. Bartlett was efficient as always. He ordered Dr Durante:

'You heard what the professor said. Trundle him into the recycler. Not the wheelchair; that may still be needed.' White-faced, Durante obeyed. The recycler was to the left of the foodfields. It was a simple matter of gently disengaging, with the help of Dr Sarah Bogardus, the spent body from its chair and pathetic apparatus, and then introducing what was once Professor Frame to the atomising chamber. They did this, closed the heavy doors, one, two, three, then set the apparatus working. There was no sound, no flashing of lights. Silently, the task of salvaging protein, carbohydrate, phosphorus, fluids cleansed and potable, and converting waste to fuel for the ancillary heating engines was completed. Frame would live in them and for them.

Bartlett said, with the brutality which they now knew was stitched into his nature, not his fault, but none the more excusable for that: 'So much for the past. Our work is nearly at its end, our work of the present. We take a deep breath and prepare for our work of the future. There will be a general meeting this evening after dinner. 2130, the usual place. Very well, dismiss.' They dismissed. Dr Maude Adams said to Vanessa:

'I don't feel at all well. Not at all well,' leaning on her.

'Come to my quarters,' Vanessa said. She gunned the frowning O'Grady with her eyes, the eyes of a woman just bereaved, and said: 'I'll look after you.'

And so, boys and girls, ladies and gentlemen, after a meal more frugal than usual, not in honour of the dead but as an earnest of the eternal space diet to come, an evening began that shall live for ever in our annals.

During dinner, the diners were aware of unaccustomed earth tremors. They all looked at each other, fearing for their ship, though it was mounted on a mound of elasticom that, theoretically at least, enabled it to ride terrestrial tempests as if it were a seaship and the earth the sea. Still, they were unaccustomed. Dr Louise Boudinot nearly ran out to check that all was well. Bartlett, the imperturbable, banged his knife-handle on high table and said: 'Calm calm calm.' They were calm.

They were, naturally, less calm at the general meeting, watching Boss Cat take his place on the dais. They feared, with justice if past experience were to be trusted, new curtailments of amenity (no concerts of phonomusic, no films) and longer working hours. They did not at all expect what Boss Cat gave them. He said:

'The time has come, as I have already intimated, to think of the future. To think, indeed, of more than our own future: of the future of the race. We have to breed a race, ladies and gentlemen,' frowning as if breeding were a hard necessity imposed upon them by the stern daughter of the voice of God. 'Before we breed, we must mate. As soon as we are under way into shallow space, the mating process will begin.' Some of them began to stare at him, open-mouthed. He said: 'I have spent time and close study on the question of mating. I have not consulted any of you on this matter; indeed, there is no one properly to consult, since we do not possess a professional zeugaromatologist on our team. But I have completed a final list in which I am confident that every relevant factor has been taken into consideration. I would ask you all to pay close attention as I read out the list and to note carefully the mate chosen for each of you. I do not imply any derogation in putting male names at first. After all, the mating process is traditionally initiated by the male.' The open mouths became more open. Not a breath was heard. The thumping earth, muffled by the sound-proofing, was forgotten. 'So then,' said Bartlett, 'in alphabetic order.

'Dr David T. Abramovitz will mate with Dr Jessica Laura Thackeray. Dr Vincent Audelan will mate with Dr Gianna Da Verrazano. Dr Paul Maxwell Bartlett, Head of Project, will mate with Dr Vanessa Mary Frame. Dr Robert F. Belluschi will mate with Dr Belle Harrison. Dr Miguel S. Cézanne will mate with –' The first one to snigger was, strangely, Dr Adams. Bartlett looked at her in total surprise. 'Please,' he said. 'Dr Cézanne, as I say, will mate with Dr Guinevere Irving. Dr Douglas C. Cornwallis will mate with Dr Minnie Farragut –' But now the single snigger had opened the door to laughter. Some laughed, then others. It was a hell of a time since any of them had had a good laugh. They laughed, some, more, more still. O'Grady frowned. Bartlett was frankly puzzled and looked for a cause of laughter – an open fly, a cat micturating against his table-leg. He tried to continue: 'Dr John R. Durante with Dr Kathleen Orlinda Eastman. Dr Mackenzie Eidlitz –' But he could not be heard. The laughter was very nearly total. Even the clinically paci-fied were laughing. Laughing, it appeared, was a solvent of even the most potent chemical conditioner. Bartlett, white, horrified, yelled: 'Silence. Silence. Silence.' That only made it worse.

Dr Eidlitz was bellowing like a sealion. Bartlett picked on him and said: 'Dr Eidlitz, control yourself. Mating is a serious business, very serious indeed.' For some reason that began to touch off a risory nerve in Dr O'Grady. Bartlett did not at first notice. He said: 'If, of course, there are any compatibility problems, Dr O'Grady will be only too happy to assist the clinical staff in effecting adjustments.' He looked at O'Grady and found, shocked, horrified, that O'Grady was showing big horse-teeth and howling. Bartlett could hardly be heard: 'O'Grady. Dr O'Grady.' O'Grady did not respond. Bartlett turned to Dr Greeley the diastemopsychologist, yelling his head off in the front row and going through the classic parameters of risory near-exhaustion: hand on ribs, finger pointing blindly at the excitatory cause. 'You,' Bartlett said, 'you, damn you,' and he came down from the dais. He hit at tear-blinded Greeley. Then the laughter stopped very abruptly. Greeley hit back. The two men tussled. 'O'Grady,' cried Bartlett. 'Dr O'Grady, put this man under close arrest.' O'Grady got up, straight-faced, and went over to the two tusslers without conviction. Then, seeing open mouths and pallor where he had recently seen universal joy, he burst into a huge cackle. This primed Jovian laughter on the back row. 'Put everybody under close arrest,' cried Bartlett. That was the end. Howls and screams and what used to be called hysteria, children. It was all the funnier because of Bartlett's fury.

It was only Bartlett who observed the main door open and Lieutenant Jolson, head of the residual platoon, come in. Jolson looked in astonishment at the fiftyfold, or nearly, laughter and was forced, by reflex, to relax his own face to a smirk. Then he recollected the apparent seriousness of his mission and said something to Bartlett's ear. Bartlett was not able to look grimmer than he already was. 'About two hundred, sir. Some have gloves and cutters and are cutting through the electric fence. We're unarmed, that's the trouble. Request permission for arms to be issued, sir.'

'Silence,' Bartlett yelled anew at the wildly laughing. 'Silence. Silence. I have disturbing news. *This* will stop your stupid laughter.' But it didn't, not yet.

Twenty-one

'As they used to say in vaudeville,' grunted Willett, *'this must be the place.'* He made certain adjustments to the controls which kept the thing hovering in the hostile winds – hostile to each other as well as to their craft. Val could still not get over his amazement that Willett, actor, eater, swiller, and praiser of the past, should be so skilful with a helicopter. Something to do with his son George, apparently. Willett did not want to say too much about it. George, before being transferred to Looncom (Lunar Communications), had done a helicopter course in connection with inspection of high cable laying or something. He had come home once, illegally, in a company chopper. His father had been charmed by it and insisted on going up and then taking over. He had taken to it, a reasonable and at the same time rather poetic machine.

They had picked up this particular helicopter near Sedalia, Missouri. Land transport had by now been thoroughly obstructed by broken roads, folds of upturned earth, perpetual jolting tremors. They had been astonished, near Sedalia, to see in broad midday a patch of air wholly taken up by helicopters engaged in crashing into each other in individual suicide combat. Madness, pumatic madness. There was a metal notice, twisted, battered, lying on scorched grass, which said US ARMY NUMBER 56 HELIBASE. Over an excessively amplified loudspeaker system joyful simple music was being discoursed:

'I scream, you scream,
We all scream
For ice cream:
Rah! Rah! Rah!'

Val and Willett went cautiously closer, to the thick net periphery. A
field day. Drink, fornication, aerial suicide. A tipsy sergeant had welcomed them in to the funeral games. What had begun, apparently,
as a helicopter square dance had turned into a dodgem course. Now
it was rank joyful suicide. Could anybody play? Well, said the sergeant, Val and Willett were civilians, not really eligible. On furlough,
Willett said, both. Meet Colonel Nutt and Major Barbara. No trouble, then. And they were zigzaggedly taken over to the helicopter
park, bottles of Scotch thrust into their hands by a singing corporal.
Then they were up and off, not really playing the game.

Over Kansas City they had been bounced up and down by hot air.
The town was in flames and ruins. They had a terrifying but fascinat-
ing view of ant-sized citizens running down buckling streets to avoid
collapsing masonry. Over Leavenworth they had a fuel problem.
They sailed down to what was clearly a vast deserted filling station,
plomped down on thin flat feet, found the pumps out of order but big
corrugated drums of polyoctana in the open store. They glugged the
volatile gold in and made for Topeka which, by some strange injustice
or miracle, seemed virtually intact. They put down outside the town
at a big mess that was full of grumbling military – gross stew being
ladled out by army orderlies, a fat drunken top-sergeant cook. They
were fed, sour-facedly but without demur. Val asked about the CAT
camp. Nobody knew it. Wait, how about Shorty? Shorty's outfit
had broken up, Shorty had been posted to this clear-up battalion,
grumbling and even tearful about being cut off from his old buddies
and full of unbelievable stories about a moonship and a guy in charge
called Boss Cat. Shorty was dragged out of the cookhouse, where he
was repairing a portable generator, and said yeah he knew the place.
They was kept in but that was okay, plenty going on, no shortage of
pussy (leering), no idea really where they was, but when they left they
went through a dump called Sloansville, which one guy, Meatball,

said he knew of 'cause his dad had worked on the drains there and
said gee what a dump, well what do you know, Sloansville.

Up in the air, Willett said:

'You were right, you see, right, right. Your book probably gave
those non-fictitious scientific bastards the idea.'

But Val was depressed. End of the line coming. Better to travel
hopefully than arrive at hope's fulfilment. Keeping on was the thing,
on, on. And now what for him really, what for poor Willett? It
suddenly dawned on him that the world was really coming to an
end: the fact was slotting into that part of his mind which dealt with
real verifiable propositions. More, it was taking on, his mind being
fundamentally poetic, the properties of a sense-datum. He could
smell, taste the end of the world like an apple. He said: 'Why the hell
should *we* be saved?'

Willett grunted, busy with his controls, and then said: 'For one
simple reason. Because that's not a question those scientific bastards
would ever dream of asking. That's why.' Val didn't quite understand. They followed the course of the Smoky Hill river, visibly
frothing like a trough of dirty champagne. Seismic immunity, eh?
No immunity anywhere now. The end of the world. A very sour
apple. His mouth felt dry as after sucking alum.

'As they used to say in vaudeville,' grunted Willett, '*this must be
the place.*' Val woke from unpleasant dreams from which he was,
anyway, lucky to be able to wake up. He looked down and saw a
great neat square, impeccably right-angled, huts, huts, huts, and in
the middle *it*, the thing, the end of the known road, big and squat and
beautiful. His heart dropped to his gross muddy worn work-boots,
full of chilled and aching feet. 'So that,' said Willett, with a school
boy's awe, 'is the spaceship. It's true, then. I wondered sometimes.
It's real. What do we do now? Land by it? Open its door? Walk in
and take a seat?'

'Wait,' said Val, with the caution of a science-fiction writer. 'It
can't be so easy. They'll shoot us down. There must be warning sys-
tems. Or it may be covered with a magnetic repulse field.' The craft
swayed perilously. 'Out, out,' said Val. 'Plenty of time. Nothing
impulsive. We'll wait. Land. Behind that clump of trees there.'

'Faint heart,' said Willett, obeying. He dropped down neatly. They sat an instant and sighed at the same time. Willett switched off his engine. 'Food,' he said. It was twilight. They opened up their hamper and pulled out a cold roast joint, a jar of English mustard, bread, an apple pie, clotted cream in a pot, three bottles of Montrachet chilled by the air-passage, and a flask of Meridian cognac (b.o.f.i.). Sad autumn lay all about them. The earth hiccupped.

The earth hiccupped. Just south of Sloansville a man called Elias Howe addressed a crowd through a loud-hailer. The crowd was about two hundred strong – men, women, children, cripples, ancients, frightened Kansans all of them. 'You know the truth of it, friends,' he said. 'I may be no more than a common carpenter, but carpenters have seen the truth before and had the message sent to them from above. Noah, Jesus Christ. There's been great silence from the governments of the earth, but some of us can read the signs. The earth,' he said prosaically, 'has had a long run for its money. It had to be finished off some day. And it's going to end as it began, with capitalists on top and workingmen ground into the dirt beneath. Make no mistake about it, friends and brothers. At that camp up there, with its electrical wires all around it to keep people out, is a ship that's going off into space, loaded with the wealthy, being served with champagne and caviare. All right, some of you will say it's scientists as well, jiggling at switchboards, but they're in the pay as they've always been of the capitalists, and it's the capitalists that has the last word. And where are they going, you may ask. Well, I'll tell you, friends and comrades. They're not going anywhere except into space up there, far away from that horrible planet and our moon that it stole to bang at us like a big white rock. They'll live out their lives in a big space hotel, looking at the stars and drinking and having it off with lovely girls they have up there, the best of everything. Not a bad life, is it, the life we've all dreamed of, no work and cruising about for ever, watching movies and eating fried chicken till they go off dying, smiling, saying that it's been a good life for them, which it has. Well, I'll tell you what's happening tonight, brothers and sisters. They're not going. The scientists that run it are going to be in the service of the workers, whether they like it or not. The lovely stewardesses are going to serve champagne and hamburgers to the workers, yes, and serve the workers in other ways, those workers that are not already served regularly in those ways, which I don't have to specify, you being all thinking people. And I say one last thing to you. If we don't go, nobody goes.'

The negative programme seemed to appeal more to the crowd than the positive one. They cheered. A one-eyed man at the front yelled: 'Who shoots first?'

'Nobody shoots, if it can be avoided, friends and comrades. Violence was always the way of the capitalists, they having the money for the violent weapons. Those of you carrying guns, don't fire till the word's given. Those of you with insulating gloves and cutters, don't be afraid of the hard work of cutting their fences down – an outer one and an inner one, as you'll know. The cutting party is to go first. The rest of us will follow quiet and in good order.' The earth hiccupped, the crowd roared. The crowd was made up of decent frightened people, but few of them were members of the industrial proletariat. Farmers and their families mostly, who had lived off the fat of the land. But everybody warmed to the notion of his or her being an underdog. Elias Howe touched the right nerve.

He was not an American but an Englishman who had led the local strike for higher wages in a spaceship body building factory in Coventry over a year before. He was not a carpenter but a skilled metalworker. But he knew the elemental appeal of the carpenter's trade in mob oratory. His true trade, however, was that of industrial obstruction. If there was no spaceship for a British scientific élite, then he was partly to blame. Cunning, a reading and listening man, he had got out of England by one of the last transatlantic flights before the destruction of most of the country, except for the tips of the Grampians and the Pennines, where men and women champed helplessly, waiting for the end. He had come to the right place, he knew. And now he, if nobody else, was going, he hoped, to the right place. The working-man's dream fulfilled: drink, fucking, and idleness. The earth hiccupped.

Calvin Gropius, his son Dashiel, the strange girl Edwina (who was, it seemed, now very near her time) drove wearily into the town of

Sloansville. It was intact but deserted, except for a small coffee-shop with the legend JACK JOE & CURLY above. It was lighted by a couple of oil-lamps, and a man who could not be Curly because of his baldness or perhaps was Curly because of it was playing checkers calmly with an old man. They did not at first look up when Calvin Gropius's party wearily shambled in. The old man finished the game with a leaping and demolishing king then looked up in toothless triumph. 'Got you there, boy,' he said. Gropius asked for coffee.

'Not properly open no more,' said the man behind the counter, 'but I can dredge up a little coffee, I guess, for tired travellers.' A literary touch, noted Edwina distractedly. She was losing faith in Calvin Gropius and gaining it in his son. She felt the child tugging within her. She would soon have to make choice of a father for it. But a literary touch, she noticed. Her trade was prevailing at the end. The old man said:

'You folks come a long way?'

'From Dallas, Texas,' said Dashiel.

'You seen strange sights?' asked the old man.

'A blood sacrifice, God help us, God forgive them, outside Ponca City,' shuddered Calvin Gropius.

'Terrible place, Ponca City. I been there once was when I was a kid; no more than knee-high to a grasshopper. Good place to keep away from, Ponca City.' The old man cackled. 'You hear much talk of the end of the world in Oklahoma?'

'Plenty,' said Dashiel, gratefully taking a mug of tepid coffee.

'Believe anything, them Okies will. Still, I reckon if it comes then it comes,' said the old man comfortably. He was, Edwina calculated, well into his eighties. 'Earthquakes, volcanoes, and the earth giving up its dead. That's in the good book, mister,' he told Calvin Gropius.

'I know all about the good book,' Calvin Gropius said irritably.

The Tagliaferro brothers now walked in, Salvatore wild-eyed, but with no gun in hand or at hip. 'Hi, Dash,' said Johnny. 'You got any coffee behind there?' he asked Jack, Joe or Curly. Salvatore had hungry eyes only for Calvin Gropius.

'You fellers come a long way?' asked the old man.

'Fort Worth, grandad,' said Johnny.

'That's longer than these folks, a mite. Grandad, you say, son. I'm a grandad twelve times over, you know that? No, reckon you don't, not having seen me afore.' The floor trembled. 'You stop that,' cackled the old man. 'A mite uppish,' he cackled.

'Are you,' said Salvatore, 'a minister?'

'Doctor of divinity,' said Calvin Gropius, 'for what it's worth now.' His eyes frowned at Dashiel. He didn't need these two Sicilians explained for him. Dashiel's bosses, colleagues, something, Mafia certainly.

'I gotta confess,' said Salvatore. 'I got sins on my soul.'

'I reject auricular confession,' said Calvin Gropius loftily. 'If you want to confess, go and confess in that dark corner there. Why should one man stand between another man and his maker?'

'You don't understand,' said Johnny, lighting a tipless cigarette and winking covertly. 'He's gotta confess. It's hell he's worried about.'

'There's no hell,' said the old man dogmatically. 'Hell's this world, my dad used to say. You two holy Romans then?'

'Not Romans, no,' said Johnny. 'And you keep out of it, grandad.'

Calvin Gropius sighed and then said: 'All right. Irregular, but I'll do it.' He motioned Salvatore to follow him to the dark end of the shop. The old man said:

'You folks come for the big rally? Well nigh on two hundred marching to it. That right, boy?' he said to Jack, Joe or Curly.

'What's this?' said Dashiel sharply.

'Big commie rally. Not seen one before in these parts. No call much for comminism this part of the world.' Calvin Gropius could be heard in the near-dark crying *Oh God God my God* at occasions during the purgative mutter. 'Up at the camp up the road. I ain't got nothing against comminism, mind. It's all men fighting one for the other, way it was put to me once by this book-learned feller in Anthony. That's South Kansas. Maybe you folks come through it?'

'Orgies,' said Edwina. Then she twitched and felt the child within kick her viciously. The old man was quick to notice. He said:

'I guess you're pretty near to your time, lady. Ain't no doctor in town, neither. Ran away with the others like a bunch of jack rabbits.

Nearest hospital's at Lossing. Know where that is?' The earth hiccupped twice and then went into violent spasm.

'He' s right,' said Edwina. 'I'm near.'

Calvin Gropius came back shivering from Salvatore's revelations. Salvatore himself was smiling. 'Don't know nothing about penitenza,' he said. 'Three Hail Marys should do it. I'll say them on the way. Where's coffee?'

'There's killing to be done,' said Johnny in dialect. 'You know that, *fratello*? Killing.'

Salvatore shrugged. 'Self-defence,' he said, following an old Pentagon policy, 'is best done by getting in first.' It sounded chilling in Sicilian, but not so chilling, children, as *anticipatory retaliation* used to sound. The old man said:

'You fellers foreigners? You talk kind of foreign.'

'Hundred per cent American,' said Johnny.

The time was nine-thirty. The gibbous moon was starting to cover gibbous Puma. The earth hiccupped.

Twenty-two

'Is that what that helicopter was about?' asked O'Grady. 'Earlier today, that chopper. Looking at our defences?'

'No problems up there,' said Bartlett. 'As long as our magnetised cover holds.'

'How far can you trust them with weapons?' He meant the CAT team, himself excluded.

'They'll never get in,' Bartlett said. Still, he gave O'Grady a Hutchinson hipman, with three ammogiros, and took one for himself. He also fixed round himself, with a long neck-strap, a bag of gas-bomblets.

'And the troops?' said O'Grady.

'Jolson's issuing them with rifles. Blanks, of course. Can't risk giving them lives.'

'They're supposed to be there to protect us.'

'We protect ourselves, O'Grady. Abramovitz, Hazard, Vanessa Frame – they're safe, I think. Reliable. I don't know, though. Guns in their hands – I never thought it would come to this.'

'There's a lot you never thought about.' Bartlett gave the astunomicologist a hard look but said nothing.

Illuminated solely by absurdly amplified moonlight, Puma being temporarily hidden by his stolen satellite, the two of them went to meet the mob, first looking in on the CAT team, now no longer laughing, that had been instructed to await instructions in the instruction-room, or lecture-theatre. There were instructions, for the moment, only for Hazard and Vanessa. Abramovitz did not look trustworthy, despite the course in pacification or selective amnesia or whatever had made him forget all about dissident books. Hazard and Vanessa were taken aside and given, respectively, a hipman and a Lescaze pistol. They handled them unhandily, wide-eyed both. 'I never thought it would come to this,' said Bartlett.

Not really a mob, they saw. There was organisation here. A group was concentrating on cutting at the electrified perimeter, one place only, no wasteful hacking all over. A British lower-class voice came with high-pitched clarity over a loud hailer. 'In the name of the oppressed,' it said, 'we order you to hand over your spacecraft to the workers. We want no violence. We ask you only to see the reasonableness of our request. You scientists there, stop being the tools of the capitalist oppressors. Come over to our side. You soldiers, you know what's going to happen. You're going to be left to die while your capitalist exploiters live on the fat of the land up there in space. Drop your weapons, open that gate, let us in. We come in peace. All we ask is what we want, that being what is the workers' rights.' The platoon sergeant, at a nod from his lieutenant, ordered the opening of fire. There was a fine ragged chorus of bangs, smoke, a fried bacon smell, but, although the members of the crowd nearest the wire rushed back, sending those behind tottering and falling, nobody went down dead. Lieutenant Jolson looked round curiously at his civilian masters. The sergeant gave the firing order again, and again there was a blind hash of harmless banging. As in rebuke of such kid's play, growling and crashing from all over the horizon, the man's stuff of real killing, hills falling, cities going down, sounded crisply.

A voice that disdained the use of a loud hailer was now heard, its possessor unseen. 'This is Calvin Gropius,' it said. 'I come as the last messenger of the Lord. I demand that your gates open in the Lord's name. I demand the Lord's right – the right to bear the Word of the Lord into the wide universe that is the Lord's own creation. Open your gates, I demand it, God demands it.' The voice of the workers loud-hailed in protest:

'The God that's the creation of the bloody capitalists. Open up for the workers.' But, because of the nonconformist tradition of British radical oratory, he couldn't help being influenced by the Gropius rhythms. 'The earth is the workers', and the richness thereof. Space for the workers.'

'Now, I think,' said Bartlett, and, with a good round aim, he sent a gas-bomb flying towards the spot where the cutters cut away, lighted goldenly by high-voltage sparks. There was a sudden cloud of immense dirtiness and a loud chorus of curses and desperate coughing. Encouraged, Bartlett sent another, towards where the loud-hailing workers' leader seemed to be placed. The bomb sailed through the air, over the fence, and there was no dirty cloud and coughing. Instead, it was fielded and returned neatly, a British cricket hand at work there. O'Grady pulled Bartlett away with quick policeman's reflexes. Both ran. Gas fumed and was carried away by the brisk wind. The earth hiccupped. The earth went into spasm. The Lord's? The workers'?

From behind the crowd Gropius resumed: 'I demand that the bearer of the Lord's Truth be admitted. *I demand.*' As if to back that up, the nervous spattering of what seemed to be machine-gun bullets started well behind him. And now some of the workers really began to go down, many screaming. Others ran. The loud hailer resumed:

'You see what the capitalists are doing, you scientists? Scientists, fellow-workers –' There was no more from him, except a howl, a gurgling, a choking, partly amplified. Then he was, presumably, down, loud hailer and all.

It is time to change our view, ladies and gentlemen, children, and see what was happening outside the CAT camp. Salvatore, abetted, by Johnny, was pumping out death into the workers, gritting in Sicilian: 'Let them die, why should they live, what right to live have they got, the bastards, when when when –' But he could not allow bereaved tears to cloud his sight. He pumped away, fine white teeth agleam in the ridiculous moonlight, while the ground trembled under him. Johnny said to Gropius, who came appalled up to their car:

'Salvatore, he'll get us all in there, reverend. All we want is the two guys that pilots the plane. The rest don't matter a shit, right? Just us and that broad and Dash and the guys that pilot the thing, and maybe a couple stewardesses.'

'No! No! No! This is murder!'

'Not murder, reverend. Self-defence. Salvatore don't have to confess that. Self-defence ain't no sin, reverend.'

Behind a tree, stretched out in the warm night asleep, were, for a time, Val and Willett. They had eaten and drunk heartily, they were very weary after their adventures. They did not respond to noise. They had had nothing but noise since their journey began. They had learned to sleep through noise. It was almost by chance that Dashiel Gropius dragged Edwina Goya to protection behind that same tree. There were not, in fact, many trees around. 'Good God,' said Edwina, forgetting her pains, 'it can't be. It's Dr Brodie.' She shook him. 'Dr Brodie, wake up. There's terrible danger.'

But it was Willett who woke first, grunting, groaning, smacking, very bleary. He did not know these two and he quickly grasped the pistol at his belt. The girl was pregnant, he noticed. Jesus, this was no time for getting pregnant. 'Friends,' the man said. 'Wait, you're –'

'Willett is the name.'

'I saw you at the Albee in –'

'*Hamlet.* They said I was too fat. But as I pointed out in a letter to the *New York Times* –'

'Edwina,' said Val, now awake. 'What the hell are you doing here?' He had last seen her in the departmental library, glooming over a big book on John Donne.

'This,' said Edwina, 'is the end of the world. I presume anybody can join in.'

'What a lot of people,' said Willett in wonder, seeing shrieking Kansans running everywhere. 'The chopper,' he said. 'It's safe?' It was not safe, not with maddened runners quite likely to take off from the carnage and the end of the world with it. Willett fired a couple of stray shots and saw people stumble, howling, scattering. Dashiel said:

'Gropius is my name. I'd suggest that –'

'You're too young for Gropius,' Val frowned.

'Dashiel Gropius. My father Calvin Gropius is over there, demanding entrance in God's name. Look, this lady's near her time, as you can see. There must be doctors inside that place –'

'It's all doctors,' said Edwina, her face clenching like a fist on her pain.

'The only way in,' said Dashiel, 'would be from the air. I'm assuming you know how to drive that thing –'

'Magnetic barrier,' said Val. 'But, Christ, my wife's in there. She ought to be able to let us in. Anyway, I've a right to be in. A duty, in fact.'

'You didn't seem so eager before,' said Willett. 'You talked about being shot down.'

'I was thinking of the two of us, if you must know,' said Val. 'I thought you were a little more sensitive than you seem to be. I wasn't going in without you. Does that make sense?'

Willett merely grunted. Then he said: 'Let's get in and up. At least we can stop that bastard from spreading death, whoever it is.'

'Salvatore Tagliaferro,' said Dashiel. 'He's gone mad. Lost his wife and his kids and has gone mad.' Meanwhile they made their way to the helicopter and got in, Edwina in pain and with difficulty.

Inside the camp area most of the CAT team, disobeying orders, had come out to see what was happening. Bartlett was concentrating on his official protectors. 'Out,' he told Lieutenant Jolson. 'Your work's finished in here. Get your men out.' Meanwhile Salvatore's bullets glanced whining off the tough wire of the perimeter.

'Out to be killed by that bastard? We're staying with you.'

'An order, lieutenant. Out. Get your men assembled by the transport lines. Take two trucks. Out.' Lightning flashed all over the horizon. Distant townships went tumbling. The hot moon seemed closer than ever.

'We're staying with you.'

The platoon sergeant came puffing towards them. 'For Chrissake, we need ammunition. Those were blanks. Some bastard made a mistake.' He looked back sweatily at the writhing bodies felled by Salvatore, Salvatore's car getting nearer the camp gate, Salvatore firing away.

'Ammunition's no good to you,' said Bartlett. 'It won't get through that fence either way. You're safe from that gun.'

'Not if we have to go out,' said Lieutenant Jolson. 'This mad swine here,' he told his sergeant, 'wants us to take the men away. Christ knows where to.'

'Get your man to the transport lines,' said Bartlett.

'See here, mister,' the sergeant said, 'we don't obey no civilian orders. We're staying.'

'You're not,' said Bartlett.

'You fucking well giving me orders, mister?'

'Not you personally,' said Bartlett. 'Not from now on.' He stepped back five paces, put his Hutchinson hipman to his hip, and fired a brief loud burst. The sergeant, with a look of utter amazement on his honest broad face, went down. The ground bounced him up an instant, like a spring mattress. Then he lay still. The lieutenant and O'Grady looked at Bartlett in awe. Bartlett said: 'I'll shoot your entire platoon, man by man, if I have to. Get them out of this camp.'

'And let the fucking invaders in?' said O'Grady.

'One thing at a time,' said calm Bartlett.

'You're mad, Bartlett. You're fucking mad.'

'Insubordination. I'll have to rehabilitate you myself, won't I? Later, of course. Lieutenant, you heard what I said.' Jolson's eyes were big as though exaggerated by blackface; he looked still at the corpse of his sergeant. He couldn't believe it. 'That corporal of yours would make a reasonable target,' said Bartlett, readying his gun. The lieutenant blew a shrill whistle, again, again, again. Raggedly his men assembled. He marched them, giving shaky orders. Salvatore had apparently done with blasting for a time. Beyond the gate could be seen Calvin Gropius, the Tagliaferro car. Gropius tried again:

'I'm not condoning this man's act of violence. These two men here are not with me. I'm asking you only in the name of the Lord to let his messenger in.'

Salvatore, of course, heard that very clearly. 'The bastard,' he said in English. 'After what I done for him, killing those guys. You mean you don't want us in there, reverend?'

'Be reasonable,' said Gropius. 'For God's sake, think. I'm not trying to save people. I'm trying to save the Word of the Lord.'

'*Protestante*,' grinned Salvatore terribly.

'Okay, okay,' said Johnny. 'He just wants in for himself. He don't trust us, *fratello*.'

'*Assoluzione, penitenza*,' said Salvatore. 'He didn't know how to do it. You,' he said rudely to Gropius. 'You sure my sins is forgiven?'

'This is not the time,' began Gropius lamely.

They looked up to the whirring of a low-hovering helicopter. Salvatore instinctively raised his heavy hipgun towards it.

'Okay, Salvatore, you can't kill the whole fucking world,' Johnny said.

Two trucks appeared, closed, tough-plated, with soldiers inside them. They lumbered, nervously it seemed, towards the gate. The gate, however, was electronically locked. Lieutenant Jolson looked nervously out of the passenger seat of the cab of the leading vehicle, making a key-turning gesture with great diffidence. 'Unlock that gate, O'Grady,' said Bartlett.

'And let those bastards in?'

'Unlock it. You know the code. Day Four, night.'

'You're mad.' But, scowling, O'Grady took out his pocket activator and set it to 0.35. The gate slowly swung open. The trucks started to move out. Some of the troops let out a feeble soldier's cheer. Calvin Gropius, who had always kept himself fit, sprinted to the opening and, crying 'In the Lord's name,' he tried to squeeze himself in. Hipfire resumed on the *bastardo*. He went down, sobbing 'In the Lord's'. The first truck went heedlessly over him, then the second. The helicopter hovered very low. It too gave off rapid fire. Salvatore Tagliaferro, screaming, dropped his gun, clutched his ruined face, and at once knew whether there was a hell or not. Another burst, to finish him, quite superrogatory, got Johnny, who looked up as at the sudden fall of gentle rain. He went down very quietly. An amplified voice came from the helicopter:

'How does the damned thing – Ah. My name is Willett.' The team, including its leader, looked up in wonder. It was over the camp, that confident histrionic voice, buoyed up by the electromagnetic barrier. 'An actor, now resting indefinitely. I have with me Dr Valentine Brodie, late in reporting for duty, but better late than never, Mr Dashiel Gropius, and Mrs Edwina Goya, who is about to give birth and urgently requires help. Kindly let us down.'

Bartlett said to O'Grady: 'Let them stay out there.'

Vanessa stood there, unable to think, breathe even. Dr Adams was near her. Gently, like taking a toy from a child who has just dropped off, Dr Adams unfolded Vanessa's fingers and let the warm little gun plop gently into her own hand. She released the safety-catch. Vanessa came to, shivering. 'Did you hear what I heard?'

'It's your husband, Dr Valentine Brodie.'

'My *husband* – how do you know?'

'You've talked of your husband often enough – before correcting yourself, of course. I think everybody will be delighted to see your husband. Better than being mated to Bartlett, Head of Enterprise.'

'I can see him – he's there, waving.' And then, fearful, knowing there was instability about, perhaps even still in sane-seeming Maude Adams: 'Why do you want that gun?'

O'Grady said to Bartlett: 'You heard what he said. There's a woman up there needs help.'

'She won't get it from us. This isn't an emergency hospital.'

'Deactivate the barrier,' said Dr Adams, pointing the gun at O'Grady. O'Grady, glad to obey, did a clumsy have-to-don't-I shrugging gesture at Bartlett and loped off towards the concrete block that bore the symbol of a sitting cat, back view, with a single thunderbolt, at which the animal seemed to warm itself, as at a fire.

Bartlett pointed his hipgun at O'Grady and shouted: 'I'm warning you, do you hear?'

'Best get it over,' said Dr Adams. 'We're short of time.' And she very neatly shot Bartlett. Bartlett spun howling, mad eyes looking for something, somebody, then just staring, holding huge twin gibbous moons. He went down very heavily. O'Grady saw, coming back, agape, going into an ape droop, unable to believe. He saw Dr Adams's smoking gun. Instinctively he went for his own, cold, as yet unused. Dr Adams said:

'Are you going to be a good boy, Dr O'Grady?'

O'Grady licked his lips. Hand went to hipgun. Dr Adams shot very neatly at a point just five centimeters in front of his left boot.

'Are you, O'Grady?'

O'Grady grinned sheepishly, shrugged. Then he threw his weapon down. It was a heavy weapon. 'Not too good,' he said. 'That pacifier.'

'Alcohol, laughter – those help,' said Dr Adams. 'And the odd dose of animal fear.' The earth moved rather urgently. The moon seemed to be breathing on them.

'He was mad,' said O'Grady, looking down at dead Bartlett. 'Clever, but mad. Who takes over?'

'Here he comes now,' said Vanessa. She ran to the helicopter, which was touching ground. Val, dirty, leaner than he had been, monstrously unshorn, went straight to her. They embraced, at first awkwardly, then not so awkwardly. Edwina, groaning, appeared, upheld by Dashiel Gropius, at the top of the ladder. Drs Fried and La Farge – her first maieutic assignment of the mission – looked at Vanessa, doubtful. A storm seemed to be blowing in from the moon. The ground felt like a ship-deck. Hecate, matron of women in child-bed, looked down menacing. 'The ship,' said Vanessa. 'The ship from now on.'

'Transportation?'

'A dickybird hop,' said Willett. 'In, ladies. I've always wanted to be in a spaceship.' And so he set the blades spinning again. Dashiel Gropius looked down at dead Bartlett and said:

'Who did that?'

Everybody looked at Dr Adams.

'Thank you,' said Dashiel. 'I didn't really want to do it. I'd promised Edwina, but still –' The corpse heaved gently on its unquiet bed. 'I didn't know him, you see.'

'Yes,' said Dr Adams. 'You have to know him. Have known him,' she corrected herself.

Twenty-three

The ship kept steady at anchor, despite the earth's raging without. In the otherwise empty hospital, Edwina sat up, suckling her child, a boy, born somewhat prematurely and no wonder, wondering what he should be called. Calvin? Nathan? Calvin Nathan? Calthan? Nalvin? Dashiel Gropius, sitting at her bedside, admired the upper curve and swell of her slim body. Not erotically, of course. Women who bared a breast for suckling were, for some natural reason, exempt from the responsibility of provoking lust. 'The name Dashiel,' he suggested, 'is a good unusual name.'

She looked at him without smiling. 'I've always believed in free will,' she said. 'And yet I seem, more than anyone I've ever known, to have been – drawn, tugged. Predestination – do you know the word?'

He grinned. 'You forget that I had a father named Calvin.'

'Sorry. You ran a big gambling hotel. That gets in the way of my seeing what you really are. What I was trying to say was – well, I had this idea of your father as a great elemental force – till I got to know him. Really, I suppose, I was being led to you. Poor Nat. He was killed for love of me. Yet he was only a sort of instrument. A premature instrument. I could have waited for you.' She put her free hand on his. The baby sucked blindly away.

'We wouldn't be here,' said Dashiel.

'We *shouldn't* be here,' she said. And then: 'Poor Nat.'

'Poor everybody. You loved this Nat of yours?'

'An interim love. The earthly father of this child. Now I love you.'

'That's returned,' he said, 'a thousandfold. But – you'll see me more and more as nothing. Among all these ologists. But if I told them that I'm a chartopaigniologist, they might be impressed and give me a laboratory.'

'What's a – whatever it is?'

'It means an expert in gambling.'

She chuckled. 'Write the word down for me and I'll learn it by heart. Then I can tell people who want to know what you are what you are. My husband is a –'

'Chartopaigniologist.' And then: 'You said *husband*. Who ties the knot?'

'The captain, I suppose. Dr Valentine Brodie.'

Dr Valentine Brodie was addressing the team in the great salon. He spoke diffidently. 'My only qualification,' he said, 'for being in charge is that I'm hardly fit for anything else. I know nothing except a useless trade – the craft of writing science fiction. But now there's no more science fiction to write. The chronicle I propose to commence writing will, I know, seem much in the tradition of science fiction, though it will be science fact. I mean, the recording of our adventures in space, a very long record which I will begin but those of our descendants who, like me, lack the *precise* talents of you ladies and gentlemen, will end. God knows when the last word of the space voyage will be written. I only know that the first word must be written soon. The earth's last annals are written, and we must forget about the earth – as a frail crust of solid matter covering hot water, I mean. The earth that gave us Shakespeare, Beethoven, Leonardo lives with us. We are, I may say, lucky that my predecessor had not yet fulfilled his intention of destroying what he called the materials of dissidence – meaning literature, music and art. The past lives on with us, and not merely a distillation of the best of the past. Our microlibraries are crammed with harmless trash as well as the best that's ever been thought and said and sung. We shall not be bored, though we may be impatient. Impatient, I mean, for real air and green and blue waters. The universe, as we all know, is vast, but it is not infinite. It is not impossible that our ship will at length touch a solar system similar to the one that, in two years or thereabouts, we shall be leaving by way of Jupiter, and there find a planet very similar to our doomed little earth. The journey will be dizzyingly long, but it will not be endless. Man will survive – not some cold steely ideal, all muscle and intellect, but, at least I may hope this, a being warm, wayward, imperfect, adaptable. Perhaps,' he grinned, 'I am making man in my own image – or in our friend Willett's. But, if I may say this, you have all had enough of heartless perfection.'

Willett was not happy. He did not care much for the food which, however imaginatively served up at table, proclaimed all too clearly its artificial origin. He was surprised to find himself full after eating, but it was a cheating kind of fullness. Real fullness was induced by bloody great hunks of beef, partridges, turkeys bursting with force-meat, plum puddings, apple tart with thick cream, cheese, crusty loaves, and there were none of those things here. Nor, after he had finished the bottles he had lugged aboard, would there be any more wine or brandy. Also it would be a no-smoking voyage. He puffed illegally some of the cigars brought on board by Dashiel Gropius, shut away in one of the handsome toilets, but each smoke was a sad farewell to smoking, not an earnest of endless smoking pleasure to come. He recited from a play he had once been in a kind of glorification of the dead world of fleshly indulgence:

'Acres of red meat spitting in the ovens,
Hissing and singing to a summer of incredible richness,
With a fat sap of gravy. Turkeys, capons,
Woodcock, stubblegeese – whole roasted aviaries.
And whole hams, pink as innocence. And all the
Junkets and flummeries and syllabubs and ice-puddings,
Sharp as a dentist's probe. And think of wine too –
Rivers of cold sun from all the provinces the sun washes;
Names like a roll of heroes: Cérons and Barsac,
Loupiac, Moulis, Madiran, Blanquette de Limoux,
Jurancon, Fleurie, Montrachet, Cumières…
We'll never see anything like that again.'

Some of the scientists, brought up on a diet of hamburgers and cokes, found the synthevedge and meat surrogate and artificial milk and juices little inferior to their old earth cuisine, but others remembered more civilised meals and cried. Willett was, Val supposed facetiously, a subversive influence.

Herman A. McGregor, first ploiarch, came to Willett while he was sitting forlornly in a beautifully designed armchair and watching, on the huge screen, the progress of Puma and his moon. 'You're Willett?' he said.

'None other.'

'Do you know a George Frederick Willett?'

'My son. Why?'

'A message coming through from Lunacapital.'

Willett ran, as well as he could, the long distance to the radio cabin. He recognised the voice, young and reedy, but his heart had already sunk to its limit. The voice said, amid static and howls:

'...Final communication from Lunacapital, Lunamerica. I say again, all stations now terminating communications. Seismic disturbances on the moon's surface and the prospect of early dissolution render further communication impracticable. I say again, this is George Frederick Willett, head of communications, Mooncap, closing down moon's final message.' There was a pause. 'That seems as banal a farewell as this very banal brain could be expected to contrive. I need better words. My father gave me such words once. If my father is still alive and, by chance, receiving this message, perhaps he will forgive my bad accentuation and faulty expression. It is not easy to do anything well at this final moment.' And then, the lines striking at Willett's heart the more for the very unprofessionalism of their utterance, he came out with:

'The cloud-capped towers, the gorgeous palaces,
The solemn temples, the great globe itself,
Yea, all which it inherit, shall dissolve
And, like this insubstantial pageant faded,
Leave not a rack behind. We are such stuff

As dreams are made on, and our little life
Is rounded with a sleep.'

The rest was silence. The two ploiarchs looked in silent sympathy at Willett, who sat for half a minute looking at his worn boots, sniffing. He blew his nose on a dirty handkerchief and said: 'Thank you, gentlemen.'
'No trouble.'
Willett found Val in his office on the lowest deck, busied with a small computer and a lot of papers. Willett said:
'I'm leaving.'
'What?'
'I'm leaving. Going down with the ship. The other ship, I mean – earth. There's nothing for me here.'
Val thought about that, eyes down, tapping a random morse message with his pen on the tough steel desk. 'There's nothing much for me, if it comes to that.'
'You've your wife. A delightful girl, if I may say so. Less – you know – self-assured than I expected. A sort of *melting* girl.'
'Yes, there's Vanessa. But at the end it's her world I join. The world of clean efficiency.'
'You'll change all that. Not too much, of course. There's plenty for you, Val. Duty, for instance.'
'Duty is only duty. Stern daughter of the voice of God. Not very seductive. So. You're leaving. I won't dissuade you, of course. If it weren't for Vanessa and this damned duty I'd be with you. We could at least die drunk. However I die, doing my duty, it won't be drunk. When are you leaving?'
'Now.'
'And where are you going?'
'Just back to earth. It doesn't much matter where.' There seemed to be an unwonted division inside Willett's heart. 'If I leave, am I letting mankind down?'
'You had a lot to give them. You had yourself to give them. And me, of course.'
'I could have acted Falstaff for them. Hamlet too, despite the

fatness and scantness of breath. But there's the other mankind out there. Mankind with its feet on earth. Mankind soon to be mixed with earth. My place is out there.'

'You'll find plenty of transport if you want to drive some place.'

'Yes. To some empty bar with bottles as yet unbroken. I shall drink whisky and gin and cognac and smoke three cigars at the same time. I may go out singing.'

'God bless you.'

'And you and you and you. Can I get somebody to let me out in that elevator thing?'

'I'll escort you to the door.'

And so, with no ceremony of farewell, Willett left safe America and returned to an America ready, with the rest of the earth, for dissolution. It was an afternoon of high winds, bilious clouds, the ground heaving. There were corpses about, but the whole world was a potential graveyard. Val saw Willett waddle towards the transport park. His helicopter had reached its last gasp of fuel. Besides, to travel through the air would be to cut himself off from the smell of the dying earth. Val shut the door, elevated himself back to his office, locked the door, then copiously wept. Natural tears. He wiped them, inspected his eyes in the wall-mirror, found them not over-blubbered. He composed himself when the knock came at the door. He opened up and welcomed the two ploiarchs in, gnarled tough young Scots whose ancestors had navigated bitter seas. They wanted instructions.

'Forty days,' said Val, 'to Cat Day. Are we ready to go?'

McGregor said: 'We can't get out of Puma's orbit till the work on the gravity apotha is finished. Dr Jumel still has to complete modifications to the megaproagon.'

Val nodded, not at all out of his depth. This was pure science fiction. 'What has to be done there?'

'Conversion of nuclear energy to jetpush,' said McEntegart. 'There's a thing she calls the epsilon link. She's having trouble.'

'How much trouble?'

'Ye'd best see her yersel.' Val looked sharply up, expecting insolence. No insolence, just a reversion to the speech of his fathers.

'Trouble or not,' said Val, 'our big day must be CAT 35. Five days from now. We can't risk staying on earth much longer. Earth is collapsing. Better to risk a tangential glide even from a turbulent Puma.'

'There'll be a lot of turbulence,' said McGregor.

'Yes,' said Val. 'I'll announce our sailing-date this evening.'

'It's a gamble.'

'Of course it's a gamble,' grinned Val. 'Tonight after dinner we may play a little roulette. Blackjack. Chemin de fer. Monte Carlo night, with Dashiel Gropius in charge. Get people into the gambling mood. Of course it's a gamble. What the hell isn't?'

Twenty-four

The Love Field Municipal Airport at Dallas was still serviceable – at least its south-eastern half, the north-western having been overwhelmed by a swollen Bachman Lake. Very little of the city itself was left standing after the last earthquake. Bidu Saarinen and Florenz Zenger were impatient to be gone, along with their President, but Skilling had his own plans. He said:

'You have those orders in writing, stamped with the Presidential Seal. I want no displays of rugged initiative on the part of either you or Heyser.' Heyser was the head of the America IV project in Richmond, Indiana. The spaceship, nearly identical, following the Frame plan, with its prototype in Kansas, had a feature known as a windstand, superior to the massive foam bed of the ship that Val now ruled: the craft hovered a kilometre over the turbid ground on an air cushion, had to be reached by helicopter (but how did you keep a helicopter safe these days?), and at least those up there already had little to worry about from the convulsive earth. It was to Richmond, Indiana, that Saarinen and Zenger were on their way. At least they were already embarking; they stood doubtful on the steps of their Montfleury 9. Their President should have been embarking with them. Instead –

'You don't have to worry about me,' Skilling said. 'Indeed, I order you not to worry. If I'm not there in three days you're to blast off without me. You have that in writing.'

'It's madness, sir,' said Zenger, and he bit his lip.

'A President has a certain duty to the territory he's been

responsible for. He has, as it were, to see it bedded down for the long night.'

Saarinen shuddered at the gallows humour. But he said, mildly: 'See you there then, sir. Good luck.' And he and Zenger got aboard. Skilling watched the little plane take off and then, hands in the pockets of his Potomac, as the rainproof was whimsically called, he strode towards his Phyfe two-seater. Like at least one other former New York City mayor he had been an aviator. Alas, no airport would be named after him. Not in this solar system. The Phyfe, an aircraft bearing no presidential logo, was nuclear-powered. Skilling loved it – the delicacy of its controls, the thrust that depended on a mere nutshell of concentrated power. It was now the only thing that he was able to love. He could now cherish his loneliness, a loneliness he had often, since his wife died, regretted. But a virtual celibacy, so his Catholic upbringing had induced him to believe, by a natural extension of the conditions for holding the sacerdotal office, was useful if not essential in a ruler of city, state, country. If he had ever loved any living being passionately, it was the city of New York. He would revisit New York before he, or it, died.

It was early morning, with a bloody sun struggling against clouds as thick and dirty as the smoke from a burning oil refinery. He achieved a sweet and birdlike take-off and took a bearing from McKinney, north of Dallas. He did not seek overmuch height: he wanted to see his distressed and dying kingdom. All below him lay stricken land, heaving in parts, displaying the open wounds of seismic shock, smoke rising from dead townships. The Red River had broken its banks and spread its own ruin. The Ozark mountains, mounted on their insubstantial base of air and water, leapt towards the sky, were pulled back, leapt again. Hot Springs was nothing but hot springs. He hovered low over Little Rock and saw what seemed a huge neglected stonemason's yard, stony rubbish, the littleness of dead rock. No life in Arkansas, the river towns of Augusta and Pocahontas drowned. And then the Mississippi, father of waters.

The width and rage of the great river was astonishing. He fancied that he could hear its roaring voices even from the height of his hover over Rosedale, even despite the sealed plexiglass of the cabin.

And in places the Mississippi leapt high from its bed in a flurry of dirty silver, leapt as a salmon leaps. He flew north-east to Holly Springs and said goodbye to the river's own name-state, crossed into Tennessee and over ruined Nashville ate his frugal lunch – a ham sandwich with English mustard, a Cadbury chocolate bar – and drank from his thermos of strong black sugarless coffee. He took the meal sacramentally, with a special relish. The comfort of the little things man would see no more – the silver wrappers of chocolate, yellow pungent mustard in a pot, the leap and plop of percolating coffee.

Kentucky shone no more purple beneath him. A gaping wound or, he thought less dramatically, a slash like the slash in a baked Idaho stretched, he judged, from Frankfort to Bowling Green. He was not sure of his bearings now, and no known landmarks remained except for a stretch of railway line, miraculously still lying patiently, with a broken and pulverised town on it: this he took to be Lexington. In the middle of the afternoon he crossed the swollen and deformed line of the Big Sandy River and was in West Virginia. He had once, briefly, courted a girl from Charleston, a lovely coffee-hued dancer called Betsy Domenico. That was in the days of comparative irresponsibility, when it was all politics, and political competence was expressed through human weakness – like courting a dancer from Charleston, getting drunk at rallies, telling coarse jokes at caucus meetings. Charleston had still a few of its prouder towers standing, which meant there was life there. He had an urge to descend, land, embrace, if it were possible, some of those hopeless frightened beings who were still his responsibility and whom he had, perhaps, conceivably, failed.

Failed? Yes, if among his responsibilities was the responsibility of speaking the truth. He had not spoken the truth. He had not even belatedly apologised for not telling the truth. There was a time when he could have spoken on such of the radio and television networks as had still been functioning and said: 'The end is coming, and I comforted you with false hopes. I lied for the sake of your short-lived happiness. I gave you no time to put your houses in order – meaning to fulfil the need of all men to prepare their souls for the end. But I was a man of politics, not of religion. My duty was to keep order, even if to keep order meant keeping you in the dark. Now you know there is an end to all things upon us, and what consolation can I offer? I can say: the world was already ending, though we tried to delude ourselves that this was not so. It was ending because there were too many people in the world and not enough to eat. Because a war was coming whose sole outcome would be to ensure that nobody in the world had anything at all to eat. If God exists, then God has perhaps been merciful. We cannot blame ourselves that the end is coming. We are bidden remember that nature is powerful and man weak. The psalmist was right: all flesh is grass. And now that grass is cast into the oven. Be brave, if you can. Remember that life is not a right but a gift. And now the gift is removed. Be thankful that you have savoured the gift of life. And now march into the dark with erect heads, eyes open.'

Nonsense. Cheap useless verbiage. There was nothing to say. There had never been anything to say.

The sun was full on his back as he rose and steered due east. He was over Virginia now, heading for dead Richmond. The James River surged and frothed. Richmond was not only dead but drowned. He made a right-angled turn and sped north. The waters of Chesapeake Bay were rampant over Maryland; Delaware, pincered by two bays, must be under the sea. It was not long before he saw what had once been Washington. He sobbed briefly, and then told himself: 'Reserve your tears.' He again steered due east and his stomach fell, knowing that he was approaching the end. He was coming to the region where it all began – the eastern seaboard where men had kissed the earth and cursed the sea and shaken fists at a Europe that had condemned them to poverty or the intolerance of religious bigots. They had come seeking a living or peace for the practising of their faith, slow in finding either. New Jersey. And then the city he had ruled, a city he could no longer recognise. From universal swirling waters the tallest towers of Manhattan, true, still grotesquely rose. It was pitiable – those proud peaks jutting from the deluge. The Newman Tower's top storeys, the central needle of stone that was the heart of the Scotus Complex, the Outride Building and the Paternoster

Convention City showing roofs white in the bloody sun, the two hundred storey Tractarian Folly, as it had been stupidly named, as if the makers were ashamed of its height or anxious to diminish their achievement in the eye of a God who had shattered the Tower of Babel. 'Mayor of New York City,' said Skilling, 'three terms running.'

God, or something, heard that and acted. An audience was needed for the final enactment, and what better audience than the three-times mayor? From the bowels of the universal waters an under-earth fist punched up a segment of a building as neat, except for the ragged edges, as any breakfast waffle. A single swipe from a thick brewis of water, mud, stone, metal smote the remaining towers and sent then under. Then that same hidden fist, then another, hit harder than before, and with each punch came up a fragment of the city as for the mayor's inspection, glowing briefly in the lurid light, hitting the air and going down in a dance of atoms. Then the earth opened and drank all the waters it could, shutting at once as if to gargle. Skilling, Mayor of New York City, the world's metropolis, three terms running, three terms, saw his ruined boroughs dry as a bone and as dead, preserving here and there by some miracle of irony the configuration of streets and avenues. Then new water galloped in, rusty in the sun, and hid everything. New York was one with all other ancient cities that had gone under the sea. Skilling wept and then wiped his eyes. He nodded goodbye to no one in particular. He put the remains of the chocolate in his mouth, relishing the thick bitter sweet gooiness, rolling the silver wrapper into a ball that he let fall among the pedal controls. Chewing, he turned the nose of his craft earthwards, waterwards, shut off the engine, and dove into New York City, going into the dark with his eyes open.

Twenty-five

The crew, or citizens, of America were hardly aware of the blast-off. The magnetic gravitation surrogate of the ship kept steady even the beaker of water that Edwina Gropius put to her lips. It was a three-day trip to growling Puma. The beast was growling, trembling, rippling at the prospect of soon leaping on his prey. What the hell was the thing made of? Pure iron ore? The mass tugged at the craft that had become a new, if diminutive, satellite, circling the hydrogen-misty planet in ninety minutes flat. Instruments took in what they could of Puma's surface – the scars of ancient wars, pockholes, a long purplish line that might, to a more credulous group of observers, be taken as an artefact, a Puman Great Wall of China. But all instruments squeaked of a dead planet. Dead? It was alive, horribly strong, ready to have its own way, beginning its long or endless sojourn in the solar system in an ellipse that was at a thirty-degree angle to earth's and, of course, most irregularly, trundling round in a direction opposite to earth's. Spinning between Puma and moon, the crew or citizens saw, on the great screen, a moon lacking all the features that every schoolboy knew, the seismic disasters having ravaged it like some dreadful disease. Meanwhile work went on in Dr Jumel's laboratory. She, a pretty fair girl, flushed with effort, her attractive low brow corrugated with effort, worked on the epsilon-link equations. Computer and automation cooperated in turning out successive versions of the tiny complex artefact that would provide the clue to more jetpush. Val was with her, but he confessed his impotence to advise, help, even set his SF-writer's fancy to work.

'It has to be soon,' said worried McEntegart. The calendar said CAT 10.

'It *will* be soon,' soothed Val.

But it was not soon. The calendar clicked, at artificial midnight, to CAT 9, then CAT 8 followed. Artificial dawns, artificial noons, artificial nights – their ingenious lighting system clung desperately to the old order they knew. Meanwhile earth grew closer, the moon was huge, blinding, but not so blinding as Puma. They drank the sun like some strength-giving potion, for attack, for resistance. It was hard, especially for Mr and Mrs Gropius, to believe that a terrible cosmic drama was in progress outside the tough walls of their world. These two cooed at the baby, who yelled in self-centred vigour. He had a name now: Joshua. Edwina crooned an ancient song that her grandfather had heard from his father as a boy:

'Joshua, Joshua,
Sweeter than lemon squash you are,
Oh by gosh you are,
Joshu, Oshu aaaaah.'

They watched old movies on television, including one called *When Worlds Collide* – mildly entertaining, but remote and incredible. The food that came from the galley seemed insubstantial, but it filled. It was tastier now, Florence Nesbit and Sven Maximilian Josiah Markelius having proved even more ingenious than Rosalba Opisso, the diaitologist, in the use of herb and spice surrogates. There seemed to be a great number of amateur cuisiniers aboard. There were even wine substitutes, made by compounding grape flavour with alcohol generated from the still useful waste, recycled, of the dead Professor Frame. Gin? No problem at all. Poor Willett should have stayed. No, perhaps not. He was no man for clean aseptic interiors.

CAT 7. Val refused to be desperate. If the job could be done, it could be done by Lilian Jumel. If the job could not be done, then they would all perish, crushed. Nobody had any right to life. Life was a free bestowal. Still, as they sailed between the Scylla of moon and Charybdis of Puma, between the steam of one and the ravaged

face of the other, animal panic grew in those few of them who saw
the movement to cataclysm on the ploiarchal screens. Val refused to
think of the speed demand being made on America in order that it
might flee the Puman orbit: something like half-a-million kilometers
an hour. He woke up in the artificial night, sweating. Vanessa slept
soundly, beautiful in the artificial old-time lunar light that ingen-
iously washed gently in from a casement that seemed to give on
to rolling lawn, with a ruined temple in the distance. Val dredged
desperately into memories of the mad books he had written, full of
fancy unjustified, undisciplined by the exigencies of scientific fact.
He found nothing.

Then, on CAT 6, Lilian Jumel collapsed – overworked, lacking
sleep, desperate. She had colleagues of course, competent, but mere
journeymen compared with her – John Durante, Fred Lopez, Louise
Boudinot. The megaproagon was her brainchild. O'Grady, quieter
than he had been, suggested a pacifier. Val said no – a mild hypnotic
only. And then he thought: why use drugs? The book he had written
so many eons ago – *The White and the Walk of the Morning* – had
an amateur hypnotist in it – Jess Hartford or Harvey or somebody.
Val had done his homework; he always had. While Lilian Jumel
writhed desperately on her bed, in the intervals of waking hysteria,
Val brought calm to her bedside, also a swinging gold watch bor-
rowed from Dashiel Gropius (his father's gift to him on graduation).
He calmed her with the rhythm of gentle light and an incantation.
He got her to deep sleep. He spoke to her mind. Calmly, always
calmly. He said:

'There are many ways out of the problem. The very bounce of
Puma as it eats the earth may provide the jolt needed, the extra
split-second boost. There are, apparently, a great number of asteroids spinning about. Who knows whether the pull of one of them,
infinitesimal though it may be, may not ease the gravitational problem that faces us? There is nothing to worry about. You have all the
time in the world. Things are not really so desperate. Nothing is all
that important. We have all known the rich life of earth. This new
space life is a mere bonus, a discardable extra. Rest, dear Lilian. Rest
as long as you will. Everything is being taken care of.'

On CAT 4 she rose from her bed without a word to anyone except a demand for what was called orange juice and coffee-surrogate. She showered, washed her hair, dressed. She walked calmly to her laboratory, where Durante, Lopez and Louise Boudinot were knotted over equations. 'All right,' she said, and they went to work.

On CAT 3, having achieved a velocity that kept the craft continually retreating from the impending point of collision, Lilian Jumel spoke hopefully. And then all work stopped as they went to the great screen to see the end of the moon.

The moon had been circling its new host in a regular satellitic rhythm. But earth was eventually going to be in the way of one arc of its revolution. This had always been evident, and there had been distracted speculation as to what the moon would do – wobble out of its course, be hurled to the condition of a sun satellite? But what happened now, the obvious, the banal, had always been the prognosis of most of the America team. They saw the moon come gracefully wheeling, approach the earth and then, not brutally, not even rapidly, shatter to fragments against it. The point of impact, they adjudged, was the dead heart of Europe. The moon shattered, and they gasped. One of the girls sobbed. Little Joshua Gropius howled, but not for the moon. The moon broke and went into gracefully sailing fragments that, slowly, slowly, changed to sunlit dust and, most beautifully, tried to become a dust-ring around Puma. But earth was in the way. A ring spun, of most lovely pearly configuration, but, at the point of impact with earth, shattered to amorphous dust, only to reform when free of that gross body.

On CAT 2, with no great fanfares of triumph, Lilian Jumel announced that they were ready to blast off.

And so, with a desperate-seeming wrenching that even caused a dysfunction of the magnetic gravitator, the spaceship America broke free of the pull of Puma and soared into free space, making for Mars. What they all had to see now, and yet did not wish to see, was the end of their own planet. As they sped away from Puma, they saw on the big screen the great hump of the predator, with its ring satellite that had been the moon of Shakespeare and Shelley and a million banal songs, growing ever more disjunct, ever more something-out-there.

Val assembled the team in the salon. He had never yet worn the black gear that was the uniform of the citizens of this new America, and he came in looking, if anything, scruffier than he had ever been – clad in the worn trousers and sports coat and torn boots of his, and Willett's, anabasis. He said:

'We are, as you know, about to witness the end of the earth. It seems to me that we ought to drink to something – ourselves, our future, perhaps our past, perhaps more than anything our past.' Dashiel Gropius, smiling, wheeled in a portable cocktail bar that had been speedily contrived in the util workshop. It bore bottles and glasses and ice. 'And I think too that we ought to demonstrate our power, our very human power, to enclose through intelligence or through the act of creation the huge but crass and stupid events that are the result of sheer blind celestial mechanics. The earth is dead, or nearly. Long live the human world.' He nodded at Vanessa, his wife, whose finger was on a golden lozenge on an instrument panel inlaid in the salon wall. She pressed, and the sound came out from the four corners of the ceiling – Mozart's *Jupiter* Symphony, the essence of human divinity or divine humanity made manifest through the gross accidents of bowed catgut and blown reeds. And on the screen they saw what that music diminished and made seem remote, even trivial, or else take on the patterns of choreography – cosmic but seemingly humanly contrived, because of the music. They saw Puma and earth meet, and the first patch of earth to catch the blow was the northern Rockies, which must already be leaping with stupid love to the claws of Puma. They tasted the heartening fire of gin, its little benignant brutality, as earth shattered – core of leaping water, crust of dust – and at once formed an outer ring satellite of its successor in the dizzying annals of the sun-dance. The moon was a ring and, a greater ring, pulverised earth spun already in perfect concentricity, luminous dust made of the dust of Skilling and Willett and the Tagliaferro brothers and Calvin Gropius and millions and millions more, all, indeed, who had scratched that fertile surface and watched the external wonders and horrors of mind rear themselves upon it.

Mozart, too, was part of that dusty ring, but, miracle, Mozart was also here, tender, triumphant, drowning even the loud howling of a child. The rhythms of Mozart bore them on into space, the beginnings of their, our, journey.

Epilogue

'Their, our, journey. That, boys and girls, ladies and gentlemen, is the story.' Valentine O'Grady stopped and looked quizzically at the twenty facing him in the classroom known as the Frame room. The story had, of course, taken more than a single session to tell. He had told it at length, dramatically, drawing on his fancy, his background reading, his knowledge of ancient films, the long unfinished chronicle that rested in the Brodie Library. He had told it to a group of young people who were not quite children, not quite adults, who were in fact hovering in that painful interim of pubescence where *ladies and gentlemen* and *boys and girls* could be used indifferently. 'What,' he said, 'do you think of the story?' They shrugged, made frog-mouths, pouted. One or two yawned. Maude Abramovitz, a cold, clever girl, said:

'It's not really history, is it? It's – it's –'

'Myth,' said Nat Irving.

'It happened like that,' Val O'Grady said, 'more or less. It's good for you to be reminded of your origins.'

'Why good?' asked Bill Harrison. 'It's all so – remote, different. I mean, it's a myth world, full of – what do you call them, buildings and clouds and trees. It's not our world. How can they be our people?'

'They're our people,' said Val. 'We sprang from them. A long long time ago, true.' He looked at them, sour, puzzled, unresponsive. 'We bear their names, we live in the world they built.'

'Why I said myth,' said Maude Abramovitz, although it was Nat

Irving who had said it for her, 'was because this Joshua character we've heard so much about was a myth. I mean, the whole story takes on its myth thing from him. He was supposed to be the son of God.'

'He was the son of Edwina and Nathan Goya, but he believed he was the son of God. He gave us our first space religion.'

'Which nobody believes in any more,' said Sylvia Ewing.

'Some do,' said Val O'Grady lamely.

'It's hard to take in,' George Eidlitz said. 'This business about a journey, for instance.'

'This *is* a journey,' said Val. 'This ship was designed for getting somewhere. A place where we can plant trees, feel the wind blowing in our faces, erect buildings.' Some of the class smiled. Sophie Farragut said:

'Your generation talks about a journey. Our generation knows we're just *here*. We've always been here, right back to what they call the mists of myth. I don't believe your story.'

'We'll always be here,' said Bill Harrison. 'It stands to reason. We've always been here, we always will. All that stuff you told is just invention.'

'Who built the ship?' asked Val desperately.

'God or somebody,' said Fred Greeley. 'It doesn't matter. It's here, that's what matters.'

'And the words of Shakespeare? The music of Mozart?'

'They were here too, a long long time ago.' Fred Greeley looked at his wristchron, a new one, straight from the utilab. 'There's nothing but this,' he concluded. 'All the rest is science fiction.'

Val sighed. A ship. It was impossible to convince them. The business of *getting somewhere* was left to computers. Had been, indeed, for the last millennium. A sceptical, tough, hard-brained generation. They would believe nothing. Science fiction, indeed. The end-of-session bell rang.

'All right,' he said. 'Class dismissed.'

They went running off for their protein and synthevedge. They had forgotten the story already.

Bracciano, January 31, 1976.

Appendix 1:
Anthony Burgess,
'Science Fiction'

In *Observer*, 31 July 1966, p. 21.

The fact is that there is not a great deal of merit in fantasy for its own sake. Anybody can invent worlds in which humanoids give birth to small cholesterium computers, or time comes out of a faucet, or the *alif*-class rulers secrete pseudo-cerebra in their intestines. But not anybody can write well, and the standard in most science fiction is lamentable.

I'm aware that SF makes no Jamesian claims (Hortense Calishre's *Ellipsia* is a freak), and that the correct image of an SF-writer is of a laboratory-man chain-smoking over a weekend typewriter, but once a piece of fiction (whatever its genre) asks to be taken seriously, it at once submits to the stringencies of straight literary criticism. And another thing: there is very little real intellectual content in SF. Neo-technological gimmicks don't really tickle the higher centres. SF resembles Jane Austen in its lack of intellectual engagement. But Jane Austen at least created amiable characters and wrote very well.

Of all this new SF batch, Frank Herbert's *Dune* (Gollancz) is the most ambitious *as literature*. The far-future Galactic Empire is a cliché of a creation, and so are the feuding dynasts, but Herbert, giving himself 430 big pages, uses length for depth. The Duke of Atreides and Baron Harkonnen and the rest of them are genuine characters whose acts emotionally involve the reader. The barren planet Dune (surely the Arabic *Dunia*, meaning the world?) is mapped in fanatical detail, and a couple of appendices summarise not only its ecology but also its religion. There is even a long glossary called 'Terminology of the Imperium'. And yet this devotion to detail and the evidence of immense literary care tend less to exalt the spirit than to depress it. What a waste, really. All this skill expended on a mere fantasy.

John Petty's *The Last Refuge* (Whiting and Wheaton) is more FF (futfic, or future-fiction) than SF. We approach A.D. 2000 and the USA and USSR are finished. In England a hierarchical civilisation is being painfully rebuilt. James Muller is a kind of Winston Smith, an uncomfortable atavistic survival whose individualism cannot be tolerated by the new regime. The book is a record of his enforced rehabilitation, recounted tersely and rather frighteningly. Give us, as here, fantasy that touches on our own political neuroses, and the prose is often sparked into urgency.

Similarly, the 1971 suicide wave depicted in Edmund Cooper's *All Fools' Day* (Hodder and Stoughton) is, though set off by Omega rays, a wholly credible extrapolation of a process we recognise *in potentia*. The weakness of the theme lies in its substitution of an external force (in other words, a kind of magic) for what can more plausibly be attributed to psychotic stresses. The writing is somewhat thrillerish but, at its best, impressively spare.

The Fury Out of Time by Lloyd Biggle Jr (Dobson) is about a time-capsule that hurtles in from outer space and is remanned by a maimed, hard-drinking, Hemingwayesque ex-major. He travels forward to a fierce future of warring cities and back to the Age of Reptiles. Wells did this better, and he induced belief in his time-traveller, as well as his machine. It is tough American typewriterese, like the stories in Robert A. Heinlein's *The Menace from Earth* (Dobson), the best of which is 'By His Bootstraps' – time-travelling which involves multiplication of identity (if you go forward and then back you must see yourself as you were).

In the Corgi *SF 6*, William Spencer's 'Horizontal Man' and Ernest Hill's 'Atrophy' are the best of a competent batch. The first poses the problem of immortality: how would we cope with the enforcement of endless consciousness when all we want to do is sleep? 'Atrophy', a far privier thesis, is about the danger of too much leisure in an automated world. The whole volume deserves to be bought and read: this is what the young SF-men, previously unpublished, are doing.

Appendix 2:
Anthony Burgess,
'The Last Day'

This poem appears in a letter sent to the editors of *Yale News* on 25 February 1975.

> *End of the World* – cosy, something thrilling
>   Read in a boy's book, heard on the radio:
>   Wells or Welles, apocalyptico-
> Cathartic, buildings crashing, voices shrilling,
>   And me outside the frame, clutching the shilling
>   Shocker, in an incandescent glow,
> Knowing this the ultimate *frisson*: below
> The cindered earth, me saved somehow, God willing.
>
> It will not be that way: no Gabriel's horn
>   Over the snarled traffic. A whimper, rather,
> Long-drawn and boring. Ravaged earth, forlorn
>   With crops parched, seas a polluted lather.
>   A man says: 'This is the end,' for days. But never
>   Sure. The End could linger on forever.

Appendix 3:
Anthony Burgess,
'The Eyes of New York'

The Italian publishing firm Mondadori commissioned Burgess to work on a film project titled *Gli Occhi di New York* in late 1976. The project was ultimately abandoned. The text that follows is Burgess's draft film script.

THE NARRATOR SPEAKS IN SOUTHERN ITALIAN WITH A STRONG NEW YORK ACCENT.

Call me Ishmael. Call me Mario. Call me Ivan Ivanovich. Call me Yan Yansen. Call me Jack Matsuki. Call me Poh Soo Jing. Call me anything you like: the name doesn't matter. But before anything, call me a New Yorker. Being a New Yorker, I'm the child of immigrants. All New Yorkers are immigrants or the sons or daughters of immigrants. The city the world knows was made by immigrants, and nearly nine million immigrants dwell in it.

   This is New York – the city that began for all immigrants in Ellis Island, at least from 1892–1943. This is Ellis Island. It stands in Upper New York Bay, southwest of the Battery of Manhattan, New York City. Eleven hectares. The Dutch called it Oyster Island. Then it was Bucking Island. Then it was Gibbet Island. Then Samuel Ellis bought it and later sold it to the state of New York. The state of New York sold it to the federal government for ten thousand dollars. It was a dump for ship's ballast, then a fort and an arsenal for gunpower. Now it's part of the Statue of Liberty National Monument. But then, then – the time of these pictures – it was where the immigrants waited for the opening of the gates – the gates to a new, and, they hoped, better life than anything that old dead suffering Europe could give.

This is New York – Fasanella's street-scenes, games in the Yankee Stadium, men and women at work, Little Italy.

This too is New York – urban loneliness, desperation, George Segal's images of alienated man.

This is New York. New York is many places, but to me it's the big vision. It gluts the eye, it overwhelms the eye. Call me a New Yorker, but also call me a man who uses his eyes. In fact, I'm a photographer. That's my trade – taking pictures with my Japanese camera, all over the city. Trying to sell those pictures to newspapers and magazines. Hoping someday to produce a book with very few words and a great many pictures – all mine, and all of New York City. And all the time looking, using my eyes, clicking away.

We talk a lot in New York, but we don't listen much. We even take in the rhythms of our music less through our ears than through the pores of our skin. This is a city built for human eyes. The eye is the ruling organ in New York.

Sometimes, in the spirit, I'm back on Ellis Island with my camera, taking it all in. Among these faces are the faces of my parents or my grandparents. Look at their eyes, drinking in the new world. Somebody's camera-eye was there recording. But none of the immigrants had cameras. None of the immigrants had known much liberty and they came without very much of anything – except children that Europe couldn't feed. They came with their bundles of clothes, a little hope and a measure of faith. They hoped things would be better in America. They believed that things could hardly be worse than they'd been in Calabria, Sicily, Warsaw, Kiev. They had names, but they weren't always allowed to keep them. Some of the Slav surnames were terrible tongue-twisters to the immigration officers who tried to write them down. Szymanowski, Walewskowka, Doktorow. Segaloworitz – the family had to be satisfied with just plain Segal. The southern Italians did better – Tagliaferro, Fasanella, Ciardi. They kept what their ancestors had had, more or less.

They also had their own language and dialects, and they expected to keep those. It's not easy to take a man's language away from him. Of course, the kids started to learn English almost as soon as they set foot on Ellis Island. But English would never be a *real* language. It would be the tongue an Italian and a Chinese would use to talk to each other, or else an Irishman and a Polish Jew. At home it would be Italian, Cantonese, Yiddish. The masters of English would always be the Anglo-Saxons, or the Irish who'd been taught English in the old country by their Anglo-Saxon masters. Or the blacks, children of slaves, who'd forgotten the speech of their ancestors in Africa. The Italians didn't want to become Shakespeare or Milton or Washington or Jefferson or Lincoln – masters of the tongue that the Pilgrim Fathers had brought over in 1620. What they wanted was something quite different.

Here's an Italian who became an American writer, a master of written English, to tell you what they *did* want – Pietro di Donato…

What did *any* immigrant want? To get in there and earn a living. To be left in peace by police and politician alike and allowed to look after his family. To fulfil the New York art of making a fast dollar. But a city can never be just an agglomeration of immigrants doing that – turning this patch of New York into Little Italy and that other patch into Chinatown, letting the other guy get on with the job so long as he leaves you alone. Cities are built out of citizens, and citizens have duties to each other. Citizens have to communicate with each other. Not just Italian with Italian and Pole with Pole – New Yorker with New Yorker.

Some citizens do more communicating than others. Though can we call them citizens? They're nameless men or the nameless bodies of men who don't just want to earn a fast dollar. They want to earn fast millions of dollars. They want to sell things – whisky, gin, cigarettes, real estate, automobiles, dishwashers, refrigerators, Coca-Cola – and they try to sell those things by shouting at you. Not really shouting, of course. Nobody listens to a man's voice in New York, no matter how loud. Words hugely written, images, huge-limbed, bright-coloured – these do the shouting. The eye again. Everything in New York is addressed to the eye. The eye drinks it in but is bewildered, overwhelmed, almost persuaded. Is this communication? Yes, but very much one-way communication. You're told and told again – all through images – and you don't have a chance to answer back.

You don't answer back? Well, shall I say there was a time when you didn't answer back. You took it for granted that all that wall space was the monopoly of the big men. These men had a kind of constitutional right to tell you what to smoke and drive and chew. And who were the big men? Not the immigrants from Calabria and Poland. They were rather the men who'd been in New York a long time – the Anglo-Saxons, the Irish, the Germans – the Teutonic Protestants and the Catholic Celts. Not the Italians, the East European Jews, the Chinese and the Japanese and the blacks and the Puerto Ricans.

The time came for the people who still thought of themselves as immigrants to take a piece of wall and answer back.

Answer back how? Not with words, of course, but with images. Let the older New York races have the words – English was their property. For the others – the eye. Always the eye. The New York eye. The eye served by colour, shape, the muscle and skill that set colour and shape to work. And what is the work? Communication, but not the hectoring urgent blaring blatant communication of the sellers. A different kind of communication, and much more subtle.

These murals say: Remember we're here as human beings, not just consumers of commodities. This is us. This is how we see ourselves. This is how we see you. The heights and angles of the geometrical city are softened and humanized by the bodies and faces of the very people whose blood was carried on the immigrant ships to the anteroom of Ellis Island.

The people who communicate on the walls of New York City are not frustrated cranks, scrawling psychopaths. They're not the people who scribble *This is me me me* on buses and subway trains and fences and toilets. Not *I*, but *we*. *We* means the family, the organization, the group, the plan, the serious intent. Not in the service of money, not to promote consumption. Just to communicate. The city is ourselves. Ourselves remembering ourselves – no longer the wide-eyed strangers with bundles, fed like the inmates of a prison, screened and examined and tested to see if we're worthy to enter the land. Instead, the people to whom the land belongs, to whom the city belongs.

This is art. Poor art sometimes, often unprofessional. Art nonetheless. Art is communication of a different kind from the advertiser's images or the politician's rhetoric. It's no good saying: what's it about, what does it mean? Ultimately it means itself. But underneath it there's a philosophy hard to put into words. Pride, resentment, fear – they're all in it. You could sum it up by saying it's a device for confronting the city. For though the city is people, it's also a juggernaut that crushes people.

These young people, at work with their paints and brushes on the walls of that city, are too busy with their sparetime art to talk much of the metaphysic behind it. To hear such talk we have to go to the individual artist, working alone. Like George Segal, who lives away from the city but is haunted by it.

Segal is a sculptor, and a sculptor of a rather special kind. An immigrant, or the son of an immigrant who sees in the desperation that makes immigrants a figure of the desperation of all men and women.

(Segal talks.)

Segal has a compassion for people which perhaps only the son of a poor immigrant can know. The compassion overflows the boundaries that art usually sets itself. The traditional sculptor makes his work out of the shapes, lines, contours of the human body – he abstracts these from the fleshly reality and sets up a pattern of his own. But Segal takes in the bodies of people and reproduces them lovingly as elements in a world that symbolizes desperation or loneliness. Man and woman on the brink of not-being. Before the world ends, before the earthquake strikes, before Vesuvius vomits its fire. This is the human condition.

It's not a condition imposed by a tyrannical economic or political system – though politics and economics may have something to do with it. Artists aren't much concerned with portraying the things that human ingenuity and clever social planning can put right.

They prefer to show the essential human condition as they see it. And, of course, there are two ways of seeing it. Segal's way is close to Kafka or Dostoevsky. Alienation. Frustration. Loneliness. The inability to communicate. The other way – well, we'll come to that later. Meanwhile, let's watch Segal at work. Clothing his models in the raw material of his art is his way of stripping mankind to the bone. And the bodies he reproduces by a kind of three-dimensional photography – these are set among real things – a bed, the sound of a phonograph, the ghostlike flickering of faces that talk but fail to communicate.

So out of failure to communicate a mode of communication is achieved.

Segal's vision is nourished by northern Europe, that of Fasanella by the south. If Segal is a kind of photographer, Fasanella relies on his eye and his hand. Not for him the glacial coldness of sculpture. He needs colour and lots of it. He has been called naïf, as Grandma Moses was called naïve, but if ever New York is destroyed by a nuclear bomb, we shall be able to reconstruct New York from his paintings.

Behind Fasanella is the sad immigrant story that still haunts Ellis Island, but in him it is a kind of faith in the city. Man does not have to be alienated. He is a creature of the community. The community has its miseries, its tyrannies, its oppressions, but it also has colour. Fasanella glories in the colours of things, he brings colours you can almost taste. New Yorkers eat their bread and salami and cheese and drink their coffee. They throng the streets for a festival. They go to the baseball game. They go to hear Pope Paul VI say mass in the Yankee Stadium in the Bronx. Most of all, they build the city.

Here, then, are some of the ways in which New Yorkers can look at New York. New York is full of eyes, like the night-sky, and it is rich in the treasures that eyes of the past have seen. All of the visual glory of the past is here, crammed into museums and art galleries donated to the city by rich men. But to express New York itself – the unique megalopolis – calls for techniques unthought of by Michelangelo and Leonardo. My camera is not enough. Nor is it enough to have been trained in the artistic modes of the countries that, through their refugees, have made New York. Here is new art. Or art so old, so beyond art, that it seems new.

Let the Anglo-Saxons speak the polished English of Washington and Jefferson. *This* is the speech of the immigrant.

And now let me click away, recording. More humbly, perhaps, than these other recorders, but still trying to make my eyes a substitute for my tongue. New York has eighteen million eyes – here are two of them.

(We see, as the credits come up, still after still, and we hear the shutter click between them.)

Appendix 4:
Anthony Burgess,
'Introduction' to *The Best Short Stories of J.G. Ballard*

First published in J.G. Ballard, *The Best Short Stories of J.G. Ballard* (New York: Henry Holt, 1978), pp. xi–xiii.

The first thing to say about J.G. Ballard is not that he is among our finest writers of science fiction but that he is among our finest writers of fiction *tout court* period. Ballard himself might retort that, granted the first claim, the second is redundant, since the only important fiction being produced today is science fiction (or the fiction of the untrammeled imagination, or of hypothesis, or of the metaphysical pushing to the limit of a scientific datum: unsatisfactory as it is, we always end up with science fiction). I understand that the only living writers Ballard really admires are Isaac Asimov and William Burroughs. This can be interpreted negatively as a rejection of the kind of fiction that pretends there has been no revolution in thought and sensibility since, say, 1945. And this, alas, means the greater part of contemporary fiction, which remains thematically and stylistically torpid, limiting itself, as to subject matter, to what can be observed and inferred from observation and, as to language, what might be regarded by George Eliot as a little advanced but, on the whole, perfectly intelligible. Ballard considers that the kind of limitation most contemporary fiction accepts is immortal, a shameful consequence of the rise of the bourgeois novel. Language exists less to record the actual than to liberate the imagination. To go forward, as Ballard does, is also to go back – scientific apocalypse and pre-scientific myth meet in the same creative region, where the great bourgeois novelists of tradition would not feel at home.

Ballard is a writer who accepts thematic limitations, but they are his own. His aesthetic instinct tells him that the task of the science fiction writer is not primarily to surprise or shock with bizarre inventions but, as with all fiction writers, to present human beings in incredible, if extreme, situations and to imagine their reactions. Ballard's characters are creatures of the earth, not from outer space. Why devise fanciful new planets when we have our own planet, on which strange things are already happening, on which the ultimate strange happening is linked to present actualities or latencies by cause and effect? There is nothing in the evolutionary theory that denies living things that ability to develop leaden carapaces as a protection against nuclear fallout. In time, the demographic explosion will bring about not only fantastic living-space regulations but a habit of mind that sees a broom closet as a desirable residence. Man will suck up oxygen from the oceans to aerate habitats in orbit, the Atlantic will be diminished to a salt pool, and in the pool will be the final fish of the world, to be battered to death by vicious boys. A new kind of man evolves, enslaved by engines of subliminal persuasion to ever-increasing consumption. Our response to Ballard's visions is two-fold: we reject this impossible world; we recognize that it is all too possible. The mediator between that world and this is a credible human being in a classic situation – tragical-stoical: he fights change on our behalf, but cannot win. Faulkner, in 'The Overloaded Man', comes closest to victory by devising an epistemological trick – reducing the objects of the detestable world to sense-data, turning the sense-data to ideas, then killing the ideas by killing himself.

It would be too easy to call Ballard a prophet of doom. It is not the fiction writer's job to moralize about Man the Overreacher, in the manner of the old Faust plays. He lays down a premise and pursues a syllogism. If we do this, then that inevitably follows: choice remains free. We associate prophecies of impending damnation, anyway, with the kind of mentality that rejects all technological progress: once admit the acoustic phonograph and the internal combustion engine and you are lost. Both H.G. Wells and Aldous Huxley built their utopias (eutopias, dystopias) on unassailable scientific knowledge. Ballard's own authority in various specialist fields seems, to this non-scientist, to be very considerable: I never see evidence of a false step in reasoning or a hypothesis untenable to an athletic enough imagination. The intellectual content of many of the stories is too stimulating for depression and so, one might add, is the unfailing grace and energy of the writing.

In my view, two of the most beautiful stories of the world canon of short fiction are to be found in this selection. They are not, in the strictest sense, science fiction stories: their premises are acceptable only in terms of storytelling as ancient as those of Homer. In 'The Drowned Giant' the corpse of a colossus of classic perfection of form is washed up on the beach. Children climb into the ears and nostrils; scientists inspect it; eventually the big commercial scavengers cart it off in fragments. The idea, perhaps, is nothing, but the skill lies in the exactness of the observation and the total credibility of the imagined human response to the presence of a drowned giant. Swift, in *Gulliver*, evaded too many physical problems, concerned as he was with a politico-satirical intention. Ballard evades nothing except the easy moral: to say that his story means this or that is to diminish it. In 'The Garden of Time' a doomed aristocrat, aptly named Axel, plucks crystalline flowers whose magic holds off for a while the advancing hordes that will destroy his castle and the civilized order it symbolizes. In an older kind of fairy story, the magic of the flowers would be potent but unspecified, vaguely apotropaic. In Ballard the flowers drug time into a brief trance – specific, and if one is a little off one's guard, almost rationally acceptable. The rhythms of poignancy which animate both stories are masterly: Ballard is a *moving* writer.

There are three short pieces at the end of this selection which show Ballard moving in a new direction. His novel *Crash* evinces a fascination with the erotic aspects of violent death, or the thanatotic elements in Eros. These little sketches, highly original in form as well as content (though Burroughs seems to be somewhere underneath) play grim love-death games with public, or pubic, figures. They will serve as a reminder that Ballard, master of traditional narrative styles, is restless to try new things. Through him only is science fiction likely to make a formal and stylistic breakthrough of the kind achieved by Joyce, for whom Vico's *La Scienza Nuova* was new science enough. That Ballard is already important literature this selection will leave you in no doubt.

Appendix 5:
Anthony Burgess,
'Galactic Cuckooland'

This essay was first published in the *Observer*, 2 July 1978, p. 26. The article subsequently appeared under the title 'The Boredom of SF' in Burgess's *Homage to Qwert Yuiop: Selected Journalism 1978–1985* (London: Hutchinson, 1986), pp. 466–8.

Why is most science fiction so damned dull? There are various possible answers. You practise the genre if you have fancy but no imagination. Bizarre things matter more than such fictional staples as character, psychological probability and credible dialogue. There is usually an atmosphere of evasion of real-life issues, occasionally qualified by dutiful lip-service shibboleths about human freedom and the embattled ecology. Content counts more than form. You are encouraged, despite the examples set by Ray Bradbury and H.G. Wells himself, still the best of the esseffers, to see yourself as working outside the literary tradition, which is artsy-schmartsy, and belonging to a category of near-popular sub-art, meaning bad typewriterese on coarse paper.

SF plots are easily devised. We are a million years into the future, and the world is run by the Krompir, who have police robots called patates under a grim chief with a grafted cybernetic cerebrum whose name is Peruna. There is a forbidden phoneme. If you utter it you divide into two entities which continue to subdivide until you become a million microessences used to feed the life system of Aardappel, the disembodied head of the Krompir. But there is a phonemic cancellant called a burgonya, obtainable on the planet Kartoffel. You can get there by Besterian teleportation, but the device for initiating the process is in the five hands of Tapuach Adamah, two-headed head of the underground Jagwaimo. Man must resist the System. The Lovers, who amate according to the banned traditional edicts of Terpomo, proclaim Love. Type it out and correct nothing. You will find yourself in the Gollancz SF constellation – along with Bob Shaw's *Ship of Strangers*, Richard Cowper's *The Road to Corlay*, *The 6th Day* by W.J. Burley, and *Roadside Picnic* by Arkady and Boris Strugatsky (genuine Russians translated into genuine American by Antonina W. Bouis).

Though *The Road to Corlay* is not bad, if not so good as Kingsley Amis's *The Alteration* and Keith Roberts's *Pavane*, which also posit a world in which the Roman Catholic Church rules England tyrannically. Thought has gone into it, there is an attempt at characterization, there is ingenuity in the notion of a waterlogged Britain of the year 3000 which has become seven island kingdoms. *Roadside Picnic*, on the other hand, which is about the Zone in Canada, where mysterious alien visitants leave debris of an advanced technology that fetches very high prices on the black market, is an excruciatingly brutal piece of writing, or translation. Theodore Sturgeon, in his introduction, tells us of a planet of Iron Curtain SF of immense size and density as yet unknown in the West. If this is a specimen, I remain unenticed. I remember a Soviet Writers' symposium I once attended whose SF specialists said, ha ha, the only trouble with their genre was that they could not keep up with the reality. But the real reality, as the Neapolitans would put it, is totalitarian injustice and the technological advances are a mere surface frippery. That SF should be a universal subliterature, ignoring the real world of police and censorship, is not a point in its favour. It is, I say again, evasive.

Ship of Strangers is about the space survey vessel *Sarafand*, which gets stranded in a distant galaxy where everything, including the *Sarafand*, is rapidly shrinking to zero size. Why not minus size while the author's hand is in it? *The 6th Day* is very plainly and decently written in the old Wells style. The members of a scientific expedition in the Galapagos Archipelago are transported into the far future, when the human race has self-destructed and a kind of highly intelligent octopus has taken over. Can humanity, in the form of these, and other, chronic Argonauts (Wells's original title, by the way, for *The Time Machine*), be persuaded to start all over again? No. Man is too violent a creature. Once you get into the violence you get out of SF, save for the technical trimmings. In other words, SF writers sooner or later have to resort to the clichés of the adventure yarn. Robert Silverberg's *Capricorn Games* also belongs to the Gollancz SF galaxy but is, for some reason, 30p dearer than its yellow fellows. The stories have quality and a few Borges touches – doubt of the viability of the form itself, for instance; a narrator from the future admitting that he is only signs on paper. There is also fine writing: 'At my back sprawls the sea, infinite, silent. The air is spangled with the frowning faces of women.' There is 30p worth of fine writing.

Robert Sheckley's *The Alchemical Marriage of Alistair Crompton* (Michael Joseph) has a beautiful cover by Peter Elson, and it also has humour – not a common commodity in the genre. The eponym is the chief tester of Psychosmell Inc., which makes psychotropic perfumes, and a cured schizophrenic who hates being whole and *robotniy*. The missing bits of his personality are leading separate lives on distant planets, so he sets out to recover them. This is, as they say, fun. *A Billion Days of Earth* (Dobson) is not fun. Its author, Doris Piserchia, 'known for the vivid dream-like quality of her prose', was trained as an educational psychologist, something of a recommendation in a novelist. It was always said that William, not Henry, should have taken up quality fiction. Here is some of Ms Piserchia's dreamlike prose:

> The Gods hurried into their ship, and there was only Vennavora remaining outside. She stood in the doorway, faced the sky, spread her arms, and with tears coursing down her cheeks, she said: 'Oh, Earth, you have become a scourge. You will go down in the record of the heavens as a world to shun. Killer of Its Babes will be your name... Farewell to the sweet winds and streams of your body, goodbye to the sky and the sun, to the paths in the mountains and the sparkling rain. Wherever we go, we will never find our home. It has cast us out.'

Then they get the hell out to the stars.

Last, there is the old master Brian Aldiss. *Enemies of the System* (Jonathan Cape – cheapest and best of the lot, note) is about the Ultimate State a million years hence and a trip by some of its more prestigious members to Lysenka II, a planet where the bestial inhabitants are degenerate capitalist humans. The utopian specimens of *Homo uniformis* are forced to find, against their will, virtues in these filthy flesh-eating mammalians and are drawn into being what the title says. It is too short a tale to say what has to be said, but it contrives to be rich, allusive, full of real people and unfailingly interesting. It is not, then, real SF.

Appendix 6:
Anthony Burgess,
'The Apocalypse and After'

Burgess's review of W. Warren Wagar's *Terminal Visions* (Bloomington, IN: Indiana University Press, 1982) was first published in the *Times Literary Supplement*, 18 March 1983, p. 256. The article subsequently appeared under the title 'Endtime' in Burgess's *Homage to Qwert Yuiop*, pp. 12–16.

We have had the end of the world with us ever since the world began, or nearly. As we are all solipsists, and we all die, the world dies with us. Of course, we suspect that our relics are going to live on, though we have no proof of it, and there is a possibility, again unprovable, that the sun will heartlessly rise the morning after we have become disposable morphology. Perhaps it is rage at the prospect of our ends that makes us want to extrapolate them onto the swirl of phenomena outside.

When I was a small Catholic boy living in the Middle Ages, the end of world was likely to come any time: I had sinned so much that the Day of Judgement could not be much longer delayed. But there were periodic doomsday threats for Protestants too, as in 1927, the year of fancy garters and the eclipse of the sun, when the Sunday papers had double-page apocalyptical scare stories. I remember a sudden puff of smoke bursting from a back alley and my running like mad: this was it. At school, with the nuns, the end of the world was in Christ's promise to the disciples – he would be with them till then though not apparently – and yet the finish of things was contradicted by the 'world without end' of the Paternoster. That though, I was told, was another world, post-terrestrial and not easy to envisage. Without benefit of biblical prophecy, much popular culture in my youth dealt with the end. The *Boy's Magazine* had a serial about it that excited me so much that my father burned it. The BBC, whose expressionistic drama was so brilliant in the 1930s and all without recorded sound effects and with only wind-up gramophones, put on a play about the consummation of all things, with an angelic bass singing *Sic transit gloria*. Terminal visions are not a speciality of the nuclear age. There seemed to be far more of the end of world around before we learned how to bring it on ourselves.

The difficulty of writing subliterature about the end of the world (for it is almost entirely that: in *Ulysses* the End of the World is a kilted octopus that sings 'The Keel Row') lies in the point of view. There has to somebody to witness it. Having refugees looking down on it from a spaceship is cheating, and so might be thought the bland narrative of Shute's *On the Beach* if that narrative were not so impersonal, like some dimwitted archangel's chronicle. There is a 717-page novel by Allan W. Eckert called *The Hab Theory* ('You'd better pray it's only a fiction,' says the blurb) in which the weight of the polar icecaps causes the earth to capsize. This has happened before, states the President of the United States in his address to the world, and it is the duty of mankind to preserve all knowledge so that civilization can be reinitiated by the possible handful of survivors. '"I therefore call on all governments and all people –"' And *then* all the power went off... *all over the world.*' So the book ends, and clearly Allan W. Eckert is still there with a typewriter. It won't do.

There never was a time when it would do. Not even Charles Dickens, who worked in the white light of theocentric fiction, would have sent the world up in comic spontaneous combustion and ended with a resounding moral paragraph. Mary Shelley, the mother of contemporary science fiction, established the principle of the solitary survivor in her little-read eschatographical novel *The Last Man*. This is a story of a monstrous plague killing everybody off except a doomed personage wandering companionless like Percy Bysshe's moon. There is thus an observer, though he is not going to observe much longer. (Incidentally, I must deplore in my old-fashioned way the custom, to which the author of *Terminal Visions* adheres, of presenting women writers with neither first name nor honorific. Mary Shelley becomes Shelley, as Doris becomes Lessing. There is only one Shelley, and he was a poet; there was only one Lessing, and he was a German.) H.G. Wells's *The Time Machine* looks at the imminent extinction of the sun, but it is only an apocalyptic vision, St John the Divine on a bicycle. The point is, if I read Professor Wagar's book right, that most of our literary world's ends are clearings away of old rubbish to make way for fresh starts. The world's great age begins anew, as Shelley wrote. St John the Divine's vision is the end of pagan Graeco-Roman civilization. The end of the world was for that; world without end was for the new faith.

The virtue of Professor Wagar's book on the endtime is that he has read so much rubbish, old and new. He is an academic historian and does not have to worry about literary considerations: indeed, style would only get in the way of the vision. He has read books we have only heard of, and some not even that – books like Robert Hugh Benson's *Lord the World* (1908); Poul Anderson's *After Doomsday* (1962); Léon Daudet's *Le Napus: Fléau de l'an 2227* (1927). He has read every book called *The Last Man*, of which there are a fair number, though he does not mention one that was very nearly called *The Last Man in Europe*. Strictly, Orwell's *Nineteen Eighty-Four* is very much a novel of the end with no resurrection. When Winston Smith is shot the visions of collective solipsism will take totally over, and the world as objective reality will cease to exist. This is a far more terrible prophecy than anything in Professor Wagar's long bibliography can provide, if we except *Brave New World*, where the last man hangs himself. It is the vision of stasis, of the impossibility of change, that is so terrifying. William Blake shuddered at heaven's sempiternal marble and reflected that in hell there is at least energy and motion. Shaw's *Back to Methuselah* (again unmentioned here) sees life itself as the great mutable élan: the human world may end, but, as servants of the life force, we should regard this consummation with indifference. Even Wells, who had begun as a scientific optimist and ended by presenting no future for humanity, saw the vital torch handed to other creatures too wise to destroy their environment. Professor Wagar's visions do not perhaps range wide enough.

More than halfway through he gives us the meaning of his title:

> Terminal visions are not just stories about the end of the world, or the end of the self. They are also stories about the nature and meaning of reality as interpreted by world views. They are propaganda for a certain understanding of life, in which the imaginary end serves to sharpen the focus and heighten the importance of certain structures of value. They are games of chance, so to speak, in which the players risk all their chips on a single hand. But games just the same.

In other words, test the *Weltanschauung* that happens to be in vogue by pushing it to the limit. Some world views have a theory of catastrophe, some don't. That of the Enlightenment did not, though the Marquis de Sade and Malthus had visions springing out of theories of sexuality which, by reason of the very atavism of their subject, had to admit catastrophe. After the Enlightened came the Romantics, who abandoned the steady-state model of reality drawn from mathematics and mechanics and thought, felt rather, in terms of volcanic changes, catastrophe for good or ill. They were succeeded by the followers of Comte and his doctrine of positivism. Without positivism there would have been no Mill, Darwin, Spencer, Engels or Marx and, in literature genuine or sub, no science fiction. Certainly no Jules Verne or H.G. Wells.

Since positivism is, except in socialist states and departments of sociology, generally discredited today, how is it that science fiction flourishes and by some writers, notably Ballard and Asimov, is regarded as the really significant imaginative florescence of our time? A cruel answer might be that practitioners of the form are hopelessly old-fashioned and do not see how the world has changed since 1914. Certainly, in respect of the techniques and insights of modernism, they cherish a peculiar blindness: there is not one SF writer whom we would read for the freshness or originality of his style. A writer who proclaims that subject matter is all, as most SF writers do, is clearly already admitting a rejection of modernism, but since modernism arose with a rejection of positivism this is probably in order. Now world catastrophe is one of the themes of science fiction, and yet science fiction is a child of positivism, which rejects catastrophe. We must leave it to Professor Wagar to resolve the anomaly.

Where there is a 'positivist terminal vision' the blame for world catastrophe is to be placed not on science but the abuse of science by people who do not understand science, or else on the blind forces of unscientific nature, which might include items like messianic Ludditism. But there is a post-positivist 'anti-intellectualism' or 'neo-Romanticism' or a new *Weltanschauung* which Professor Wagar, with misgivings, calls 'irrationalism'. This posits a new beginning after disaster, a system which rejects science and accepts superstition, primitive pastoralism, pragmatic cannibalism of technological debris. What both kinds of vision find impossible to accept is total and irreparable destruction, which is an extrapolation of the individual's inability to accept the death of consciousness. Sleep is in order, but death is only a kind of sleep. Nothing, thou elder brother e'en to shade, cannot be a conclusion for even the lowest order of literature.

It is the fact that Professor Wagar's survey covers only the lower order which makes one unwilling to grant too much importance to his theme. Frank Kermode saw, in his *The Sense of an Ending*, that what Professor Wagar calls the public endtime had to be 'radically immanentized... reduced merely to an individual's death or to a time of personal crisis or of waiting for crisis, a waiting for Godot.' That 'merely' is surely out of order. The end of the world is, alas, a very trivial theme. If Henry James had written a story about a group of people awaiting the end in an English country house, his concern with personal relations would have rendered the final catastrophe highly irrelevant, the mere blank part of the page after the end not of time but of the story. When Professor Wagar writes of Moxley's *Red Snow*, Southwold's *The Seventh Bowl*, Spitz's *La Guerre des Mouches*, Vidal's *Kalki*, Vonnegut's *Cat's Cradle*, George's *Dr Strangelove* (or *Red Alert*), Moore's *Greener than You*

Think, Disch's *The Genocides* and Roshwald's *Level 7*, he is dealing with electronic games. The genuine crises that face us – the death of the topsoil, the population explosion, the chance of the wrong button being pressed – are not strictly material for fiction. Fiction is not about what happens to the world but what happens to a select group of human souls, with crisis or catastrophe as the mere pretext for an exquisitely painful probing, as in James, of personal agonies and elations. If books have to be written about the end of the world, they should be speculative as science and not as subliterary criticism.

And if H.G. Wells emerges in this survey as the only giant in a genre which he virtually invented, it is, almost in spite of himself, because he was interestingly ambiguous, which few of his successors are, and because he dealt in the minutiae of human experience. The man in *The War of the Worlds* who, facing the probable endtime, mourns the loss of tinned salmon with vinegar remains more memorable than the Martian death rays. Only very minor literature dares to aim at apocalypse.

Notes

23   **Catday:** 'Cat Day', meaning 'day of catastrophe', was the
      working title of the *Puma* project. The title appears on the
      title page of the first version of the screenplay: 'Film script
      of *Puma* (Cat Day) by Burgess', International Anthony
      Burgess Foundation (hereafter IABF), Manchester, GB 3104
      AB/ARCH/A/PUM/1.

24   **Here on the final pyre:** an allusion to Seneca's play *Medea*:
      'Heap up a final pyre, Jason,/for your sons, and build a
      burial mound for them' (lines 997–8). In Lucius Annaeus
      Seneca, *The Complete Tragedies: Volume One*, edited by
      Shadi Bartsch, translated by Shadi Bartsch, Susanna Braund,
      Alex Dressler and Elaine Fantham (Chicago: The University
      of Chicago Press, 2017), p. 47.

24   **This is the way the world ends/Not with a whimper.**
      BANG: a reworking of the final lines of T.S. Eliot's 'The
      Hollow Men' (1925). See T.S. Eliot, *Collected Poems, 1909–
      1962* (London: Faber, 1963): '*This is the way the world ends/
      Not with a bang but a whimper*' (p. 92).

25   **All this happened a long time ago, children:** this open-
      ing frame recalls the concluding chapter of *The Clockwork
      Testament: or, Enderby's End* (London: Hart-Davis,
      MacGibbon, 1974): 'THIS, children, is New York' (p. 124).

25   **St Bede's Primary:** there is no primary school of this name
      in Nowra. This is likely an allusion to St Bede's College,
      an independent Roman Catholic school on Alexandra Road

South in Whalley Range, Manchester. Burgess recalls making an application to St Bede's in the first volume of his autobiography *Little Wilson and Big God* (London: Heinemann, 1987), p. 78.

25   **Tamworth**: a city in New South Wales, Australia.

25   **Joey**: a young kangaroo.

25   **Warwick**: a town and locality in south-east Queensland, Australia.

25   **Bertie Domville**: a reference to the play *Guy Domville* (1895) by Henry James. Burgess relates the story of James's dismay at the failure of the play in his novel *Earthly Powers* (London: Hutchinson, 1980), p. 90. The name Ron Domville is given to a television announcer in the first version of the *Puma* screenplay, 'Film script of *Puma* (Cat day)', p. 7.

25   **watching their flocks by night**: from the Christmas carol 'While Shepherds Watched Their Flocks', attributed to Nahum Tate (1652–1692).

25   **Southern Cross**: part of the Crux constellation. This well-known asterism, easily visible in the southern hemisphere, is composed of five stars that form the shape of a cross.

25   **Lithgow**: a city in New South Wales, Australia.

25   **poddy-dodger**: 'a person who steals unbranded calves, a cattle rustler; hence as a general term of abuse' (*Oxford English Dictionary*). Australian slang. For Burgess on the Australian language, see *Enderby Outside* (London: Heinemann, 1968) and *A Mouthful of Air: Language and Languages, Especially English* (London: Hutchinson, 1992).

25   **Birchip**: a town in Victoria, Australia.

25   **Australian Labour Party salute**: 'Australian salute' is a slang term for the act of brushing flies away.

25   **pommy bastard**: Australian and New Zealand slang (usually derogatory): 'An immigrant (usually a recent one) to Australia or New Zealand from Britain; a British (esp. an English) person' (*OED*).

26   **Maitland**: a city in New South Wales, Australia.

26   **Bathurst**: a city in New South Wales, Australia.

26 *Wagga Wagga Sentinel*: Wagga Wagga is a city in the Riverina region of New South Wales, Australia.

26 **Channel 37**: an unused television channel set aside for radio astronomy. Channel 37 occupies a band spanning from 608 to 614 MHz.

26 **three schooners and a rusty nail**: in South Australia, 'schooner' refers to a beer glass with a capacity of 285 ml. A Rusty Nail is a cocktail made by mixing Drambuie and Scotch whisky.

26 **Hector**: '624 Hektor', a D-type asteroid, is one of the most elongated bodies of its size in the Solar System.

26 **Ajax**: '1404 Ajax' is a C-type asteroid named after Ajax from Greek mythology.

26 **Hercules**: a constellation, rather than an asteroid, named after the Roman god Hercules.

26 **Vesta**: '4 Vesta' is a large asteroid named after the Roman goddess of the hearth. Vesta Bainbridge is the name of Enderby's wife in *Inside Mr Enderby* (London: Heinemann, 1963) and *Enderby Outside*. The association of 'Vesta' with toilet cleanser is perhaps another allusion to Enderby, who composes much of his poetry while seated on the lavatory.

26 **Juno**: '3 Juno' is an asteroid named after the Roman goddess.

26 **Victoria**: '12 Victoria' is a large main-belt asteroid. Named after the Roman goddess of victory, the name also honours Queen Victoria (1819–1901) who adopted the title Empress of India in 1876. In *The End of the World News* (London: Hutchinson, 1982) Burgess confirms the connection, adding 'named after an ancient empress of India' (p. 21).

26 **Brucia**: the asteroid '323 Brucia' was named after the American philanthropist, and supporter of astronomy, Catherine Wolfe Bruce (1816–1900).

27 **Marilyn**: '1486 Marilyn' is a main-belt asteroid discovered by the Belgian astronomer Eugène Delporte (1882–1955) on 23 August 1938 and is named after Marilyn Herget, daughter of American astronomer Paul Herget (1908–1981).

27 **American Relief Administration ... ARA**: an American

relief programme to Europe and post-revolutionary Russia after the First World War. The ARA, directed by Herbert Hoover, operated from 1919 to 1923.

27   **vermin of the sky**: term for asteroids coined by Edmund Weiss (1837–1917), the director of the Vienna Observatory.

27   **USAMC**: acronym. See note to p. 32, United States of America, Mexico and Canada.

27   **Lilienthal**: Lilienthal is a town Lower Saxony (Germany) close to Bremen. The name perhaps appealed to Burgess for its connection to the German aviation pioneer Karl Wilhelm Otto Lilienthal (1848–1896).

27   **Teutphone**: German speaker, from 'Teutonic'. Not in *OED*. The Teutphone Province is therefore the Germanic speaking area of Europe. Burgess employs a similar device in his novel *The Wanting Seed* (London: Heinemann, 1962) in which the superpowers are named Enspun, Ruspun and Chinspun – English, Russian and Chinese Speaking Unions (pp. 61, 220).

27   **Pickeringia**: '784 Pickeringia' is a main-belt asteroid orbiting the Sun, named after American astronomer Edward Charles Pickering (1846–1919).

27   **Blenkinsopia**: there is no asteroid of this name listed in NASA's Center for Near Earth Object Studies database. This may be an allusion to the cartoon character Bertie Blenkinsop who first appeared in the *Beano* in 1953.

27   **Piazzia**: '1000 Piazzia' is an asteroid named after Italian Catholic priest and astronomer Giuseppe Piazzi (1746–1826).

27   **Gaussia**: '1001 Gaussia' is an asteroid named after the German mathematician Carl Friedrich Gauss (1777–1855).

27   **Global Astronomic Sodality, GAS**: GAS is a creation of Burgess's own. Sodality, 'A society, association, or fraternity of any kind' (*OED*), has religious connotations: 'In the Roman Catholic Church, a religious guild or brotherhood established for purposes of devotion or mutual help or action' (*OED*). The term appears throughout James Joyce's novel *A Portrait of the Artist as a Young Man* (1916).

27   **megasteroid:** Mega Asteroid. Not in *OED*.

27   **blepophone:** telecommunications device combining sound
and screen. An allusion to the 1968 science fiction film
2001: A Space Odyssey (1968), directed by Stanley Kubrick.
Burgess recalls meeting Kubrick's daughter in *You've Had
Your Time* (London: Heinemann, 1990): 'I met first his guard
dogs, then the daughter, now grown, who had been the lisp-
ing infant on the blepophone screen in *A Space Odyssey*'
(p. 246). Not in *OED*.

27   **Professor Bateman:** Reginald Bate was Burgess's contemporary at Manchester University (1937–1940). See *Little
Wilson and Big God*, pp. 170–1.

28   **Sector G476:** a possible allusion to the television series *Star
Trek* created by Gene Roddenberry, in which the galaxy is
navigated in terms of quadrants and sectors. There are two
books relating to the series in the archives of the IABF in
Manchester, both of which might have been obtained with
the Puma project in mind: *Star Trek Blueprints* (New York:
Ballantine, 1975) and *Star Trek Star Fleet Technical Manual*
(New York: Ballantine, 1975).

28   **Hubert Frame:** an allusion to Janet Frame, the pen name
of New Zealand author Nene Janet Paterson Clutha (1924–
2004). Frame was awarded the Hubert Church Memorial
Award for her collection *The Lagoon and Other Stories*
(1952). Burgess reviewed Janet Frame's novel *Faces in the
Water* (*Yorkshire Post*, 8 February 1962, p. 4) and writes
of his time in New Zealand, making reference to Frame, in
You've Had Your Time (pp. 215–18).

28   **University of Westchester:** Westchester is a county in New
York, situated in the Hudson Valley. While there is a West
Chester University of Pennsylvania, this is more likely an
allusion to the University of Manchester where Burgess stud-
ied for his degree in English Literature. A similar phrasing
occurs in Burgess's novel *One Hand Clapping* (London: Peter
Davis, 1961) in which Manchester becomes 'Bradcaster'.

28   **ouranologist:** the Greek term for physical universe is

'ouranos'. Described later by Bartlett as 'the discipline that binds together the various specialisations necessary to the building of a space microcosm' (p. 99). The *Puma* MS shows Burgess reworking this word, the original spelling (later corrected by hand) reads 'houranologist'. The closest word in the *OED*, sharing the same Greek root, is 'uranography': 'The branch of astronomy concerned with the description and mapping of the stars or the heavens'.

28   **Israel Goodman Memorial Lecture**: Israel Goodman (1904–1952) was the president of the Miami Zionist Council and a member of the executive of the Zionist Organization of America.

28   **astrolabes**: 'portable instruments formerly used for making astronomical measurements' (*OED*).

28   **Rasps Extra Strong**: fictitious brand of cigarettes. The name suggests the damaged (rasping) voice associated with smoking.

28   **Cataract**: fictitious brand of cigarettes. Smoking has been directly linked to the development of cataracts (an impairment of vision).

29   **Fourth Estate**: the press.

29   **Sufficient unto the day**: 'Sufficient unto the day is the evil thereof' (Matthew 6:34). James Joyce rewrites this aphorism in *Ulysses* as 'Sufficient for the day is the newspaper thereof' (p. 133). Burgess often quotes Joyce's version, for example in *The Ink Trade* (Manchester: Carcanet, 2018), p. 259.

29   *Beware of French imitations*: Lea & Perrins' Worcestershire Sauce, a classic English fermented sauce originating in the nineteenth century, was advertised with the slogan 'Beware of Imitations'. See William Shurtleff and Akiko Aoyagi, *History of Worcestershire Sauce* (Lafayette, CA: Soyinfo, 2012). Applied here to Australian cognac, the same slogan is later connected to Untermeyer New York cognac (p. 42).

29   **President's son Jimmy**: an allusion to Jimmy Carter (1924–), the thirty-ninth President of the United States (1977–1981). The foreword to *The End of the World News*, a fiction

penned under the name John B. Wilson, attributes the inspiration for the novel's tripartite structure (one part of which is a version of the *Puma* text) to a photograph of President Carter 'watching three screens simultaneously' (p. ix).

29   **West Point**: the United States Military Academy, approximately 50 miles north of New York.

29   **God works in a mysterious way**: an allusion to William Cowper's poem 'God moves in a mysterious way' (1774).

30   **Legrand**: an allusion to the pianist and composer Michel Legrand, with whom Burgess was to work on a stage musical adaptation of the French film *Les Enfants du Paradis* (written by Carné and Prévert). While Legrand's music failed to materialise, Burgess completed the lyrics. The unpublished libretto is in the archives of the IABF.

30   *L'Univers*: This newspaper title ['The Universe'], Burgess's own creation, combines allusions to the French daily afternoon newspaper *Le Monde* ['The World'] and the Catholic newspaper *The Universe*, founded in 1860.

30   *Figaro*: *Le Figaro* is a French daily morning newspaper.

30   **Burgos is preaching doom in Valparaiso**: an allusion to both Burgess himself, and to Luis Borges (1899–1986), an author he describes in *Little Wilson and Big God* as his 'Argentine Namesake' (p. 175).

30   **seawindsuntanned**: weathered by sea, wind and sun. Not in *OED*.

30   **Robotti**: allusion to the Italian engineer Aurelio Robotti (1913–1994).

30   **Milton, thou shouldst be living at this hour**: first line of William Wordsworth's poem 'London, 1802' (composed 1802, published 1807).

31   **disembogued**: 'To come forth as from a river's mouth, to emerge; to discharge itself as a river' (*OED*).

31   **telescreen**: telescreens, which are both televisions and security cameras, appear in Chapter 1 of George Orwell's *Nineteen Eighty-Four* (London: Secker & Warburg, 1949): 'The telescreen received and transmitted simultaneously.'

31   **rainbowed:** 'Coloured like a rainbow; surrounded or illuminated with a rainbow or rainbows' (*OED*).

31   **poms without brains:** Burgess uses the same phrase in *You've Had Your Time*: 'There was a fair amount of resentment down there [New Zealand], resentment of big Australia, which called Kiwis "Poms without brynes"' (p. 216).

31   **Vanessa:** the name, closely associated by its initials in the novel with Valentine, perhaps recalls Venus, the Roman goddess of love.

31   **generators and genetrices:** *OED* lists 'generator' as 'male parent, a father', and 'genetrice' as an obsolete form of 'genetrix' meaning 'female parent, a mother'.

32   **Ouranological:** see note to p. 28, ouranologist. Not in *OED*.

32   **Sidney Carton:** Sydney Carton, central character in Charles Dickens's *A Tale of Two Cities* (1859), is recalled here for his self-sacrifice at the end of that novel. Burgess adapted *A Tale of Two Cities* for the Tyrone Guthrie Theatre in Minneapolis in the early 1970s (ultimately unproduced).

32   **Traflane F:** 'traffic lane', a contraction of 'traffic' and 'lane'. Not in *OED*.

32   **United States of America, Mexico and Canada:** the superpowers in *Puma* recall those in *The Wanting Seed*. For a discussion of superpowers in that novel, see *You've Had Your Time*, p. 33.

32   **an hour or so:** the typescript reads 'quieten the cough for an hour so'. This is amended in *The End of the World News* to 'an hour or so' and the same is done here.

33   **palinlogue:** words that, when read backwards, produce other words. Similar to the palindrome (words that read the same both forwards or backwards), the palinlogue is perhaps derived from the Latin *palillogia*, meaning repetition, and *logos*, meaning 'word, speech, discourse' (*OED*). Burgess uses the term in *MF* (London: Cape, 1971), with the sense of 'riddle': 'He had talked no more of Sib Legeru but I had, of course, like you, read his palinlogue' (pp. 182–3). Palinlogue

appears again in *You've Had Your Time*: 'I was in time to hear Tom dealing with my first hero, Sgt R. Ennis of *A Vision of Battlements*. The name R. Ennis, Tom said, was a palinlogue of "sinner." I was surprised to hear this, since I had chosen "Ennis" because, signifying an island, it pointed at the loneliness of the possessor of the name' (p. 206). Not in *OED*.

33   **Lombard cigarettes:** perhaps a reference to Lambert & Butler, this fictitious brand of cigarettes might allude to the screen actress Carole Lombard (1908–1942) who featured in advertising campaigns for Old Gold and Lucky Strike in the 1930s.

33   **Pmrhuaaet:** this throat clearing, an anagram of Earth Puma, recalls Burgess's 1963 novel *Inside Mr Enderby*, which begins with the sound of Enderby's snoring: 'Pfffrrrummmp' (p. 9).

33   **Newman:** John Henry Newman (1801–1890), theologian and cardinal, was a key figure in the Tractarian movement. An extract from Newman's *The Idea of a University* appears in the second volume of Burgess's *They Wrote in English* (Milan: Tramontana, 1979).

33   **Patmore:** Coventry Kersey Deighton Patmore (1823–1896), poet and essayist, best known for his poem *The Angel in the House* (1854). Patmore would convert to Catholicism in 1864. Burgess discusses Patmore's poem 'The Toys' in relation to the prospect of his own death in *You've Had Your Time* (p. 388).

33   **Scotus:** John Duns Scotus (*c.*1265–1308), Franciscan friar and master of theology at Oxford University. Given the frequency of allusions to Gerard Manley Hopkins (1844–1889), this is likely a reference to his poem 'Duns Scotus's Oxford' (1918).

33   **Outride Building:** possibly an allusion to Gerard Manley Hopkins: 'Two licences are natural to Sprung Rhythm. The one is rests, as in music; ... The other is *hangers* or *outrides*, that is one, two, or three slack syllables added to a foot and not counting in the nominal scanning' (Preface to *Poems* 1918).

33   **Paternoster:** the Lord's Prayer (in Latin) of the Roman Catholic Church.

33   **dun hell smoke:** an allusion to Lady Macbeth's line 'And pall thee in the dunnest smoke of hell', *Macbeth* (I, v, 49). Quotations from Shakespeare in these endnotes are taken from the third edition of *The Norton Shakespeare* (New York & London: Norton, 2016). The line also recalls the British cigarette brand Dunhill.

33   **dragons' teeth:** The typescript reads 'dragon's teeth'. This appears to be a typographical error and has been amended here (Burgess makes this correction in *The End of the World News*).

34   **Valentine Brodie:** Valentine is a name readily associated with romantic love. The surname is perhaps an allusion to Miss Brodie of Muriel Spark's novel *The Prime of Miss Jean Brodie* (1961), a character Burgess described as 'no narrow clinger to the curriculum' in his review in the *Yorkshire Post* (2 November 1961, p. 4).

34   *Eyelid of Slumber, Maenefa the Mountain, Cuspclasp and Flukefang, Desirable Sight, The Moon Dwindled* **and** *The White and the Walk of the Morning*: the titles of Brodie's books are derived from Gerard Manley Hopkins's poem 'Moonrise, June 19 1876'. Burgess makes similar use of Hopkins's work in Chapter 12 of *The Doctor is Sick* (London: Heinemann, 1960), taking the titles of magazines seen through a stationer's window from his poem 'The Windhover' (p. 84) and again in *The Clockwork Testament* in which the titles of Ermine Elderley's films are derived from a series of Hopkins's poems (p. 81).

34   **Cyrano de Bergerac:** Savinien de Cyrano de Bergerac (1619–1655), French novelist and playwright. Burgess translated Rostrand's *Cyrano* in 1971 and adapted it as a Broadway musical in 1973.

34   **Galindez:** Jesús de Galíndez (1915–1956), a Basque nationalist writer who taught political science at Columbia

University. Galindez disappeared from Manhattan, New York, in 1956.

35   **Scifi or Futfic**: abbreviations of 'Science Fiction' and 'Future Fiction', respectively. In his article 'Science Fiction' (*Observer*, 31 July 1966, reproduced here as Appendix 1) Burgess uses SF (rather than scifi) and gives John Petty's *The Last Refuge* as an example of 'FF (futfic, or future-fiction)'. Burgess uses the phrase again in *You've Had Your Time* (pp. 354–5).

35   **Daniel Defoe's *Journal of the Plague Year***: Burgess wrote the introduction to the Penguin edition of Defoe's *Journal of the Plague Year* in 1966. For more details of his connection of Defoe and apocalypse, see William M. Murray, 'Anthony Burgess on Apocalypse', *Iowa Review*, vol. 8, no. 3 (1977), 37–45 (p. 44).

35   **Dan French**: Daniel Chester French (1850–1931), American sculptor best known for his statue of Abraham Lincoln (1920) in the Lincoln Memorial, Washington DC.

35   **that old Anglo-American guy, Harry no Henry James**: Henry James (1843–1916), American-born writer who became a British citizen in 1915.

35   **Judd Gray**: Henry Judd Gray (1892–1928) was executed by electric chair for the murder of Albert Snyder in January 1928. Ruth Snyder (1895–1928), Albert's wife, was also executed. A photograph of Ruth Snyder's execution, the first picture of execution by electric chair, was published on the front page of the *New York Daily News* (13 January 1928). The case inspired James M. Cain's 1943 novel *Double Indemnity* and appears in Burgess's *New York* (Amsterdam: Time-Life, 1976), p. 185.

36   **Harrison**: Harry Max Harrison (1925–2012), American science fiction author. Burgess suggests in *You've Had Your Time* that Harrison 'stole the ending [of Burgess's *The Wanting Seed*] for the film of his *No Room! No Room!*, called *Soylent Green*' (p. 64). The correct title of Harrison's novel is *Make Room! Make Room!*

36 **Abramovitz**: allusion to the American architect Max Abramovitz (1908–2004). His work includes the David Geffen Hall in New York City's Lincoln Center for the Performing Arts. See *New York*, p. 126.

36 **the nonsense of running university courses in science fiction**: In *The End of the World News* these lines become more critical: 'this nonsense – a university course in, let's face it, trash' (p. 30). This is perhaps a deliberate reference to Kingsley Amis, who delivered a series of lectures on science fiction at Princeton in spring 1959. Those lectures were published as *New Maps of Hell: A Survey of Science Fiction* (New York: Harcourt, Brace, 1960).

36 **Tamsen Disney**: the surname suggests the characteristics associated with Walt Disney cartoons: 'simplified, sanitized, or romanticized' (*OED*).

37 **watching invisibly, by courtesy of an old SF writer called H.G. Wells**: a reference to H.G. Wells's novella *The Invisible Man* (1897).

37 **Margaret Hammerstein**: Oscar Hammerstein II (1895–1960), American librettist who worked with Richard Rodgers on popular musicals such as *Oklahoma!*, *South Pacific* and *The Sound of Music*. See *New York*, p. 123.

37 *Paradise Lost*: epic poem about the fall of man written in blank verse by the English poet John Milton (1608–1674). For Burgess on Milton, see *They Wrote in English*, vol. 2, pp. 131–2.

38 **Otis L.**: an allusion to the American industrialist Elisha Graves Otis (1811–1861) (the 'L' here reprises the initial sound of Elisha). Writing in *New York*, Burgess describes Elisha Graves Otis as 'a master mechanic in a bedstead factory in Albany, New York' (p. 17).

38 **Grosso**: Grosso is a *comune* (municipality) in the Metropolitan City of Turin, Italy.

38 **Parachronic Fantasy**: A parachronism is an error in chronology, similar to an anachronism. The word appears in Burgess's 1965 novel *A Vision of Battlements* (Manchester,

Manchester University Press, 2017, p. 190), *The Wanting Seed* (p. 42) and *The Kingdom of the Wicked* (London: Hutchinson, 1985): 'It seemed more logical to pass from earthly time to a region which might be termed parachronic but not achronic' (p. 306). Burgess's use of the word to mean 'outside of time' is at slight variance with the *OED* definition.

38   **I want an A**: an allusion to Nathaniel Hawthorne's *The Scarlet Letter: A Romance* (1850), in which the letter 'A' stands for adulteress. This scene recalls a similar encounter with a student in *The Clockwork Testament* (p. 36).

38   **Paradisaical fruit, lovely in waning but lustreless ... parted me leaf and leaf**: These lines are based on the poem 'Moonrise' by Gerard Manley Hopkins. See note to p. 34.

38   **flue**: 'A woolly or downy substance' (*OED*).

38   **coynte**: archaic: 'The female genitals' (*OED*).

38   ***Wesches***: abbreviation of Westchester.

38   **Gracie Flagg, singer**: a reference to Dame Gracie Fields, born Grace Stansfield (1898–1979), Lancashire-born music-hall entertainer and film actress.

38   **Doris Cosby, actress**: likely a reference to the American actress and singer Doris Day, born Doris Mary Ann Kappelhoff (1922–).

39   ***Hamsun Three***: Knut Hamsun (1859–1952), Nobel Prize-winning Norwegian author, recognised for his literary brilliance and reviled for his far-right politics. Hamsun's novel *Pan* (1896) is notable for its discussions of sexuality and sexual deviation. Burgess gives the name 'Sig Hamsun' to one of Enderby's students in *The Clockwork Testament*, a 'sloppy viking' who writes sexually charged poetry (p. 61).

39   **Gropius**: Walter Adolph Georg Gropius (1883–1969), German architect and founder of the Bauhaus School (see *New York*, p. 17). The name, connected with the character's sexuality, recalls the word 'groping'.

39   **Red wines *chambré***: the typescript reads 'Red wines *chambrés*' with the accent added in Burgess's hand. The text has

been corrected here, following *The End of the World News*, to *chambré*.

40   **All that thunder about hell and damnation.** Miserable sinners writhing in the unquenchable fire: an allusion to Father Arnall's sermon in Chapter 3 of James Joyce's *A Portrait of the Artist as a Young Man* (1916). For a discussion of Burgess's use of sermons in his fiction, see Andrew Biswell, *The Real Life of Anthony Burgess* (London: Picador, 2005), pp. 35–6.

41   **Frick Giant:** fictitious brand of cigarettes, the name of which is an allusion to Henry Clay Frick (1849–1919), American industrialist. In *New York* the Frick Collection is among a list of New York art galleries and museums that Burgess declares himself 'heretical or philistine enough to ignore' (p. 166). In *The Worm and the Ring* (London: Heinemann, 1961), Frick is 'the affectionate shortening of Frederica' (p. 30).

41   **Muriel Pollock:** American pianist and composer of popular music Muriel Pollock (1895–1971), best known for her ragtime composition 'Rooster Rag' (1917).

41   **Bonicelli:** possibly a combination of the Italian early Renaissance painter Sandro Botticelli (1445–1510) and Vittorio Bonicelli (1919–1994), an Italian writer and producer known for the SF film *Barbarella* (1968).

41   **Paxton:** William McGregor Paxton (1869–1941), American painter and founder of the Guild of Boston Artists.

41   **Loewy:** Raymond Loewy (1893–1986), French-born American designer. Loewy's designs included Lucky Strike packaging and Coca-Cola vending machines.

41   **Treboux:** Robert Marcel Treboux (1924–2012), owner of the renowned Manhattan bistro Le Veau d'Or.

41   **Voorhees:** an allusion to the architect Stephen Francis Voorhees (1878–1965). Voorhees joined Andrew C. McKenzie's architectural firm (previously Eidlitz & McKenzie) in 1910. See note to p. 73, Eidlitz, Mackenzie.

41   **Hebald:** an allusion to the New York born sculptor Milton Elting Hebald (1917–2015). Burgess and his second wife,

Liana, bought a house from Hebald in Bracciano, near Rome, and remained friends with the sculptor while they lived in Italy. Burgess writes about Hebald in *You've Had Your Time* (pp. 219–20), and reviewed Frank Getlein's illustrated book *Milton Hebald* (New York: Viking, 1971) in the *New York Times* (24 October 1971, p. 26).

41 **Stereotelescreen**: see note to p. 31, telescreen. The addition of 'Stereo-' is Burgess's own. Not in *OED*.

41 **Piers Widener**: possible allusion to the American art collector Peter Arrell Browne Widener (1834–1915), whose family fortune funded the Widener Library in Cambridge, Massachusetts.

41 **Whitney-Stanford cabinet**: allusion to the American architect Stanford White (1853–1906), whose murder Burgess recounts in *New York* (pp. 181–2). Also a possible allusion to the Whitney Museum of Modern Art, in Manhattan, New York City; see *New York*, p. 123. The Oedipus cantata, written by Burgess and Stanley Silverman, was performed at the Whitney Museum in 1973.

41 **Franchot Tilyou**: a merging of Stanislaus Pascal Franchot Tone (1905–1968), known as Franchot Tone, and George C. Tilyou (1862–1914). Tone was an American stage, film and television actor best known for his role in *Mutiny on the Bounty* (1935). Tilyou was a New York businessman who founded Steeplechase Park in 1897.

42 **Untermeyer New York cognac**: allusion to the American poet Louis Untermeyer (1885–1977). Also possibly an allusion to Untermyer Park, a park of 43 acres in Yonkers, New York.

44 **smalling in the heavens**: possible allusion to Thomas Hardy's 'Departure' (1899): 'While the far farewell music thins and fails/And the broad bottoms rip the bearing brine—/All smalling slowly to the gray sea line—/And each significant red smoke-shaft pales.' Burgess uses the word in a different context in the first version of the *Puma* script: 'Willett, smalling in the distance, goes off' (p. 102).

45 **Frobisher's Hypothesis:** Sir Martin Frobisher (1535?–1594), privateer, explorer and naval commander.

45 **Deuteroastral Doctrine:** combining 'Deutero-' (from Deuteronomy) and 'astral' (pertaining to the stars), this doctrine is concerned with the exodus of humankind into space. Not in *OED*.

45 **Montrachet:** a French dry white wine.

45 *Nostalgie de la Boue:* a borrowing from French, lit. 'yearning for mud', coined by the French poet and dramatist Émile Augier (1820–1889) in *Le Mariage d'Olympe* (1855): 'A longing for sexual or social degradation; a desire to regress to more primitive social conditions or behaviour than those to which a person is accustomed' (*OED*).

45 **Peter Nichols:** English playwright Peter Nichols (1927–).

47 **Roelantsen Station:** Born in the Netherlands, Adam Roelantsen (*c.*1606–1653) was the first schoolteacher and the first headmaster of what is now the Collegiate School in New York.

47 **Teutprot:** neologism formed by merging of Teutonic and Protestant. Burgess uses the term a number of times in *New York* where he speaks of 'the Teutprot element, now strongly Germanic' (p. 35). See also *New York*, pp. 120, 124.

47 **sniff in the krotevar:** the initial sound of 'krotevar' (not in the *OED*) is suggestive of the word crotch. Sniff, given the context, is used to indicate violence of some kind. The language of the Teutprot youth in this chapter recalls the more extensive use of NADSAT in *A Clockwork Orange* (London: Heinemann, 1962).

47 **yeled:** child (Hebrew).

47 **A prert on the dumpendebat:** an allusion to the thirteenth-century Latin hymn *Stabat Mater* which includes the line 'Dum pendebat filius' ['While the Son was hanging']. As 'dumpendebat', the word is used by Burgess as a euphemism for penis. See *ABBA ABBA* (London: Faber, 1977), p. 15, and *You've Had Your Time*, pp. 328–30.

47   **GNYs**: Greater New York, a cocktail that Burgess describes in *New York* as 'a variation, naturally, of a Manhattan – whiskey and vermouth, plus four olives' (p. 181).

47   **Yamasaki's**: Minoru Yamasaki (1912–1986), American architect of the World Trade Center. The same name appears in *The Pianoplayers* (Manchester: Manchester University Press, 2017), where it relates to the Yamasaki method of learning to play the piano (p. 194).

47   **jall his little bell up his yahma and flute his beard up his rucksuck**: more Teutprot phrasing: 'jall', 'yahma', 'flute' and 'rucksuck' do not appear in the *OED* in the senses intended here.

47   **scudding**: 'to run or move briskly' (*OED*).

47   **Astoria district of Queens**: writing in *New York*, Burgess describes Queens as 'a borough of refugees from decay and decline – decent people who have moved out of Manhattan or Brooklyn or the Bronx, unwilling either to tolerate or to fight urban deterioration there, who now find the problem has pursued them into their supposed sanctuary' (p. 66).

47   **Willett**: the name, read as a diminutive form of William, recalls William Shakespeare, whose work Willett has performed on stage. The name perhaps also alludes to the British translator and editor John Willett (1917–2002), who reviewed Burgess's novel *Tremor of Intent* (London: Heinemann, 1966) for the *Times Literary Supplement* in 1966.

48   **a slabberdegullion druggel, a doddipol jolthead, a blockish grutnol and a turdgut ... shitabed and lousy rascal**: Willett's tirade of abuse is taken from Chapter 25 of Thomas Urquhart and Peter Anthony Motteux's translation of François Rabelais's *The Heroic Deeds of Gargantua and of Pantagruel* (London: Dent, 1929). There is a copy of volume two of the Dent edition in the archives of the IABF in Manchester, inscribed 'J.B. Wilson'.

48   **galliard**: 'Valiant, hardy, "stout", sturdy' (*OED*).

48   **fat Jack**: Falstaff. Shakespeare's popular 'fat rogue', *1 Henry*

IV (I, ii, 284) is regularly referred to as 'Jack', a diminutive of his given name John. Burgess wrote a Falstaff play – *Sir John Falstaff va alla guerra, or Sir John Falstaff goes to war* – for the Italian actor Mario Maranzana. See *You've Had Your Time*, p. 328.

48   **in poison:** in person. Burgess uses the same phonetic spelling in Part 1, Chapter 2 of *A Clockwork Orange*: 'if it isn't fat stinking Billyboy in poison' (p. 15). The association with New York American accents is made clear in an early draft of Burgess's *New York*: '"Don't eat dat sandwich, son, it's doidy," I heard a fond father say in, or on, Coney Island. There is something Dutch in that rejection of *th* and that deformation of *dirty*' (typescript draft of *New York*, IABF, Manchester, AAT/8, p. 3).

48   **onomastic:** 'an assumed name' (*OED*).

48   **Robert Courtland van Caulaert Willett:** Willett's middle names allude to the artist Jean-Dominique van Caulaert (1897–1979) and, less precisely but recalling the New York connection, Van Cortlandt Park in the Bronx in New York City (see *New York*, p. 68).

48   **Gargantua once in a stage-version of Rabelais's bawdy masterpiece:** Gargantua is one of two giants, the other being his son Pantagruel, who appear in Rabelais's *Gargantua and of Pantagruel*. See note to p. 48, a slabberdegullion druggel.

48   **Too fat, they said, too scant of breath:** 'He's fat, and scant of breath –' Lines spoken by Gertrude to Claudius in Shakespeare's *Hamlet* (V, ii).

49   **talk programme on the stereotel:** this programme recalls the Sperr Lansing Show on which Enderby appears in Chapter 7 of *The Clockwork Testament* (pp. 75–88). Stereotel is an abbreviation of stereotelescreen (see note to p. 41).

49   **stereoscopic:** 'having an appearance of solidity or relief like an object viewed in a stereoscope' (*OED*). Burgess uses the same term in *The Wanting Seed* (p. 45).

49   **Sycophant-varlets … ninny lobcocks:** from Rabelais. See note to p. 48, a slabberdegullion druggel.

49   **Roundy Cupcakes, Kingfisher Kingfish in Eggbatter**:
       allusion to Gerard Manley Hopkins's poem 'As Kingfishers
       Catch Fire' (1918), which begins: 'As kingfishers catch fire,
       dragonflies draw flame;/As tumbled over rim in roundy
       wells.'

49   **Beadbonny**: from Gerard Manley Hopkins's poem
       'Inversnaid' (1881): 'Degged with dew, dappled with dew/
       Are the groins of the braes that the brook treads through,/
       Wiry heathpacks, flitches of fern,/And the beadbonny ash
       that sits over the burn.'

49   **Calvin**: Gropius's forename is an allusion to the Protestant
       reformer John Calvin (1509–1564).

49   **Codshead loobies ... lubberly ... gnat-squeak**: from
       Rabelais. See note to p. 48, a slabberdegullion druggel.

49   **Heart, you round me right/With: our evening is over
       us; our night whelms, whelms and will end us**: lines
       from Gerard Manley Hopkins's sonnet 'Spelt from Sibyl's
       Leaves'.

50   **Puma in the heavens greets Christ the tiger**: allusion to
       T.S. Eliot's poem 'Gerontion' (1920): 'In the juvescence
       of the year/Came Christ the tiger'. 'Christ the Tiger' was
       Burgess's working title for his novel *Man of Nazareth*
       (London: McGraw-Hill, 1979).

50   **Star of wonder, star of light**: lyrics from the Christmas
       carol 'We Three Kings', written by John Henry Hopkins, Jr.
       in 1857.

50   **Turkeys as big as sheep and Christmas puddings like can-
       non-balls, and the flaming sauce reeking like a blaze in a
       brandy-cellar**: allusion to 'Stave III' of Charles Dickens's
       A Christmas Carol (1843): 'Mrs Cratchit entered: flushed,
       but smiling proudly: with the pudding, like a speckled can-
       non-ball, so hard and firm, blazing in half of half-a-quartern
       of ignited brandy, and bedight with Christmas holly stuck
       into the top.'

50   **working on the railroad**: American folk song. The first
       published version appeared in 1894.

51   **teleauditors**: telescreen viewers. Not in *OED*.

51   **Zwingli Gilroy, D.D.**: allusion to Huldrych (Ulrich) Zwingli (1484–1531), a leader of the Reformation in Switzerland.

51   **hot gospeller**: preacher, evangelist (slang).

51   **Fireballs blazing in the intestines ...**: Gropius's address draws on the book of Revelation. His rhetoric is close to that of the sermon in Chapter 3 of James Joyce's *A Portrait of the Artist as a Young Man* (1916).

51   **condign**: 'Worthy, deserving' (*OED*).

52   **I have seen, have smelt, tasted, heard, touched**: allusion to T.S. Eliot's poem 'Gerontion': 'I have lost my sight, smell, hearing, taste and touch.'

52   **Wyclif Wilcock**: allusion to John Wyclif (d.1384), theologian, philosopher and religious reformer.

52   **We fear thy anger, Lord,/Less than we love our sin./O may we soon begin/To cut the devil's cord/And let thy goodness in**: In *A Clockwork Orange: A Play With Music* (1987; 2nd edition, 1998), the prisoners sing a similar hymn: 'But may we all begin/To curse the strength of sin/And all the devil's brood/And let thy goodness in' (p. 16).

53   **Watts**: Isaac Watts (1674–1748), independent minister, poet and hymn writer.

53   **Wesley**: Charles Wesley (1707–1788), Church of England clergyman and founder of Methodism, 'regarded as the greatest of English hymn writers' (*Oxford Dictionary of National Biography*).

53   *Sewanee Review*: Established in 1892, the *Sewanee Review* is the longest-running literary quarterly in America.

53   **the true meaning of the sticking of the lance into Christ's side when he was dying on the cross**: an allusion to homosexuality. A trial for moral corruption in poetry (again suggestive of Christ's homosexuality) is depicted in Chapter 64 of Burgess's novel *Earthly Powers*.

53   **Goya**: Francisco de Goya (1746–1828), Spanish painter and etcher. The connection to Goya is confirmed when, unable to recall Nat's name, Melanie Putnam says to her son Jonathan,

'A Spanish kind of name. There was some big painter with it' (p. 151).

53   **Mouth D**: an exit from the stadium.

53   **crupper**: 'The human buttocks: jocularly Coll., from late C. 16. Ex a horses rump', Eric Partridge, *Dictionary of Slang and Unconventional English* (London: Routledge, 1961).

53   **Gottlieb Way**: allusion to Robert Gottlieb, Burgess's former editor at Knopf in New York. See *You've Had Your Time*, p. 203.

53   **Greeley Street**: an allusion to *New York Tribune* editor Horace Greeley (1811–1872).

54   **Microagronomy**: agronomy is the 'science of science of crop production and soil management' (*OED*). Not in *OED*.

54   **HOOC (CH_2)$_2$ CH (NH_2) COONa ... *book chacha coona book chacha coona***: The appearance of this chemical formula as a song recalls the dream of Mr Lodge, the chemistry teacher in *The Worm and the Ring*: 'C and H and O danced before his eyes to the gas fire's music, taking dwarf partners, changing partners, 12 22 11 5 10 5, 6 12 6. Square or cube dancing, like that they had in the school hall on Fridays, Linda CHO, smashing lumps with sugar hair' (p. 58).

54   **wore a bright star on his brow**: an allusion to the Star of Bethlehem, and also a possible reference to John Keats' sonnet 'Bright star' (1884), which Burgess includes under the title 'Last Sonnet' in *They Wrote in English*, vol. 2, pp. 323–4.

54   **The second coming**: poem by W.B. Yeats, written in 1919 and published in 1920. The poem is included in *They Wrote in English*, vol. 2, pp. 496–7.

54   **And what rough beast, its hour come round at last, slouches towards Bethlehem to be born?**: The final two lines of W.B. Yeats's 'The Second Coming'.

54   **Belial**: the devil. '[W]hat concord hath Christ with Belial? or what part hath he that believeth with an infidel?' 2 Corinthians 6:15.

54   **Beelzebub:** prince of demons. See Matthew 12:25–8: 'if I drive out demons by the Spirit of God, then the kingdom of God has come upon you.'

55   **Salome and John the Baptist [...] Galilean court:** in the New Testament, Salome, the daughter of Herod II and Herodias, demanded and received the head of John the Baptist (Mark 6: 21–9).

55   **DeWitt Towers:** Dwight Towers is the captain of the American nuclear submarine in Nevil Shute's post-apocalyptic novel *On the Beach* (London: Heinemann, 1957). Shute's novel includes an extract from T.S. Eliot's 'The Hollow Men' (1925) on its title page, including the concluding lines, '*This is the way the world ends/Not with a bang but a whimper.*' These lines were reworked by Burgess for inclusion in *Puma* (see p. 24). For Burgess on Shute, see *Ninety-Nine Novels: The Best in English Since 1939* (London: Alison Busby, 1984), p. 44.

56   **the sort of scene Michelangelo painted on the wall of the Sistine Chapel:** Burgess made a film about the Sistine Chapel for Italian television, broadcast by RAI in July 1974. Burgess discusses Michelangelo's work in 'Working on Apocalypse', 45.

56   **a black youth, called Stanley Baldwin:** an allusion to the writer and playwright James Baldwin (1924–1987) whose *Blues for Mister Charley* Burgess discusses in *You've Had Your Time*, p. 117.

57   **overpopulated world:** Overpopulation is the theme of Burgess's dystopian novel *The Wanting Seed*.

57   **this coming year is out:** The *Puma* typescript is missing a line here. The word 'out', present in *The End of the World News*, is added here.

58   **Feast of Childermass or Holy Innocents:** Christian festival celebrated on 28 December, commemorating the massacre of children by King Herod in his attempt to kill the infant Jesus. *Childermass* (1928) is the first novel in Wyndham Lewis's 'The Human Age' trilogy.

58   **Feast of St Stephen:** Christian festival celebrated on 26
      December. Also known as St Stephen's Day.

58   **Gibraltar:** Burgess was stationed on Gibraltar between 1943
      and 1946 during his time in the British army. He writes about
      the island in his novel *A Vision of Battlements*, and in the
      essay 'Gibraltar' (1967), reprinted in *A Vision of Battlements*
      (pp. 200–10).

59   **ПУМА – АМЕРИКАНСКИЙ ЗВЕРЬ:** 'Puma – American
      beast' (Russian). 'In the sky' is Frame's addition.

59   **Year of the Cat:** In the Vietnamese and Gurung zodiacs
      (replacing the rabbit of the Chinese zodiac) the Year of
      the Cat ran from 11 February 1975 until 30 January 1976.
      Burgess completed the typescript of this novel on 31 January
      1976.

59   **perigee:** 'The point in the orbit of the moon, an artificial
      satellite, etc., at which it is nearest to the earth' (*OED*).

60   **'Humankind,' he said, 'cannot bear very much reality. A
      poet said that:** Lines from T.S. Eliot's 'Burnt Norton' (1935)
      in his *Collected Poems*: 'Go, go, go, said the bird: human
      kind/Cannot bear very much reality' (p. 190).

61   **Ararat:** the place at which Noah's Ark landed after the
      Flood (Genesis 8:4).

61   **Space Race:** 'the competition between nations to be first
      to achieve any of various objectives in space exploration'
      (*OED*). Specifically, the term refers to the competition for
      supremacy in space flight between the United States and the
      Soviet Union during the Cold War.

62   **Tallis:** allusion to the composer Thomas Tallis (d.1585)
      whose work Burgess admired. Another Tallis (William)
      appears in Aldous Huxley's novel *Ape and Essence* (1948).
      That novel, like *Puma*, is concerned with the end of the
      world and, like Burgess's novel, is presented as a framed
      narrative constructed by a deceased writer.

63   **Mayflowers and Speedwells and Santa Marias:** The
      Mayflower and the *Speedwell* were two of the ships that
      transported the Pilgrims to America in 1620. *La Santa María*

de la Inmaculada Concepción was the largest of the three ships used by Christopher Columbus in his voyage to the Americas in 1492.

65 **anagraphic fiction**: the rewriting of the past. A coinage combining 'ana-' ('up, in place or time, back, again, anew', *OED*) and '-graphic' ('writing'). Not in *OED*.

65 **chicken Marengo**: French dish consisting of a chicken sautéed in oil with garlic and tomato and garnished with a fried egg. Legend has it that the dish was first created for Napoleon Bonaparte following his victory at the Battle of Marengo (14 June 1800). In *New York*, Burgess writes: 'In Europe even eating and drinking are somehow acts of communication with the past. This is literally so in France, where some country soup-kettles have simmered away since the time of Richelieu. To eat chicken Marengo is to be eucaristically linked with a Napoleonic victory' (p. 157).

65 *nom de jeune femme*: maiden name (French). This should read '*nom de jeune fille*'.

66 *nusus*: the word to which Vanessa is referring is likely 'nushus/nushuz' [نشوز], meaning recalcitrance.

66 **frowning like Napoleon**: Napoleon Bonaparte (1769–1821), French military leader and emperor. Likely an allusion to Hippolyte Paul Delaroche's 1846 portrait 'Napoleon at Fontainebleau, 31 March 1814'. Burgess wrote a fictionalised life of Napoleon in his novel *Napoleon Symphony* (London: Cape, 1974).

67 **selenologist**: from selenology: 'The science relating to the moon; chiefly, the science of the movements and astronomical relations of the moon' (*OED*).

68 **rags of poetry**: an allusion to the 'Shakespeherian Rag' (line 128) of T.S. Eliot's *The Waste Land* (1922).

68 **big stone wedding-cakes**: churches. The tiered wedding cake is said to have been inspired by St Bride's Church in London, designed by Christopher Wren and built in 1675.

68 **postlude**: 'A concluding piece or movement played at the

end of an oratorio or the like' (*OED*). Burgess includes 'postludes' in some of his musical compositions, such as the song cycle 'A Man Who Has Come Through' (1985).

69   **hangtrain**: 'hanging train', formed by a contraction of 'hanging' and 'train'. Not in *OED*.

69   **Dr Emile Fouilhoux**: Jacques André Fouilhoux (1879–1945), French engineer and architect. Fouilhoux worked in New York on projects including the American Radiator Building and the St Vincent de Paul Asylum.

69   **carcinomologist**: cancer specialist. From 'carcinoma', meaning cancer. Not in *OED*.

69   **röntgen image**: Wilhelm Conrad Röntgen (1845–1923), German physicist remembered for his discovery of X-rays in 1895.

69   **pneumometaphyteusis**: neologism (meaning lung transplant) apparently created by merging 'pneumo' (air) and 'emphyteusis' (leasehold). Not in *OED*.

69   **Bodenheim**: Maxwell Bodenheim (1892–1954), American poet and novelist known as the King of the Greenwich Village Bohemians.

70   **pneumosurrog**: an artificial lung. The word combines 'pneumo' (air) and 'surrogate' (deputy). The device is described in the first version of the *Puma* screenplay as 'a kind of miniature iron lung, fitted to his chest, plugged into the mains, but capable of being worked by battery' (p. 28). In this novel: 'The machine strapped to his body was an ingenious device that, with the aid of a catalyst known as DCT3, converted oxides to oxygen which rhythmically flooded his bloodstream but enabled him to expire the wastes orally, so that he had a normal supply of breathed-out gases for the speech process' (p. 84). Not in *OED*.

70   **Tomorrow will be love for the loveless, and for the lover love**: The poem is a translation of the Latin poem *Pervigilium Veneris* (third century BC). The translation here is Burgess's own, taken from his novel *The Eve of St Venus* (London: Sidgwick & Jackson, 1964), pp. 124–5.

70   **The next transit of Venus was due in 2004:** Burgess is correct in this, then-future, dating.

70   **Madame Aphrodite's:** allusion to Tad Mosel and Jerry Herman's off-Broadway musical *Madame Aphrodite* (1961).

71   **a plaster statuette of love's goddess (Botticelli version):** a reference to Sandro Botticelli's painting 'The Birth of Venus' (*c*.1486).

71   **Stella:** possible allusion to Philip Sidney's sonnet sequence *Astrophil and Stella* (1591).

72   **Pounce on me, Puma:** a composition of Burgess's own.

73   **Abramovitz:** Max Abramovitz (1908–2004), American architect and founder of the New York City firm Harrison & Abramovitz.

73   **bibliothecologist:** library specialist. Combining the French 'bibliotec' (library) with '-ologist' (expert). Not in *OED*.

73   **Adams, Maude Quincy:** Maude Adams (1872–1953), full name Maude Ewing Adams Kiskadden, was an American actress best known for her appearance as Peter Pan in the 1905 Broadway production.

73   **ouranoclinician:** (space) doctor. See note to p. 28, ouranologist.

73   **hydroponist:** hydroponics is '[t]he process of growing plants without soil' (*OED*).

73   **Belluschi:** allusion to Pietro Belluschi (1899–1994). Italian architect working in America. Belluschi and Walter Gropius worked as design consultants on the Pan Am Building in 1963.

73   **Boudinot, Louise:** allusion to statesman Elias Boudinot (1740–1821), who served as President of Congress from 1782 to 1783.

73   **Cézanne:** allusion to the French artist Paul Cézanne (1839–1906).

73   **electronologist:** specialist in electrons (subatomic particles with negative electric charge). Not in *OED*.

73   **heliergonomist:** specialist in power. 'Heliergs' are glossed

later in the novel as 'power generators' (p. 119). Not in *OED*.

73   **Cornwallis:** allusion to Charles Cornwallis (1738–1805), a leading British general in the American War of Independence.

73   **Da Verrazano, Gianna:** allusion to the Italian explorer Giovanni da Verrazzano (1485–1528) who was mentioned by Burgess in *New York*: '1524 Italian navigator Giovanni da Verrazano [*sic*] discovers bay where New York City now stands' (p. 40).

73   **microbibliothecologist:** see note to p. 73, bibliothecologist. 'Micro-' meaning small, as in 'microcomputer'.

73   **DeWitt, Felicia:** see note to p. 55, DeWitt Towers.

73   **Durante:** allusion to the American singer, pianist and comedian James Francis Durante (1893–1980).

73   **Eastman, K.O.:** allusion to Eastman Kodak, an American company specialising in photographic equipment and film, founded by the New York-born George Eastman (1854–1932).

73   **Eidlitz, Mackenzie:** an allusion to the architectural firm Eidlitz & McKenzie, whose buildings included One Times Square, the former headquarters of the *New York Times*.

73   **energiologist:** specialist in energy. Not in *OED*.

73   **Ewing, Georges Auguste:** allusion to the French chef and culinary writer, Georges Auguste Escoffier (1846–1935).

73   **diastemiconographer:** specialist in the study of the physical properties of space. Likely derived from the Latin *diastēma*, meaning 'space between' (*OED*) pertaining to the space between planets. In the *Puma* script (first version) the term 'diastemicroecon' is used by Frame to describe the spaceship *America I* (p. 20). Not in *OED*.

73   **Farragut:** Farragut is a neighbourhood in the New York City borough of Brooklyn, named after the American Civil War Admiral, David Farragut (1801–1870).

73   **Forster:** allusion to the English novelist E.M. Forster (1879–1970). Forster's own post-apocalyptic science fiction story

'The Machine Stops' was published in *The Oxford and Cambridge Review* (November 1909), 83–122.

73 **hupologistics**: a coinage of unclear meaning, perhaps 'hupo', used as a prefix, comes from the Greek 'hypo' – 'with sense "under, beneath, below"' (*OED*): hence denoting a subordinate rank of logistics engineer. Not in *OED*.

73 **Fried**: an allusion to Henry Fried, described in an unpublished draft of *New York* as 'head of a building firm, Commissioner of Correction for New York State and a director of the National Democratic Club', 'Draft of New York City (NYC)', IABF, Manchester, AAQ/14, p. 86.

73 **Nathaniel**: allusion to the American novelist Nathaniel Hawthorne (1804–1864).

73 **microagronomist**: see note to p. 54, Microagronomy.

73 **Greeley, William**: see note to p. 53, Greeley Street.

73 **diastemopsychologist**: see note to p. 73, diastemiconographer. Not in *OED*.

74 **cybernetologist**: specialist in cybernetics. Not in *OED*.

74 **Hazard, Ebenezer, supplies coordinator**: humorous allusion to the tight-fisted character Ebenezer Scrooge from Charles Dickens's *A Christmas Carol* (1843).

74 **Herodotus, Alger**: allusion to the popular American author Horatio Alger (1832–1899), whose work was 'steeped in Xenophon and Plato, Thucydides and Herodotus'. Carol Nackenoff, *The Fictional Republic: Horatio Alger and American Political Discourse* (New York and Oxford: Oxford University Press, 1994), p. 16.

74 **Irving, Guinevere**: an allusion to the English stage actor Sir Henry Irving (1838–1905) who played King Arthur, alongside Dame Alice Ellen Terry's (1847–1928) Guinevere, in a production of Joseph Comyns Carr's *King Arthur: A Drama* (1895).

74 **atmospherologist**: atmospheric specialist. Later in the novel this is confirmed: 'Dr Guinevere Irving was in charge of the air' (p. 120). Not in *OED*.

74 **Jumel**: Eliza Jumel (1775–1865), American socialite. Her

name is associated with the Jumel Terrace Historic District historic district in Manhattan.

74   **Kopple, Grayson**: an allusion to the documentary film makers Barbara Kopple and Helen Grayson.

74   **mellonologist**: expert in chemistry, exact meaning unclear. In chemistry, mellon is 'A cyclic organic compound, [(CN)2NH]3, obtained as a yellow powder by heating certain cyanogenic compounds such as melam' (*OED*). Not in *OED*.

74   **La Farge, Gertrude**: allusion to the American writer Gertrude Stein (1874–1946) and John La Farge (1880–1962), son of the American painter of the same name (1835–1910), the editor of the Jesuit weekly *America*, who reviewed the opera *Four Saints in Three Acts* for which Stein had written the libretto.

74   **maieutist**: midwife. Derived from the ancient Greek 'maieutic', meaning 'obstetric' (*OED*). Not in *OED*.

74   **Markelius, Sven Maximilian Josiah**: allusion to the Swedish architect Sven Gottfrid Markelius (1889–1972).

74   **oicodomicologist**: specialist in resource management. From 'economy', which has the Latin root 'oeconomia': 'The management or administration of the material resources' (*OED*). Not in *OED*.

74   **Moshowitz, Israel**: allusion to Israel Mowshowitz (1914–1991), Rabbi of the Hillcrest Jewish Center in Queens, New York City.

74   **morphoticist**: expert in chemistry, exact meaning unclear. From 'morphotic': 'Involved in the formation, development, or change in form of an organic structure; relating to or characterized by the adoption of a distinct form' (*OED*). Not in *OED*.

74   **ploiarch**: navigator. The term, explained on p. 119, comes from 'ploion', a Greek generic term for ship or boat. Not in *OED*.

74   **Nesbit, Florence**: Florence Evelyn Nesbit (1884–1967), an American 'Show girl' whose part in the 'Trial of the Century'

is dramatised by Burgess in *New York* (p. 182). Burgess served alongside a Mr Nesbit during his time in the army (see *Little Wilson and Big God*, pp. 250–1).

74 **mageirist**: cook. From the Ancient Greek 'mágeiros'. Not in *OED*.

74 **O'Farrell, Terence**: possibly an allusion to the English music-hall singer Talbot O'Farrell (1878–1952), or to the writer J.G. Farrell, whose novel about Ireland, *Troubles*, was published by Cape in 1970.

74 **rapticologist**: a coinage of unclear meaning. Not in *OED*.

74 **O'Grady, Lee Harvey**: allusion to Lee Harvey Oswald (1939–1963), the former United States Marine who assassinated President John F. Kennedy on 22 November 1963. See *New York*, p. 189.

74 **astunomicologist**: expert in pacification. Professor Hubert Frame tells Vanessa later in the book: 'It comes from the Greek for policeman. The Natsci committee, as you'll remember, was worried about space hysteria, hysterical dissidence, the need for an expert in pacification. One can never be sure. Policeman sounds horrible, of course. O'Grady is highly qualified in techniques of pacification' (p. 143). Not in *OED*.

74 **diaitologist**: a specialist in diet. Later in the novel it is confirmed that Rosalba Opisso is in charge of the ship's galley (p. 119). Not in *OED*.

74 **Parkhurst, Ethel Armand**: allusion to Emmeline Pankhurst (1858–1928), the leader of the British suffragette movement.

74 **Piccirilli, Attilia**: an allusion to Attilio Piccirilli (1866–1945). Piccirilli, one of the renowned Piccirilli brothers, was an American architectural modeller, carver and sculptor working in New York. The forename Attilia is feminine.

74 **Prometeo**: Italian rendering of Prometheus, the creator of mankind in Greek myth.

74 **anacoinotic**: a coinage of unclear meaning. Not in *OED*.

74 **Reiser, Deborah**: perhaps, combining the initial 'D' and

the surname 'Reiser', an allusion to the American author Theodore Herman Albert Dreiser (1871–1945). See *New York*, pp. 41, 78.

74   **Roelantsen, Julius C.C.**: see note to p. 47, Roelantsen Station.

74   **Sennacherib**: King of Assyria (705 BC–681 BC).

74   **Skidmore, Owings Merrill**: Skidmore, Owings & Merrill is an American architectural firm founded in 1936.

74   **scediastics**: likely pertaining to the study of shade/darkness, formed from the Old English 'sced'. Not in *OED*.

74   **Thackeray**: allusion to the British author William Makepeace Thackeray (1811–1863).

74   **Velasquez**: allusion to Spanish painter Diego Rodríguez de Silva y Velázquez (1599–1660).

74   **Wouter van Twiller**: Wouter van Twiller (1606–1654), the Director-General of the Dutch colony New Netherland in North America from 1633 until 1638.

74   **diastemographer**: see note to p. 73, diastemiconographer. Not in *OED*.

74   **Wolheim**: allusion to the American actor Louis R. Wolheim (1880–1931). The majority of Wolheim's work was in silent films, though he did act in *All Quiet on the Western Front*.

74   **petrologist**: 'An expert in or student of petrology [the branch of geology concerned with the origin, structure, and composition of rocks]' (*OED*).

74   **Yamasaki, Minoru**: see note to p. 47, Yamasaki's.

74   **Paul Maxwell Bartlett**: an allusion to the American sculptor Paul Wayland Bartlett (1865–1925). This connection is perhaps confirmed by the novel's allusions to the Piccirilli brothers (see notes to p. 74, Piccirilli, Attilia, and p. 135, Piccirilli Pasta Treats) who carved the sculptures designed by Bartlett and John Quincy Adams Ward for the pediment of the New York Stock Exchange. Another Bartlett appears in *The Wanting Seed*: 'Q.M.S.I [Quartermaster Sergeant Instructor] Bartlett' (p. 225).

75   **Boss Cat**: an allusion to the American animated television

series *Top Cat*, made by the Hanna-Barbera studios between 1961 and 1962. The series was renamed *Boss Cat* when it was released in the United Kingdom.

75   ***Who's Who***: Established in 1849 and published annually, *Who's Who* contains autobiographical listings of people from around the globe who have an impact on British life. Its unique quality is that details are provided by the biographees. Burgess writes of being asked to submit his details to *Who's Who* in *You've Had Your Time* (pp. 97–8).

75   **Choate School**: Choate Rosemary Hall, often abbreviated to Choate, is a private school in Connecticut whose alumni include the United States President John F. Kennedy.

75   **Achilles ... Philoctetes**: from Greek myth, participants in the Trojan War.

75   **M.I.T.**: Massachusetts Institute of Technology.

75   **Global Diastemic Organisation**: see note to p. 73, diastemiconographer.

75   **Into Space**: a possible allusion to the BBC Radio science fiction programme *Journey Into Space*, written by Charles Chilton (1917–2013), which aired between 1953 and 1958.

75   **The Future of Man**: title of a book, published in 1964, by the French philosopher and Jesuit priest Pierre Teilhard de Chardin (1881–1955).

75   **Critique of the Hopkinsian Radiation Belt Doctrine**: an allusion to the poet Gerard Manley Hopkins, whose work features throughout *Puma*, and to the work of James Van Allen, whose team at the University of Iowa discovered the earth's radiation belts (the Van Allen Belts) and with whom Burgess discussed astronomy while researching of *Puma* (see *You've Had Your Time*, p. 326).

75   **366 West End Avenue, New York City**: During his time in New York, Burgess lived at Apartment 10-D, 670 West End Avenue, NY 10025.

76   **Heidegger**: Martin Heidegger (1889–1976), German philosopher.

76   **Reich**: Wilhelm Reich (1897–1957), Austrian psychoanalyst,

credited with coining the term 'the sexual revolution'. Reich appears briefly in the Freud narrative in *The End of the World News* (p. 131).

76 **Jung**: Carl Gustav Jung (1875–1961), Swiss psychiatrist and psychoanalyst.

76 **Teilhard de Chardin**: see note to p. 75, The Future of Man.

76 **Metternich**: Klemens von Metternich (1773–1859), Austrian politician and diplomat.

76 **All these men**: the typescript reads 'All these man'. This grammatical error is corrected here (Burgess makes the same correction in *The End of the World News*).

76 ***The Republic* of Plato**: Socratic dialogue, written around 380 BC.

76 **Hobbes's *Leviathan***: Thomas Hobbes's book, *Leviathan or The Matter, Forme and Power of a Common-Wealth Ecclesiasticall and Civil* (1651).

76 **Prauschnitz**: In *Little Wilson and Big God* Burgess writes of a 'Karl Prauschnitz', one of the few foreigners he encountered at Manchester University: 'Our foreigners were mostly Germans' (p. 201). The name appears again as the 'tempestuous *diva*' Maria Prauschnitz in Burgess's *Byrne: A Novel* (London: Hutchinson, 1995), p. 25.

76 ***Demos*, after all, meant 'the mob'**: a borrowing from Ancient Greek referring to 'the common people of an ancient Greek state' (*OED*).

77 ***Mutiny on the Bounty***: 1962 film directed by Lewis Milestone and starring Marlon Brando. For Burgess on the mutiny, see his essay 'Two Hundred Years of the Bounty' in *One Man's Chorus*, edited by Ben Forkner (New York: Caroll & Graf, 1998), pp. 337–40.

77 **Dalrymple Hall on the Columbia campus**: Burgess taught literature and creative writing at Columbia University in the City of New York in the academic year 1970/71.

77 **Lindsay Airport**: airport named after 'the glamorous Mayor John Lindsay' (*New York*, p. 70). Lindsay (1921–2000), was

Mayor of New York between January 1966 and December 1973.

77   **satyriasis**: 'Excessively great venereal desire in the male' (*OED*). The word also appears in *Tremor of Intent* (London: Heineman, 1966), p. 1.

78   **Librium**: proprietary name of the sedative Chlordiazepoxide. The drug appears in Naomi Mitchison's *All change Here: Girlhood and Marriage* (London: Bodley Head, 1975), p. 92.

78   **Mens, Sana, Corpore**: an allusion to Juvenal's *Satire X*: 'Mens sana in corpore sano' [a healthy mind in a healthy body].

78   **SF man**: Burgess uses the phrase 'SF-men' in his article 'Science Fiction'. See Appendix 1.

78   **soak**: 'A heavy drinker' (*OED*).

80   **telenewsummary**: contraction of 'television news summary'. Not in *OED*.

81   **Kuo-Yü**: 'a form of Mandarin adopted for official use' (*OED*). Burgess's first wife Lynne spoke Kuo-Yü (see *You've Had Your Time*, pp. 150–1).

83   **United Free Nations Building**: a reference to the United Nations Headquarters in New York City.

83   **Bedford-Stuyvesant district of Brooklyn**: historic district, described by Burgess in *New York*: 'The blacks have their impenetrable strongholds of Harlem and Bedford-Stuyvesant' (p. 46).

83   **habituated to calamity**: Writing of New Yorkers in *New York*, Burgess notes that, among many other qualities, they are 'world-wise, resigned, incapable of registering surprise' (p. 50) and that they 'do best in times of crisis' (p. 51).

83   **Malay archipelago**: Burgess lived in Malaya between 1954 and 1957, working as a teacher at the Malay College in Kuala Kangsar and at the Malayan Teachers' Training College at Kota Bharu. His experience there fed directly into his early novels *Time for a Tiger* (London: Heinemann, 1956), *The Enemy in the Blanket* (London: Heinemann, 1958) and *Beds in the East* (London: Heinemann, 1959), known collectively

as 'The Malayan Trilogy'. Burgess writes of his time in
Malaya in Chapter 6 of *Little Wilson and Big God*.

84   **Pygmalion and Galatea**: In Greek myth Pygmalion is a
sculptor who falls in love with a beautiful statue of a woman
he has created. The goddess Aphrodite brings the statue,
Galatea, to life and Pygmalion and Galatea marry.

85   **Iowa City**: Burgess lived in Iowa City while working as a visiting professor at the University of Iowa in
1975.

85   **Windhover Press**: private press established by Kim K.
Merker in 1967 and sponsored by the University of Iowa.
'Windhover' is also the title of a poem by Gerard Manley
Hopkins.

85   *Searfskin*: the typescript appears to read 'Searfskin', with the
'e' added in Burgess's hand over a typed 'c'.

86   **St Patrick's Cathedral**: designed by James Renwick Jr.
(1818–1895) and opened in 1879. In *New York* Burgess
writes of the 'neo-Gothic grandeur (or is it horror?) of St.
Patrick's Cathedral' (p. 16).

86   **Jack's Tavern**: an allusion perhaps to the Boar's Head
Tavern in Shakespeare's *1 Henry IV* where Hal and Falstaff
often meet, their relationship perhaps providing a model for
that of Val and Willett.

86   **he had played Orson Welles in a dramatisation ... of that
ancient radio adaptation of the other Wells's *War of the
Worlds***: a reference to the 1975 film *The Night That Panicked
America*, directed by Joseph Sargent. The film dramatises
the mass panic inspired by Welles's radio play of H.G.
Wells's novel *The War of the Worlds* (1898) on 30 October
1938. Orson Welles (1915–1985) was played by Paul Shenar
(1936–1989). Burgess had written a musical about Houdini
for Welles in 1972.

86   **Shitabed scoundrel, slapsauce druggel, jobbernol
gnatsnapper, codshead looby, turdgut**: from Rabelais. See
note to p. 48, a slabberdegullion druggel.

86   **each and every one**: the typescript reads 'each and every-

one'. This is amended in *The End of the World News* to 'each and every one' and the same is done here.

86   **LIVEDOG**: 'god evil' reversed. The name appears in Burgess's novel *The Wanting Seed*: '"We are both God and the Devil, though not at the same time. Only Mr Livedog can be that, and Mr Livedog, of course, is a mere fictional symbol." All the boys smiled. They all loved *The Adventures of Mr Livedog* in the *Cosmicomic*. Mr Livedog was a big fubsy demiurge who, *sufflaminandus* like Shakespeare, spawned unwanted life all over the earth' (p. 12). See also *Little Wilson and Big God*, p. 63, and *This Man and Music* (London: Hutchinson, 1982), pp. 176–7.

87   **California, seedbed of crank faiths**: Discussing *Puma* in his 1975 interview 'Working on Apocalypse', Burgess says of California, 'it's always been associated in my mind with apocalypse and magic and astrology and the like' (p. 44).

87   **codshead jobbernols**: from Rabelais. See note to p. 48, a slabberdegullion druggel.

87   **Sixth Avenue (which had once been called the Avenue of the Americas)**: Burgess notes in *New York* that New Yorkers evince 'a certain pride in refusing to accept the renaming of Sixth Avenue as the Avenue of the Americas' (p. 49).

87   **Man is born to trouble**: 'Yet man is born unto trouble, as the sparks fly upward' (Job 5:7).

87   **wordman**: Writing in *Nothing Like the Sun: A Story of Shakespeare's Love-Life* (London: Heinemann, 1964), Burgess describes the young Shakespeare as a 'word-boy' (p. 12).

88   **Oh I have been to Ludlow Fair/And left my necktie God knows where/And carried halfway home or near/Pints and quarts of Ludlow beer**: lines from the second verse of A.E. Housman's poem 'Terence, this is stupid stuff' in *A Shropshire Lad* (1896).

88   **Lob-dotterel**: from Rabelais. See note to p. 48, a slabberdegullion druggel.

88   **Noddie-peak simpleton. Idle lusk. Saucy coxcomb:** from
      Rabelais. See note to p. 48, a slabberdegullion druggel.

89   **millicents:** a slang term for 'police'. The word appears in *A
      Clockwork Orange* with the same meaning. Likely derived
      from the Russian 'Militsiya' (police force). Discussing his
      time in Russia in *You've Had Your Time*, Burgess writes of
      'uniformed *militsioners*' (p. 45). Not in *OED*.

89   **minutemen:** militiamen ready for immediate military ser-
      vice (*OED*).

89   **emergies:** police/emergency services. Not in *OED*.

89   **specials:** an abbreviation of 'special constable'. 'B-Specials'
      was a slang term for the Ulster Special Constabulary, formed
      in 1920 and disbanded in 1970 following allegations of polit-
      ical bias. Not in *OED*.

89   **It's trunch trunch truncheon does the trick, wrote
      somebody, Kipling, Beerbohm, somebody:** from Max
      Beerbohm's parody of Rudyard Kipling, 'P.C., X, 36 by
      R*d**rd K*pl*ng', in *A Christmas Garland* (1912).

89   **gog:** 'A euphemistic substitute for *God*' (*OED*).

89   **shitabed scrotflogs:** from Rabelais. See note to p. 48, a slab-
      berdegullion druggel.

89   **'Dark dark dark,' quoted Willett, 'we all go into the dark.':**
      Willett, and his unnamed respondent, are quoting the first
      lines of the third section of Eliot's 'East Coker' (1940). Eliot
      himself is probably alluding to Milton's dramatic poem
      Samson Agonistes (published 1671): 'O dark, dark, dark,
      amid the blaze of noon' (line 80).

89   **Thou toilest not, neither dost thou spin:** from Matthew
      6:28: 'Consider the lilies of the field, how they grow; they
      toil not, neither do they spin.'

89   **nicks and lockups:** slang (orig. Austral.): 'A prison; a
      lock-up, *esp.* one at a police station. Also: a police station'
      (*OED*). In British slang 'nick' is commonly used both as a
      verb 'to capture' and as a noun 'police station'.

90   **Tide-time ... Wait for no man:** allusion to the well-known
      phrase, 'Time and tide wait for no man'.

90   **gooseturd colour**: a yellowish green. Mentioned in scene two of Ben Jonson's *The Alchemist*: 'The citizens gape at her, and praise her tires,/And my lord's goose-turd bands, that rides with her!'

90   **'Go, devil ... Toilest'**: wordplay, God – evil. 'Toilest' is a reversal of 'T.S. Eliot'.

91   **A tavern in the village. The Minetta**: Minetta Tavern was opened in Greenwich Village in 1937. The Minetta is also referenced in Burgess's 1968 novel *Enderby Outside* (p. 9).

92   **megalal**: aeroplane's public address system. Not in *OED*.

92   **Standard Yankee**: for Burgess on American English, see his essays 'English as an America' in *Urgent Copy: Literary Studies* (London: Cape, 1968), pp. 213–21, and 'Anglo-American' in *Homage to Qwert Yuiop: Selected Journalism 1978–1985* (London: Hutchinson, 1986), pp. 143–5, and his book *A Mouthful of Air*.

92   **magical mystery tour**: EP, song and film by the Beatles released in 1967. Burgess was not a fan. See *You've Had Your Time*, p. 77.

92   **scediastist**: see note to p. 74, scediastics.

93   **'All intrepid captains and mates,' he trolled, 'and those who went down, doing their duty.' ... a regular sea symphony**: Willett is quoting from Walt Whitman's poem 'Song for All Seas, All Ships' (1855). The poem provided the words to Ralph Vaughan Williams's 'A Sea Symphony', first performed in 1910.

93   *molto accel.*: Italian musical terms *molto* 'very much' and *accelerando* 'gradually getting faster'.

93   **'An eighteenth-century sailor's life,' said Willett. 'A jail sentence with the risk of drowning added ...'**: Willett is quoting from James Boswell's *The Life of Samuel Johnson* (1791).

94   **Politian**: an allusion to an unfinished play by Edgar Allan Poe, 'Scenes from Politian, an unpublished Drama. By Edgar A. Poe', *Southern Literary Messenger*, December 1835, pp. 17–26.

94   **diarrheally**: a reference to diarrhoea. Not in *OED*.

95   **Götterdämmerung**: the last in Richard Wagner's cycle of four music dramas *Der Ring des Nibelungen*. The same reference to Wagner appears in *The Enemy in the Blanket* (p. 117), where it refers to the end of the British Empire.

95   **THOTHMES**: the third pharaoh of the 18th dynasty of Egypt.

96   **time and the hour running through the roughest night**: lines spoken by Macbeth: 'Time and the hour runs through the roughest day' (I, iii).

96   **Laocoön**: 'The name of a legendary Trojan priest who, with his two sons, was crushed to death by two sea-serpents' (*OED*).

99   **philosophy was once regarded as the clearing-house, or interpretative unifier, of the various sciences**: an allusion to discussions of the nature of scientific rationalism in the work of positivist philosophers in the 1960s.

100   **Kazan**: Elia Kazan (1909–2003), an influential Greek-American director, producer, writer and actor.

100   **Barnum**: Phineas Taylor Barnum (1810–1891), American showman.

100   **Wollcott**: Hotel Wolcott in Manhattan, New York City, designed by the architect John H. Duncan.

101   **Lieutenant Wetmore**: *The Lieutenant Governor* (1904) is a novel by Guy Wetmore Carryl (1873–1904).

102   **Will Rogers airport**: Will Rogers World Airport, in Oklahoma City, Oklahoma, is named after the actor, vaudeville performer and writer Will Rogers (1879–1935).

102   **Toscanini**: Arturo Toscanini (1867–1957), Italian conductor.

103   **Sullivan's 'Lost Chord'**: a song composed in 1877 by the English composer Arthur Seymour Sullivan (1842–1900). For Burgess on Sullivan, see his review of the biography *Arthur Sullivan: A Victorian Musician by Arthur Jacobs*, reprinted as 'S. Without G.' in *Homage to Qwert Yuiop*, pp. 569–72.

103   **Maria Gropius**: The typescript reads 'Maria Calvin'; this apparent error is amended here.

104   *'E vidi,'* he recited, filling them with Sharpas Super. *'Ed ecco una nube bianca, e sopra la nube uno seduto simile a un figlio d'uomo, avente sopra la sua testa una corona d'oro ...'*: from Revelation 14:14: 'And I looked, and behold a white cloud, and upon the cloud one sat like unto the Son of man, having on his head a golden crown' (Italian).

104   **Bibbia**: the Bible (Italian).

104   **an Italian Protestant, one of the Mid-West Florio congregation**: an allusion to the author and teacher of languages John Florio (1553–1625). Florio, the London-born son of an Italian protestant, appears in Burgess's novels *Nothing Like the Sun* and *ABBA ABBA*.

104   **pornograph**: a pornographic work. Burgess uses the term in the preface to *You've Had Your Time*: 'There is never any self-indulgence in writing, unless it be a pornograph for personal use' (p. vii). The word first appears in Burgess's lecture 'Obscenity and the Arts', delivered in June 1970 and later published as a pamphlet by the Malta Library Association (1973). The word, listed in the *OED*, has fallen out of current usage.

104   **Tiziano**: allusion to the Italian painter Tiziano Vecelli (c.1488/90–1576), better known in English as Titian.

105   **telecams**: television cameras. Not in *OED*.

105   **dogfaces**: foot soldiers in the United States army (military slang).

106   **Tagliaferro**: 'Iron-cutter' from the Italian *tagliare* (to cut) and *ferro* (iron). Burgess writes of his experience of the New York Mafia in *You've Had Your Time*, noting, 'one of [Burgess's son] Andrea's teachers had actually married on to the outer rim of the Tagliaferro family' (p. 233), and later being warned that Paolo Andrea was 'on the kidnap list' (p. 321) by an Italian member of the Tagliaferro family. Burgess would reuse the name in *Earthly Powers*, where he writes of 'the late Mrs Tagliaferro' (p. 13). In February 1975 Burgess wrote the outline for a novel, provisionally titled *The Mafia Tree* (the outline is held in archives of the IABF, Manchester, AAT/10).

106   **Salvatore**: saviour (Italian).

106   *sacra merda*: holy shit (Italian).

106   **Princeton, New Jersey**: Burgess was a Visiting Fellow at Princeton (1970/71) where he instructed students in creative writing.

106   **Jack the Seer**: a possible play on the name 'Shakespeare'. Burgess playfully explores the possible variants of Shakespeare's name at length in his illustrated biography *Shakespeare* (London: Cape, 1970).

106   **Lady Day**: Feast of the Annunciation (25 March).

106   **go west, young men**: 'Go west, young man', a popular American saying of the nineteenth century. Of uncertain origin, the phrase is usually credited to *New York Tribune* editor Horace Greeley (1811–1872). See *New York*, p. 80.

106   **The Florentine Hotel**: in the first version of the *Puma* script this becomes 'The Fiorentina': 'an ornate building, like Caesar's Palace, Las Vegas' (p. 57).

106   **a rapid quietus**: ending of life, an allusion to Hamlet's famous 'To be, or not to be?' soliloquy: 'When he himself might his quietus make/With a bare bodkin' (III, I, 74–5).

106   **death-mechanics**: assassins. *OED* lists 'mechanic' as a slang for 'hired killer'.

106   **Fontainebleau Hotel**: allusion to the Fontainebleau Miami Beach, designed by Morris Lapidus and opened in 1954.

106   **Protestants, it was known, could be trusted more than Catholics**: here Burgess echoes a sentiment expressed in *New York* where, talking of the immigrants to the city in the 1900s, he notes that: 'The Irish, although English-speaking and legal children of Great Britain, were looked down upon because they were Catholic, while the Germans, knowing no English, were acceptable because they were Protestant. Protestantism was the religion of hard work, cleanliness, education, advancement' (p. 34).

107   **sky-pilot**: a chaplain (slang), 'esp. one serving in the armed

forces or among sailors' (*OED*). The term 'sky pilot' appears in the 'Cyclops' episode of James Joyce's *Ulysses* (Paris: Shakespeare and Company, 1922), p. 298.

107 **Maranzana family**: an allusion to Salvatore Maranzano (1886–1931), one of the most powerful of the New York Mafiosi. Also a joking reference to the actor Mario Maranzana, a friend of Burgess's from Rome.

107 *Babbo*: daddy, informal (Italian).

107 *puttane*: whores (Italian).

107 *Un whisky liscio*: a neat whiskey (Italian).

108 **male Scottish evening dress**: Burgess recounts his son Paolo Andrea's adoption of the Scottish identity in *You've Had Your Time*: 'He wore the tartan of the Wilson sept of the Gunn clan ... He was to be called Andrew Burgess Wilson' (p. 344).

108 *Ptolemy* **suite**: The Ptolemaic dynasty ruled Hellenistic Egypt from 305 BC to 30 BC. This is misspelt in the typescript where it reads 'Ptolomy'; the error, corrected in *The End of the World News* (p. 199), is also corrected here.

108 **b.o.f.i**: This acronym, which appears throughout the novel, stands here for 'Beware of French imitations'. See also note to p. 29.

109 **Tchaikovsky panatelas**: allusion to the Russian composer Pyotr Ilyich Tchaikovsky (1840–1893).

109 **THE GARDENS OF ALLAH MOST HIGH**: an allusion to the Garden of Allah hotel, California.

109 **New Yorkers have seen everything and live in a perpetual state of fear**: an allusion to General Douglas MacArthur's Address to the Annual Stockholders Sperry Rand Corporation (30 July 1957): 'Our government has kept us in a perpetual state of fear — kept us in a continuous stampede of patriotic fervor — with the cry of grave national emergency. Always there has been some terrible evil at home or some monstrous foreign power that was going to gobble us up if we did not blindly rally behind it by furnishing the exorbitant funds demanded. Yet, in retrospect, these disas-

ters seem never to have happened, seem never to have been quite real.' Edward T. Imparato (ed.), *General MacArthur Speeches and Reports 1908–1964* (Nashville, TN: Turner Publishing Company, 2000), p. 206.

109 **Valentino**: an allusion to Rudolph Valentino, the stage name of the Italian-American actor Rodolfo Alfonso Raffaello Pierre Filibert Guglielmi di Valentina d'Antonguella (1895–1926).

109 **durovit**: a reinforced glass, the initial sound likely derived from 'durable'. Not in *OED*.

109 **Brooklyn Bridge**: Burgess discusses the political significance of the Brooklyn Bridge in *New York* (pp. 63–4).

109 **a new savage disruptor of western civilisation from the fierce lands of barbaric warriors**: the Goths, the Germanic tribes that invaded the Eastern and Western Empires in the third, fourth and fifth centuries.

110 **Ezra Winter**: Ezra Augustus Winter (1886–1949), American muralist.

111 **Puma, lord and vassal**: the typescript reads 'Puma, lord and vassal'. This appears to be a typographical error on Burgess's part (*The End of the World News* has 'vassal') and has been changed here.

111 **JACOB RIIS BALLROOM**: Jacob Riis (1849–1914), was a Danish-American writer, photographer and social reformer. His book *How the Other Half Lives* (1890) documented the lives of New York's poor. Riis discusses the dancing and ball-rooms of the poor in Chapter 14 of *The Battle With the Slum* (1902). See *New York*, p. 46.

111 **massy**: 'Solid and weighty' (*OED*).

112 *Blue Danube*: English title of Johann Strauss II's 'An der schönen blauen Donau', Op. 314 (1866).

112 **Time and the hour run through the roughest**: an aside spoken by Macbeth (I, iii, 150). For a fuller discussion of this passage, see the chapter 'How did Shakespeare speak his lines?' in *A Mouthful of Air*, pp. 217–21.

112 **the old Guthrie**: the Guthrie Theatre was founded in 1963

by Sir Tyrone Guthrie. Burgess writes of his work for the Guthrie in *You've Had Your Time* (p. 210).

112   **Pickwick Coffee Shop**: an allusion to Charles Dickens's first novel *The Posthumous Papers of the Pickwick Club* (1836–1837).

113   **Mr Weill**: allusion to the German composer Kurt Julian Weill (1900–1950). Weill became an American citizen in 1943 and lived in New York.

113   **Mrs Wolheim**: allusion to the New York-born American actor Louis R. Wolheim (1880–1931).

113   **Mr Terhune**: allusion to the American author Albert Payson Terhune (1872–1942).

113   **Steinway**: Steinway & Sons are an American-German piano company, founded in 1853 by Heinrich Engelhard Steinweg in Manhattan, New York. Burgess bought a new Steinway upright piano in 1975 and installed it in his Bracciano house.

114   **two sons, twins**: the typescript reads 'two sins, twins'. This is amended in *The End of the World News* to 'sons' and the same is done here. However, the rhyme 'sins/twins' might suggest that Burgess intended this as a Freudian slip on Willett's part.

114   **Maupertius, Clausius, Cassini, even Hell**: these are all names of lunar craters. 'Maupertius' is misspelt – it should read 'Maupertuis'. The error stands in *The End of the World News* and is left uncorrected here.

114   **There seems to be some ancient inexplicable law**: Val is referring to the Titius–Bode Law.

115   **Ptolemaic terms, not Copernican**: the Ptolemaic is an Earth-centred model of the universe, while the Copernican model places the sun at the centre of the solar system. Burgess writes in *Little Wilson and Big God* (p. 187) that, as a schoolboy, he planned an opera about Copernicus and his discovery of the heliocentric universe. The typescript reads 'Ptolomaic', this is corrected here.

115   **AWOL**: absent without leave (army slang).

The Desirable Sight: this book title is taken from the sixth line of Gerard Manley Hopkins's poem 'Moonrise'.

115 **The future hasn't come into being yet ... profusion of its flowers**: an allusion to the discussion of time in book eleven of Augustine's *Confessions*, perhaps as it comes to influence Eliot's *Four Quartets*. See Eliot, *Collected Poems*, pp. 187–223.

116 **mazurka**: a Polish folk dance.

116 **dirty grey-green-white sloggering knouts**: Burgess uses a similar phrasing to describe the sea in his novel *A Vision of Battlements*: 'Over the decks salty knouts of broken sea lunged and sloggered' (p. 23) and again in *The Clockwork Testament* where he writes of 'the rash-smart sloggering brine' (p. 45). This last example is a line from Gerard Manley Hopkins's poem 'The Wreck of the Deutschland' (1918).

119 **uricon-based**: Uricon is a city in the poem 'On Wenlock Edge' from A.E. Housman's *A Shropshire Lad*.

119 **crack of doom**: 'The last or great Judgement at the end of the world' (*OED*). An allusion to Shakespeare's *Macbeth*, 'What will the line stretch out to' th' cracke of Doome?' (IV, i, 133). In the Foreword to *Here Comes Everybody: An Introduction to James Joyce for the Ordinary Reader* (London: Faber, 1965), Burgess remarks: 'Another book about James Joyce? Yes, and very far from being the last or anywhere near the last. Indeed (What, will the line stretch out till crack of Bloom?) it must be regarded as coming very early in the series' (p. 11).

119 **protoploion**: (first) spaceship. Formed by combining 'proto-' meaning original and 'ploion', a Greek generic term for ship or boat. Not in *OED*.

119 **ploiarchal**: see note to p. 74, ploiarch.

119 **heliergs**: power generators. A combination of *hēlios* (sun, Greek) and 'erg' (unit of energy). Not in *OED*.

120 **magnetotechnasma**: technology based on magnetism. Not in *OED*.

120 **To burrow under the wire was a dream derived from old**

scratched movies about prisoner-of-war camps in World War whatever-it-was, I, II, III: likely an allusion to film *The Great Escape* (1963) directed by John Sturges.

120   **Stanford Everard Whiteboy:** the Whiteboys were a secret Irish organisation who defended tenant farmer rights. The connection to Ireland is supported by the name Everard which reprises the title of Matthew Archdeacon's novel *Everard: An Irish Tale of 19th Century* (1835).

121   **Colonel Fernando Jefferson:** allusion to Thomas Jefferson (1743–1826), third President of the United States of America, and the principal author of the Declaration of Independence.

121   **Captain Truslove:** a character from Evelyn Waugh's 1952 novel *Men at Arms*. Burgess includes the 'Sword of Honour' trilogy (of which *Men at Arms* forms the first part) in his *Ninety-Nine Novels.*

121   **Speight van:** John [Johnny] Speight (1920–1998), British comedy scriptwriter best known for his work on *The Arthur Haynes Show* (ITV, 1957–1966) and *Till Death Us Do Part* (BBC, 1966–1975).

121   **booby hatch:** used here as to indicate an access door, the term is American slang for 'a home for the insane' (*OED*).

121   **auzesis trays:** presumably from the biological 'auxesis' from the Greek for growth. In plant physiology, auxetic substances increase cell growth.

121   **heliodiscs:** a coinage of Burgess's own. From the Greek *hēlios*, meaning sun.

123   **Jack, Joe and Curly:** allusion to the American vaudeville act 'The Three Stooges', whose line-up in the 1930s and 1940s featured Larry, Moe and Curly (Larry Fine, Moe Howard and Curly Howard).

123   **Stokes:** allusion to the American publisher Frederick Abbott Stokes (1857–1939), the founder of the Frederick A. Stokes Company.

123   **dangerous Geoff Grigson:** allusion to the British poet and editor Geoffrey Edward Harvey Grigson (1905–1985). Grigson reviewed Burgess's work unfavourably, a fact that

clearly upset Burgess who recalls the review of *Urgent Copy* ('Insatiable Liking?' in *Listener*, 7 November 1968, pp. 618–9) in *You've Had Your Time*: 'Grigson is now dead, but I abate none of my resentment at his allegation of my coarseness' (p. 243).

125 **Scribner**: allusion to the New York publisher Charles Scribner's Sons.

125 *Trophimonistics*: relating to food production/consumption. 'Trophi' is defined in the *OED* as: 'A mouthpart or feeding organ in certain other invertebrates'. Not in *OED*.

126 *a happy ship*: an allusion to Lord Louis Mountbatten's speech to the crew of the HMS *Kelly*, reproduced in Noël Coward's 1942 film *In Which We Serve*: 'In my experience, you cannot have an efficient ship unless you have a happy ship, and you cannot have a happy ship unless you have an efficient ship … and that is the way I intend to go on – with a happy and an efficient ship.'

126 **never never never**: allusion to the patriotic British song 'Rule, Britannia!' written by James Thomson and set to music by Thomas Arne in 1740. The song, often associated with the navy, includes the refrain: 'Rule, Britannia! rule the waves:/Britons never shall be slaves.'

128 **selenostations of earth**: see note to p. 67, selenologist.

128 **Vitruvius, Zagut and Schneckenberg … Sheepshanks**: areas on earth's moon.

128 **Day of Independence**: American holiday celebrating the Declaration of Independence on 4 July 1776.

128 **Bidu Saarinen**: allusion to the Finnish-American architect Eero Saarinen (1910–1961). Saarinen designed New York City's Trans World Flight Center (opened 1962).

128 **Florenz Zenger**: this name is an amalgamation of Florenz Ziegfeld (1867–1932) and John Peter Zenger (1697–1746). Ziegfeld was a Broadway impresario remembered for his *Ziegfeld Follies*. Zenger was the publisher and editor of the *New York Weekly Journal*. The two names follow one another in the index to Burgess's *New York* (p. 200).

129   **Toynbee:** (Theodore) Philip Toynbee (1916–1981), an English writer named by Burgess in *You've Had Your Time* in a list of 'the cream of the British Littérateurs' (p. 104). Toynbee had published an unfavourable review of *The Clockwork Testament* a few months before Burgess wrote *Puma*. See 'Kicking the Bucket', *Observer*, 2 June 1974, p. 33.

129   **dollars' worth:** the typescript reads 'dollars worth'.

129   **womanising handsome clever bastard ... a man who had been assassinated in his forties in this very town:** John F. Kennedy (1917–1963), thirty-fifth President of the United States of America, was assassinated in Dallas, Texas, on 22 November 1963.

130   **Jello:** Jell-O, a brand name of a gelatine-based dessert. Established in the United States in 1897.

130   **The dream; Jennifer never tired of recounting her dream:** Burgess discusses his own experience of 'psychic visions' in *You've Had Your Time* (pp. 85–8).

130   **Go ye then to Dallas, safe in the Lord:** allusion to Psalm 91.

131   **in Geneva, Switzerland, under the man whose name was given to me at the font:** allusion to the French theologian John Calvin (1509–1564).

131   **And once in New England, many centuries ago:** an allusion to the Toleration Act (1689) by which nonconformists were granted the right to worship freely.

132   **Genesis 6:** Chapter 6 of Genesis tells the story of the destruction of humankind and the construction Noah's Ark.

132   **for it repenteth me that I have made them:** Genesis 6:7.

132   **But Noah found grace in the eyes of the Lord ... And Noah begat three sons:** Genesis 6: 8–10.

133   **And God said unto Noah ... Make thee an ark of gopher wood:** Genesis 6: 13–14.

133   **The animals went in two by two, hurrah, hurrah:** children's song sung to the tune of Patrick Gilmore's popular American Civil War song 'When Johnny Comes Marching Home' (1863).

135 **Peter Minuit Hotel:** Peter Minuit (*c.*1580–1638), director of the Dutch colony of New Netherland (1621–1631), is described by Burgess in *New York* as 'director-general of what was to become not only New York but also Connecticut, New Jersey and Long Island' (p. 10).

135 **Big Apple:** nickname for New York made popular in the 1920s by *New York Morning Telegraph* sportswriter John J. FitzGerald.

135 **Hiss Soups:** an allusion to Alger Hiss (1904–1996), an American State Department official convicted for perjury in 1950 following accusations that he had acted as a spy for the former Soviet Union. A picture of Hiss appears in Burgess's *New York* (p. 189).

135 **Seth Low Tasty Stews:** Seth Low (1850–1916) was the ninety-second mayor of New York City.

135 **Mensch Spongemeats:** a borrowing from the Yiddish 'mensh', meaning 'a person of integrity or rectitude' (*OED*). This is an allusion to the cannibalism in Burgess's novel *The Wanting Seed*; as Burgess remarks in *You've Had Your Time*, 'One of these days we may well buy *Munch* and discover that it is *Mensch*' (p. 34). In *The Clockwork Testament* Enderby cooks himself a meal of 'slices of spongy canned meat called Mensch or Munch or something' (p. 41).

135 **Piccirilli Pasta Treats:** see note to p. 74, Piccirilli, Attilia.

135 **Moshowitz Kosher Puddings:** another allusion to New York's Jewish population, which Burgess discusses in *New York* (p. 41).

135 **Marquis de Lafayette:** allusion to the French military officer Marie-Joseph Paul Yves Roch Gilbert du Motier, Marquis de Lafayette (1757–1834). Lafayette fought in the American Revolutionary War.

136 **bookspinstand in the skyreceplevel smokestore:** Burgess is combining words here (not in *OED*) to describe the bookstands outside a tobacconist store on the sky reception level.

136 ***Astronomy, Folks*:** perhaps an allusion to Isabel Martin Lewis's book *Astronomy for Young Folks* (1922).

136   **catchpenny titles**: 'Something (esp. a publication) of little value, designed to attract purchasers' (*OED*).

136   **moygashel**: a fine Irish linen produced in the mill town of the same name in County Tyrone, Northern Ireland.

136   **Joe Papps**: allusion to the American theatrical producer and director Joseph 'Joe' Papp (1921–1991), who established the Public Theatre in lower Manhattan in 1954.

137   **Chemical Bank**: an American bank chartered in 1824 in New York City. Chemical Bank merged with the Chase Manhattan Corporation in 1996.

138   **OLMSTEAD**: allusion to the American landscape architect Frederick Law Olmsted (1822–1903). Olmsted was the chief architect of Central Park. See *New York*, pp. 161–2.

138   **ISIDOR STRAUS**: Isidor Straus (1845–1912), American businessman and co-owner of Macy's Department Store.

139   **by his skin and teeth**: from Job 19:20: 'My bone cleaveth to my skin and to my flesh, and I am escaped with the skin of my teeth.'

139   **CRUNCHTHUMP GRAVELATORS**: the 'CRUNCH-THUMP' appears to be a fictitious brand of stone-crushing machine.

139   **WARREN AND WETMORE WETMIX**: Warren and Wetmore, an architecture firm in New York City known for their work on hotels.

139   **IF IT'S GOODY'S IT'S GOOD**: Goody Products, Inc., a producer of hair accessories for the American market founded in in 1907 by Henry Goodman. Also a possible allusion to Goody's Bar in Greenwich Village, New York. Burgess references Goody's Bar in his 1968 novel *Enderby Outside* (p. 9).

140   **flutch calf-lollies, turdy-guts and shitten shepherds**: from Rabelais. See note to p. 48, a slabberdegullion druggel.

140   **gat-toothed**: 'Having the teeth set wide apart' (*OED*). In *The Clockwork Testament* Enderby notes that his enemies include 'a gat-toothed black writer and his wife' (p. 10). 'Gat-tothed' is used in Chaucer's 'The Wife of Bath's Tale'.

140   'Honeybunch,' he called her, 'piggesnie, heartsease, bedworthy bundlesnuggle,': terms of endearment. 'Piggesnye' is used in Chaucer's *Miller's Tale*, and again, as 'Piggesnie', in Burgess's short story 'The Muse' in *Hudson Review*, vol. 21, no. 1 (1968), 109–26.

140   **collar-dogs or breast-badge**: military badges.

142   **astunomological**: see note to p. 74, astunomicologist.

143   **I've been thinking**: the typescript reads 'I'm been thinking'. This is amended in *The End of the World News* to 'I've been thinking' and the same is done here.

144   **eireneutis 6a**: a fictitious medication related to sterilisation or the suppression of sexual appetite. The word combines 'eire', a Middle English form of 'heir', and 'neuter' (castrate/ spay). Not in *OED*.

145   **gravity apotha**: a means by which to escape earth's gravitational pull. The prefix 'apo' is used here in the sense of 'standing off or away from each other, detached, separate' (*OED*). In the second *Puma* screenplay the gravity apotha is responsible for '[t]he increased atomic thrust that will make all the difference' (p. 94). Not in *OED*.

145   **megaproagon**: mega-thruster. 'Proag' has the meaning 'thrust' (*OED*). Not in *OED*.

145   **America Nova**: New America.

145   **conspectus**: 'A general view or comprehensive survey (with the mind's eye)' (*OED*).

145   **dyspneal**: 'of or belonging to dyspnœa', meaning 'Difficulty of breathing' (*OED*).

146   **The end justifies the means, but the means determines the nature of the end**: an allusion to Leon Trotsky's phrase: 'A means can be justified only by its end. But the end in its turn needs to be justified.' *Their Morals and Ours* (New York: Pathfinder Press, 5th edn, 1973), p. 48.

146   **A corporal work of mercy**: the seven corporal works of mercy are those tending to the bodily, material and physical needs of others.

146   **taps**: a corruption of 'tattoo'. 'Taps' is United

States military slang for a bugle call played at dusk.

147 **We few, we happy few, we band of brothers**: lines spoken by Henry V during the St Crispin's Day speech in Shakespeare's *Henry V* (IV, iii, 18–67).

147 **zombyishly**: a coinage meaning 'in the style of a zombie'. Not in *OED*.

148 *arrant* **thief**: from Shakespeare's *Timon of Athens*: 'The moon's an arrant thief,/And her pale fire she snatches from the sun' (IV, iii, 430–1).

148 **Dr McBean**: allusion to the American architect Thomas McBean, the designer of St Paul's Chapel in Manhattan.

149 **tigrine**: 'Of, pertaining to, or resembling a tiger' (*OED*).

151 **Poe Speedbird, Edgar Allan as he called it**: a reference to American writer Edgar Allan Poe (1809–1849). The Speedbird is the corporate logo of Imperial Airways, later British Airways, designed by Theyre Lee-Elliott in 1932.

151 **Sagamore Hill**: the residence of Theodore Roosevelt, twenty-sixth President of the United States, from 1885 until 1919.

152 *Baa Lamb's Ass*: an allusion to Numbers 22:21–38 in which Balaam's ass speaks. The sonnet 'Balaam's Ass', translated from Belli, appears in Burgess's novel *ABBA ABBA* (p. 107).

152 **Woolworth**: an allusion to the neo-gothic Woolworth Building in Manhattan, designed by Cass Gilbert (1859–1934) and completed in 1913 (for Burgess on Gilbert and New York skyscrapers, see *New York*, p. 16). The building features in a song in Burgess's musical *Trotsky's in New York!* The vocal score for this unproduced musical is held in the archives of the IABF, Manchester, MUS/1/7.

152 **C-notes**: 100-dollar bill (informal).

152 **Chivas Regal ... Claymore**: brands of blended Scotch whiskey.

154 **Ghersom**: Gershom was the first-born son of Moses and Zipporah (Exodus 2:22).

154   **Marquet:** Albert Marquet (1875–1947), French Fauvist painter.

154   **Dorothy Draper Museum:** Dorothy Draper (1889–1969), an American interior decorator, established the interior design company Dorothy Draper & Company in 1923. Among her commissions was the restaurant at the Metropolitan Museum of Art in 1954.

154   *Not to Call Night*: the title of Val's novel is taken from Gerard Manley Hopkins's poem 'Moonrise'.

155   **Angus Wilson:** Sir Angus Frank Johnstone Wilson (1913–1991), English novelist and biographer. Burgess includes Wilson's *The Old Men at the Zoo* (1961) and *Late Call* (1964) in his *Ninety-Nine Novels*. *The Old Men at the Zoo*, which is set in a future in which 'a federated Europe [is] growling at isolated Britain' (p. 82) provides a possible source of the Europe that Burgess explores in *Puma*.

155   **Bodley:** an allusion to the Bodley Head Press.

155   **The critics were always quick to leap on writers who hadn't done their homework:** Burgess would feel this first-hand when critics attacked him for inaccuracies in his historical novel *The Kingdom of the Wicked*. His response, 'The Anachronist Strikes Back', was published in the *Times Literary Supplement*, 2 August 1985, p. 850.

155   **Shitabed lobnoddy, foolish loggerhead ... turdstrewed:** from Rabelais. See note to p. 48, a slabberdegullion druggel.

156   **Arabology:** the study of Arabic texts and/or peoples. Not in *OED*.

156   **buddiuddy:** close to the colloquial 'buddy buddy' meaning pal or friend. Not in *OED*.

156   **The inalienable right of all Americans. Guaranteed by the Constitution. The pursuit of happiness, also of enemies and harmless uneatable animals:** an allusion to the Second Amendment of the United States Constitution, which guarantees 'the right of the people to keep and bear Arms'.

157   **bever:** 'A small repast between meals' (*OED*).

157   **long Columbus panatelas**: Columbus Cigars are produced in Honduras. A panatela is a thin cigar (a long panatela would be a lancero).

157   *moderato*: musical term meaning moderate speed.

158   **Aupnia**: from apnœa, 'the suspension of breathing' (*OED*). Not in *OED*.

158   **snakelong check**: presumably a long bill of sale. 'Snakelong' is not in *OED*.

158   **omniclef**: a device for lock picking. From 'omni-', meaning 'of all things' (*OED*), and 'clef', meaning 'key' (French). In *A Clockwork Orange*, Alex picks locks with a device called a 'polyclef'. Not in *OED*.

158   **stage Britishry**: exaggerated British accent. *OED* records 'Englishry' as a synonym for 'Englishness'. 'Britishry' is not in *OED*.

158   **Christ pedicate the bastard**: Burgess appears fond of the word pedicate, 'To practise pedication [anal intercourse] on (a person)' (*OED*). It occurs again in the song 'Copulation Without Population' in *Blooms of Dublin* (completed 1975) and in the novel *Earthly Powers*.

158   **Tophet**: a theological and poetic synonym for hell.

159   **chiliastic**: 'relating to, or holding the doctrine of the millennium' (*OED*). This doctrine is largely derived from Revelation 20: 1–6.

160   **David felled Goliath with a boy's catapult. Joshua ordered the moon to stand still. Moses fought.**: see 1 Samuel 17, Joshua 10:12 and Exodus 2:12.

161   *Quo Vadis*: a 1951 American epic film directed by Mervyn LeRoy.

161   *Ben Hur*: a 1959 American epic film directed by William Wyler and starring Charlton Heston.

161   *The Exorcist*: a 1973 American horror film directed by William Friedkin. Burgess reviewed William Peter Blatty's novel *The Exorcist*, on which the 1973 film is based, for the *New York Times* (11 February 1973).

161   **separated his neck from his shirt-collar**: the typescript

reads 'spearated.' This becomes 'separated' in *The End of the World News* (p. 294) and is likewise amended here.

161   **We have this little party**: In *The End of the World News* this line is followed by: 'Edwina said nothing. Nobody said anything. Then Edwina tightened her raincoat belt about her lost waist and said to Gropius:' (p. 294). This addition, not added here, makes clearer who is speaking the next lines.

163   **People get shot**: the typescript reads 'People got shot'. This is amended in *The End of the World News* to 'People get shot' and the same is done here.

165   **Berlioz orchestra**: French composer Louis-Hector Berlioz (1803–1869), author of the influential *Treatise on Instrumentation* (1844).

166   **supererogatorily**: a rare form of 'supererogatory': meaning 'beyond what is required or needed' (*OED*).

166   **and a gross black cat**: the typescript omits 'and'. The conjunction is added in *The End of the World News* and the same is done here.

166   **applejack**: a North American apple brandy. In African American slang, applejack is 'a generic name for a dance, esp. the current vogue step'. See Jonathon Green, *Chambers Slang Dictionary* (Edinburgh: Chambers, 2008).

166   **an eternal sensorium just to hold the memory**: While the phrasing appears to recall Isaac Newton's 'the sensorium of God' in *Opticks* (1704) Query 28 and Query 31, Appendix A, a more likely connection is to Augustine's discussion of memory and time in books 10 and 11 of his *Confessions* (c.397–400). Marshall McLuhan famously claimed that he wanted to cultivate 'the total sensorium of man' (*New York Times*, 29 January 1967). For Burgess on McLuhan, see his essay 'The Modicum is the Messuage' in *Spectator*, 13 October 1967, p. 427; reprinted in *Urgent Copy*, pp. 250–4.

166   **gentians**: plants belonging to the genus Gentiana. Perhaps an allusion to D.H. Lawrence's poem 'Bavarian Gentians' (1932), a poem Burgess set to music in 1985. Lawrence's

poem, written late in his life, is suffused with imagery about impending death.

166   **in the not to call night, the white and the walk of the morning:** from Gerald Manley Hopkins's poem 'Moonrise': 'I AWOKE in the Midsummer not to call night,/in the white and the walk of the morning'.

167   **Prophet. Zoroaster. Met his own. Image Walking. In the garden:** from Act 1 of Percy Bysshe Shelly's drama *Prometheus Unbound* (1820): 'Ere Babylon was dust,/The Magus Zoroaster, my dear child,/Met his own image walking in the garden.'

167   **I am *dying, Egypt, dying*:** lines spoken by Mark Antony in Shakespeare's *Antony and Cleopatra* (IV, xv, 19).

167   **1616:** the year of Shakespeare's death. Also the year in which Nicolaus Copernicus's *De revolutionibus orbium coelestium* [On the Revolutions of the Heavenly Spheres] (1543) was placed on the Index of Forbidden Books by decree of the Sacred Congregation.

168   **Shyly the sun rose:** recalling Charles Dickens's *A Tale of Two Cities* (1859): 'Sadly, sadly, the sun rose' (Book 2, Chapter 5).

168   **They left the nameless farm in the old way of picaresque novels – one, Willett the heavy, on horseback, Val, lighter, on the placid donkey:** a reference to Miguel de Cervantes Saavedra's Spanish novel *The Ingenious Nobleman Mister Quixote of La Mancha* (1605–1615). In the novel Don Quixote rides a horse (Rocinante), while his squire, Sancho Panza, rides a donkey (Dapple). The allusion is made clearer in the first version of the *Puma* script in which 'Willett carries a tree-branch as a lance' (p. 78).

168   **claw-buttock dance:** mimicking sexual intercourse. Likely derived from Rabelais's 'close buttock game' in Chapter 3 of the first volume of *Gargantua and Pantagruel*.

168   **Roma Rocket:** Burgess describes Roma Rocket, a fortified Californian red wine, in *You've Had Your Time*: 'a mixture of grape juice and raw alcohol' (p. 206).

168   **mots:** *OED* has 'mot' as an alternative spelling of 'mort': 'A promiscuous woman or girl.'

169   **Howard Johnson motel:** an American chain of hotels. In an early example of product placement, Howard Johnson's logos appear in the film *2001: A Space Odyssey* (1968).

170   **Oldsmobile:** brand of American car produced by General Motors.

171   **'I could lie down,' quoted Willett unconvincingly, 'like a tired child and weep away this life of care.':** Willett is quoting Percy Bysshe Shelley's 'Stanzas Written in Dejection, near Naples' (1818).

171   **Albergo:** hotel (Italian).

171   **Havana Hermositos:** Cuban cigars. The Cuban brand Romeo y Julieta produce a cigar called the 'Hermosa' (Spanish, meaning 'beautiful').

171   **.45 Beaufort:** a fictitious brand of .45 calibre handgun whose name recalls the Beaufort Scale by which wind speed is measured.

173   **Your duty as a wife, as the helpmeet of the last living servant of the Lord:** see Genesis 2:20: 'And Adam gave names to all cattle, and to the fowl of the air, and to every beast of the field; but for Adam there was not found an help meet for him.'

173   **by-blow:** 'an illegitimate child, a bastard' (*OED*)

174   **Bloomsday, boomsday, doomsday:** Bloomsday (16 June) is a celebration of the life and works of James Joyce. Burgess's operetta *Blooms of Dublin* was first performed on BBC Radio during the centenary celebrations in 1982.

176   **pumatic asylums:** a play on words; 'lunatic asylums'.

176   **won'tcocks:** a play on words that alludes to the woodcock, a migratory bird allied to the snipe. Here the 'fat young man' could be suggesting that he knows that Val is being disingenuous: the *OED* notes the use of woodcock as 'a type of gullibility or folly' (obsolete.).

177   **scintillacy:** from 'scintilla' meaning a spark or sparkling. Not in *OED*.

177   **Thunder spoke ... DAAAAAA**: The Sanskrit words spoken by the thunder in Eliot's poem *The Waste Land* ('Datta, Dayadhvam, Damyata') translate into English as 'Give, Sympathise, Control'. Nabby Adams, Fenella Crabbe and Alladad Khan discuss this passage in Burgess's novel *Time for a Tiger* (p. 134).

177   **Drawlatch hoydens ... Christ All Grouthead Gnatsnapper Mighty**: from Rabelais. See note to p. 48, a slabberdegullion druggel.

177   **Somme mustard**: mustard gas, a chemical weapon used during the First World War at the Battle of the Somme (1916).

177   **These, in the day that heaven was falling,/The our when earth's foundations fled,/Followed their military calling/ And took their wages, and are dead**: Willett is quoting from A.E. Housman's poem 'Epitaph on an Army of Mercenaries' (1917).

177   **Houseman**: an allusion to the English poet Alfred Edward Housman (1859–1936). There isn't a town called Houseman in Missouri.

177   **carpark**: typescript has 'carpack'. Corrected here.

177   **ILLIONS**: allusion to Marcus Charles Illions (1871–1949), the renowned American carver of wooden carousel horses who lived in New York City.

178   **white-robed end-of-the-worlders**: Revelation 6:11. 'And white robes were given unto every one of them; and it was said unto them, that they should rest yet for a little season, until their fellow servants also and their brethren, that should be killed as they were, should be fulfilled.'

178   **And I saw a new heaven and a new earth**: Revelation 21:1–2.

178   **the mountains in the Song that is Solomon's**: Song of Solomon 2:8, 'The voice of my beloved! behold, he cometh leaping upon the mountains, skipping upon the hills.'

178   **gewgaws**: 'A gaudy trifle, plaything, or ornament, a pretty thing of little value, a toy or bauble' (*OED*).

178   **Kopple sub-machine guns**: allusion to the American film director Barbara Kopple (1946–).

178   **Lefferts hipfirers, a Munsey Angel**: the names of these guns allude to areas in New York. Prospect Lefferts Gardens is a residential area in New York City. Munsey Park is a village in Nassau County, New York.

178   **Why should a fucking mouse have life and they be fucking dead?**: 'Why should a dog, a horse, a rat have life,/And thou no breath at all?' *King Lear* (V, iii, 282–3).

179   **Oh Jesus, oh Jesus lover of my soul**: allusion to Charles Wesley's hymn 'Jesus, Lover of My Soul' (1740).

180   **The sweet by-and-by**: *In the Sweet By and By* (1868), a Christian hymn written by S. Fillmore Bennett with music by Joseph P. Webster.

181   **woman's perfidy**: an allusion to Chapter 56 of Charles Dickens' *The Old Curiosity Shop* (1841) in which Dick Swiveller remarks, 'I shall wear this emblem of woman's perfidy, in remembrance of her with whom I shall never again thread the windings of the mazy'.

181   **Lot's wife Sara, looking back**: allusion to Genesis 19, in which Lot's wife is turned into a pillar of salt.

183   **Franco-German-Italian Defrit**: the name of this space ship is derived from the first two letters of the native-language names of each of the three countries involved in its construction: Deutschland, France, Italia.

184   **'... *Scientia non satis est*. Knowledge,' he translated, 'is not enough ...'**: perhaps an allusion to Sir Francis Bacon's 'scientia ipsa potentia est' [knowledge itself is power] in *Meditationes Sacrae* (1597). Also, possibly, an allusion to the *Satires* of Horace, Book 1, Satire 4, line 54: 'Non satis est puris versum perscribere verbis' [It is not enough to write out a line of simple words].

184   **Eat me, drink me. Rather sacramental**: an allusion to John 6:53–7.

185   **elasticom**: a material with elastic properties. Not in *OED*.

185   **the stern daughter of the voice of God**: the first line of

William Wordsworth's 'Ode to Duty' (written 1805, published 1807).

185   **zeugaromatologist**: an expert in match-making or breeding. From the Ancient Greek 'zeugma' [ζεῦγμα] 'a yoking' (*OED*). Not in *OED*.

186   **showing big horse-teeth**: the phrase appears in Thomas Wolfe's 1937 novella *The Lost Boy* (Chapel Hill: University of North Carolina Press, 1992): 'He saw Grover and bared his big horse teeth' (p. 5). Burgess spent a semester as a visiting professor at the State University of North Carolina at Chapel Hill where Wolfe was educated, writing in *You've Had Your Time*: 'to my shock I found, on my campus wanderings, a plaque dedicated to him buried in the long grass. He had been forgotten' (p. 205).

189   **I scream, you scream,/We all scream/For ice cream:/Rah! Rah! Rah!**: lyrics from 'Ice Cream' (1927), a novelty song with words and music by Howard Johnson, Billy Moll and Robert A.K. King.

189   **Colonel Nutt**: an allusion to the American entertainer Commodore Nutt (1848–1881). Nutt was a dwarf who was hired by P.T. Barnum and appeared at the American Museum in New York.

189   **Major Barbara**: the title of a play by George Bernard Shaw, premiered in 1905 and published in 1907.

189   **Shorty**: possibly confirming, and continuing, the allusion to Commodore Nutt.

189   **Meatball**: In American slang, a meatball is 'a stupid person'. The earliest recorded usage is from the 1920s. Green lists it as a variation of 'meathead'. 'Meat balls' are the testicles.

190   **Better to travel hopefully than arrive at hope's fulfilment**: an allusion to Robert Louis Stevenson's *Virginibus Puerisque and Other Papers* (1881), where he writes: 'To travel hopefully is a better thing than to arrive.'

191   **Faint heart**: given Willett's proclivity to quote Shakespeare, this is likely an allusion to *Venus and Adonis* (1593), 'The thought of it doth make my faint heart bleed' (line 669), or

his *Rape of Lucrece* (1594), 'Faint not, faint heart, but stoutly say "So be it:"' (line 1209).

191   **Elias Howe**: American inventor (1819–1867). In *New York* Burgess discusses 'the sewing machine that Howe fathered in 1846' (p. 97).

193   **playing checkers**: an allusion perhaps to the Three Stooges short *Tassels in the Air* (1938), in which Curly and Larry play checkers.

195   *fratello*: brother (Italian).

195   **'Self-defence,' he said, following an old Pentagon policy, 'is best done by getting in first.'**: an allusion to the Pentagon's 'first strike' (or pre-emptive strike) policy in relation to the use of nuclear weapons.

195   *anticipatory retaliation*: in *1985* (London: Hutchinson, 1978), Burgess writes: 'The Pentagon is given to using expressions like "anticipatory retaliation", meaning unprovoked assault' (p. 44).

196   **Hutchinson hipman**: an allusion to the British publisher Hutchinson who would publish much of Burgess's fiction from the late 1970s onwards.

196   **ammogiros**: rotating ammunition magazine. Formed by combining 'ammo' (ammunition) and 'giro' (from 'gyre' meaning revolving). Not in *OED*.

197   **Lescaze**: allusion to Swiss-born American architect William Edmond Lescaze (1896–1969). Lescaze was one of the pioneers of modernism in American architecture.

199   **Albee**: allusion to Edward Franklin Albee III (1928–2016), an American playwright who was awarded Pulitzer prizes for his plays *A Delicate Balance* (1967), *Seascape* (1975) and *Three Tall Women* (1994).

199   **John Donne**: English poet and Church of England clergyman (1572–1631).

201   **Jolson's eyes were big as though exaggerated by blackface**: an allusion to American singer and actor Al Jolson (1886–1950). Jolson performed in blackface, theatrical make-up used by non-black performers representing black charac-

ters, in *The Jazz Singer* (1927). For Burgess on Jolson and blackface, see *New York*, p. 120. Jolson also features in *The Pianoplayers* (p. 72).

202   ***Assoluzione, penitenza***: Absolution, penance (Italian).

204   **Hecate**: from Greek myth, a goddess, daughter of Perses and Asteria associated with the moon and, among many other things, childbirth.

204   **dickybird hop**: 'Dicky Bird Hop' (1926) was a children's song with words by Leslie Sarony and music by Ronald Gourley. Popular versions were sung by Gracie Fields in 1938 and Ann Stephens in 1941. 'Bird' is aviation slang for helicopter, hence a dickybird hop is a ride in a helicopter.

206   **chartopaigniologist**: a neologism that Burgess glosses in the novel as 'an expert in gambling' (p. 206). The word combines 'charto' (from the Latin charta 'paper, leaf of paper', which, in fourteenth-century Italian has the equivalent 'carta' meaning 'playing-card'), 'paignion' (the Greek equivalent of *jeu d'esprit* [game of the mind]) and '-ologist' (expert).

207   **He recited from a play**: the passage that follows is taken from Burgess's *The Eve of St Venus* (p. 11).

208   **synthevedge**: a contraction of synthetic vegetables, this coinage is similar to 'synthemesc' (synthetic mescaline), one of the fictional drugs which appears in *A Clockwork Orange*. Not in *OED*.

208   **George Frederick Willett**: allusion to the composer George Frederick Handel (born Georg Friedrich Händel) (1685–1759).

208   **The cloud-capped towers, the gorgeous palaces**: Willett is quoting from Shakespeare's *The Tempest* (IV, i, 152–8).

209   **The rest was silence**: Hamlet's final words were 'the rest is silence' (V, ii, 336).

210   **epsilon**: a possible allusion to Aldous Huxley's novel *Brave New World* (1932) in which the Epsilons are the lowest of society's castes.

211   **Chemin de fer**: French card game derived from baccarat.

212   **Montfleury**: character in Edmond Rostand's play *Cyrano de Bergerac* (1897).

213   **Phyfe two-seater**: This fictitious aeroplane takes its name from Duncan Phyfe (1768–1854), one of America's foremost cabinetmakers. The joke here presumably relates to Phyfe's sofas.

213   **Like at least one other former New York City mayor he had been an aviator**: Fiorello Henry La Guardia (1882–1947), the ninety-ninth mayor of New York City (1934–1945), was a bomber pilot in the First World War. As New York's mayor he opened New York Municipal Airport No. 2 in 1939 (now LaGuardia Airport).

213   **stony rubbish, the littleness of dead rock**: allusion to the first part of T.S. Eliot's *The Waste Land*: 'What are the roots that clutch, what branches grow/Out of this stony rubbish?' (lines 19–20).

214   **baked Idaho**: baked potato (North American slang).

214   **Big Sandy River**: this reads 'Big Sanay River' in the type-script. Corrected here.

215   **all flesh is grass**: Isaiah 40:6. *All Flesh is Grass* is the title of a science-fiction novel by Clifford D. Simak published in 1965.

215   **Reserve your tears**: lines from William Leman Rede's song 'Hush'd be Sorrow's Sigh'. The song is about lovers parting.

216   **brewis**: broth.

218   **Joshua, Joshua,/Sweeter than lemon squash you are,/ Oh by gosh you are,/Joshu, Oshu, aaaaah**: lines from the music hall song 'Joshua' (1910), written and composed by George Arthurs and Bert Lee.

218   **When Worlds Collide**: 1951 science fiction film directed by Rudolph Maté and based on Philip Wylie and Edwin Balmer's 1932 novel of the same name. See Introduction (pp. 1–5) for details of the connection of *Puma* and Maté's film.

218   **Scylla of moon and Charybdis of Puma**: Scylla and

Charybdis are monsters in Greek mythology. Odysseus and his men must navigate the straits between Scylla and Charybdis in book XII of Homer's *Odyssey*. To be between Scylla and Charybdis means being caught between two evils.

221 **Mozart's *Jupiter* Symphony**: Wolfgang Amadeus Mozart's Symphony No. 41 in C major (1788).

224 **'Some do,' [...] Val sighed**: In the typescript Burgess misnames his characters in this passage, substituting 'Nat' for 'Val'. The error is corrected in *The End of the World News* and is corrected here.

224 **wristchron**: wrist watch. 'Chron' from the Latin *chronologia* (time). Not in *OED*.

224 **Bracciano, January 31, 1976**: Burgess and Liana owned a house in Bracciano, a small town north of Rome, Italy in 1970. For details of their time there, see *You've Had Your Time*, pp. 289–90.

225 **Jamesian claims**: an allusion to the American novelist Henry James (1843–1916), used here as shorthand for literary quality.

225 **Hortense Calishre's *Ellipsia* is a freak**: an allusion to Calishre's satirical novel *Journal from Ellipsia* (New York: Little, Brown, 1965).

225 **Gollancz**: British publishing house founded in 1927 by Victor Gollancz. Famed for its yellow-jacketed SF series, Gollancz became a science fiction imprint, owned by Orion Publishing Group, in 1998.

226 **Dunia**: the name of the imaginary caliphate in Burgess's *Devil of a State* (London: Heinemann, 1961).

226 **Corgi *SF* 6**: Edited by John Carnell and published by Denis Dobson in 1965 under the title *New Writings in SF6*, this anthology was published by Corgi in paperback in 1966.

228 ***Yale News***: The *Yale Daily News* is a student newspaper published by students at Yale University.

228 **Wells or Welles**: Burgess is referring to the writer H.G.

Wells (1866–1946), author of *The War of the Worlds* (1898), and the actor and director Orson Welles who directed and narrated an adaptation of that novel on American radio in 1938.

228   **Gabriel's horn**: an allusion to the Archangel Gabriel, a figure associated the blowing of a trumpet to announce God's return to earth.

229   **'The Eyes of New York'**: The project is described by Burgess in *You've Had Your Time* (pp. 339–40).

229   **Call me Ishmael. Call me Mario. Call me Ivan Ivanovich. Call me Yan Yansen. Call me Jack Matsuki. Call me Poh Soo Jing.**: here the narrator signals the diversity of New York's population offering names of Jewish, Italian, Russian, Swedish, Japanese and Chinese origin. 'Call me Ishmael' is the first line of Herman Melville's Moby-Dick (1851). Jen Jenson is the name of a Swedish lumberjack in W.H. Auden's libretto for Benjamin Britten's opera *Paul Bunyan*, first performed at Columbia University in May 1941.

230   **Fasanella's street-scenes**: Italian-American painter Ralph Fasanella (1914–1997).

230   **George Segal**: American painter and sculptor (1924–2000).

230   **Doktorow**: allusion to the American author E.L. Doctorow (1931–2015).

230   **Segaloworitz**: allusion to Segal's East European heritage.

230   **Tagliaferro**: see note to p. 106.

230   **Ciardi**: Italian-American poet John Ciardi (1916–1986).

231   **Pietro di Donato**: Italian-American novelist (1911–1992).

237   **Man the Overreacher**: an allusion to Harry Levin's book *Christopher Marlowe: Overreacher* (Cambridge, MA: Harvard University Press, 1952). Levin argues that all of the protagonists in Marlowe's plays are over-reachers.

238   **H.G. Wells and Aldous Huxley built their utopias (eutopias, dystopias)**: Burgess discusses dystopia and utopia at length in the first part of his novel *1985*.

238   **the thanatotic elements in Eros**: in Freudian theory, Thanatos, the death drive, opposes Eros, the drive of life.

241   Kartoffel: potato (German). It also appears in *A Clockwork Orange*, Part 1, Chapter 1 (p. 2).

241   Besterian: allusion to the American science fiction author Alfred Bester (1913–1987).

241   Keith Roberts's *Pavane*: this novel is listed amongst Burgess's *Ninety Nine Novels* (p. 104).

242   a few Borges touches: Burgess was a fan of Jorge Luis Borges (1899–1986). See *You've Had Your Time*, p. 336.

242   William, not Henry: here Burgess distinguishes between William James (the philosopher and psychologist) and his brother Henry James, the author.

245   *Sic transit Gloria*: a Latin phrase, *Sic transit gloria mundi* means 'Thus passes the glory of the world'.

245   in *Ulysses* the End of the World is a kilted octopus that sings 'The Keel Row': see *Ulysses*, 'Lestrygonians'.

246   St John the Divine: the presumed author of the Book of Revelation.

246   *The Last Man in Europe*: the proposed title of George Orwell's *Nineteen Eighty-Four*.

247   *Weltanschauung*: world view (German).

248   Nothing, thou elder brother e'en to shade: allusion to John Wilmot, Earl of Rochester's poem 'Upon Nothing'.